NORTH STAR

Hammond Innes's highly individual and successful novels are the result of travel in the outback parts of the world. Many of them follow the central character to strange countries where the forces of nature, as much as people, provide the conflict. He has also written two books of travel and one of history. His international reputation as a story-teller keeps his books in print; they have been translated into over thirty foreign languages.

This story of infiltration and sabotage in the North Sea was conceived while Hammond Innes was on board the Shell rig *Staflo*. It was the autumn of 1972, when few people knew much about North Sea oil, fewer still were alerted to the dangers. But it was then that the first anti-sabotage orders were issued.

North Star stems from this, and from the long night hours Hammond Innes spent in a polar air-stream east of Shetland, watching the anchors being lifted on the Brent field and laid again two hundred miles to the south on the Auk.

HAMMOND INNES

North Star

FONTANA/Collins

First published in 1974 by William Collins Sons & Co Ltd
First issued in Fontana Books 1977

© Hammond Innes 1974

Made and printed in Great Britain by
William Collins Sons & Co Ltd Glasgow

For Nora and Jim
whose assistance was invaluable

No, when the fight begins within himself,
A man's worth something.

BROWNING

CONTENTS

Area of the
larger map

N

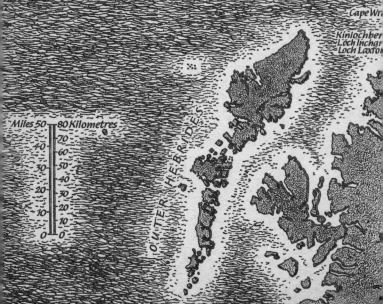

A T L A N T I C   O C E A N

Cape Wr

Kinlochber
Loch Inchar
Loch Laxfor

Miles 50 — 80 Kilometres

40 — 70
— 60
30 — 50
— 40
20 — 30
10 — 20
— 10
0 — 0

O U T E R   H E B R I D E S

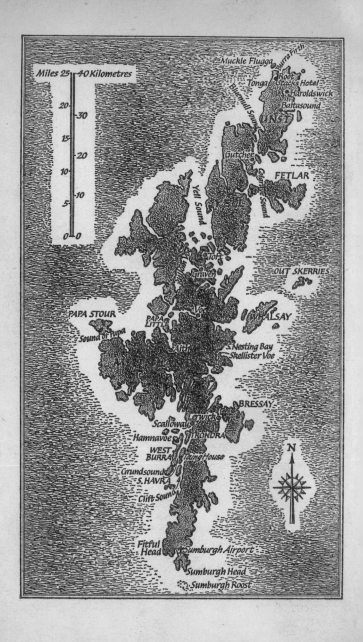

PART ONE

THE TRAWLER

CHAPTER ONE

It was March, the wind cold from the north-east and the *Fisher Maid* plunging down the waves with a wicked twist to her tail. I shut the door of the bridge behind me, leaving the skipper to listen to the forecast, and went down the ladder, heading aft to check the gear. I knew the forecast would be bad. But it couldn't be any worse than the weather we had had off Bear Island. I paused in the shelter of the superstructure. Here on the starboard side I was out of the wind and I took out my pipe, filling it automatically, standing there, staring out across the darkening sea.

I had seen to the stowage of the gear myself, a thousand miles back when we had finished trawling; it was just an excuse to be out in the open, away from the smell of oil and stale food, the blare of the radio and the company of men I had been locked up with for too long. On a trawler it's bloody difficult to be alone when you want to.

Shetland was still just visible, the black humps of the distant hills like wave patterns against a cold green strip of sky, and the light on Sumburgh Head blinking above the hard line of the horizon. Only that pale green strip to mark the bitter cold we'd been steaming through; the rest of the sky was clouded over now. A flurry of sleet drove like a veil across the starboard navigation light. Inside of two days we would be back in Hull, and still I hadn't made up my mind, the shadowy figures, the crash of glass, the sudden blaze of bottled petrol, and that child's face at the upstairs window . . . It had haunted me throughout the voyage.

Slowly the pale light faded in the west. I stood there watching it until that last vestige of the dying day was engulfed by night, wondering whether the strike would still be on, what the hell I was going to do. Waves were breaking against the stern, the driven spume white in the gathering dark, and the wind whistling in the top hamper. I was thinking of my father then, wondering what he would have done, giving his life for a cause in a country not his own. Would he have allowed his principles to be totally destroyed by a single cruel and senseless action?

The match made a small flared arc as I tossed it over the side, my hands gripping the rail, the metal cold to the touch, my eyes staring westward to Shetland, fifteen miles away. He had been born in Shetland, and I had never been there. I hadn't even known him, only the legend. My mind slipped back, my life in flashes, and always that legend, a guiding light to everything I had done – and I wasn't sure any more. A door opened, the muffled sound of the radio reminding me of the industrial world just two days' steaming away, the docks, the stuffy smoky meetings, the arguments, the pickets, the turmoil of over-population, man in the mass. Christ! How could one man, one individual speck, find his way in the tangle of motives and pressures?

'Mike!'

I turned, glancing upwards to see Sparks standing at the top of the ladder, his thin hair blowing in the wind. The bridge door slammed behind him as he came down to stand beside me, a sheet of paper thrust towards me.

I pushed it away. 'I don't need a forecast to tell me it'll be Force 9 before the night's out.'

'It's not the forecast.' His thin, rather high-pitched voice was half blown away by the wind. 'A message for the skipper.'

'Well, give it to him then,' I said irritably.

'I have. But since it concerns you –' I could smell the beer on his breath as his pale face thrust closer, the eyes bright behind his glasses. 'You in trouble?'

'How d'you mean?'

'Look, Mike,' he said, 'you were shipped at the last minute after Les Sinclair had gone down with a virus. You and the skipper – you're not buddies like Les, so he may not tell you. I thought I'd warn you, that's all. The police will be waiting for you when we dock. A Detective-Sergeant Wright. Here's a copy of the message.' And he pressed the piece of paper into my hands.

'Thanks.'

'They want to interview you. I suppose you know why?'

'Yes, I know why.' I stuffed the paper into my pocket, staring out into the night, saying nothing. I had been afraid of this all through the voyage. Somebody must have recognized me, and now, when I stepped ashore, the police would be there, wanting a statement. And if I gave it to them, if I admitted I knew who the men were, then I would be a witness for the prosecution, and the decision would no longer be a personal one, something between me and my conscience and made of my own volition. It would be the result of police interrogation. At least it would seem like that to everybody but me.

'D'you want any sort of a message sent, a private message – lawyers or anything like that?' He was still standing there at my elbow, a man whose world was the ether, who fed on information dragged out of the air on invisible wavelengths, his curiosity glowing in his owlish eyes.

'No,' I said. 'There's nothing a lawyer can do.'

He hesitated, standing there beside me, waiting. Doubtless it was kind of him, but radio operators are all the same. They want to be in everybody's confidence. In the end he left me and I was alone again, watching as the ice-battered trawler plunged southward down the North Sea, each surge and twist carrying me closer to the moment of decision. But you don't change the whole direction of your life because a child is nearly burned alive. Or do you?

The storm was rising, and in the end I gave up thinking about it and went to my cabin, lying there, sleepless and fully clothed, the ship's plates writhing to the violence of the movement. I was back on the bridge in time to get the news. It came right at the end, the talks broken off and the strike still on. Weeks now and every shipyard in Hull at a standstill. Did that mean Pierson & Watt were out, too?

The skipper was there and he turned and looked at me. 'You hear that? And the poomps going full bat.'

They'd been going flat out ever since we'd hit the ice. 'They'll get us home,' I said.

He didn't answer, moving to the port side of the bridge, his carpet slippers flapping loosely. He wasn't a big man, but there was a lot of strength in that short, long-armed body, the round bullet head almost neckless on broad shoulders. And he had an inner strength, his silences more telling than words. He stood there for a while, staring out into the murk ahead. 'Better get some sleep. It's going to be a long night.'

I nodded. It was his watch now and I went below, checking the engine-room and the hold. The fish pounds were just about full, almost two thousand kit – that would be about 20,000 stone landed, a lot of it high-priced. Worth the bashing we had taken up there on the edge of the pack and my share as mate looking good. The fact that she was low in the water did not matter now. We were running with a quartering sea and the pumps were holding. If we'd been steaming into it things might have been different.

It was a long night all right. At four in the morning I was back on the bridge, visibility almost nil and the big deckie they called the Porpoise with his eyes glued to the radar screen. The skipper was in the chartroom working out a Decca position. His thick hairy hands juggled with the parallel rule, pencilling a cross just east of our intended course. 'Wind's veered a point, pooshing us more than I thought.' He ordered a correction to the helm as he entered up the log, and then, instead of leaving me to my watch, he slid the chartroom door shut. 'Three weeks now. You heard what they said on the news. Every yard in Hooll at a standstill.' He had his broad bottom wedged against the chart table, his slightly protuberant eyes fixed on me. 'Every blasted yard.' He pulled his pipe and and began to fill it. 'When did you first go into trawling?'

'Some years back now.'

'Ah asked when.'

'Spring of 1969 – the *Lady Betty*.'

'Old Harcourt. Shipped as a deckie, did you?'

I nodded.

'And your mate's ticket four years later.' He lit his pipe, solid and immovable as the ship fell off a wavetop, sending the rule and dividers skidding across the chart. 'Ah doan't understand you, and that's the truth. A bloke with your education – ' He shook his head, frowning. 'Still got your union card an' all?'

'Yes.'

'But not the Hooll Trawlers' Officers – shipyard, isn't it?'

I didn't say anything and he grunted. 'What made you switch to trawling?'

'My own business,' I said.

'Aye.' He took the pipe out of his mouth, his eyes staring. 'But just tell me. Ah'd laike t'knaw.'

I laughed. What could I tell him? 'The sea,' I said. 'It's in my blood, I suppose.'

'You were at the Marston Yard on Clydebank, a member of the strike committee in 1968. And before that you were in prison, result of a demo that tangled with the police.[3]

'That's a long time ago.'

'You're still the same bloke, aren't you?'

'Come to the point,' I said.

'Orl raight, Ah will. Pierson & Watt now, if they've coom oot . . . Sounds laike it, an' they're non-union, all of them. Young Watt won't employ union men. So where do we go for a refit?'

'Not my problem,' I said.

'No. Not your problem. But you're doing, I reck'n.[3]

'Then you're wrong.'

He shook his head, an obstinate look on his face. 'You're a good mate. I grant you that. But you're a trouble-maker. I wouldn't have shipped you if – ' He stuffed his pipe firmly back into his mouth.

'If what?' I asked.

'I was doing you a favour.'

'You were short of a mate.'

'Aye. But it didn't have to be you.' And then he shrugged and said, 'Orl raight, Ah'll tell you – Jimmy Watt asked me to take you. Get the bugger off our backs, that's how he put it.' And then his big forefinger was jabbing me in the chest. 'Do you deny you were on the Committee?'

'Not on the Committee. I was called in to advise them.'

'Advise them, eh?' His voice was still quiet and under control, but the Hull accent was stronger now, something building up in him, an undercurrent of menace. 'Advise them on what? Intimidation?' He leaned his round head closer, the grey eyes cold and fishlike in the hard light. 'Or did they call you in to get at Jimmy's foreman, to get Bob Entwhisle to – '

'What the hell are you talking about?' I was suddenly angry, remembering how I'd walked out of that crowded meeting, the little Congregational Hall thick with smoke and full of violence. 'You know nothing about it.'

'Doan't I? Well I know this – '

'You listen to me.' I was shouting and I reached out and grabbed hold of his shoulder.

'Doan't you dare.' He slammed his big fists down on my arms, wrenching himself free. 'Keep your hands off.'

'Just listen,' I said. 'It was the economics of the strike – the future of the yards, the financial state of shipbuilding in the North East. They were scared about their jobs.'

He glared at me. 'They doan't care about their jobs. They

doan't care about anything – just so long as they can smash us all to hell.'

'You may be right.' What was the point of arguing with him? I suddenly felt tired. 'My watch,' I said. 'You'd better get some sleep yourself now.'

'Why would they ask you about the financial state of the shipbuilding industry?'

'I was trained as an economist. London School of Economics. You know so much about me you should know that.' I turned to the chart. 'What do you intend to do? You can't make another trip without a refit. There's a leak for'ard where we hit that growler –'

'Ah doan't need you to tell me that.' He relit his pipe, staring down at the chart. 'There's no roosh. Ah'll have a word with Jimmy in the morning. Aye.' He nodded to himself. 'We've a little time yet.' And he turned abruptly, without another word, and left me alone to my watch.

It was a long four hours; nothing to relieve the monotony but the slowly changing position of an oil rig seen only as a blip on the radar screen. The wind was gusting 50 knots, the ship standing on her head and no visibility in the blinding murk of sleet and spray. Plenty of time to think, and my brain too tired, too numbed by the battering to work out what I was going to tell the police when we docked. There had been two of them, two shadowy figures, and then the crash of glass, the sudden blaze, their faces lit as they turned and ran.

I switched on the Decca Navigator, concentrating on the clicking dials to get a fix, doing it automatically, knowing I could identify them both and worrying about Bucknall. Claxby I didn't care about; he was an older man, a hardline militant brought in to cause trouble. If it had been just Claxby, there on his own, I wouldn't have hesitated. But young Harry Bucknall was the son of a good honest shipyard worker who had marched to London with the Jarrow boys in the thirties. A post-graduate university student, intelligent and an anarchist. At least he had done it out of conviction, believing that violence was the path to revolution. And I had no doubt who had been the ringleader.

I entered up the fix and went back to stand by the wheel, staring out into the black night. All I had to do was tell the police. Tell them the truth. But it was the charge that worried me. If I hadn't been there, if the little girl had died in that fire, it would have been murder. The charge could still be attempted

16

murder and myself in the witness box, the full glare of publicity, and everybody knowing I had been interrogated by the police. It would be my evidence, my evidence alone, that convicted them. I would be cast in the role of a Judas. And they hadn't meant to harm the little girl. They hadn't known she was there.

All this time I was pacing up and down, the bridge tumbling under my feet, the noise of the storm beating at my ears, the elements in tune with my mood – everything in chaos, the world, my life, everything. Was this a sort of crossroads in the long journey from womb to grave? If only there were somebody I could turn to, somebody to lean on, to give me strength, to tell me what the hell to do.

I was thinking of Fiona then, wishing to God that just something in my life had turned out right. And then a rogue wave came out of the night, hitting us on the quarter, water roaring along the port side, and as the ship fell off the top of it with a slam that hurled me against the man at the wheel I heard him cursing under his breath. Our eyes met and his big mouth opened in a grin: 'Them lads ashore . . . all toocked oop in bed with their womenfolk. Makes me laff on a night like this.'

'Why?'

' 'Cos they doan't know when they're well off, always itching for something. Me, I joost want what they've got – raight now I'd settle for the missis, all warm and cosy laike, naice soft bed that didn't move unless I made it.' He grinned, winking an eye, the longing of weeks at sea on his face.

My watch ended and I went to my bunk, lying in the dark, thinking wearily. I was an idealist, and idealists get cut down to size when ideals are transposed into politics. Maybe I wasn't tough enough. When it came to the crunch . . . Was I a coward then, my ideals shattered by a petrol bomb? But the doubts had started long before that. When was it? At that Clydeside meeting when a small group of militants screamed 'Fascist!' at me because I had tried to spell out for them what would happen? I had dried up and handed the mike over to a man, who talked their language, not the logic of falling orders and redundancies. Was that when the doubts had started? I couldn't be sure. It was such an accumulation of things.

It was just on ten when I went back on to the bridge, daylight now, a grey world, cloud and sea all one in colour and the whitecaps rolling in from dead astern. I glanced at the gyro and then at the skipper. 'You've altered course.'

'Aye.'

'Aberdeen?'

He nodded, his eyes on a small freighter headed for Norway and making heavy weather of it as she butted the tail end of the storm.

'Did you talk to Watt?'

He didn't answer me and after a moment I ducked out of the bridge to the door of the radio room. The fug in that little cubbyhole was overpowering, the air thick with smoke. Sparks was thumbing the key, tapping out a message in his shirt sleeves, a cigarette burning beside him in a rusty tobacco tin full of stubs. I waited, sweating there, until he had finished 'Any news for me?' I asked.

He picked up his cigarette, turning in his chair and looking at me, his dark eyes large behind the steel-rimmed glasses. 'You know we're headed for Aberdeen?' Morse crackled from the loudspeaker and he reached out tobacco-stained fingers for his message pad, listening with his pencil poised. Then he relaxed. 'That rig again. So much traffic for *Redco 2* I've hardly been able to send at all, and the old man desperate to jump the queue and get us slipped.'

'He hasn't notified the Aberdeen police?'

'Not his job to do that. The office knows, of course, so maybe they have.' He leaned back, his eyes fixed on me, but half his mind on the Morse. 'They're waiting to haul anchors so I suppose they got no joy on the Bressay Bank. Les is fit again, by the way.' And he added, 'Sorry about that. The old man'll be sorry, too, in a way. Les isn't the best mate in the fleet. What'll you do when we get in?'

I hesitated, wondering whether the police would be waiting for me at Aberdeen. 'Go on the club again, I suppose.' One trip in six months. I was hating myself for being so dependent on trawler owners for employment, conscious of a deep-seated urge to start something on my own.

'Why don't you switch to oil – supply ships, something like that? That's where the future is. Trawling . . .' He shrugged his shoulders. 'Doesn't matter to me. I go where Marconi send me. But a man like you, with a master's certificate, you want to go where the future is.' He jerked his head at the sound of the Morse. 'He's talking to the tug owners now, a big German job steaming north from Heligoland. The forecast's good, so they'll be under tow tomorrow night. Every trip it's the same; down past Brent and Auk, all this area of the North Sea, nothing but rig talk – *Bluewater, Staflo, North Star, Glomar.* Take my advice – I listen and I know. There'll be more rig supply ships than trawlers soon.'

'Maybe.' I stood there for a moment listening to the crackle of the Morse. Clydebank, Newcastle, Hull, all the political involvement of my life . . . My mind switched to Shetland, to the islands now far down below the horizon. Was it the island blood in my veins that had made me abandon capitalist America as a kid? Was that why I had started on my wanderings, seeking the values I could not find in the rich world my mother had embraced? Or was it the legendary figure of my father? Had I built him up as a hero in my mind simply because she had tried to bury him? I didn't know. My mind was confused. All I knew for certain was that everything I had done, everything I had believed in, had suddenly turned sour.

And then Sparks murmured, 'The offshore capital of the world.' He coughed over his cigarette. 'Aberdeen – you know it?'

I shook my head. 'Never been there.'

He smiled. 'Well, that's what they call it.' The Morse ceased and he glanced at the clock, his fingers reaching for the dials, turning to the emergency waveband. 'Take a walk round the harbour when you get there. Have a look at the pipe storage depots, the diving outfits, all the clutter of stuff the oil rigs need. You'll get the message then all right. Aberdeen's no longer a fish port. It's an oil rig supply base, and if I were in your shoes . . .' He stopped then, his body suddenly tense as a ghostly voice, calling in clear, began repeating the single word – 'Mayday, Mayday, Mayday . . .' The voice was urgent, giving details now . . . It was a trawler with its engines out of order being swept on to a rock-bound coast in heavy seas.

'Shetland.' Sparks was scribbling it down on his pad, and as the voice began to repeat the vessel's position, he glanced up at a large-scale map. 'Looks like he'll drive ashore on Whalsay Island.' He ripped the sheet off his pad and got to his feet. 'Nothing we can do about it, but the old man better know.' And he hurried past me through into the bridge.

The name of the trawler was the *Duchess of Norfolk.* We looked her up out of curiosity. She was just under 200 tons, built at Lowestoft in 1939 and owned now by G. Petersen of

Hamnavoe, Shetland. New engines 1968, Paxman diesels, so what had gone wrong? All the Chief said was, 'Bloody Shetlanders, they wouldn't know a crankshaft from a camshaft.' He didn't like the Shetlanders, having been stuck there once with gales and a leaking ship.

The *Duchess of Norfolk* was in fact south of Whalsay and, with the wind backed into the north-east, she drove towards South Nesting. We caught snatches of radio talk, very faint, as the trawler *Ranger* steamed to her assistance. It gave me something to occupy my mind, following her progress on the Shetland Isles chart No. 3059. She cleared Muckle Fladdicap, a bare three cables to the eastward, drifted inside Muckla Billan and Litla Billan, missed the rock islet of Climnie by a shift of the tide and hit Fiska Skerry at 13.46. By then the trawler *Ranger* was almost up with her and inside of half an hour had a line aboard. That was the last I heard of her, for we were already in sight of Aberdeen's North Pier, with the city showing grey through the murk above the pale line of the Links, and I was busy getting ready to dock.

The skipper took us in, heading straight for Albert Basin, where the trawlers lay. As we approached Point Law, a survey vessel sweeping past us began to open up. Sparks appeared at my elbow. 'See what I mean?' He nodded towards a cluster of tanks to starboard with supply ships moored alongside. 'Mud silos,' he said. The area beyond was being developed, the sound of reconstruction work coming to us across the water. 'That's the future you're looking at.'

It was an extraordinary sight, the whole harbour area crowded with ships, drilling ships, survey vessels, seismic ships, tugs and ancillary craft all jam-packed among the fishing vessels. And, upriver from Torry Harbour, a litter of pipes and buoys, equipment of all sorts, lay piled up on the quay, more mud silos and a new berth nearly completed. As we moved slowly into Albert Basin we passed very close to Point Law and the supply ship bunkering there. It was the first time I had been really close to one of these flat-bottomed, tug-like vessels that keep the rigs drilling.

'I only know trawlers,' I said. Moored there, the ship looked very sleek, very efficient, but I had seen one once heading out to the Brent in a strong westerly gale, seas breaking over the flat, open afterdeck. 'I'd rather have the *Fisher Maid* up around Bear Island than one of those in a North Sea gale.'

He shrugged, his eyes smiling behind his glasses. 'All I'm

saying is, if you got in on the act, you wouldn't be short of a ship for years, not the way new rigs are coming into service.'

A trawler passed us very close, another just ahead of us, as we nosed our way down the length of Albert Quay, searching for a berth. I could see the fish market now, and then a gap opened up and the skipper said quietly, 'Looks a laikely hole. Reckon there's just room for us.' He ordered port wheel, our bows swinging, and I took the loudhailer out on to the wing of the bridge.

We were tied up by 14.00, the lumpers offloading the catch Since Aberdeen was not our home port, there was no pay, only subs from the local agent to see the boys home. They had a long rail journey ahead of them and most of them were away by the time the first pound boards were being replaced and the emptied compartments hosed down. The skipper called me to his cabin. He was packing his bag. 'You in a hurry to get back?' He knew I was the only officer who hadn't got a wife waiting for him in Hull.

I shook my head.

He was standing holding a shirt and a bundle of dirty socks in his hand, a slug of whisky on the locker behind him. 'Ah thought not.' The bulging eyeballs stared at me. 'Take it then you won't object to staying the night aboard. We've no ship's husband here, you see, and Les doesn't arrive till tomorrow.' He waited a moment and then nodded. 'Good. That's settled then. Better use my cabin so's you can keep an eye on things laike.'

The lumpers packed it in shortly before 19.00 and then I had the ship to myself. I sat on the bridge smoking a pipe and watching the lights come on as dusk descended over the city and the high land behind it. A stillness had settled on the Basin, the quay deserted except for the occasional figure moving along the shadowed wall of the sheds. A siren blared briefly and a trawler up near the entrance started backing out. I watched her as she backed for the open sea, thinking of the mate preparing his gear and the ice ahead and the skipper wondering where the hell he'd get a catch that would satisfy his gaffers.

After that the port seemed dead, nothing stirring. Night had closed down on Aberdeen. I tapped out my pipe and went to the galley to collect a plateful of shepherd's pie and veg the cook had left for me. The galley stove was still warm and I put a kettle on for coffee. With the coffee I had a glass of brandy from the officers' ex-bond locker. A cat had come aboard and as I drank I watched it stalk its prey in the shadows cast by the deck lights.

To be suddenly alone on a ship gives one an odd feeling of isolation. All during the voyage the *Fisher Maid* had been alive with men, an organized unit of activity, her hull vibrating to the pulse of her engines, resounding to the noise of the sea. Now it was deserted, a hollow shell, inactive, still and strangely quiet. I had time to think now, but somehow I seemed unable to concentrate. I was tired, of course, but I think it was the stillness and the quiet that prevented my mind from focusing clearly. I finished my drink, went down to my cabin and packed my gear, shifting it to the skipper's cabin in the bridge housing. Then I turned in.

I was in my pyjamas, having a last smoke, when I heard footsteps crossing the gangway, the murmur of voices. I went through into the bridge and out on to the wing. Two figures stood talking on the deck below. 'Looking for somebody?'

They turned at the sound of my voice, their faces pale in shadow, something slightly menacing as they stared up at me. Then one of them moved, coming out of the shadows to the foot of the ladder. 'Heard you were still aboard. We'd like a word with you.' He started up the ladder, a short, burly figure, his round, pugnacious face framed in dark sideburns, eyes deep-set and a full-lipped mouth. 'Remember me?'

I nodded, the sight of him taking me back to that angry meeting in Hull. He was a Newark man and nothing to do with the shipyards. His name was Bob Scunton and he had confronted me when I was still trying to address the meeting, prodding me in the stomach and telling me to belt up and stop talking a load of statistical rubbish the lads didn't want to know. The other man I had never seen before. 'All right,' I said. 'You can come up.' And I led them into the bridge. There was only one seat, so we stood facing each other, and I didn't like it. I had the feeling of being cornered. 'Well, what is it?'

'Last month, the night of the shipyard workers' meeting.' Scunton's voice was slow and deliberate, his eyes watching me. 'You got a little girl out of a burning house and handed her over to the neighbours. Didn't give your name. Just handed her over and slipped away. Right?'

I didn't say anything, standing there, waiting, conscious of the other man with a slight cast in the left eye that made his gaze oddly disconcerting.

'Thought no doubt you wouldn't be recognized.'

My mouth felt dry, all my fears now suddenly realized. I knew Scunton, knew his reputation. These were men who operated in the shadows, manœuvring and motivating others, controlling events. They weren't union men. They weren't members of any political party. But they were always there, in the background, whenever there was trouble. 'Come to the point,' I said.

'All right, I will.' He licked his lips, his eyes darting round the bridge. 'What about a drink while we're discussing it?'

'It's been a hard trip,' I told him. 'I'm tired.'

'So are we,' he growled. 'Soon as we heard you weren't putting into Hull we came north.' He thrust his head forward. 'You haven't talked to the police yet, have you?'

'No.'

He nodded. 'Okay, but when you do, what are you going to tell them? That's what we want to know.'

'It's no business of yours.' But I knew it was. I could see it in the way the two of them glanced at each other, and suddenly all the turmoil and the doubts exploded in anger. 'You bastards put them up to it, is that it? Is that what you're scared of – that I'll identify them and they'll involve you?'

Scunton moved towards me. 'You shop them and we'll – '

But the other man interrupted him. 'I'll handle this, Bob.' His voice was quiet, a hard, flat voice. 'You were recognized. One of the neighbours, a man. The police will expect a statement.' He paused, the disconcerting gaze sliding past me. Then suddenly he asked, 'What were you doing standing there in the rain outside No. 5 Washbrook Road?'

I hesitated, unwilling to explain myself to men I knew would never understand. 'You weren't at the meeting that night.'

'No.'

'There was a mood of violence,' I said. 'A lot of threats were made, mainly directed at Pierson & Watt and the yard foreman – '

'We believe in solidarity,' Scunton growled in that thick voice of his. 'Pierson & Watt were the one yard – '

'You believe in violence,' I told him.

'All right. Maybe we do, when it's necessary.'

I turned back to face the other man. 'If I hadn't been there, Bucknall and that fellow Claxby might well be facing a murder charge.'

'So you know who it was,' Scunton cut in.

'Yes,' I said. 'I know who they were.' And suddenly I didn't care. 'If you want to throw petrol bombs, why the hell don't you have the guts to do it yourselves? And to risk innocent lives – a little girl . . .'

'You threw it.' His voice was so quiet it stopped me like a bucket of ice-cold water. 'That's what we came to tell you.'

Staring at him, seeing the hard, bitter line of his mouth, the cold grey eyes glinting in the gleam of deck lights, I felt suddenly scared of him. 'Who are you?' I asked him.

He gave a little shrug, a shut look on his face. 'We have a witness.' He pulled a packet of cigarettes from his pocket and offered me one, and when I pushed it away, he said, 'You were alone, nobody to corroborate your evidence.' He took out a cigarette and lit it, the movement of his hands deliberate. He was giving me time to take it in. 'So it will be your word against his, and the man who will say you threw the petrol bomb is a local man. He'll make a good witness.'

'Get out!' My hands were clenched, the words coming through my teeth.

He didn't move, drawing in a lungful of smoke and staring at me. 'Bucknall doesn't matter. But Claxby is too useful a man to be thrown away.'

'Get out of here!'

'You could be useful, too.' He said it reflectively, as though considering the matter. Then he shrugged. 'But at the moment we're concerned with the East Coast yards. We've failed with the trawlermen. The fisheries officer of their union won't play. But if we can hold the strike long enough, then there'll be very little fish coming in anyway. That will give the unions the leverage they need in their negotiations. A trial, with two militants in dock, wouldn't suit us at all.' He paused, and then added, 'We were able to have a word with your radio operator before coming here. In a pub. You're out of a job again, it seems.' And when I didn't say anything, he smiled. 'He told us he thought you ought to be commanding a supply ship. That's where the future lies, isn't it?'

He was looking at me again and the expression of his eyes had a speculative quality. 'Get into oil,' he said quietly. 'And forget about what you saw in Washbrook Road.' He stubbed out his cigarette, then turned abruptly towards the door, jerking his head at Scunton. 'Think about it,' he said over his shoulder. 'All you need tell the police is that it was too dark to see who they were.'

'And if I tell them the truth?'

He swung round on me. 'Then you'd be a fool.' And he added, 'You keep your mouth shut and I'll see our witness does the same. You understand?' He stared at me a moment. Then he nodded and went out, Scunton following, their footsteps sounding hollow as they went down the ladder and across the deck to the gangway. And after that I was alone again, still in my pyjamas and feeling cold.

I got myself a drink, my hands trembling, wishing, as I had done so often in my life, that I had somebody to fall back on, not just the legendary figure of my father, but somebody, something, to give me strength. And suddenly I was thinking of the islands seen the previous evening black against that green strip of sky. Shetland, the land where my father had been born. I had never been so close to Shetland before, and sitting there, the brandy warming my guts, it gradually came to me that now was the moment. I would go north to the islands – now while I had the chance.

CHAPTER TWO

My first sight of Shetland was a lighthouse sliding by the window and green lawn slopes falling from rock outcrops, everything fresh and clean, touched with the luminosity of evening light. The *Highlander* landed and I saw the remains of old wartime buildings as we taxied in to park beside a large British Airways helicopter. There was a light drizzle falling, and as I stood waiting on the apron for my baggage, the smell of the grass and the sea all about me, I had a deep sense of peace, something I hadn't felt for a long time.

Most of my fellow passengers were oil men returning to the Redco rig. For ten minutes or so they filled the little prefab terminal with colour and the babble of their accents; then they trooped out to the waiting chopper and in a buzz-saw whirr of engines and blades they were lifted up and whirled away. Suddenly everything was very quiet, only the rattle of crockery as a woman went round the tables collecting empty cups, the murmur of voices from the BA desk where the dispatch clerk was talking to the crew of the *Highlander*. There was an Ordnance Survey map on the wall. I got myself another cup of coffee and stood looking at it, refreshing my memory based on the Shetland charts I had pored over on the bridge of *Fisher Maid*.

Sumburgh Head is the southernmost point of the whole island chain, the tip of a long finger of mountainous land jutting south from the main port of Lerwick. The distance by road looked about 30 miles. A voice at my side said, 'Can I help you?' He was a small man in blue dungarees, dark-haired with bright blue eyes and a ruddy face.

'I want to get to Hamnavoe,' I said and pointed to the little port, which was at the north end of the island of West Burra, a little below Lerwick, but on the west coast.

He ran a car hire business, but when I said I couldn't afford to rent a car, that didn't seem to worry him. 'Hamnavoe.' He shook his head. 'Don't know anyone going to Hamnavoe. You'll have to go to Lerwick first. There's a bus in the morning, or maybe I can fix you a lift. Either way it means staying the night.' And he added, 'My wife can fix you bed and breakfast if that's any help.'

His name was Wishart and I stayed the night with them, in a small house above Sumburgh village with breeze-block outbuildings in which he kept his cars. He had been a mechanic servicing local farm vehicles until the oil companies started drilling off Shetland. 'Now I've got a real good business, not just tourists, you see – it's all the year round, oil executives, contractors, technicians, commercial travellers. We've never known it so good.' His face was beaming.

'Yes, but how long is it going to last?' his wife said quietly, and behind her words was the experience of hard times.

'Ah!' His eyes glanced quickly round the neat little parlour with its gleaming new furniture and bright chintz curtains. 'That's the question, isn't it?' We had finished the meal and were sitting drinking whisky out of a gin bottle. The whisky had a strong peaty flavour. 'You being from Aberdeen, maybe you know the answer to that.'

I shook my head. 'I'm a trawlerman.'

'Trawlers, eh? You looking for a job up at Hamnavoe?'

'Maybe,' I replied cautiously.

'It's a lot smaller than Lerwick, you know. You'd do better in Lerwick.' He poured himself another finger of the pale liquor, topping my glass up at the same time. 'Only this morning I rented a car to a man wanting to get hold of a trawler chap – something to do with one of the rigs. But there aren't any big boats up here, only peerie ones, and there's none of them going cheap. Anyway, the fishermen here, they hate the oil companies. They're scared of what could happen. The *Torrey Canyon* was bad enough, but suppose one of these production rigs blows? Particularly if they strike oil to the west; then all of the Shetland fisheries could be destroyed, millions of tons of oil polluting the seas for miles around. That's what scares them.' He looked at me, his eyes very bright. 'Dangerous bloody game, anyway. Trawling, I mean. There's just been one of them wrecked, went ashore yesterday in a north-easterly gale. Skipper dead and two of the crew injured.'

'The *Duchess of Norfolk*?'

He nodded. 'That's right. Drifted into South Nesting Bay ... Hear they beached her in the East Voe of Skellister. That's all right until another north-easter piles the seas in. You mentioning Hamnavoe reminded me of it. The skipper came from Hamnavoe. Now what the hell was his name? Not a Shetlander. Norwegian, I think. You ever been up to Graven?' And when I told him I had never been in Shetland before, he nodded, staring into his glass. 'An old wartime base, like Sumburgh here. But bigger. They had seaplanes – Catalinas – and a big airfield. And Scalloway, that's where the Norwegian boats were based after they moved from Lunna, landing men and arms in Norway, bringing refugees out. I was only a peerie boy at the time, but my Dad was up there. A blacksmith, fixing armaments, all sorts of odd jobs.' And he went on to talk of his father, the stories he had told, until it was almost midnight and his wife chased him off to bed.

It rained all night. I could hear it drumming on the slates. But in the morning the sun was shining, a magnificent view of sea and rocks and greensward, all sparkling in the freshness of that early northern light. I left with the post van that had brought the mail down from Lerwick, the washed brightness of land and sea calling to something deep within me. We passed under Ward of Scousburgh, Mosey Hill and Hallilee, the road dropping down to the sea, vistas of blue water stretching away to Bressay and the Isle of Noss. It was all new, an island world, yet I felt at home, and the remoteness of it seemed suddenly to cut me off from all the rest of my life. It was a strange feeling, and I sat there beside the postman hardly saying a word.

He dropped me about three miles from Lerwick, where the Scalloway road came in from the west. 'You won't have to wait long. Anybody will give you a lift.' A breeze had sprung up, a cold little wind from the north. I lit my pipe, watching the red van disappear. I was alone then, the hills all around me, sheep noises and the sea down in the valley. Would anybody at Hamnavoe remember my father? I didn't even know when he had left the place. My mother might have been able to tell me, but I hadn't written to her in years, and anyway she was dead now. She had never been to Shetland, never talked to me about his early life.

A builder's truck loaded with breeze-blocks took me to the outskirts of Scalloway, where the road to Hamnavoe turned off to the south along the placid waters of the East Voe. A small drifter was anchored under the castle, sea birds lying to their own reflections, and I could see water stretching away beyond the bridge that joined Trondra Island to the Mainland shore. I was there about twenty minutes before a tourist gave me a lift into Hamnavoe. It was lunchtime then. I bought some biscuits and cheese, left my bags at the stores, and strolled up a grass track to sit on a bank below some cottages. A purse-seine fishing boat was coming in round the headland, another moored at the concrete pier, both of them wooden-hulled and painted black.

The woman in the stores had told me there was nobody of the name of Randall in Hamnavoe now. She had said something about a plaque in the church, but when I went there after my lunch, it was locked. There was no pub and the few people I met had never heard of him. It was the teacher up at the school who suggested I talk to Miss Manson, an elderly spinster living at Brough, about a mile down the road towards Grund Sound. But the wind had backed westerly and it was raining then. I found lodgings in a little house on the hill that had a Bed and Breakfast sign in the window and was full of children. It was a bleak place looking north to a scattering of islands half hidden in the rain. The man was away at sea, the woman uncommunicative, and the radio blared incessantly.

As darkness fell I walked down to the pier. But there was nobody there, the two fishing vessels silent and deserted, and Hamnavoe itself a dead place wrapped in a wet blanket of low cloud. I was walking slowly back, my head tucked into the collar of my anorak, when a shaft of light shone out from a cottage doorway and a voice said, 'You the stranger been asking about Alistair Randall?'

'Yes,' I said, and he invited me in. He was a beaky, tired-looking man with thin white hair and a nervous blink to his eyes. The door closed behind me and I was in a cosy little room with a peat fire. A little old woman, very plump, sat in her knitting chair, the needles clicking, bright eyes watching me out of a round face that showed scarcely a wrinkle.

'My wife,' he said and I was conscious of an atmosphere in the room, an undercurrent of strain. 'Mrs Sandford knew the Randalls.'

She nodded, an almost imperceptible movement of the head, the knitting needles clicking away and her eyes fixed on me with a strange eagerness.

'Can you tell me about Alistair Randall?' I asked.

Her eyes dropped to her knitting and there was an uncomfortable silence. Her husband smiled at me blinking his eyes. 'He was here all one summer.'

It was very warm in the room and I unzipped my anorak. 'You did know him then?'

The knitting needles stopped, the room very still, and she was staring at me again. 'Who are you?' she asked.

I hesitated before replying. Since leaving the *Fisher Maid* I had been using my mother's maiden name of Fraser – just in case they tried to follow me. But now . . . 'My name is Mike Randall,' I said. 'Alistair Randall was my father.'

The sound of her breath was like a sigh and she nodded slowly. 'Yes, I see now – the eyes, of course. We did wonder, Albert and me – when we heard you had been making enquiries . . .' That strange eagerness was back in her eyes as she gazed up at me. 'From America, aren't you?'

'I was brought up there. I left when I was twenty.'

She seemed disappointed. 'But your mother . . . She went out as governess to a rich business man and then married him. During the war I think.'

'Yes, during the war.'

'Muriel.' She nodded. 'Her name was Muriel. Is she still alive?' I didn't say anything and she turned to her husband. 'Give Mr Randall a chair, Albert. And a glass of whisky to keep out the damp.'

She asked me at lot more questions then, about myself and what I had done with my life. 'So you didn't come to see me?'

'I came to find out about my father.'

'Did you know I wrote to your mother?'

'No.'

'It must be three or four years ago now.'

'She shouldn't have written like that,' her husband said, his voice gentle, almost apologetic. 'I told her not to.'

'Life hasn't been easy for us,' she muttered angrily. 'Both of us getting old now, and Albert hasn't worked in twenty years. It was my son insisted I write. Did your mother never mention I had written to her? Mrs Graber, Bay View, Narragansett, Rhode Island, USA. That's right, isn't it?'

I think she must have written to her for money, and because she was disappointed that I hadn't come to Hamnavoe in answer to that letter, it took time and patience to get her to talk about my father. Her husband hardly said a word. He was from Scalloway and I don't think he had ever met Alistair Randall. But she had virtually grown up with him, for the Randalls had had a small farm at Houss on East Burra and her eldest brother had kept a lobster boat down in the Voe of North Houss. 'Alistair often came out in the boat with us.' The softness of her voice, the faraway look in her eyes . . . I sensed there was something more, but all she said was, 'He was a very wild boy.'

He had gone to sea at the age of fifteen, on an inshore boat fishing out from Hamnavoe. Then his father had died, the farm was sold and his mother had gone to live at Easter Quarff, which was where she had come from. 'I didn't see him for a long time after that. He got a job on a Lerwick drifter. And when the *Shetland Times* printed his views on the working conditions of the island drifters he started writing for the papers regularly, you see.'

She produced some faded cuttings from her work bag, and while I was glancing through them, she told me how he had shipped in a Danish cargo boat bound for Svendborg and hadn't come back for a long time.

'Did he go on to Russia?' I asked, for the last of the cuttings was about whaling in the Barents Sea.

But she didn't know. 'He only spoke of Denmark and Norway. Oh, and Finland – he had been to Finland.'

'How long was he away?'

'Almost three years.'

'And then he came back to Lerwick?'

'No, to Hamnavoe. Of course I was married by then . . .'

'But you saw him again?'

She glanced across at her husband, a smile that had a quality of sadness. 'Yes, I saw him again.'

'Did he talk about Russia at all? He was a Communist, you know.'

She shook her head. 'No, he never talked to me about Russia.'

'How old was he then?'

She paused while she worked it out. 'He was a year younger than me, so he would have been twenty-three.'

That made it 1930, for he had been born in 1907. I asked her how long he had stayed in Hamnavoe. 'Just the summer, that was all. He was writing most of the time – a book, I think. But I never heard it was published. And he was gone before winter. He was a very restless man.'

'Was that when he went to America?'

But she wasn't sure. 'I never heard from him again – only at the end.' She delved into her work bag again, an envelope this time. She held it out to me, her small hand trembling slightly. 'It was because of this I asked Albert to bring you in. I thought you must be a relative, you making enquiries of him here. He will have written it just before he was killed. You can read it if you like. I don't mind.'

The envelope was dirty and torn and it had no stamp on it. The address was in pencil, barely readable. Mrs Anne Sandford, Hamnavoe, Shetland. The letter inside consisted of two sheets of ruled paper taken from some sort of notebook, a thin pencilled scrawl that had obviously been written under great tension. It was headed 'Somewhere outside Madrid' and dated February 25, 1939.

Darling Anna –

We are cut off and being shelled to hell. We have held on now for twenty-eight weary months. Not much food and bitterly cold. The Communists have pulled back, our flank exposed. Tomorrow or the next day I shall probably be dead. In these last hours I think of Shetland, and of you. There's not been much of happiness in my life, and what little there has been I had with you. A pity I ever left the islands, but a man's destiny lies in himself and is unavoidable. It has led me inevitably to Spain where we have played out the overture for a new world war, the bright hopes of youth lost in this mess of blood and cordite.

You may think it strange that my thoughts are with you now and not with my wife. But Muriel is a realist, whereas you are the essential woman, the Mother Earth of my native islands. God keep you, and Shetland, in peace during the holocaust to come. I pray for you as I hope you will sometimes pray for me.

Your loving
Alistair

I read it through twice, trying to visualize his circumstances at the time of writing, crouching in a trench on the crumbling perimeter of Madrid. And the writing, so overcharged with emotion – the Highland half of him crying out for pity. For prayer, too.

I looked across at the woman so still beside the fire. 'My mother said he used to write poetry.'

She took the letter from me, staring down at the two faded pages. 'During that summer . . . Yes, I suppose it was poetry. It didn't rhyme and I didn't understand it, you see. So he never showed me any more.' Her eyes were beginning to weep and she turned away, stuffing the letter back into her work bag. 'One of his brigade brought it more than a year later . . . That was just after our troops had been evacuated from Norway. He was an RAF sergeant then, stationed up at Graven. Brought us some sugar, too, didn't he, Albert?'

Her husband blinked and nodded. 'His name was Pettit. A kind man.'

'We were very short of sugar, you see, and with a growing boy . . .' Her voice trailed away. 'Those were difficult times here in Shetland, you know.' And she began knitting again. 'It's for my son,' she said. 'He was here today.' And her husband said, 'The first time in more than a year.'

That undercurrent again, and as soon as I had finished my whisky I left them, hurrying back to my lodgings while the words of that letter were still fresh in my mind. In the bare little room I wrote it down, I think exactly, and then I went to bed and for a long time lay awake in the dark thinking of his disillusionment and how it matched my own. To die on a battlefield for something you no longer believed in . . . And his last letter, not to my mother, but to this woman in Shetland. *The Mother Earth of my native islands.* The call of his homeland perhaps. Is that what we cling to at the point of death?

The only picture I had ever seen of him was in my mother's

sitting-room in the big house on Rhode Island. It had been tucked away in a drawer full of odds and ends, a photograph taken outside the Registry Office in Edinburgh where they had been married. I remember my mother coming in and finding me standing there with it in my hand, the cold, contained fury with which she had whipped it away from me and torn it up. So long ago now that I could barely remember what he looked like, only the eyes, which had seemed to stare at me out of the print, and the fact that he was shorter than she was and his suit crumpled.

The wind blew all night. It was still blowing in the morning, But the clouds broken now and fitful gleams of sunshine. I started out for Brough shortly after nine, walking south along the back of West Burra, the grass all green and the sea sparkling. I found Miss Manson feeding chickens in the backyard of her cottage, a tall gaunt woman with steel-rimmed spectacles and a waspish tongue. The schoolteacher had warned me she was 'as full of gossip as a cat with kittens', so I didn't tell her who I was, only that I was a relative. It didn't satisfy her, of course, but she couldn't stop talking – chiefly about Anna Sandford and the dance she had led her husband, running all over the island after Alistair Randall so soon after they were married. 'And that son of hers – serves her right. He was always a hard boy and now he's up in Unst and hardly bothers with them at all . . . Well, there's little of Albert there, you know, the poor devil.'

I don't think she had known my father at all, only the gossip. She was a good deal younger. But she could remember the farm being sold and she showed me the dower chest her mother had bought at the auction, a plain oak piece carefully polished. Some people called Eunson lived there now and she told me how to find it. She also told me that the plaque I had heard about was not in Hamnavoe church, but in Grund Sound.

Grundsound was another mile down the road. There was a little war memorial where the road to Houss branched off to the left across a stone bridge and the view down the South Voe was a bright vista of water, flat as a mirror in the sun. The church was just beyond the bridge, a small stone building close by the school. Fresh-dug earth, black as peat, was piled in one corner of the graveyard and the church door stood open. It was dark inside and stark in its plainness. The plaque was at the west end and the inscription, etched black on the plain brass, read:

ALISTAIR MOUAT RANDALL
*Journalist and soldier who died
in the Spanish Civil War, 1939*

'No, when the fight begins within himself,
A man's worth something.' – *Browning*

I stared at it a long time, wondering who had put it there – the date of death not given, nor the side he had fought on, and those lines from Browning. Was it my mother? Had she made that strange choice of an epitaph? I turned to the nearest pew and sat down, wishing I knew the rest of that poem.

Footsteps on the gravel outside and a single bell in the roof struck an uncertain note. It struck again, and then again, a slow toll, rhythmic as the strokes of an oar. The door swung open, the sunshine flooding in, and then four men bearing a coffin on their shoulders. There was no music, only the tread of their feet to act as a dirge. They laid the coffin down before the altar, the daffodils on it a blaze of spring in a shaft of sunlight. The men took a pew to the left and then a Presbyterian minister came in, followed by a young woman in a tweed skirt and a monkey jacket, a brown scarf tied over her head. Her face was set and very brown. Behind her was a shambling giant of a man, blond and bearded, and several others, all ill-at-ease in their Sunday best.

They were fishermen by the look of it. The girl didn't notice me, her gaze on the coffin, but the big man did, his eyes steel blue and his huge hands clenched. I waited until they had settled and then slipped away out into the sunshine, back to the little war memorial where I sat on the grass looking down the long vista of the voe to Houss Ness.

I was still there when they came out of the church. I saw the coffin laid to rest in its grave, and then they all left in a Land-Rover, heading south down East Burra towards Houss, the girl driving. The minister locked up and followed them in his car, leaving only the gravedigger shovelling at the peat-black earth.

The sad little scene and the two lines of that poem . . . Death the solution to everything. Who had known him so well that he had revealed to them an inner conflict that matched my own? Who had cared enough to blazon it to the world, and understood enough to claim that, and not his death for a cause, as the real worth? Not Anna Sandford surely. Not my mother. But somebody. I stared blindly at the stone cross, bare against the blue sky, and wished I had known him. And then a car came from the direction of Hamnavoe and stopped in front of me, its bright red body blocking the view.

'You're Randall, aren't you?' The driver was a man of about my own age, perhaps a little more, his dark hair greying at the temples and blown by the wind. He wore a fisherman's jersey and his face was round and plump, the eyes slightly bloodshot. 'I was told I'd find you along the road to Grund Sound. Can I give you a lift?' And he pushed the door open for me. 'I'm Ian Sandford.'

I hesitated, wondering what he wanted. 'I'd as soon walk,' I said.

'Aye, it's a fine day, and we've not had many of those this last fortnight.' He was leaning towards me across the passenger seat, his face framed in long sideburns. 'Mother said you were a trawlerman. That right?'

I didn't say anything, trying to recall what else I had told her; the islands were an enclosed world and gossip travelled fast.

'Would you know the worth of a trawler lying beached with a hole in her bottom?' There was a speculative glint in his eyes.

'Depends how badly she's holed and what it's going to cost to get her off.'

He nodded. 'Jump in then and I'll drive you over. Take about an hour, that's all.'

I hesitated, thinking it was probably just an excuse to find out more about me. But the wind was blowing from the north-west now. It was cold, and anyway it would be interesting to have a look at that trawler; there couldn't be more than one beached on Shetland. I got in beside him, but instead of turning the car, he said suddenly, 'What made you come to Grund Sound?'

'There's a plaque in the church here. I wanted to see it.'

He stared at me suspiciously. Then he laughed. 'Oh, that.' He nodded towards the graveyard and the man shovelling earth. 'There was a funeral here today. I thought perhaps . . . You saw it, did you?' And he added, 'It was the trawler's skipper they buried. Old man Petersen. Owed money in Lerwick, a finance company mortgage.' He backed and turned the car. 'The wreck's up for sale now.'

Just outside Hamnavoe we turned right, across the bridge to Trondra. 'You ever been to Unst?' he asked. 'I've got a bit of a hotel at the end of Burra Firth where the north road stops. Trolls, Vikings and stone circles, that's what they come for. And it's only two miles to the top of Herma Ness. They can see Muckle Flugga from there and go home with pictures of the northernmost point of the British Isles.' He had a quick, energetic way of talking, as though needing to convince himself all the time that he was possessed of a dynamic personality. 'Birdwatchers in summer. Gales in winter.' He laughed. 'It's a bloody hell of a place.'

'Then why are you up there?' I asked.

'Oil. I'm waiting for the oil to come ashore, that's why.' He leaned towards me, his manner becoming confidential. 'I've got a company now. And I've just landed a contract to supply two of the rigs – food mainly. But to ship the stuff out I need a boat, you see.'

We crossed the Scalloway-Lerwick road, heading north alongside Loch of Tingwall towards the eastern shore. It was shortly after midday when we drove through Skellister, South Nesting Bay blue under a blue sky and the voes, sheltered in the lee of the land, calm as silk. The *Duchess of Norfolk* lay in the East Voe, so close against a narrow spit of land she might have been moored there. She was low in the water aft, but still neat and trim, not too much rust and her brasswork gleaming in the sun.

'Looks in good condition,' Sandford said.

I nodded, thinking of the men following that coffin. So much care, and their ship stranded here and up for sale. 'She's holed below the waterline, is she?' I couldn't see any damage, part of her bulwarks stove in, that was all.

'It's on the other side,' he said, and we left the car, walking through little mounded hills of sheep-cropped grass until we stood on the spit only a few yards from her. I could see it then, a ragged tear in the plating by the stern. It was about five feet long and only just showing above the surface of the water.

'Well, what do you think?'

I barely heard him. I was day-dreaming – thinking how it would be possible to repair that rent and get her off. Down by the stern like that, her engine-room would be flooded. But if that was the only damage a single pump would soon float her, once the hole was patched. 'You don't know how far the damage extends below the water, do you?'

'About two feet – three feet at the after end.'

'Somebody took you out?' There was no sign of a boat.

He laughed. 'Nobody here last night. It was almost dark. I just stripped off my clothes and swam out.' There were ropes trailing from her deck aft, but he had not climbed on board. 'Well, what do you reckon she'll fetch at auction?' He was watching me closely.

She was soundly built and those Paxmans . . . 'Have you got enough money?' I was wishing to God I had.

'No,' he said. 'Of course I haven't. But I can borrow it, can't I? Same as I did when I converted those old wartime buildings up at Burra Firth.'

I stood there, looking at the chunky vessel with her high straight stem, the rounded stern. She had been drifting before the gale all the time until she struck. It was the bulwarks for'ard that were damaged, nothing much else – a window broken and one of the trawl doors missing, that was all I could see. And if a man who'd never been to sea in his life could borrow the money . . .

'How much would she be worth down south?' His voice was eager, greed in his eyes as he stared at me. 'Slipped and repaired with the engines in proper order.'

'She was built in 1939.' I was remembering prices paid for old trawlers in Hull, but most of them distant water boats and much bigger than this one. 'Somewhere around fifty thousand,' I said. 'Sixty at the most.'

'And lying here, just as she is, beached in the voe and her engines full of seawater?'

He wanted a low figure, of course, hoping for a bargain. 'It depends if anybody else is as keen as you. You might get her for as low as fifteen. But you'd be lucky.'

'Fifteen – that's about what I thought. Less maybe.' He was staring at the black hull and I knew he was working out the probable cost of repairs. He didn't see her as a ship, only as a means of making money.

'When will they fix the date for the auction?' I asked.

'It's fixed already – next Monday.' And this was Friday. The haste seemed almost indecent, but as he pointed out, it only needed a strong nor'easter, and the finance company wanted their money. 'They don't care what she fetches so long as it covers the mortgage. That's the beauty of it.'

We walked back to the car then, both of us too preoccupied with our thoughts to say much as we drove back through Skellister and along the road to the south. We were in country that was as much water as land, loch and sea all quiet in the lee, the hills smiling in the sun, and my mind on that trawler resting on her bed of boulders. If he hadn't been so cold-blooded about it, regarding her, not as a ship, but simply as a means of making money, I don't think I would have done what I did. Or if he had asked me to skipper her . . . But he was so bloody anxious to get to his bank before it closed that he hardly said a word as he drove straight to Lerwick and parked the car on the Esplanade not far from the steamer quay. 'Meet me here in an hour's time and I'll drive you back.'

But by then I had made up my mind. 'Don't bother,' I said. 'I have to see somebody here anyway.'

'Just as you wish.' He hesitated, then slammed the car door. 'Well, thanks for your help.' And he hurried away, across the road and up a steep little alley.

It was a crazy idea. I had rather less than £100 in my pocket. But to hell with that. To hell with the police. Hull was a long way away and I was thinking of the future now, and Providence in the shape of that trawler beckoning irresistibly. A bank might not give me a loan, but there were companies operating up here now that had the cash if I could provide them with what they wanted. I walked along the Esplanade to the Queen's Hotel, got myself a beer and a sandwich and phoned Wishart in Sumburgh. I was lucky, he was in and he knew where the oil man who had rented a car from him was staying – at the Lerwick Hotel. 'His name's Fuller and he's got it till Monday.'

'Monday evening?' I asked.

'No, morning. He's booked out on the early flight to Dyce.'

'And he hasn't changed his booking?'

But he didn't know about that. 'If he has, he can't have the car.'

I thanked him and rang off. Either Fuller didn't know about the auction, or else he wasn't interested. An oil company looking for a trawler would hardly concern itself with a wreck, and wanting one on the cheap was a relative term. I had another beer, enquired the way to the hotel, and set off up the hill behind the port.

The Lerwick Hotel was out by the hospital, a low building standing well back, with Bressay and the open sea behind it. Fuller wasn't there. He had left immediately after breakfast, taking a packed lunch with him. I wrote him a note telling him I would call back at six that evening and went down to the port again. In the raised pedestrian way above the Esplanade I found a newsagents and bought an Ordnance Survey map and a copy of the *Shetland Times*. The local paper was datelined 28th March. It had come out that morning and the wreck of the *Duchess of Norfolk* was its lead story.

I read about the wreck sitting on a bollard with the gulls screaming above the fish quay. The engines had apparently been shut down due to overheating, the pipe supplying sea-water to the cooling system having sprung a leak. They had been used briefly in an attempt to get her past Fiska Skerry, but had generated insufficient power and a big sea had slammed her sideways against the rock. The *Ranger* had towed her off and got her as far as the East Voe of Skellister, but had had to abandon the tow just short of Vadill of Garth. The engines had been used again to beach her in the lee of the spit. Unfortunately, both the chief engineer and his assistant were in hospital. They were the two men who had been injured, so there was no indication as to whether the overheating had seriously damaged the engines. At least they had not seized up solid.

The most surprising information in the report was that the insurance on the vessel had been allowed to lapse. It was owned apparently by Gertrude Petersen and skippered by her father-in-law, Olav Petersen, 81, who had died of a heart attack during the gale while they were steaming south between Whalsay and the Out Skerries. It was the lack of insurance that had decided the mortgagees to foreclose. 'We naturally presumed the insurance had been maintained,' the manager was reported as saying. 'When we learned that the premium had not been paid we had no alternative.' The amount of the mortgage was not given.

On the back page, under 'Auctioneers' Announcements', was a notice of the sale – *At the Queen's Hotel on Monday, 31st March, at 12 noon, the trawler* Duchess of Norfolk *of 190 tons presently lying aground in the East Voe of Skellister, by order of the owner, Mrs G. Petersen of Taing House, East Burra, and of the mortgagees, North Scottish Land and Securities.*

It took me the rest of the afternoon to track down the equipment I thought I might need and to establish some sort of relationship with the yards. The smallest proved the most helpful. It was out beyond the breeze-block plant on a dirt road that led to the old gun emplacements on Green Head. The owner, a cheerful, bald-headed man named Jim Halcrow, had been an engineer in the Navy. It was little more than a workshop with no slip and only four men employed. He serviced engines and deck gear, and as luck would have it one of the boats he was working on at the moment was an oil rig supply vessel in for emergency replacement of a fractured prop shaft. 'We'll be going for trials about a week from now, and who's to care if I take her up to South Nesting on test? If I did, an' if we hapt on yon trawler lying afloat, it'd be natural for us to take her in tow, now wouldn't it?' He gave me a broad wink. 'Provided, of course, we're doing the engine repairs for you.'

'How much?' I asked.

'Say fifty for the tow, cash and nobody breathing a word, and the rate for the job on her engines.'

It was a little after six before I got back to the hotel. Fuller was waiting for me in the entrance lounge, a solid man with grey hair and a grey face. He smiled when I asked him if he had found the trawler he was looking for. 'We'll be needing two and with summer coming there's not many owners interested in chartering. I've got the offer of one, but it's old and available only at the end of July. That's too late.' He offered me a drink, and when he had given the order, he enquired whether I was a trawler owner.

'Not at the moment,' I said.

'Your note said you had a proposition.' He had a faintly harassed air.

For answer I handed him my copy of the *Shetland Times*. But he had already seen it and he knew about the auction. Briefly he explained his requirements: a vessel in commission and complete with crew to act as watchdog to a drilling rig his company would start operating in Shetland waters about a month from now. It would probably be drilling through into the late summer, early autumn; the stand-by boat was required to keep station, whatever the weather, which was why he had wanted trawlers rather than small coasters. 'And we don't want to own them. We just want to charter.'

'I wasn't suggesting you bought it.' The drinks came and I asked him what the charter rate would be. His figure was too low and I told him so. 'You loan me twenty thousand for six months at a nominal 2 per cent and I'll accept the charter at your rate.' And I went on to give my qualifications and the general outline of how I thought I could get the stranded trawler serviceable enough to pass survey inside of a month.

His questions were mainly financial. I think he had been trained in accountancy. He had that sort of a mind and he knew very little about ships. But he was desperate to get something settled. That was obvious when he invited me to stay on for dinner. The reason emerged during the meal. He worked at the Head Office of a shipping line that had just been taken over by a City finance company run by a man who, as he put it, had a flair for getting into the right thing at the right moment. This man was arriving at Sumburgh next day, flying his own plane, and as soon as he mentioned the name I understood his need to have something to show for the two days he had been up here. Vic Villiers had been acquiring a reputation for the ruthless exploitation of under-developed assets when I was still at the LSE. This was his first venture into oil.

'One of our subsidiaries has a rig operating in the North Sea. The present contract has less than a month to run. After that Mr Villiers plans a crash exploration programme of the two licences we acquired in 1971, both of them licences to drill on the continental shelf west of Shetland.'

I didn't care what their plans were. All I wanted was the money to bid for the *Duchess,* but when I suggested he take Villiers down to see the trawler tomorrow, he smiled at me sourly. 'I don't think he'd appreciate that. He'll have the chairman of one of the big merchant banks with him and will be travelling on to Unst for a weekend's birdwatching. He's a very keen ornithologist.'

'Then come down and see it for yourself,' I said. 'Now, tonight – then at least you'll be able to tell him what the proposition is.'

He was a creature of settled habits and not at all keen on a night visit to a lonely inlet. But he was even less enthusiastic about my coming with him to Sumburgh in the morning and putting my proposition to Villiers direct. He borrowed a torch from the management and half an hour later we were walking the grass verge of the voe. The hills to our left were black against the night sky, the trawler a dark shadow in the pale sheen of the water. I took him out to the spit, playing the beam of the torch over the hull and superstructure explaining again, and in detail, how I thought I could salvage her.

He didn't say much, but I hardly noticed I was so keyed up; a mood of excitement, of elation almost, that I hadn't felt in years. And suddenly I was stripping off my clothes. If Sandford could swim out to her, then so could I, and the desire to stand on her bridge for a moment was urgent and overwhelming. Also I wanted to check the size of the hole in her hull and make certain there was nothing else seriously wrong with her.

'Wait here,' I said. 'I won't be long.'

I think he tried to dissuade me, but by then I was wading naked into the water. It was cold, but not as cold as it had been on the edge of the pack up by Bear Island. It didn't take more than a few strokes to bring me alongside the hull. The torch was rubber covered, virtually watertight, so that I was able to dive down and examine the rent. It was much as Sandford had described it, but the plates were buckled over a wider area. I dived to the bottom, saw that she was grounded at the stern, and then swam all round her, checking the hull. But that was the only damage. I came back to the rent, cold now and feeling tired. I wasn't at all sure I could pull myself up by the rope dangling over the side, and with the hole gaping in front of me, I took a chance and swam through, wary of the jagged edges of the plating.

I surfaced in the engine-room, the taste of oil on my lips the water black and scummy, full of floating debris. The two banks of diesels were awash, the coupling to the single screw completely submerged. I floated cautiously to the ladder leading up past the header tank into the crew's quarters and clambered out. The air was warm and stale, smelling faintly of diesel oil. I stayed there for a moment, wondering how the hell those diesels had functioned at all with the engine-room half under water. But then, of course, she was on the bottom now and the tide making. Afloat, most of that rent would have been above the waterline.

I was beginning to shiver; rubbing my hands over my body, I could feel the goose-pimples below the film of oil. I started up the ladder then, unwilling to dive down again into the black murk of dirty water out of which the engines protruded like rocks awash. The ladder led up to an alleyway, and I went aft, past the galley and the messroom, to a door that opened on to the deck, with toilet and showers right in the stern. I moved for'ard, making a quick tour of the ship, careful of my feet and trying to memorize every item of damage. It was dark now, a cold breeze fluttering the flag of a dan buoy, all the nets neatly stowed along the inside of the bulwarks. Up on the road a car's headlights blazed and then vanished.

'You all right?' Fuller called.

I shouted back to him that I wouldn't be long and made my way to the bridge. It was an old-fashioned lay-out, a telegraph on the starboard side and the wheel at the back. But new equipment had been added, most of it ranged haphazardly under the half-circle of insloping windows – Decca radar, navigator and recorder, echo-sounder, log and speed indicator. The skipper's seat was fixed to a piece of metal piping socketed into the floor, and on the wall behind was the VHF set and the Warden receiver.

It was old equipment, probably secondhand. Leading off the starboard gangway, to the right of the companionway down to the quarters, was an enclosed space with a shelf for chartwork, and on it was the main R/T set, a big Cresta-Vega double-sideband. The door to the master's cabin was not locked. Inside, I found the bedding neatly piled on the bunk, all vestige of its dead occupant removed. Somebody – the girl probably, or that shambling giant of a man, who might well be the mate – had been on board and collected the old man's things, all except an aged reefer jacket hanging on the back of the door, salt marks white on the dark cloth and traces of mildew. I put it on and went back into the bridge, standing for a moment with my hands on the wheel, trying to visualize how she would be in a seaway with the diesels at half ahead and her crew shooting the trawl, myself the owner and skipper. It was a dream, no more, and I was too cold to think very clearly, but the longing was there, deep inside me.

It was only a moment I stood at the wheel, but I can still remember the odd feeling of companionship I experienced, as though there was a presence beside me in the darkness of the bridge. Not hostile, just watchful. I let go of the wheel and it was gone, as though it were the helm itself that had communicated with me. How long, I wondered, had the 81-year-old Olav Petersen been master on this bridge?

I went back to the radio shelf outside the skipper's cabin, remembering I had seen charts there. I thought perhaps the log might be there too, hoping that, if it went back far enough, it might give some indication of why Petersen's daughter-in-law had become the owner. Had her husband also died on board?

But there was no log book, only the charts. These were the two Shetland Isles charts, Nos. 1118A and B, and I opened them out, laying them flat along the shelf and following the pencil marks of their last cruise. They had been trawling off

Ramna Stacks on the 23rd, off Gloup Holm and The Clapper on the 24th, and had started south down Bluemull Sound at 05.35 on the 25th. It was all there, every fix, every change of course, the pencilled figures thin and shaky. But on the 25th the writing had changed. It was larger, firmer, and there were erasures, as though whoever had taken over was unaccustomed to making chart entries.

I was shivering by then, my teeth chattering uncontrollably. I put the charts back in the drawer and with a last glance round the bridge, I went out along the starboard gangway into the chill of the night breeze. I had forgotten about the reefer and I took it off and hung it in the shower compartment at the stern. The freeboard was so small with the tide near the high that I did not bother about a rope, but dived straight over the side and headed for the spit. The coldness of the water took my breath away and I was gasping for air as my feet touched bottom. I heard Fuller speaking, but I didn't catch the words. Then the beam of a torch stabbed the night and a voice demanded, 'Who are you? What are you doing here?' It was a woman's voice, loud and very clear, vibrant with anger.

I stopped, blinded by the glare and shivering. 'I've no clothes on,' I said, feeling foolish.

She laughed, a furious snorting sound. 'Do you think I haven't seen a man naked before? Now come on. Get out and explain what you've been up to.' And she kept the torch full on me all the time I was stumbling ashore over the boulders. I heard Fuller trying to explain, but by then I was past caring. I just reached for my clothes and dragged them on without bothering to dry myself. I thought she was some farmer's wife out after sheep or ponies, and then I heard her say, 'Sharks. You're like sharks, coming out here in the dark – ' Her voice was wild and high – 'sniffing round the ship as though it is a bloody carcass.'

I grabbed the torch and turned it on her, the violence of her emotions warning me. Her face was no longer that of the young woman I had seen following the coffin that morning. Gone was the serenity, the tight-lipped control. 'I'm sorry,' I said. What else? I knew how she must feel. I could see it in her eyes, the blaze of anger brightened by tears. And she was right. Sandford, Fuller, myself, others probably – all of us for our different reasons wanting to know whether the trawler could be floated again. 'You shouldn't have come – '

'Shouldn't have come! My ship, an' you tell me – '

'Feeling the way you do about her.' I lowered the beam of the torch, not wishing to intrude into the private world of her emotions. 'We'll go now.' I heard a sob in the darkness. That was all. She didn't say anything. 'If I had known . . .' I murmured, then left it at that. No good making excuses when to her we were sharks with our teeth into the prey. But whether the ship was just an outlet for her grief, or something more, I don't know. Men grieve over the loss of their ships, but for a woman . . .

I was thinking about her most of the time Fuller was driving me back to Hamnavoe. I'd never met a woman owner before. I was still thinking about her next morning as I took the road to Brough again, walking through a light drizzle. Fuller had said he would put my proposition to Villiers and I was remembering the blaze of anger in her eyes, wondering whether she would attend the auction. I was quite sure she had been on board when her father-in-law had died, and this I was able to confirm when I stopped at Miss Manson's cottage. 'She has always gone out with them, even when Jan was alive. He was her husband and she had to, him being so sickly, you see.'

She couldn't tell me very much. The Petersens had only been on East Burra four or five years. Jan Petersen had died about two years ago – of pneumonia, she thought. He had been in hospital at Lerwick, and after his death the trawler had anchored between voyages in the shelter of The Taing instead of at Hamnavoe. 'So it's not often we see Gertrude now.' And she added, 'She's Norwegian, you know. The old man, too, and most of the crew, they're all Norwegians.'

I walked on then to Grund Sound and the little church, but it was the grave with its bunches of daffodils I saw; I wasn't thinking about my father. I paused for a moment on the bridge, gazing across at the mound of fresh earth. I think I had half hoped to find her there. I could have explained to her then . . . But perhaps not. I went slowly on and ate my lunch in a field with three Shetland ponies watching me and a view of the calm circle of water sheltered by a tongue of land that was marked on my map as The Taing. Her house, which was an old farmhouse little bigger than a cottage, stood at the base of the tongue. It was built of stone with a slate roof, superbly set against the steep backdrop of the hills beyond Clift Sound. I could just imagine how it would have been for her, coming back after a week's trawling and waking up in the morning to look out of the window at her own ship lying snug to its reflection. But the inlet was empty now and the house looked deserted, no sign of life.

I walked on through Houss, across Ayre Dyke and over the Ward of Symbister to a view of the Stacks of Houssness and South Havra beyond, and all the time I was thinking about the ship, how much she would fetch at auction, what it would feel like to be an owner and in business for myself. The urge to achieve something constructive, that creative instinct I had ignored for so long . . . It had all suddenly become focused on that trawler.

I was so full of plans that it never occurred to me Villiers would turn down my proposition. God! How simple everything is when you are walking alone with the sea all round you and dreaming dreams!

But when I got back to my lodgings late in the afternoon I found a long envelope waiting for me; inside were documents for signature with a note from Fuller explaining them. Instead of a loan, Villiers had instructed him to acquire the mortgage. This he had done and he was now offering to assign it to me as advance payment for a three-month charter on the terms I had already turned down. But after that he would be prepared to renew it monthly at progressively higher rates. The documents enclosed with his letter were the Charter Agreement and the Deed of Assignment for the mortgage, and there were three copies of each. *All copies require the signature of both yourself and the legal owner of the vessel, one copy to be retained by her, one by yourself and the third to be returned to me at the Lerwick Hotel by tomorrow evening at the latest.* And the letter went on: *We think it best that you negotiate direct with Mrs Petersen. She may well be reluctant to accept you as the mortgagee, or – and this is equally essential to what Mr Villiers and I have in mind – to agree to your captaining the vessel once it is in commission again. In which case, the auction will proceed and the vessel will become the property of the highest bidder.*

The mortgage was for £12,000 at twelve per cent interest, and sitting in my bare little room, going over those documents in the fading light, I found it difficult to concentrate on the legal phrases. Was it Villiers or Fuller who had devised the scheme? Not that it mattered, but Villiers I thought – it was so simple, so damnably clever. A cheap charter that committed me to getting the trawler into commission by 20th April and then running her on a shoestring to keep out of debt . . . and leaving me to fix it all with Gertrude Petersen.

I saw her the following morning and by then I had been over all the arguments. To my surprise she was waiting for me when I came down the track to Taing House. It was blowing hard from the south-west, her fair hair flying in the wind as she took me inside. 'I was told to expect you.' She didn't offer me a chair, and she didn't sit down herself, but stood facing me, her legs slightly apart as though the floor of the sitting-room was a deck that might heave under her feet at any moment. 'I saw Mr Fuller yesterday. In the evening. He explained the arrangement to me.' Her manner was cold and distant and her voice controlled. 'You have the deeds with you?'

'Yes,' I said, surprised and relieved that I didn't have to explain it all to her. 'What made you see Fuller?'

'I heard he was looking for a trawler.' No emotion now, and the grey eyes fixed on me, hard and businesslike. 'You're not the only one with ideas about refloating her. Johan is down there working on her now and I have talked with Jim Halcrow.'

'I see.' So she had reached some other arrangement with Fuller. But when I suggested this, she shook her head. 'You think I cut you out?' A flicker of a smile showed at the corners of her mouth. 'Hardly. I do not have a master's ticket, nor does Johan, and neither of us has worked in a shipyard. Jim Halcrow says you have. Is that right, Mr Randall?' And she added, her eyes narrowed as though trying to make up her mind about me, 'It is Randall, isn't it? I understand when you arrived in Sumburgh – '

'Randall,' I said. 'Mike Randall.'

She gave a little shrug. 'Well, Mr Randall, the question is, can you get her sufficiently watertight to float her off?'

'I think so,' I said.

She looked at me a moment and then she nodded. 'Good. Then let us start with the Deed of Agreement. I am told it is the simpler of the two.'

She made room on the table by the window and I spread the three copies out for her. 'I should warn you,' I said, 'there is a clause in it making its validity dependent on your signing the Charter Agreement.'

'Of course.' She was bending over the documents and she didn't look up, her hair falling over her face. Her hands, palms down on the table, supporting her weight, were short and capable, the skin burned brown with salt, the nails cut short, and the gold circle of her wedding ring glinting in the light. Directly in front of her was a photograph in a plain oak frame. The print, blotched with damp mould, faded by exposure to light, showed a man with a thin face under a peaked cap bent over the gun of a whale catcher. Beside him an older man with back and roaring with laughter. 'My husband, Jan,' she said. 'With his father. It was just after the war, the first whale he harpooned after he became schutter. They were very happy then I think.' She signed her name quickly on all three copies. 'Now the other documents please.' And she held out her hand.

But this time she did not sign her name as soon as she had read it through. Instead, she looked up at me. 'Do you agree with the terms these people are offering?'

'I haven't much choice.'

'No?' She stared at me, the eyes gone cold again and the hostility back in her voice. 'Well, I do have a choice, Mr Randall, and they need a stand-by boat very badly. All rigs operating in the North Sea have to have one, by law. I check on that before I see Mr Fuller.' She nodded emphatically, as though expressing satisfaction at her good sense. 'So, he has agreed to some alterations. I am to write them on all the copies, each alteration to be initialled by both of us.'

What she had got out of him was a small increase in the charter rate and an interest-free loan sufficient to cover salvage, repairs, insurance, and with luck most of the victualling. 'I do not intend, you see, to get into the hands of the money-lenders again.'

'I wonder you ever did,' I murmured.

'You think I get into their hands?' There was sudden bitterness in her voice. 'You think I forget the insurance premium! Oh, no! But business – that is a man's job. So my father-in-law always say. My husband, too. They must deal with the chandlers, the buyers, everything to do with money. And they never haggle.' She gave an exasperated laugh. 'Too proud to behave like fishwives, I guess. But now . . .' She stared at me very determinedly. 'You captain the ship. But that is all. You understand? I look after the business.'

I hesitated, thinking of all that had to be done to get the trawler on station by 20th April. It would be hard, slogging work, and the one thing I would have fought Fuller over she hadn't even raised. 'You realize you have committed the ship to standing by the rig for three months in all weathers without any relief boat.'

'That is why I was able to get an improved charter rate.'

'No crew will stand for it. Three months out there—'

'Johan says they agree. I have offered a bonus of course.'

'And the engineers?'

'Per is already discharged. Some burns, that is all. Duncan has two cracked ribs. I saw him at the hospital last night.'

'And he undertakes to keep those engines running for three months?'

She nodded, a little defiantly I thought. 'Yes, he does.' I forebore to mention that it was a failure of the engines that had lost her ship, but she must have guessed what was in my mind for she said quickly, 'Duncan was away sick for almost a month. Per Kalvik, the assistant engineer, is not so good. He is a young man and on his own he do not maintain the engines properly.' And she added, 'Duncan has never been away from the ship before, not since we installed the new engines.'

She had it all worked out, the crew, the engineers, everything, quite prepared to ignore the fact that under the terms of the agreement we had to provide a replacement if for any reason I was forced to run for shelter. But when I pointed this out to her, she flared up at me: 'It is you who are raising difficulties, nobody else. Fuel and stores, anything you want, is to be delivered free of any transport charge by the supply ship, and I have arranged for the transportation of men on leave by helicopter from the rig, also free. Since you will not be fishing you will need less crew. Minimum crew for stand-by boats is six—captain, mate, chief engineer, assistant engineer, cook and one deckhand. You, Duncan and Johan will not get relief.' She had been talking very fast. Now she stopped abruptly, standing staring at me, her manner suddenly awkward. 'It is a very difficult situation, between us. We do not know anything about each other. And this agreement—' She made a motion of her hand towards the document. 'As soon as I sign, then you are the mortgagee and I am in your hands. Even the loan I arrange—it is made to you, not to me. He insists on that.'

It was certainly an odd arrangement and the division of any profits left to us. 'I imagine you will require some sort of an agreement drawn up between us,' I said.

She didn't seem to hear me, her head turned to the window,

gazing out at the water. 'These business men are very clever.' There was a long pause, and then suddenly she was facing me again. 'Two complete strangers. And they have hung us round each other's neck.' She smiled, a gleam of humour that was gone in a flash. 'Well, there it is. Neither of us can argue, we have no money.' She pulled up a chair and sat down. 'I agree. We shall need to have an agreement. But not now. Later.' And she began writing in the alterations.

She wrote fast, as though by concentrating on the words she could relieve the tension and frustration that was in her, initialling each alteration as she made it and signing the copies at the bottom. Then she pushed the whole lot over to me. When I had signed she said, 'Johan is living on board. I suggest you do the same now.'

'And the crew?'

'They are at the Seaman's Mission, available whenever you want them.' She collected the papers together and put them in the envelope. 'Now if you are ready, we will pick up your things and I will drive you down to the boat.'

CHAPTER THREE

It took me four days to complete the welding of a steel patch. The biggest problem was rigging a secure platform on which to work in the cramped space between the starboard engine and the hull. After that it was a question of following each tide down as the water poured out of the engine-room through the rent in the hull. The job was slow and dirty, and though we had spring tides, the last six inches or so of steel sheet had to be left unwelded. It was on the Tuesday morning, just as Johan and two of the crew were holding the first sheet in position and I was spot-welding it to the hull plates, that Sandford arrived.

No doubt he called my name several times before he tapped me on the shoulder. The arc of the welding torch made a hell of a row in the confined space of the engine-room. I swung round, the arc sputtering in my hand so that I nearly knocked him off the single plank we had rigged as a walkway from the ladder. 'What do you want?'

'That mortgage. I'm told you own it.' He had to yell to make himself heard. 'I'll buy it off you.'

I turned back towards the hull plating. With the tide falling, and the sheet not yet fixed, this was no time for interruptions. His hand gripped my shoulder. 'How much do you want?'

I pushed my visor up. 'Talk to Mrs Petersen,' I said. 'She's the business brains.' His eyes, bright in the spotlight, reminded me of the way his mother had looked when she thought there might be money in my visit.

'I have. I saw her last night.'

'Then you know the answer.'

'She isn't the mortgagee.'

I glanced at my watch. Just over an hour of tide to go. I turned my back on him, pulling the visor down and flicking the jet full on. He shouted something at me as I bent to my welding again, the bearded face of Johan watching with his big hands on the plate, dangerously close as the gobs of molten steel flew out. I forgot about him then, my mind concentrated on the job.

Before the tide was up again I had the whole plate welded, except for the last six inches which had still been underwater at the bottom of the tide. It was late afternoon then and we went up to the bridge, the four of us sweating and tired and dirty. 'You want tea?' Johan asked as we reached the top of the ladder and felt the cold air of the deck.

'No, beer I think.'

'Ja. Beer.' His blond beard, all grimed with oil and slightly singed, cracked open in a grin. 'Beer for me also. Lars? Henrik?' The two seamen nodded and he sent Lars to raid the pantry. We had left our jerseys in the bridge and we entered to find Sandford seated in the skipper's chair, a pile of cigarette butts in the ashtray behind the wheel housing. 'I've been watching the tide on the rocks. Thought you wouldn't be able to work down there much longer.'

I pulled on my jersey, chilled now with the sweat drying on me. 'You been waiting here all the time?'

He nodded. 'Can't discuss business with a man waving a welding torch in my face.'

'There's no business to discuss,' I said.

'No?' He swivelled the chair as though enjoying the feel of being in the master's seat. 'I've been thinking. It was clever of you. I never thought of buying the mortgage. Nor did any of us. There were five of us turned up at the auction yesterday morning, all of us with money to bid for her, and nobody was exactly pleased when they told us it was off.' He lit a cigarette from the butt of the one he had just finished and stubbed the old one out in the ashtray. 'Can we go somewhere where we can talk?'

'I'm living on board,' I told him. 'If you want to talk it will have to be here.' Lars appeared with four cans of beer.

Sandford got to his feet. 'Come into the master's cabin then. We can talk there.'

'There's nothing to talk about,' I said. But he insisted and in the end I followed him. 'Well, what is it?' I said as we faced each other alone with the door closed.

'It took me most of yesterday to find out just how you'd fixed it.'

'I didn't fix it.'

'No, it was that oil man Fuller. But you're the mortgagee and I'm willing to buy you out.'

'It's all tied up with the charter agreement.'

'I know that. But it suits my plans. I'll give you a thousand — cash. So long as you get her floated.'

Within two minutes he had raised his offer to fifteen hundred and I wondered why. Cash meant he knew all about fiddling tax. It wasn't only that I was suspicious; it went against the grain. And when I asked him who would skipper her, he said he had his own man and a crew as well.

'You'd still have to complete the charter,' I said.

He nodded. 'Of course.'

It didn't make sense. 'What's behind your offer?'

He laughed. 'I told you. I need a ship. And this is the only one available.' And he added, 'Fifteen hundred isn't a bad offer just for getting her afloat and towed into Bressay Sound.'

'You're wasting your time,' I said. 'Money doesn't mean very much to me.' And it was true. If I had stayed in the States I could have had all the money I wanted, but not on my terms. And what the hell is life about if you don't live it on your own terms? But to explain that to Sandford, who had inherited a solid streak of peasant greed from his mother, would be like explaining Marxism to a Hull trawler owner. I pulled the door open. 'I need another beer,' I said.

He stood for a moment uncertainly. But he knew it was no good. 'I thought you were clever.' His voice reflected his disappointment. 'You're just a bloody fool,' he said angrily. And then, as he was going out, he turned and asked me why, after all these years, I had come to Shetland making enquiries about my father. 'You never knew him. You never cared what happened to him. Why now?'

'That's my business,' I said and I pushed him out into the gangway, ordering Henrik to take him ashore in the work boat we now had alongside. Gertrude Petersen arrived shortly afterwards with a meal she had prepared at home, and when I told her what had happened, she said, 'I don't like that man. I don't like the people he employs. Last December, when we are stormbound in Burra Firth for two days, we are in the hotel and there is this Irish behind the bar – he make trouble for Johan.' She didn't say what trouble, but there was a slight flush on her face as she added, 'It is the last time we drink in his hotel.'

I forgot about Sandford after that. We lived by the tide, our heads aching after every shift, falling into our bunks as soon as we had fed and sleeping until the alarm woke us. And when, in the early hours of the Friday morning, it was done and we began pumping, I just stood there on the deck staring at the dark shadow of the hills, feeling utterly exhausted. I was like a surgeon who has performed a difficult operation. All I wanted now was for the patient to live, and so identified had I become with the ship that I felt it was part of me.

We breakfasted late to the racket of the pump, and afterwards Gertrude drove me to Halcrow's yard. They were behind schedule, and with the drilling contractors screaming for their supply ship, the trials were set for Sunday afternoon. That gave us two clear days. We got the anchor out on the port beam, with the chain linked by a big block and tackle to the trawl winch hawser, then at low water on the Saturday morning, with the Land-Rover hitched to the tail end of the purchase guy, and all of us pulling, some of the locals as well, we managed to roll her about 12 degrees. This list to port was just sufficient to bring the whole patch clear of the water at the bottom of the tide. But it still took two tides to cut the plate edges of the hull, beat out the dents and weld the last six inches of the patch. Even when that was done the pump could only just hold its own.

'We'll have to slip and patch her properly from the outside,' I told Gertrude as we stood that evening in the engine-room, the sound of the pump drumming at the deck overhead and the water gurgling in the bilges. She didn't argue. On the port side the floor gratings ran down into water. Even when we had released the purchase tackle and the trawler was floating upright on the top of the tide, water sloshed and gurgled over the gratings as the ship moved in the wind, dancing to a slight swell coming in round the end of the spit. She knew the hull had to be absolutely watertight if we were to keep the sea in all weathers for three weary months.

All this time the wind had been westerly and the water in the voe quiet under the lee of mainland. Now the forecast was for changeable weather, the last of the depressions moving away towards Iceland and a High coming in behind it, with a Low over France. That slight swell was a warning of north-easterly winds. Duncan appeared at my side and stood sniffing the air as though he, too, sensed the change. He was a dour man with a long nose and a sandy moustache. The hospital had discharged him the previous afternoon and he had been down in the engine-room ever since cleaning the place up with the help of his assistant, Per, and the youngest member of the crew, a big bull of a boy known as Sperm. 'Pump holding?' I asked him.

'Aye.'

'And the engines?'

'They'll no get her oot o' here, if that's what you mean.'

So we just had to hope Jim Halcrow would risk bringing the supply ship right in on the tide. 'Mrs Petersen told you the parts you ordered have arrived by air?' He nodded and I asked him how his ribs were.

'Strapped so tight I can't hardly breathe. But it's the electrics I'm worried aboot. That pipe to the cooling system is nothing by comparison. It could be the dynamos will have to be stripped down, or even replaced, and God knows what's happened to the wiring.' He sniffed again at the breeze coming in down the voe. 'Ach weel, I'll get back doon again noo. That bluidy boy dinna ken the difference between an oil line and a fuel pipe.'

'You'd better get some sleep,' I told him.

'A week in that bluidy morgue – what the hell ye think I been doing?' And he disappeared into the night, heading for the door to the engine-room, his left arm held awkwardly to his body.

It was still only a breeze when dawn broke. But by 09.00 it had strengthened to Force 4 and there were waves breaking on the seaward side of the spit. We grounded shortly after-wards, the keel bumping on boulders. The grating and clanging lasted almost half an hour. All we could do after that was wait, and hope that the wind wouldn't increase before high water, which was at 16.05.

But by then I had something else to worry about. Gertrude arrived just as we were completing the lifting of the anchor and she came aboard as soon as the work boat had dropped the anchor and chain under the bows. 'Jim Halcrow says he will bring the supply ship in whatever the weather. He has the power and the manœuvrability, also he draws much less than we do. But he needs to know the exact time you expect to be afloat.'

'Tell him we'll be bumping the bottom at about 15.35 and clear to tow off any time after 16.00.'

She nodded. 'Okay. I tell him that.' There was a pause and then she said, 'There was a man at the yard this morning. He was making enquiries.'

We were standing in the starboard bridge gangway, watching the crew heaving in on the anchor chain, the trawler lying still now and the hills behind a diorama of shifting light as the clouds scudded over. An island scene, and all so peaceful that the industrial world I had lived in seemed unreal. 'What sort of a man?'

'A police inspector, but in plain clothes.'

Not Bob Scunton then or the other man. That was something. Unless this inspector insisted on my going back to Hull. 'What did he want?'

'Just enquiring about you. What you were doing.'

'Did he ask you any questions?'

'No. He did not need to. He had already talked to me the previous day.'

'Where?'

'At Taing.'

'You didn't tell me.'

'No.'

'Why?'

She looked at me then. 'Why do you think? I don't want to distract you.' And she added, 'He will see you when the ship is afloat and lying off the yard.'

God! What a practical, soulless woman she was, not caring a damn about anything but her trawler.

'What is it about?' she asked. 'You have done something?'

I looked at her, feeling suddenly cold and hard inside. Was this what a whaling station did to you? She had been brought up in the stench of the flensing deck, and her father had rubbed his hands with glee and said it smelled of money. She had told me that herself, laughing, and I had seen her in my mind as a young girl with the guts and urine of dead whales spilling out at her feet, and her father beaming and rubbing his hands. 'A little girl was nearly killed,' I said.

'And you were involved?'

'No.'

'Then why is this inspector here from London?'

'Better ask him,' I said, and went down the ladder to give a hand for'ard.

Gertrude Petersen left shortly after that. The warps were all ready aft, the anchor stowed and the chain flaked neatly on the foredeck, heaving lines and fenders handy. Nothing to do after lunch but watch the tide making and the sea slowly building as the wind increased – and think about what happened next, why they should have sent an inspector from London. In the privacy of my cabin I poured myself a stiff whisky. I should have been worrying about the tow. Instead, I was thinking how hard she was, my mind going back to the problem that had been with me ever since that night in Hull. A local matter surely, not something for Scotland Yard. Unless . . . But I shied away from the thought. It was just a matter of intimidation. Intimidation that had got out of control. I must concentrate on that. Did I identify the men or not? That was all that mattered.

Johan poked his head round the door. 'We can see the tug now. It is steaming out in the bay. Fixed courses, so he is making speed trials.'

I followed him into the bridge, relieved to get away from my thoughts. The sky had cleared, the whitecaps in the bay bright in the sun. The supply ship was just turning at the extremity of her northward run up by Stany Hog. The high superstructure for'ard and the flat run aft certainly gave her the look of a tug. She completed the turn and started south. The time was 14.55. Less than an hour to go. I went all round the ship with Johan, checking that everything was ready and that each man knew what he had to do. Then I went back to the bridge and tested the loudhailer. No sign of the ship. She was lost to view behind the dune-like hills of Ward of Brough.

Ten minutes later she poked her bluff fendered bows round Cunning Holm islet, moving slowly now, coming in on her echo-sounder. A few minutes and she was in full view, turning and pointing her bows straight at us. And at almost the same moment I felt a slight lift to the deck under my feet, heard the first faint rumble of the keel knocking on boulders. She came in very slowly, feeling her way, until her bows were level with the spit. She hung there for a while, her engines throwing a froth of water for'ard along her sides as she maintained station against the wind funnelling down the voe. I could see Jim Halcrow seated at the controls high up in the little glass wheelhouse, Gertrude Petersen beside him. He put a microphone to his lips and loud across the water came his query— 'Are you off the bottom yet?'

I was out on the bridge gangway then and I called through the loudhailer for him to come and get us. He gave me a thumbs-up and drifted round the end of the spit, turning on his own axis and bringing his stern right against ours. I had never seen one of these vessels operating in a confined space; it was like driving a Dodgem. We didn't need heaving lines. Johan just passed the end of our big warp straight into the hands of the man hanging out over the stern roller. He hitched it on to the winch hawser and my men hardly had time to make fast before the supply ship was going ahead, rope and hawser taking the strain. There was an ugly grinding noise, a jar on the soles of my feet as we came up against rock, then we were off, our bows swinging away downwind.

It was the neatest thing; one moment we were aground, hammering on boulders, the next we were out in the channel, clear of the spit and stern-on to the voe. The supply ship had 6000 h.p. and Jim Halcrow used the wind to get us positioned, then he just plucked us out stern-first into the bay. The tail end of our warp was already made fast at the bows. All we had to do was cast off astern. As soon as our bows were round the tow began.

We had to go round Bressay and enter Lerwick from the south, but even so, we were anchored off the Halcrow yard before dark. A constable in uniform was standing on the boat jetty watching us.

By the time we had finished flaking down the tow warp the work boat was alongside, Jim Halcrow coming on board, followed by Gertrude Petersen, her eyes shining. 'It worked,' she said laughing. 'Your patch is all right.'

'So long as the pump keeps going.' My voice sounded sharp. I was quite incapable of responding to her mood. I hadn't expected a constable. 'Trials go off satisfactorily?' I asked Halcrow.

'Fine. Manœuvring and towing made a good test for the new shaft.' He glanced at the sky upwind of us, then at his watch. 'Well, let's have a look at your problems. Where's your Chief, in the engine-room?'

I nodded and led him below. We could hear the water sloshing about in the bilges as we went down the ladder. The sound of it was loud now the ship was floating to her marks. Duncan appeared out of the gloom. 'Ye'll have to have a resairve pump on board.' Apparently we had made 5 inches during the tow. I introduced him to Halcrow and left them to it. When I got back to the deck the yard boat had arrived and the constable was waiting for me. He was a big, tow-headed young islander with a friendly face. 'You the captain?'

'Yes.'

He had his notebook open in his hand. 'Michael Mouat Randall. Would that be the name?' And when I nodded, he said, 'I must ask you to accompany me to the station.'

'Any reason?'

'No, sir. Only that Inspector Garrard would like a word with you.'

So their witness hadn't perjured himself yet and there was no warrant. 'I've a lot to do,' I said. 'If the Inspector wants to talk to me he's welcome to come on board.'

The young man hesitated. 'I'll tell him that if you like, sir. But he's not one of us, y'know, so I'd advise you to come along and see what it's all about.'

I didn't like it. Sending a constable to fetch me to the station, instead of coming down to the ship himself . . . 'Oh, for God's sake!' Gertrude Petersen exclaimed. 'Go on down to the station with him and get it over. We've got a lot to do.'

'Well, you get on with it then,' I told her. I wasn't in the best of moods as I went ashore. The constable had his police car parked behind the yard, and as we started down the shore road, I asked him what branch Inspector Garrard was assigned to.

'Ye'll have to ask him, sir.'

'Does that mean you don't know?'

I think he knew, but he had his orders and he didn't talk as we drove into Lerwick.

The police station was in the County Buildings up on Town Hall Brae, a brown sandstone building opposite the Garrison Theatre. I was taken straight through into a small bare room. The constable switched the light on. 'I'll tell the Inspector ye're here.' The door closed and I resigned myself to a long wait. Stupidly I had left my pipe on the bridge. I felt lost without it now that my mind had to grapple once again with problems of conscience and expedience. Did they really have a local witness who would get up in court and swear he'd seen me throw that petrol bomb? I could remember the hard line of the man's mouth, the shut face pale in the deck lights, and Aberdeen harbour glimmering in the rain. Where was he now, I wondered?

I was still thinking about him, and why an inspector was checking on my movements, when the door opened and a slightly stooped man in a tweed jacket entered. 'Sorry to keep you waiting.' He had the tired air of a man who has been up all night, but his eyes were bright as he put the briefcase he was carrying down and sat at the table, waving me to the chair opposite. 'I gather you're busy trying to get that wrecked trawler back into commission.'

I nodded.

'Any particular reason?'

'Reason?' It wasn't the opening I had expected.

'Yes. Why are you doing it?'

'I don't see that it concerns the police.'

'No? Well, maybe it doesn't.' He reached into the briefcase, pulled out several files and laid them on the table in front of him. 'But motivation is something that does concern me. If you know what motivates a man, then you are at least halfway to solving a case – or avoiding trouble.' He was soft-spoken, his manner quiet and relaxed, almost conversational. 'We'll come back to that in a moment. Meanwhile – ' He opened the slimmest of the files in front of him – 'let us take a look at your record.' He fished out a pair of gilt-rimmed half-glasses; these and the slight stoop gave him a somewhat academic air. 'I would guess you have never done anything without strong motivation.' He looked across at me. 'Not perhaps the right word. Without ideological convictions. Would that be a reasonable assessment of your somewhat unusual shifts of work and environment?' He was staring at me over the half-glasses. 'I see you don't want to admit to that. Is it the word ideological you object to?'

'My ideological convictions, presuming I have any, are my own concern.'

He nodded. 'Perhaps. But there are things I don't understand and I would appreciate your co-operation.'

'What about?'

'Why you suddenly decided to come up here, for instance?' The academic air had receded, the pale eyes watching me. 'You know the Hull police were waiting to interview you – a question of intimidation.'

'I had nothing to do with that.'

'Then what were you doing there?' He didn't seem surprised at my not answering. 'Lucky you were,' he murmured. 'For the little girl, anyway.' He paused, letting the silence run on. Finally he said, 'Would you like to tell me about it?'

'Not your department,' I said. 'You're not from Hull.' That question about ideological convictions . . . 'What department are you – Special Branch?'

He smiled. 'Let us say I am a police officer who knows quite a lot about you, has learned more since he has been here and now wants to know what the hell you're up to.'

'Do I have to be up to something?' But he'd see it differently, of course. Once a man has been in trouble with the police . . . 'You're part of the Establishment,' I said. 'You don't have to worry about finding a job. It's always there. But for others it's different. Do you find that difficult to understand?' I was being sarcastic, but it didn't seem to upset him.

'You don't have to worry about a job either, Randall. You're not just a trawlerman. You're a highly intelligent, highly trained individual. But your record, if I may say so, is a somewhat unusual one.' He picked up the top page of the file, leaning back with it in his hand. 'This is a summary. Shall I read it to you?' He did not wait for me to reply, but went straight on: 'You were born on 2nd April, 1937. Your mother, Muriel Caroline Randall, taught in kindergarten in Aberdeen. In November 1938, following the Munich crisis, she took a course in nursing at Glasgow Infirmary. There she met Henry Wilkin Graber, a wealthy American business man. In fact, she was one of the nurses who looked after him when he was brought into the hospital in February 1939 following a car accident. Shortly after his return to the States he offered her the job of governess to his two children. She turned him down then, but just over a year later, in July 1940, she took passage on one of the refugee ships to the States. That was after the fall of France, so presumably her concern was for you. Would that be right?'

'You work out your own answers,' I said.

He smiled. 'I'm only trying to get at the motivation. Your father, for instance. Have you ever visited Shetland before?' And when I shook my head, he said, 'Now, suddenly, you go to West Burra, where he was born, and start making enquiries. Why?'

'A man ought to know something about his father,' I murmured.

'He was a Communist. But you knew that before you came up here.'

'Yes.'

'Where is he now?' He was leaning forward, his eyes on my face.

'Don't be silly,' I said. 'You've been to Hamnavoe, and to Ground Sound too. You know damn well he died just before Madrid fell to Franco's forces.'

He nodded. 'Of course. The plaque. Who put it there?'

'I've no idea.'

'Your mother perhaps?'

'I don't think so.'

'And you're an only child – no brothers or sisters.'

'No.'

'But it was somebody who knew him well, eh? That line from Browning – the conflict within himself. Are you sure you've never met him?' My bewilderment must have shown, for he added, 'The plaque was sent to the Clerk of the Presbytery of Shetland in 1958 by an anonymous donor with instructions where it was to be placed and a sum that more than covered the cost of the work.'

'I only saw it just over a week ago. I had no idea how it came to be up there.'

He stared at me for a moment, looking me straight in the eyes. He was still staring at me when he suddenly said, 'Are you a Communist?'

'No.'

'But you believe in Communism?'

'I also believe in Christianity.'

He smiled and I caught a flicker of interest, even sympathy, in those pale eyes. 'And there is a difference between the Christian faith and the Christian church. Is that what you mean?'

I shrugged.

'Just as there is a difference between the Communist ideal

and Communism itself, say the Russian brand?'

'You don't need to get me down to a police station to state the obvious.'

He laughed, leaning back in his chair and relaxing again. 'Well, let's get back to your file. And please pick me up if they've got it wrong at all. In January 1941 your mother took up residence in Graber's house on Rhode Island. You were then three-and-a-half years old. Did you like Henry Graber?'

'I don't remember.'

'And you don't remember your father either?'

'No.'

'Yet you accepted the one and rejected the other. Was that because of your mother's marriage? Were you jealous of Graber?'

I reached into my pocket for my pipe, realized it wasn't there and heard him say something about the physical relationship of a mother and her only son. 'For Christ's sake, where's this leading?' I demanded angrily.

His strangely quiet face looked suddenly grim. 'I'll tell you where it's leading – to your record. It's here in this file, two dozen separate items at least – shop floor convener, agitator, union organizer and militant. You've been in prison, you've been charged with inciting others to create a disturbance, resisting arrest, intent to cause grievous bodily harm, and in your public speeches, your writings, in the way you have incited pickets and moved bodies of strikers, you've demonstrated a degree of violent reaction to or from something that is quite abnormal. Now, let's get back to your mother's marriage. It was her second marriage and Graber's third. The date is given here as 5th November, 1944 – is that right?'

I nodded. 'I think my stepfather was very lonely. His wife had just died.' But it had started before then. 'She had been ill for a long time – a mental illness. And my mother –' I checked myself. No point in telling him about that moment of appalment when, as a little boy, I had discovered she didn't regard me as her entire world. 'It was natural enough, I guess.'

'But a shock to you?'

'I imagine so.'

'He had an explosives and small arms factory and made a fortune out of the war. Is that why you suddenly left home?'

'I wanted to travel.'

'To Calcutta – Düsseldorf?'

I felt my muscles tense, the past turning over in my mind,

'My God, you've done your homework.'

'Not me,' he said. 'It's all here.' And he reached for the second file. 'You were educated very expensively – the Phillips Exeter Academy, then Princeton. At Princeton you studied economics. Do you remember a Professor Hansbacher?'

I nodded, the thick glasses, the round beaming face leaping to mind, his brilliant lectures on the nature and defects of capitalism.

'You should, because he remembered you. *One of the cleverest students I ever had.* That's how he describes you. He was a Communist, wasn't he?'

'I've no idea. I was just a kid.'

'That was what he was accused of. He lost his job in the McCarthy witch-hunt.' He leaned towards me. 'You were at an impressionable age. He must have had considerable influence on you.'

'He had a very logical, very clear mind.'

'A brilliant teacher, in fact. Yet within a year you left. Why?'

'I told you. I wanted to travel.'

'To Calcutta? Isn't that where the dropouts go? What did you use for money?' I don't think he expected an answer and I sat there, silent, knowing what was coming: '4th January, 1957 – you were twenty then and in Düsseldorf. What were you doing in Düsseldorf?'

'Why ask me since you've got it all there?'

He nodded. 'You were charged with being in the possession of drugs and you had one of the leading German advocates to defend you. Who paid for that? Was it your stepfather?'

'His lawyers. Yes, he paid for it.'

'You got three months. A year later you had reached India. And then, suddenly, you pulled yourself together. You came to England and studied at the London School of Economics. Did he pay for that too?'

But by then I'd had enough. 'I don't have to sit here going over my past with you.' I got to my feet. 'It's over and done with, and I've got work to do.'

'You're here quite voluntarily.'

'You sent an officer to bring me in.'

He sighed. 'Well, if you're not prepared to co-operate, why did you come?' He leaned back, the pale eyes staring up at me. 'Was it because you knew I'd been making enquiries about you?'

'Why should that worry me? And if you want to know, I

paid my own way while studying at the LSE. Nothing to do with Graber.'

'And when you got your degree you joined the staff of a national daily as a financial journalist.'

'I specialized in industrial relations.'

'You were earning good money. Then suddenly you abandoned your well-paid job, moved to the Clyde and became a shipyard worker. Any particular reason?'

'I found I only knew the management side. I didn't know what it was like from the worker's point of view.'

'Nothing to do with your father?'

'No.'

'And two years later you were a convener, fomenting wildcat strikes and organizing picket lines. Three charges in four years and a short prison sentence. Then you dropped out of that, went to Grimsby and got a job on a trawler. That was after your marriage had broken up. Four years later you had your mate's ticket, then your master's. And now you've dropped out again – into Shetland, enquiring about your father, refloating an old trawler with a contract to act as stand-by boat to an oil rig.' He put the sheet of paper down. 'What was your motive in all this?' He got to his feet then and stood facing me. 'That's all I want to know – your motive.'

'Does there have to be one?'

'I think so.'

'Life isn't like that,' I told him. 'There's no logic in human behaviour.'

'Not always, I agree. But there's often a pattern.' He paused, looking meditatively down at the file. 'I could pull you in for questioning,' he said.

'You've got no warrant.'

He looked at me. 'I could get one.' His voice was suddenly hard. 'Did you start that blaze?'

'No.'

'But you were there. You know who did.'

I didn't answer.

'And you've no intention of going to Hull to help the police in their enquiries.'

'I've got a job to do and there's a lot of work getting that trawler ready for use.'

He nodded. 'I'll tell them. They may issue a warrant or they may not.' He considered me for a moment, frowning, as though uncertain what to do next. 'All right. We'll leave it at that then. But if they make an arrest, you'll be called as a witness. You realize that?' He gave me time to think about it, and then he said, 'I'm going to give you some advice. A warning, rather.' He was suddenly very still, the pale eyes fixed on me. 'The stakes up here in the North Sea are big now,' he said, speaking slowly and with emphasis. 'Big enough to attract a lot of interest, not all of it welcome. Do you understand what I'm talking about?'

'I think so.' I suddenly wanted to get out of there, the little office very quiet and his eyes fixed on me.

'Good.' He hesitated, then reached for the pad and pencil on the desk and wrote down a number. 'If you find yourself getting out of your depth –'

'Why should I?'

He looked at me for a moment. Then he said, 'You're vulnerable, that's why. You're tough physically, but you're vulnerable.' He didn't explain. He didn't have to. 'If you want to talk to me again, go to any police station and have them ring that number. Or you can telephone direct.' He handed me the sheet of paper. It was an 01 number – London. 'What's the name of the rig you're going to work with?'

'North Star.'

'And the company?'

'Star-Trion, a subsidiary of Villiers Finance and Industrial.'

He nodded. 'Well, just remember what I said, and stay out of trouble.' He went to the door and opened it for me. But as I was going out he stopped me. 'One other thing. Your father. He wasn't killed in 1939.'

I stared at him incredulously. 'What the hell are you talking about?'

'Just that. They picked him up in Norway in 1942.' The door closed and I was in the passage leading out of the County Buildings, past the flagpole into Town Hall Brae.

CHAPTER FOUR

I should have gone back and asked him what else he knew. But I was scared. Those files, that dossier on me. The offences I had committed were all minor ones, but he had made them sound formidable, stringing them together like that. A pattern

. . . Of course, there had been a pattern. And once the authorities get their teeth into you – Christ! they had taken a lot of trouble.

And my father . . . That plaque. Who the hell had erected that plaque? And why? Why should anybody do that if he hadn't been killed in the defence of Madrid?

He would have been 68 now, if he were still alive. Too old to be involved in anything very active. But in 1942, when Norway was occupied by the Germans and the Russians were our allies . . . So many questions, and my mind in turmoil as we sweated to get that trawler fit for sea. And all the time that feeling of something hanging over me, a frightening sense of insecurity as I tried to grapple with a mental change of life that seemed to have altered my whole outlook. Work was a panacea, and God knows there was plenty of that.

We slipped on the evening of Friday, 11th April, working through the weekend to get her off at dawn on the Monday. It was the only patent slip in Lerwick and we were lucky to get the use of it, even though it meant doing most of the work ourselves. By then I had had a telegram from the Star-Trion office in Aberdeen requesting confirmation that we would be on station by 20th April as required under the terms of the charter. The location was also given – 60° 22′ N, 2° 40′ W, which was some 30 miles west of Papa Stour, in Block 206/17. We went for sea trials on the Thursday immediately after survey, steaming north as far as Rams Ness, the southern point of Fetlar, in a nor'westerly Force 5-6 with a dirty sea spilling down through Colgrave Sound.

There was still a lot that needed doing. But the repairs to the hull stood up to it and the engines gave full power. We were back off Halcrow's yard by 10.30 on the Friday morning and Gertrude got a telegram off to Star-Trion confirming. We were in business, provided we could keep the vessel going for three months at a stretch.

I was at the chart shelf outside my cabin, working out an ETD based on steaming time required to reach the location, when she returned. 'You'll go south round Sumburgh Head?'

'Yes.'

'Then you can anchor at Taing and sail out to the rig from there.'

It was a thought. A last peaceful night and the chance of a final check on the way round. We could even get delivery of anything we had forgotten.

'Then perhaps you will have time to discuss the agreement between us.'

I looked at her, standing in the doorway at the top of the companionway, a solid figure in an oilskin jacket. Clouds were scudding in over the brown stone smudge of Lerwick town. I couldn't see the expression on her face, but her voice had sounded a little tense. 'I'm afraid I had forgotten about that.'

'You are not very businesslike.' There was a pause, and then, a little hesitantly, she said, 'How do I know you will not go off with the ship?'

'You have Johan, Duncan, the crew – I'm the only outsider.'

'Three months is a long time.'

I turned on her, flinging down my pencil. 'We both signed that charter agreement,' I said, keeping a tight hold on my tongue.

'A piece of paper.'

'Any agreement we draw up between us is still only a piece of paper.'

'Ja.' She had turned back into the bridge, leaning on the telegraph and staring out through the windows. The forecast was bad and a rainstorm was curtaining the higher part of the town. 'I'm sorry.' She made a little movement of her hand. 'We do not work very easily together. My fault, I think. But this ship has so many memories. We come to Shetland in her, Jan and I. When Selmvaag Vaal closed down. Jan bought her in Bergen. It cost us every penny we had, and some of our friends' money as well.'

'What was a Lowestoft trawler doing in Bergen?'

'She was an MFV I think you call them. Right at the beginning of the war she was brought north to Scapa Flow as a fleet supply ship. Later she did some patrols and after that she was with the fleet in Norway. I have the logs at Taing. Then, in 1941, she is in Shetland, sailing again to Norway. It was this ship that brought Far Petersen off, from one of the fjords just east of Tromsö. He had Jan with him. They often talked about that voyage. They were almost trapped by a patrol boat, but the fog saved them. A thick fog just when the bullets were hitting all round. There are some marks if you know where to look.'

'When was this?' I asked.

'In 1942. It was winter. I remember the date – 27th January. That was when they land in Shetland that first time.'

'And you have the logs?'

'Yes. The early ones. Jan found them, tucked away at the back of a locker in the cabin there. I'll show you when you bring her into Taing.' She turned abruptly, moving a step towards me. 'You will bring her in? Please.'

'In case I run off with her?'

But she didn't smile. 'I'll feel easier, that's all.' And she added, 'I saw Sandford when I was ashore. He was driving past me along the Esplanade in a red car. Has he been on board?'

'No.'

'You haven't seen him again?'

I shook my head, turning back to the chart shelf and measuring off the distance to Clift Sound.

'What is he doing here in Lerwick, do you think?'

'If you run a hotel I suppose you need supplies.' Just over forty miles to The Taing. Say five hours' steaming. 'If we left at noon tomorrow –'

'He doesn't need to come to Lerwick for stores. He can order by telephone.' Her voice had risen slightly, a note of tension. 'Why does he need a ship so badly he is prepared to buy the mortgage?'

'I told you, he's got a contract to supply two rigs.'

'Do you believe him?' She had moved towards me and I could see her face now in the chart cabin light. She was frowning. 'I think he is here because we are ready to sail.' And, on a note of urgency, she added, 'You must leave for Taing now. Immediately. Can you do that? Otherwise, I think perhaps we are not permitted to sail at all.'

'Nonsense,' I said. 'She may not be classed A1, but the survey went off all right. And even if she didn't pass survey, we would still have our temporary certificate of seaworthiness.'

But it wasn't the survey she was worried about. It was the crew. Apparently she had been warned by her local councillor that Johan and the three other Norwegians might be ordered to leave Shetland. 'Somebody has been enquiring about their work permits. We never bother about work permits before. Not for fishing. But, now that we are going to work for an oil rig, it may be different.'

'Then you'd better apply for them.'

She nodded. 'Of course. I have the papers already. But Mr Tulloch thinks it will be opposed and they will be ordered to leave.'

'But if they didn't need work permits before –'

'He says it is politics. The fishermen here are a very strong community and they don't like the oil companies. So, you see, it is not very difficult to stir up trouble.'

'And you think Sandford is behind it?'

She gave a little shrug. 'Perhaps. I don't know. But it is one way of ensuring that we lose this charter.' She was so urgent about it that I agreed to sail as soon as we had taken on fuel and water.

We moored at the quay, alongside a Lerwick trawler, shortly after 13.00. I think we were lucky in that it was lunch-time and the rain teeming down. All the offices were closed. Nobody bothered us and at 14.42 we slipped our warps and stood out into Bressay Sound. Visibility was bad in low cloud and rain squalls, but by 15.05 we were clear of Kirkabister Ness with Bard Head a grey lump bearing 85°.

Sea conditions were fairly good as we steamed south under the lee of the long mountain spine running down to Sumburgh Head and I had time to take a look at the Admiralty Sailing Directions. I had never before had need of Part I of the North Sea Pilot, which covers the Faroes, Shetlands and Orkneys, and I was appalled at the force of the tidal streams. The main stream was south-east-going and between Orkney and Shetland it reached a speed of 8-10 knots at the margin headlands of North Ronaldsay and Sumburgh Head. The result, of course, was violent tide races. Known as roosts in Shetland, they were to be encountered off all the major headlands, with the Sumburgh Roost the most dangerous of all – 'As in the confused, tumbling and bursting sea, vessels often become entirely un-manageable, and sometimes founder, while others have been tossed about for days in light weather, the roost should be given a wide berth.'

I looked at the spine of the faded and dog-eared Pilot. It was dated 1921. Obviously the warning was for sailing vessels. I was checking the tide data on the chart when Johan appeared at my side. 'You take Sumburgh very close, ja. It is the last hour of the south-going tide, so the wind is with the tide and we get a lift on the eddy by Fitful.'

I left it to him and he took the wheel himself, turning the headland so close that we seemed in imminent danger of hitting the islet of Little Tind. The wind was westerly, force 6, the sea lumpy and full of holes, but not breaking heavily. It took us a long time to round Hog of the Holm and claw our way up to Head of the Holm with wind and tide both against us. But with Johan piloting I had no worries, except perhaps when we turned due north up the long sheer slate-grey line of Fitful Head. We were on a lee shore then, no place for an engine failure, and so close in that we were back-winded by the towering cliffs, the burst of the waves sounding like gunfire.

The tide turned and we were inside the Havras by 19.30 with the Stacks of Houssness just visible and Clift Sound opening up ahead. The light was fading, and, as we came into the shelter of East Burra, Johan sent Henrik for'ard to call the leading marks into the voe.

That first view of Taing from the sea will always remain, the evening light dulled by rain, the clouds sweeping low and the narrow tongue of land suddenly revealed as being separate from the green slopes behind. And then, as we nosed slowly in, the house suddenly appearing, a grey ghost of a building and the water below it a leaden sheet barely touched by the wind. And when we had let go our anchor, and the echo of the chain running out had died away, our engines stopped, everything so still, so absolutely quiet.

I thought Gertrude Petersen would have been down at the water's edge to welcome her ship home, but though there was a light on in the house, nothing stirred. I had the Zodiac inflated and got over the side and rowed myself ashore, not bothering about the outboard. It was warm rowing in oilskins and farther than I thought. The rain had stopped, the evening strangely luminous with fish rising. I could hear the slap of them hitting the water and the circles rippling out were so numerous that sometimes they interlocked. I couldn't see the entrance to the voe, it was blocked by the lit shape of the trawler, and with the low arm of The Taing stretching out from the shore, and the steep mountain slopes beyond, it was more like a loch than an indent open to the sea.

The beach below the house was sand and rock with a small boat jetty of cemented boulder. The cement was crumbling, the boulders loose, and it was already half awash on the tide. I pulled the inflatable up on to higher ground, made fast the painter and then stood for a moment looking back at the voe and the trawler lying there, the ship, the house, the land-encircled water, everything so perfect. I was thinking of Jan Petersen then, wondering how he had acquired such a place. And a wife who would go to sea with him, stand by him through thick and thin. A refugee from another country. And

I had started with so much, achieved so little. No matter that the ship was mortgaged, the house, too, probably. They were his. He had owned them. And now he was dead and I was going up to his house to make an agreement with his wife, sitting probably at that table in the window with the photograph of him and his father on their catcher.

I got out my pipe and filled it. But I didn't light it. I just stood there, holding it in my hand as though for comfort in that quiet remoteness of the darkening landscape. The moment between light and dark, just as night closes in, is a time of silence when the soul is touched by doubts. I had that feeling now, the past a nothingness, the future all uncertain – and myself not knowing, or even understanding, what I was doing here.

I put my pipe away and turned abruptly, walking up to the house and knocking on the door. I wanted to get this over and get to sea. Three months in the loneliness of command, seeing nothing but the same patch of sea and the ugly superstructure of a floating rig – three months of that should be enough to sort myself out. The sound of my fist on the door was loud in the stillness and the lamplight streaming out from the window on my right became a muted glow as the curtains were drawn. The sound of footsteps clacking on stone, then the door opened and she was there. But not as I had expected her, in the denim slacks and faded jersey I had become accustomed to. Now she was wearing a long dress and high heeled shoes, and her fair hair, limned by the light of an oil lamp on the chest behind her, fell to her shoulders.

I stood there for a moment, not saying anything, her appearance so unexpected. She had always seemed to me a sturdy, solid Norwegian, and Fuller's phrase, 'the legal owner', had fitted her exactly. 'Well, are you coming in or not?'

I went in slowly, feeling uncomfortable. 'I'm afraid I haven't changed.'

'Does it matter?' She was smiling as she closed the door.

'No, I suppose not.' I was staring at her as she turned into the lamplight, her long dress flowing and her eyes bright. This was the first time I had seen her with any make-up on. 'Takes a bit of getting used to.'

She laughed. 'Tonight I am celebrating.' And she added over her shoulder as she took me into the living-room, 'I've not had much to celebrate these last few years. But when I saw the *Duchess* coming in round the end of The Taing . . .' She stopped, turning and facing me. 'You will never know what that meant to me.' And then she asked me whether I had fed. 'I hope you haven't.'

'No, I've come straight ashore as you suggested.'

'Good. Because otherwise you would have to eat two meals.'

'It's not impossible.'

She laughed. 'You don't know what I've cooked.' Her teeth flashed white, her eyes sparkling. It crossed my mind that she was a widow now and flying some sort of flag, with the table laid for two, lace mats and rough-carved wooden candlesticks. And then she said, 'If Jan were here, how he would have enjoyed it. Don't you feel you deserve a celebration after all the work you have done? Now, take off your oilskins please and we will have a drink.'

She went into the kitchen, returning with glasses and a bottle. 'I found this when I am going through Far's things – it is aquavit, real live aquavit. I think it came with the ship from Norway and he kept it against some happy day.'

She was in a mood of strange elation, gripped by a sort of feverish belief that now the ship was back at her old mooring everything would be all right. 'You bring me luck,' she said, raising her glass, the too-wide mouth smiling at me. 'Skal!' And she tossed the drink back, her eyes on me, watching to see that I did the same.

'Are you trying to drink me under the table?' I asked as she refilled my glass.

'Maybe. I don't know.' She was laughing, but at herself I think, at the invitation in her eyes that she didn't bother to conceal. 'You haven't wished us luck.'

I got up then, remembering how formal Scandinavian ships' officers could be, and made a little speech. She clapped her hands, and after she had drunk, she put her glass down carefully, holding it cupped in her capable brown hands, her head a little bowed so that the fair hair cascaded over her face. 'I think we are very strange partners, you and I, neither of us knowing what we want of life or where we are going. All I know is what I feel inside me, that tonight is different – the start of something. But I don't know what.' She raised her head and looked at me questioningly. 'Don't you feel that?'

I shrugged. 'Maybe,' I said guardedly.

'I think for you also this is a new beginning.'

'What about that agreement?' I asked her.

'Have you thought about it?'

'No. I haven't had time. But I think we should discuss it now, while we are still sober.'

'There is nothing to discuss.' Her hand reached out to the bottle. 'Will you have another drink?'

I shook my head. 'Not now. When we've settled this maybe.'

'There is some wine to follow. What you would call plonk, I think. I bought it at the stores this morning. But now – ' She filled my glass again. 'Now I think we have one last aquavit and drink to a partnership.' She picked up her glass, not looking at me, but staring down into the heavy pale liquor. 'You see, I have had time to think about it. There is no way that I can see to draw up a legal document between us that is of any use. I am the owner. You hold the mortgage. Either we are partners or one of us must find the money to buy the other out. How much money have you got?'

'Less than fifty pounds.'

'You see? You cannot buy me out. And I have nothing. I am living on borrowed money. So what is the point of an agreement?'

'I thought you didn't trust me?'

'I don't. Your head is too full of strange ideas – about people and politics and economics of the world. Oh, don't think I have been spying on you, but they tell me everything, about what you eat, how much you sleep, what you talk about. And there is the gossip here, too. You came to see Hilda Manson, making enquiries about your father. The house where he was born is just up the road, and there is that tablet in the church, so I know something about him.' She was looking at me, a gleam of humour back in her eyes. 'I think probably you suffer from some sort of a father complex.' Her hand reached out and touched my arm. 'Do not please be offended. I am an expert on this subject. Jan, you see, had a father complex, so that in a sense I married two men. Far Petersen . . . I always called him that, it is the Norwegian word for Father . . . Far was with us always, from the very beginning of our marriage. But it did not matter. I loved that dear gentle old man very much, even though he is so stupid about money.' She moved her hand to the bottle. 'So, you see, I know,' she said, filling my glass, but not her own, and then rising to her feet. 'Now we will eat. It is fish, do you mind?'

I shook my head.

'Fish to start with, then meat.' She bent towards me, laughing. 'Cheer up! It is not the end of the world that another person knows something about what is going on in your mind. For me, it gives you a certain integrity. And because of that you get no agreement, but a celebration dinner instead.' And she turned to go to the kitchen.

I offered to help her, but she waved me back into my chair. 'Have your drink and relax. About five minutes I think. And if you are bored with your own company, there are the logs over there.' She indicated the table by the window. 'I looked them out for you this afternoon. The voyage which brought Far Petersen and Jan to Shetland is in the second book.'

I took my drink over to the table, moving the lamp so that it shone on the little pile of books tied up with string. There were seven of them, and all but two were hardbound books like ledgers. These covered the voyages from 1966, when Jan Petersen and his father began fishing out of Lerwick and Hamnavoe. Courses, speeds, fixes, weather, everything was recorded, including the time spent trawling and the catches for each voyage. Mostly they were fishing around Shetland, occasionally Orkney or Fair Isle. These voyages were a week, or ten days at the most. But in the summer they had fished up to Faroe and then the voyages had been longer.

I glanced only briefly at these logs. It was the two others, both exercise books, that interested me. They were not proper logs, but a personal record of patrols, incidents and voyages completed in the early part of the war. They had been kept by a Lt Adrian Farrant. The first covered the Scapa Flow period and the evacuation of British troops from the Narvik area of Norway in June, 1940. The second was a record of voyages made in the winter of 1941/42, mostly to rendezvous with local fishing boats off the coast of Norway, but a few to the coast itself north of the Arctic Circle. It was one of those that Gertrude had marked with a slip of paper: *Three men and a small boy were taken off from Lyngenfjord at 01.00, the time agreed; Mark Johnston, a mining saboteur with SOE, Knut Hansen, a business man from Trondheim, Olav Petersen, a whaling captain from Selmvaag, and Jan Petersen, his son, aged 8. The worst conditions possible, clear sky and bright moonlight. I wished the agent who had radioed a report of inshore fog could have been with me for we were spotted before we were even clear of the fjord . . .*

No wonder Lt Farrant had hidden the books at the back of the locker. In every case he had given the names and occupations of those he had landed in Norway and those he had brought out, a highly secret record.

I began from the beginning then, turning the pages quickly, reading only the names with a growing certainty of what I would find. And in the voyage that began: *Sailed from Graven at 19.00 on January 6,* I found it: *Arrived off the RV near Oksfjord in Finnmark at 21.33, weather ideal with low cloud and drizzle, wind light from WNW. Took off Nils Storkson as arranged. He is an officer of the Company Linge, I think, but there is another man with him, Alistair Randall, who claims he is a British citizen. Storkson says he is an agent, but not one of ours, and insists I put him under guard. Both are suffering from exposure and Randall from slight frostbite. He is a much older man and badly scarred, an old injury. Only Storkson is armed. I have taken away his gun and given them the cabin for'ard of the galley.*

Then followed a brief account of the voyage back to Shetland. It concluded: *Berthed alongside the quay at Graven 09.45, January 12, and handed passengers over for interrogation. Both are fully recovered and both tell different stories. A matter for Intelligence. I am only the bus driver . . .*

I sat back, staring at that page, reading it through again. Garrard had been right and the confirmation that my father had not died in Spain left me confused and more than a little puzzled. *An agent, but not one of ours.* Whose then? Not the Germans. Had the Russians had agents in North Norway at the beginning of 1942?

The door to the kitchen opened. 'Finish your drink and come and eat.' She put the plates she was carrying on the table. 'It is steamed halibut. I hope you like.' I sat down, remembering the presence I had felt on the bridge, that strange sense of companionship when I had stood alone at the wheel that first time. 'Is it all right?' she asked. 'You are very silent.'

'It's fine,' I said. Could it have been his presence I had felt? Had he been in such a state of nerves that it had left an indelible impression?

'You are thinking about their voyage to Shetland. It was very dangerous, to come right into the coast like that. The *Duchess* is not a Norwegian ship like the boats they had sailing out of Lunna and Scalloway. She was based at Graven in Sullom Voe and it was her speed and range that made them use her. But she only went in to the coast in an emergency or when it was something very important. It wasn't Far Petersen they went in to get on that trip, it was the man Johnston, an

English agent; also to land explosives and equipment.'

If she had seen the name Randall in the log she didn't mention it. Probably she didn't remember, and when I had opened the bottle of red wine, and the joint of lamb was on the table, I forgot about it, too. I remember I talked a lot about my early life in America and how I had worked my way from Germany across the Middle East to India. She was curious about me, and in the candlelight, with the drink inside me and her large eyes staring, I even told her about Düsseldorf. To be able to talk freely like that, to have somebody listen – it was something I found I needed very badly. And to add to the enjoyment, there was the knowledge that the evening could only end one way, and that there was all the next day ahead of us. Our hands touched once as I took the tray with the coffee on it and a bottle of Glen Morangie. I felt the movement of her fingers and my blood leapt. We sat, very properly, on two separate chairs, facing each other and sipped our coffee and our whisky, talking gently in the lamplight, each of us knowing what was going to happen and the delay making the sense of anticipation almost unbearable. I hadn't had a woman for a long time. And now, with all the work behind me . . .

The knock on the door was sudden and very loud. I thought it must be Johan or somebody from the ship. Gertrude must have thought so, too, for she said as she got up, 'They are becoming too dependent on you.' But it wasn't anybody from the ship. It was Sandford, and he had a policeman with him. He came in smiling, his sharp eyes taking in the cosy intimacy of the room at a glance. 'I thought we'd find you'd slipped round here.'

'What do you want?' I asked him, but with the constable there we both knew.

It was the same man who had escorted me to the police station. 'You have foreign nationals working on your boat. Is that correct?'

I nodded, and he read out the four names.

'They're Norwegian,' Gertrude said. 'I am Norwegian, too. We have residents' permits.'

'Aye, I know that. But what about work permits?'

'Those have been applied for.'

'Would that be for renewal, or are they new applications? We have checked with the Department of Employment and there is no record – '

'My fault,' she said quickly. 'Well, Mr Petersen's really, and nobody ever troubled us about it. But now the applications for permits are in and I have seen the Fisheries Inspector in Lerwick. He has agreed to recommend them, so you don't have to worry.'

'Not if you send the men ashore,' Sandford said. 'And when the Inspector has had time to think about it, I doubt very much if he will support your applications.' He looked pleased with himself as he turned to me. 'You're sailing tomorrow, or is it Sunday? You'll be short of a crew. I could help you there.'

'We'll manage,' I said.

'You can't act as stand-by boat to an oil rig if your manning strength is below the regulation minimum.'

I stared at him, wondering what was behind it. 'You're quite a sea lawyer,' I said. And then I turned to the constable. 'Have you a warrant?'

He shook his head. 'There'll be no charges so long as you send them ashore. Those are my instructions.' And when I asked him to produce them, his face took on a stolid look. 'Verbal instructions, from my sergeant,' he said. 'I'm to see that those four men are brought ashore. They may have to be deported.'

'But that's ridiculous,' Gertrude said. 'They live on board. It's their home.'

'It will be for the Home Office to decide.'

I got my oilskins from the door where I had hung them. I was boiling with anger, but I had too much experience of the slow inexorable process of the law to argue. I just wondered what that little bastard Sandford was up to.

Gertrude came at me as I was zipping up my oilskin jacket. 'You are not going to bring them ashore?' Her voice was high and strident, her eyes blazing. 'You can't. I forbid it.'

'Just leave it to me,' I told her. 'It's my responsibility.' I reached for my cap and put it on. Then I went across to Sandford. 'You've been to a lot of trouble over this – why?'

'You got that ship by a trick.'

'It's not the ship you're after now,' I said. 'It's the crew. You want your own men on board. Why?'

He hesitated, his eyes gone dead and I knew there was something else, something he hadn't told me. 'It should be a Shetland crew,' he murmured. 'Shetlanders have a right to exploit their own oil.' But he couldn't look me in the face, his eyes shifting. 'I offered to help, that's all. Crews aren't easy to get.'

'But you have one willing and ready to take over. Your own skipper, too?' There was something here I didn't understand. But I couldn't take hold of him and shake the truth out of him, not with the constable standing there. I glanced at Gertrude. Her long dress looked suddenly incongruous, the candles behind her guttering in the draught from the open door. 'I'll tell them,' I said, and I went out, walking quickly down to the landing beach with the aid of my torch. It was very dark now, a soft rain falling and only the riding light of the trawler showing blurred in the night. The constable came with me and helped me launch the Zodiac.

'How long before we get the permits?' I asked him.

'Normally it's a matter of a few days. But in this case –' He straightened up, facing me in the darkness. 'It's politics, you see, sir.'

'You mean Sandford is right and the applications will be refused.'

'It's only what I hear.'

'And who instructed your sergeant to send you down at this time of the evening?'

'I don't know, sir.'

'But it was Sandford who was pressing the matter.'

'Several councillors, too.'

I was in the boat then. Fortunately he didn't insist on coming with me. He pushed me off clear of the boulders and then I was out from the land, rowing towards the ship. Halfway there I stopped and lit my pipe, the rain drifting in the flare of the match. The sound of an accordion and men's voices singing came to me across the water. I sat there for a moment thinking about what I was going to do, about Shetland politics and how I would stand in law. But Block 206 was in international waters. Out there I was my own master, and if the permits were refused, then I could still send the men ashore when Gertrude had found replacements. I started rowing again, the rain coming in flurries, hissing on the bowl of my pipe.

It was Duncan who answered my hail as I came alongside. He helped me climb aboard and I told him to get the engines started. 'We'll be leaving as soon as we've fetched our anchor.'

He didn't argue, just nodded and said, 'Aye. But ye'd better break it gently to the lads. They've got a bellyful of beer and they'll no' think much of the idea.'

They were crammed into the mess room aft, their faces sweating in the naked light, the table littered with beer cans and young Per swaying to the tune he was queezing out of the box. The song died as I looked at Johan sitting by the galley hatch. 'You've got out of here at night before, haven't you?' I asked him.

'You want to leave now?'

'If we don't go now, we don't go at all.' And I told him what had happened.

He finished the can of beer he was drinking and got slowly to his feet. 'Ja. We can try.' He pushed his hand up over his face, rubbing at his eyes and swaying slightly. 'What is the weather?'

'Dark,' I said. 'And raining.'

'And the wind?'

'Still from the south-west.'

'Gud. Then we know when we clear Houss Ness.' The thrum of the diesels started and he turned. 'Lars. Henrik.' He said something to them in Norwegian, then went down the alleyway, pushed open the door to the deck and went out into the night, not bothering about oilskins. Henrik followed him and Lars came up to the bridge with me. I didn't switch the deck lights on. We needed night vision. It was very dark, so dark I could barely see them working on the foredeck, the winch clattering and the chain beginning to come in.

A light shone out from the shore. Gertrude had drawn the curtains back, and when the winch had stopped and Johan had joined me in the bridge, he got us out past the end of The Taing on compass bearings taken on the faint glimmer of that light. We lost it as soon as we were out into Clift Sound, a slight swell under us and everything black. We headed south on a compass course of 175° with myself at the radar and Johan watching the glimmer of the waves breaking against the cliffs. I think he distrusted electronics, for he conned the ship by eye, and when we began to feel the full weight of the sea, he ordered a change of course to the west.

He wasn't a navigator. He couldn't handle a sextant. He could barely plot a course on the chart. But he came from Luro and had learned how to pilot a boat fishing the Inner Lead up towards the Lofotens. We passed so close to Houss Ness that we could hear the roar of the waves breaking against the Stacks. He came in from the starboard gangway then. 'Okay. We are clear now on due west. In one mile Groot Ness is to starboard. After that there is nothing between you and the bottom of Greenland.'

Lars was already steering 270°. I went into the chart recess and switched on the light. Foula was the obvious choice. 'What's the holding like in Ham Voe?'

'In this wind, gud.' He leaned over the chart beside me, his jersey sodden. 'Foula is okay. Nobody bother us there.'

He went below then and I switched on the bridge radio. It was 23.36 and I got the tail-end of the late news, something about an oil slick off the Northumberland coast and the local MP to table a motion in the House about pollution and firmer Government control of oil rigs. *In Hull a meeting of shipyard workers to consider the latest offer was disrupted by militants. With fish being imported to augment supplies and prices soaring the Government is being pressed to intervene in the dispute* . . . I switched on one of the heaters and removed my oilskins, waiting for the inshore forecast. The news seemed remote, another world, as I listened to the sounds of the ship, the slam of the bows as she fell off the tops of the waves. All your life you work for something you believe in, then three weeks of hard, concentrated effort, and it means nothing. I crossed to the radar set, but nothing showed and I stood there, staring out at the black night with the waves coming at us as smudges of grey in the darkness, the radio drowning the plunging impact of the bows. Three months, and what at the end of it? I was thinking of Gertrude, wondering what our relationship would have been now if Sandford hadn't turned up. A partnership, she had said, but the only experience I had had of partnership with a woman had disintegrated into ideological arguments and recriminations.

I switched the Decca to maximum range and as the radius lines changed the outline of Foula appeared little more than 22 miles ahead. Speed 7 knots. In three hours' time . . . *Gale warnings Hebrides, Rockall and Malin: westerly gale Force 8 may be expected in the next 2 hours* . . . We would have to anchor close in to be under the lee and Ham was sure to have a police station. Why was it that everything I did seemed to lead inevitably to a clash with authority? And Sandford – there was something about him, something familiar that I didn't understand. I tried to see behind the bright aggressive eyes, the truculence of his manner, but instead I found my mind switching to the entry in that exercise book. *An agent, but not one of ours.* And he had been on this ship, in the cabin for'ard of the galley. *A matter for Intelligence.* Somewhere, in some record office, there would be an Intelligence report. I tried to imagine what it said, but I couldn't think clearly. I was tired, my stomach queasy. It was always like this at the start of a voyage. Just nausea. I was never sick. I leaned on the chart shelf, pushing back my cap and wiping the sweat from my forehead.

Two hours later, the large comforting bulk of Johan appeared at my side. He had been into Ham Voe before, so I left it to him, and at 03.07 we let go our anchor about a cable off the end of the pier. It was still and very peaceful in the lee of the towering mass of Hamnafjeld and I went to my bunk, thinking I was clear of trouble tucked away here under Foula.

We lay there all Saturday and nobody bothered us until a fishing boat came in late that afternoon. She had the letters LK and her number painted white on her bows, and instead of making for the pier, she headed straight for us, the crew on deck putting fenders out. I watched her come alongside, and as Henrik and Lars took her warps, I called down to the skipper to ask him where he came from, what he wanted.

'From Scalloway,' he said, leaning his head out of the wooden wheelhouse. 'You're Randall, are you? I've brought a Mr Stevens to see you.' He said something over his shoulder and a man came out of the door at the back of the wheelhouse, a short man with thinning hair dressed in a dark suit. He looked up at me and I saw the steel-trap mouth, the hard unfriendly eyes, the slight cast of the eye. He didn't ask permission to come on board, but went straight to the side and hauled himself up on to our deck. A moment later he was on the bridge facing me. Johan was there, and Henrik, too. We had been playing cribbage. 'These two of your Norwegians?' The same quiet voice, hard and flat, and the odd sidelong look of the left eye. 'You should have put them ashore.'

'What's it got to do with you?' My hands were clenched, my voice strained. 'How did you know where to find me?' I was remembering the cold-blooded way he had threatened me, wondering whether he thought I'd made a statement to the police as he stood there facing me, saying nothing. 'What made you follow me out here?'

'We'll talk about that in your cabin.' He turned abruptly and started down the companionway, then realized it was at the back of the bridge.

'I don't want you on board.' But he had already disappeared inside, and the fishing boat had recovered her warps and was going astern. I watched her sheer away from our side and head for the pier, the name *Island Girl* on her stern, then I followed him to my cabin. He was sitting on my bunk with a packet of cigarettes in his hand. He didn't offer me one this time. 'Shut the door.' He waved me to the single upright chair. 'I take it you know something about the background of this drilling operation. Have you met Villiers?'

'No.'

'But you've heard of him – you know the way he operates, the sort of man he is?'

'I know he runs a very successful finance company.'

'You admire success?' It wasn't a question, more a sneer, the word success made to sound obscene. 'He makes money – at the expense of others, of course. And ultimately it's the workers who suffer.'

'You don't need to give me the propaganda line.'

'No?' He was watching me as he took a cigarette out of the packet and lit it. 'Just thought I'd remind you, that's all. It's some time since you were a shipyard worker. You were one of the leaders then. A shop floor convener with a gift for turning on the heat when it was needed.' He paused, drawing on his cigarette. Then he said, 'Before that you worked as a journalist in the City. You didn't like it, did you?'

'There are two sides to everything,' I said, wondering where this was leading.

He smiled. 'Seeing things two ways can be confusing.'

'You didn't come out here in a fishing boat to tell me that.'

'No. But you've been confused for some time, and that's a pity. You're in a very unique position at the moment. Unique from our point of view.' He was staring at me as though trying to make up his mind, and I wasn't certain which of his eyes was focused on my face. 'But then if you weren't confused, you wouldn't be here, would you?' He said it reflectively, the sound of the radio on the bridge almost drowning his words. 'You wouldn't have come to Shetland, trying to find out about your father, and landed yourself with this trawler.'

So it was the trawler that had brought him here. 'What's the trawler got to do with it?'

But he ignored my question. 'Villiers now,' he murmured. 'Would you say Villiers is typical of the City?'

'One aspect of it, yes. But not the City as a whole. That's pretty mundane.'

'Of course. Banks and insurance and unit trusts.' He smiled quietly to himself. 'But that's not how the public sees it. All they read about is the property developers, the land speculators, the ones that hit the headlines getting rich too quick, while workers are declared redundant or fight management and government for increased wages that never catch up with inflation. Look at Villiers, with his finance companies and his villa in Bermuda, as well as his Hampshire estate, two aircraft and a flat in Belgravia. That's the capitalist image the public understands. Girls, parties, villas abroad – and who pays? They do in the end.' He leaned suddenly forward. 'That's why we're interested in Villiers. The face of capitalism at its ugliest.'

He was very different from the militants I had met – no warmth, and talking in clichés. 'Villiers is happily married with two kids,' I said wearily. 'And he works – '

'I thought you said you'd never met him?' He was still leaning forward, his eyes gone hard.

'I haven't. But I read the newspapers.'

'I see.' He stared at his cigarette, his mouth a thin line. 'You *are* confused, aren't you?' He gave a little shrug. 'Well, it can't be helped. Villiers is very suitable to our purpose. And so are you. It doesn't really matter that you think him so commendable.'

'I didn't say that. You're twisting my words.'

A silence then, a long, uncomfortable silence. Finally he said, speaking slowly, 'It may help you to understand the importance we attach to this if I fill you in on the background. You know, of course, that we can call on the services of quite a few journalists, wittingly or unwittingly. Recently we have had a very good man looking into the Villiers take-over technique and the companies he has grabbed. It's the latest that concerns you, an offer by Villiers Finance and Industrial, known as VFI, for the whole of the capital of Neven-Clyde Shipping. The offer was very astutely timed – last January, when Neven-Clyde had just reported heavy losses on a harbour construction contract in Brazil.'

'It's of no interest to me,' I said. 'I'm running a trawler now.'

He jabbed a cigarette at me. 'You think you can escape after all these years?' He was watching me, the slant of his eyes more disconcerting than ever. 'It's not as simple as that, Randall. We all have our backgrounds, and the past produces its own obligations.' The hard mouth managed a smile. 'As a boy you can run away to sea. Not as a man.'

He leaned back slowly and his voice was quiet and relaxed as he continued: 'Neven-Clyde's trouble was that they diversified, mostly into fields where their expertise was limited. They lost money, and they lost the support of their shareholders. The VFI offer was declared unconditional on 14th March. The attraction for Villiers was the shipping offices in various parts of the world and the losses built up over the years, which he can now offset against profits for tax purposes. The construction business has already been sold off. N-C Ceramics is on the market. So, too, are N-C Textiles, a small company specializing in panties and bras with a factory in Belfast, N-C Plastics, producing dolls and garden furnishings, and N-C Musicals, a pop record company.'

It took me back to my days as a journalist, the wheeling and dealing that was part of the background to life in the City. It had coloured all my thinking, affected my whole outlook. But now – it didn't concern me now. Only the sea. The sea at least was clean, clear-cut, impersonal, without hate or greed or bitterness. An elemental force, nothing more, nothing complicated. But I couldn't explain it to a man like this, his voice droning on: 'All this is much too complicated to capture public imagination. Stripping, property-dealing, even redundancies – they've had it all before. And anyway a lot of it is above their heads. But an oil rig . . .' He paused, his eyes watching for my reaction as he drew on his cigarette. 'Two years ago Neven-Clyde bought their way into North Sea oil with the acquisition of a company called Star-Trion. Its only tangible asset was one of the first sea-going rigs built in this country – a rig called *North Star* which they purchased second-hand. This is the rig that will be drilling here in Block 206. Star-Trion operated it as drilling contractors. But as far back as the 1971 auction they put in a bid for two areas west of Shetland. At that time the major oil companies were concentrating on the North Sea proper. North East Atlantic areas were regarded as hazardous for the rigs then available. Also, geophysically, they were not fully evaluated. Star-Trion got them both on a very low bid.'

'Are you implying that the rig is unsafe in these waters?' I asked.

'Yes, I think so. Where they're going to drill the sea is almost two hundred metres deep – about the limit for *North Star*. Certainly the public can be made to see it that way. Fishermen particularly, if the result was heavy oil pollution.'

'Result of what?' I demanded. 'What the hell are you suggesting?'

'A strike on board. That for a start.'

'There's never been a strike on a sea-going rig, not that I've heard.'

'No – not yet, not a proper one.' He drew slowly on his cigarette. 'What did you think I meant?'

'Anybody who can arrange for a man's house to be deliberately set on fire – '

'You were never in Northern Ireland, were you? Anyway, they didn't know the little girl was in the house.'

'Would it have made any difference if they had?'

He shrugged, watching the smoke curling up from his cigarette. 'You send those four Norwegians ashore and replace them with our men,' he said quietly. 'That's all you have to do.'

I shook my head, Garrard's warning clear in my mind. 'It's not a strike you're calling, it's something else, isn't it?'

He raised his eyes and stared at me. 'Is it your future you're worrying about?' He didn't wait for me to reply but went straight on: 'You're wrong when you say there's never been a strike on a North Sea rig. There was one last October, but the contractor managed to keep it out of the papers. They were Scots mainly, so he flew in two new drilling crews, all Americans. There was a fight on board and one or two men got hurt. But he got the strikers off his rig.' He was smiling quietly to himself. 'The only trouble is nobody will work on the rig now, except foreigners, so it costs a lot more.'

'What rig was that?'

'Never mind what rig. We've infiltrated several drilling teams. As a result, we've got our foot in the door of three rigs, maybe four if *North Star* accepts our men as replacements for two roustabouts who've got into trouble ashore.'

'Then why do you want your men on board my ship?'

He looked at me, hesitating. Then he said, 'I told you, *North Star* is an old rig and unsuitable for the North East Atlantic. If it breaks loose and drags . . . The threat of a disaster at sea is always news and we get a chance to publicize our demands on grounds of danger. Drillers would be glad of some publicity on rates of pay. The public thinks even a roustabout gets paid a fortune. He doesn't. He works twelve hours on, twelve hours off and every other week he's ashore. He doesn't get paid for that, so you have to divide his weekly pay packet by two.'

'And your men will ensure that the anchors drag, is that it?'

He shrugged. 'They'll probably drag anyway.'

'But you're going to make sure they do.' I stared at him.

Who was he, this cold, hard little man, always working in the background? 'That's sabotage.'

He didn't deny it. All he said was, 'Nobody's going to get hurt.'

'How do you know? How can you possibly know?'

'When you've seen the size of the rig, you'll realize it's out of the question. But it will make the headlines, and then Villiers will be seen as a capitalist gambler operating with obsolete equipment in dangerous waters.'

'It's not your neck you're risking,' I said.

'Nor yours.' The flat, hard voice was suddenly sharp. 'You send those four Norwegians ashore and replace them with our men. That's all you have to do.'

I shook my head, my hands sweating, my body cold inside. 'There's something more, isn't there?' That reference to Northern Ireland. He was cold-blooded enough for that, too. 'There has to be something more, or you wouldn't be going to all this trouble.'

He stubbed out his cigarette. 'Not for you. Not as we've planned it.' He was watching me, and now the squint had a strangely menacing quality, so that I had the feeling that it was this slight physical disability – and it was only slight – that had warped him mentally. 'A pay dispute, a halt to operations – that would focus attention on the rig. And if we can involve Villiers directly, so much the better. Then, if the rig drags at the moment they strike oil – ' He shrugged. 'A lot of ifs . . . But the seismic survey, completed just after Villiers took the company over, makes an oil strike a strong possibility.' He was talking quietly, but there was an urgency in his voice, his mind locked on his plans. 'Then we could have a major environmental disaster and Villiers would be branded as a man intent on making millions by cashing in on oil without any regard to the environment, or to the fishermen who earn a living by the sea.' And he added, emphasizing his words, 'He's tailor-made to our purpose.'

He paused then, stubbing out his cigarette. 'I've told you more than I intended. But you would have to know in the end. And it's better that it comes from me, so that you understand what is at stake.' His head jerked forward. 'Something else you should understand. Nothing – not you or anybody else – is going to stand in the way.' His hand came down on the locker beside him. 'Nothing. You hear? This ship of yours, and you the master of it – we'll never have an opportunity as good as this again. You're on charter out here for three months. In less than a month nobody will even notice you're there. You'll be accepted as part of the scenery.' He got to his feet. 'The first hole will take about five weeks to drill. That's our information. I'll send the replacement crew and the equipment we'll need out by a local boat in about three weeks' time.'

I reminded him that Mrs Petersen was responsible for crew replacements. 'You won't get her to accept your men.'

But he brushed that aside. 'She'll have no alternative. Sandford will see to it that your Norwegians don't get their work permits, and with the pressure we'll be putting on the fishing community, no Shetlander will volunteer.'

I was standing facing him then, a deep void inside me. A small, insignificant little man with a cast in his eye, and I was afraid of him. Deep inside he had me scared. 'Who are you?' I asked him. A name didn't matter. But where had he come from? What was his background? His face was blank, not a muscle moved. 'That skipper said your name was Stevens.' Even a name might make him seem more human.

'Alf Stevens.' The voice so quiet and that thin smile. It might just as well have been Bill Smith.

'You realize the police know I'm here. An Inspector Garrard from London –'

'They've nothing against you.'

'They have my record, a dossier, several files.'

He laughed. 'It's like I told you. The past sticks with you. There's no escape.' And with brutal frankness, he added, 'They can't charge you, not unless our witness talks. And he won't do that so long as you co-operate. All right?' He looked at me, one-eyed, the left squinting off into the corner where I had been sitting. 'Now, if you'd sound two blasts on your siren . . .' He turned to the door then, so sure of me apparently that he didn't need an answer. It was that absolute blind assurance that turned my fear of him to anger.

Two steps and I had him by the shoulder, spinning him round, my face close to his. 'I could sail out of here, straight to Aberdeen, and hand you over.'

'You could indeed.' His face was without expression, no fear, nothing. 'My word against yours and political power behind me. You can try it if you like, but you wouldn't win.'

'There'll be fifty or more men on that rig. You expect me to endanger their lives . . .'

'I told you. Nobody is going to get hurt.' He took my hand

87

from his shoulder, looking at me as though I was somehow to be pitied. 'Take after your father, don't you?'

'How do you mean?'

'I think you know. You've been making enquiries.'

'I know he was brought out of Norway—'

'He was compromised. And afterwards . . .' He shrugged. 'Rehabilitation can be a long process. Not many survived.'

I stood there, rooted to the spot. 'What are you trying to tell me?' My voice sounded strained, my mind gone numb. 'He's alive—is that what you're saying?'

He looked at me intently. 'Would that make any difference?' he asked softly. But I was too surprised, too shocked to say anything. 'Suppose you were able to talk to him?'

I couldn't believe it. I didn't want to believe it. Those lines from Browning, the little plaque—'It's not true,' I heard myself say and there was a tightness in my throat. 'It's not possible.'

He laughed. 'I think your Inspector Garrard would tell you differently.' And he added, his voice gone hard again, 'But you can't go to him, can you? He knows too much about you. You can't go to the police, anybody. So you do as we tell you. Otherwise, you'll never know another moment's peace. And that's what you want, isn't it? To be left alone.' He nodded. 'Well, after this you will be, so long as you co-operate.' He stared at me a moment, then turned and went out of the cabin. I heard him ask Henrik to sound two blasts, the sound of his footsteps in the gangway, and I stood there, unable to move, unable to think.

I didn't go to the bridge until I heard the fishing boat alongside. He was already on board. He turned and looked at me, and then he disappeared into the wheelhouse and the boat pulled away from us. I watched as it steamed down Ham Voe, the tonk-tonk of its diesel echoing back until it disappeared beyond Baa Head. It was past six then and the crew were already feeding. I had mine on the bridge, alone, and afterwards I went to my bunk. But I didn't get much sleep, and at 03.30 we got our anchor and left Foula for our rendezvous with *North Star*.

PART TWO

THE RIG

CHAPTER ONE

There was no sign of the rig when we arrived at the location shortly after 11.00 on Sunday, 20th April. The Decca ship was lying hove-to ahead of two marker buoys in line. The dan-buoys marking the position of the eight anchors were already laid, spread uniformly round the drilling site, which itself was marked with a yellow-flagged buoy. All the dan-buoys had lights. I steamed within hailing distance of the Decca ship and asked her skipper when the rig would arrive.

'You on stand-by?' He was a small man with a bright red woollen cap on a round bullet head. 'Last I heard the ETA was 17.00. But she'll be later than that. The tug's under-powered for the job, and even with the two supply ships towing they made barely a knot and a half yesterday. The wind veering may help.'

'They'll be anchoring at night then?'

'Sure they will, and that could be a fine balls-up, so keep well clear unless they start hollering for help. Only a few weeks ago I fished one poor bugger out. It was black as a crow's arse and when we did get him we found the anchor hawser had taken half his head off. You tell your crew to watch those boys doing their stuff on the flat-iron decks of the supply ships, then they'll realize what cushy jobs they got.' He grinned, waving and turning back into his bridge.

The cook was standing at the rail below me and I heard him say, 'Aye, but they're in town several nights a week, not stuck out here for three bluidy months.' His name was Flett and he came from Orkney.

We could hear the rig's radio traffic, but none of it Voice, and shortly after midday we picked the blip of it up on our radar. By then the sea had gone down, only a slight swell. The wind was south-easterly, light, visibility good, and about an hour later she began to come up over the horizon. The shape of her grew very slowly and we lay wallowing in the swell playing cribbage until late in the afternoon the Decca ship steamed up alongside and asked us to take station 4 cables on her port side to form a 'gate' leading to the location marker buoys. By then the rig was standing out of the sea like a colossal steel water beetle, her size accentuated by the fact that she was riding high on her four 'torpedoes', which had been de-ballasted to within about 20 feet of the surface. She was still more than two miles away, and as we moved into position, a last watery gleam from the setting sun shone on the high antenna of the drill tower, the name *North Star* showing clear on the side of the platform. She was turning now, very gradually, to enter the 'gate' against the tide, our radio picking up the barge engineer's instructions to the two supply ships and the tug, which was already dropping its tow.

'*North Star* to *Bowstring* – as soon as we are in position over ze marker I tell you, then you leave *Rattler* to hold us and lay out ze first anchor, is it?'

'Roger *North Star*.'

'Is Number Two anchor ze virst one.' A Dutchman by the sound of it, and in that last gleam we could see two figures on the helicopter deck, one with a walkie-talkie to his mouth as he acted as towmaster.

'Roger – out.'

And then the other ship's captain: 'You're relying on the tide to hold her, but suppose we get a cross-wind?'

'Ze forecast is good – so ve lay anchors vast and everyzing okay, is it.'

'Is it?' The voice crackled with emphasis. 'You don't have to lay the bloody anchors in the dark, mate.'

'Then ve lay them again tomorrow if zey are no good,' the Dutchman replied imperturbably. And, much fainter, another voice – 'See they lay them right first time, Pieter. I don't want any hold-up when the drilling crews . . .' The voice faded, but something in the crispness of it made me wonder if that was Villiers standing up there beside the barge engineer. I remembered reading some years back that he had had a narrow escape when the prototype belonging to a small aircraft company he had acquired crashed while doing landing and take-off tests. He was the sort of a man who would get a kick out of being on the spot at the start of a new venture.

The lurid gleam of sunlight vanished, the rig moving ponderously. Dusk came fast with low cloud rolling in, the huge structure abreast of us, 20 steel columns riding high on submerged pontoons with the derrick a latticed finger thrusting at the overcast, the ruby glow of its warning lights giving it a festive air. *Decca to North Star, North Star to Rattler* – our bridge radio crackled with instructions as the rig, a blaze of lights now, approached the tiny pinpoint of the location buoy.

It was night before *North Star* was in position and *Bowstring,* the smaller of the two supply ships, closed stern-on for her towing hawser to be let go. The time was 21.17. An arc light swung as the rig's crane moved, one of the crew clinging like a fly to the deck rails, hand on the heavy hook, guiding it into the eye of an anchor pennant. The brontosaurus-like head of the crane reared up to lift the anchor clear of its housing on the underwater section of the column, then bowed downwards as *Bowstring* backed in, men moving on the flat deck of the supply ship, balanced on the stern just clear of the roller, reaching out with gloved hands to connect the pennant to their winch hawser, and the mate standing with his walkie-talkie to his ear.

I had closed in to watch how it was done, the crane head rising again and *Bowstring* pouring a white froth from her stern as the winch roared, the pennant dragging at the 15-ton anchor till the big shackle at the top of its stock came clear of the water, held hard against the fat round barrel of the stern-roller. The heavy clamp, secured by a strop to the bulwarks, was snapped on, the men on deck shackling on the long pennant wire attached to one of the 3-ton anchor buoys and a winch drum high up on the corner of the rig paying out cable as the tow began, out to the pinprick light of the anchor position marker rising and falling in the swell.

It took almost an hour to lay that one anchor, the men on the supply ship never still, moving so nimbly as their flat craft wallowed with its load that they looked like ballet dancers on the lit stage of the after deck. By midnight the second anchor was down and *Rattler,* released from her tow, had joined *Bowstring,* the crane in almost constant motion as it fed pennants and buoys to the two of them. And all the time we lay hove-to and rolling just clear of the anchor cable lines, our radio tuned to the walkie-talkie talk. There was only one hitch, and that was towards dawn.

'*North Star* to *Duchess* . . . close in to No. 5 – ve haf No. 5 anchor jammed and are zending divers down.'

Two divers in wet suits, with aqualungs on their backs, were lowered by crane in a steel cage, their torches shining like sea luminosity as they swam around the column housing of No. 5. The pennant wire had wrapped itself round one of the anchor flukes and we lay there, with the rig towering above us, while the pennant was cleared and dropped and a new pennant shackled on, the anchor hoisted clear by an auxiliary winch on the rig's deck.

It was daylight by the time that last anchor was laid and the rig held by all eight winches under correct tension. *Bowstring* was already over the horizon, *Rattler* hull-down, both on their way back to Aberdeen. The Decca ship had gone during the night. Only ourselves left now, a lone trawler keeping watch around the rig. It was 06.28 and I handed over to Johan and turned in.

I had hardly closed my eyes, it seemed, before a hand was shaking me and Henrik's voice said, 'The rig has sent a boat for you.' It was an inflatable rescue boat with one of the divers at the outboard motor, an Italian with dark curly hair and thin olive features. 'Issa Mr Villiers. 'E wanta speak wiz you.'

It was a bumpy ride, the boat driven at speed and the northerly breeze kicking up small waves, only snatches of talk possible. His name was Alfredo and he was one of the divers who had been down clearing the anchor. 'Issa very cold, si . . . Where is my 'ome? It is Milano. But not in a long time, I mean.' He had been in the North Sea for two years now, before that in Nigeria. 'Si, I have a wife and two bambini. Those-a boys, they are growing with a Scotch accent.' White teeth flashing with laughter and the bows dropping as we swept in under the giant pier-shadow of the rig. The slop of waves against the columns, the swirl of the tide running, and then the rusty iron of an endless stairway embracing a column and rising to the distant glint of sky high above. 'You go to toolpusher's office. They tella you where is Mr Villiers. Okay?'

Even though the ballast tanks had been blown and the torpedo-shaped pontoons sunk from the towing to the drilling depth of almost 60 feet, I reckoned it was well over 50 feet from sea level to the helicopter deck. I came out just beside the monstrous drum of No. 4 winch. The toolpusher's office was a steel shack, the entrance leading off the helicopter deck, and behind it was the pipe deck piled high with pipe, steel casing, drill bits, all the ironmongery of drilling, some 2,000 tons of it. Beyond the pipe deck was the steel skid for lifting pipe to the derrick floor, and reared above it, like an enormous pylon, the derrick tower itself.

I pushed open the door of the toolpusher's office and a leathery-faced man wearing a bright red peaked cap looked up from the girlie picture mag he was reading. Behind him was a complicated diagram with the emergency indicators for blow-out prevention. Of course, they would have precautions, and that diagram, so detailed, so comprehensive – I stood there for a moment staring up at it. Pipe rams, blind shear – I can't remember all of them, but four or five fail-safes, each with a red warning light to beam out its danger signals once action had been taken. With all those safety measures there did not seem much danger of a dragging anchor causing oil pollution.

'You looking for somebody?' The man in the peaked cap was regarding me suspiciously.

'Mr Villiers,' I said. More than anything else, the sight of that diagram brought home to me the nature of this colossal machine, the complications of operating deep under water and deeper still into layers of rock below the seabed.

Offhandedly he directed me to the barge engineer's office. This was one deck down into the crew's quarters, right opposite the ballast control room. I caught a glimpse of an engineer seated at an enormous console full of pressure gauges and the whole wall facing him taken up by a diagram panel with red and green lights, flanked by ballast indicators that looked like giant temperature gauges. Then I was into the office and two men were standing at a table in the corner, poring over a large design sheet, their white safety helmets perched on a pile of books. They turned as I entered and one of them, a short bulky man with hair that stood up like a brush and very blue eyes in a crinkled sun-worn face, folded the design, leaning on it with his hands. He wore a faded anorak over a grubby T-shirt. The other was dressed in a sky-blue sweater, with the clean collar of a white shirt showing above it, and neatly creased, immaculate trousers. He was taller, thinner, with livelier features. 'You the skipper of that trawler?' he asked. I nodded and he held out his hand. 'Vic Villiers.' His grip was firm, his eyes on my face, summing me up. 'A long night, eh?'

'I had just turned in,' I said.

'Sorry about that. How would you like to be running one of those supply ships?'

'I think I might have a nervous breakdown.'

He laughed. 'You've never seen a rig laying anchors before?'

'No.'

'Nor had I. Fascinating!' There was an undercurrent of

excitement in his voice. 'This is Pieter van Dam.' He turned to the man beside him. 'God knows how many times he's done it, eh, Pieter? And not an ulcer in his belly.'

The Dutchman's stolid face broke into a smile as he made an exaggerated effort to pull in his protruding stomach. 'The ulcers only come ven you begin losing lifes, is it?'

'Well, you're not losing any here.' There was a subtle change in Villiers's manner, the smile gone and the moment of humour with it. 'You're off on the first flight, aren't you? I'll see you before you go.' He gave a brief nod of dismissal and turned to me. 'Sit down.' He waved me to one of the chairs drawn up round a low table littered with empty coffee cups and oil industry magazines. The door closed behind the Dutchman and we were alone. The room was stuffy, full of stale cigarette and cigar smoke, the glare of fluorescent lighting. I was nervous and suddenly very tired, the all-pervading hum of machinery a soporific.

'You wanted to see me,' I murmured. He was standing there, staring at me, and I wondered whether he suspected anything. 'Is it about the work permits?' If it wasn't about the work permits . . .

'We had a report, of course. Putting to sea like that was a little high-handed, the sort of thing that upsets the locals.' But he was smiling as he sat down opposite me. 'I've had Fuller open an office in Scalloway now. He'll fix it for you. In any case, you don't have to worry about work permits here.' He stretched out his legs, leaning back, the light on the dark stubble of his jaw. 'What did you think of Fuller by the way?'

I shrugged. What the hell did he expect me to say? 'He's a good man from your point of view.'

'No hard feelings?'

'What about?'

His hand had moved to the table, long sensitive fingers beating a light tattoo. 'That charter. He pulled a fast one on you, didn't he?'

'I imagined it was your idea to buy the mortgage.'

'Well that much of it is to your advantage, so long as you do the job and stay on station.' He sat there for a moment, staring at me, not saying anything, and I had a feeling he was trying to make up his mind about something, the fingers still tapping at the table top. 'You're wondering why I got you over here, after we've both of us been up all night.' His tanned face was handsome, almost boyish, his eyes dark under dark brows, his hair almost black. 'You probably think that because I deal in company finance I'm not interested in people. But running a business or running a trawler, it's the same thing – everybody's got to fit. You, for instance.' He shifted a little forward in his chair. 'What made you salvage that boat and then take on a three-month charter?'

'It's suitable employment for an old trawler.'

'And you like the sea.' He smiled, leaning back again. He knew it didn't answer his question, but he let it go, asking me instead about the salvage and how we had managed to get her off the rocks and repaired in time. He seemed genuinely interested. It was a side of him I hadn't expected, an enthusiasm for physical practicalities, and as I tried to answer his detailed questions, I began to understand what it was that had induced him to gamble in oil, why he was out here taking a personal interest in the anchoring of this rig he had acquired more or less by chance. And because he seemed impressed by what we had done, I found myself warming to him.

It was very naïve of me, but I was tired and the atmosphere relaxed. And when he progressed to enquiring about my background, it seemed quite natural. I suppose I was a little flattered, too, and because I thought his questions stemmed from a business man's desire to make the fullest use of anybody associated with him, I told him just enough about myself to give him confidence.

'So your stepfather was an industrialist?'

'Yes – a small arms factory. That was during the war. Afterwards he switched to consumer durables.'

'And you came over to England to study at the LSE and work as a financial journalist.' But instead of asking me why I hadn't stayed in journalism, he began discussing the present economic outlook, the fuel situation and the future of the country in a monetary world dominated by the oil revenues of Middle East potentates. He was even more optimistic than the press, or even the politicians, believing that offshore oil could solve Britain's whole balance of payment problems. It was a long time since I had talked to anybody of his calibre and, tired as I was, I found it immensely stimulating.

'So we have this chance to become rich again, to change the whole economic climate of the country. But what about the political climate? Will that change?' And without thinking I said, 'Yes. The political climate depends on the economic, doesn't it?' And I added, conscious that I was now giving form to thoughts that had been vaguely in my mind for some time, 'This is something our political leaders, certainly our union leaders, have been slow to grasp. The mass of the people, of course, they haven't a clue – not about economics. But the political climate, that's different. They are the political climate, and in some subtle way they sense a change without understanding the cause.'

'You really think that?'

'Yes, I do. You change the economic climate, then the political climate must change, too.'

He shook his head. 'I see your point. But I can't go along with you. It's the chicken and the egg. The economic climate is dependent on union co-operation. No union co-operation, no change in the country's economy. Maybe that's what they want, eh?'

'The militants, yes,' I said. 'They want anarchy. But that's not what the rank and file of the trade union movement wants. I'm convinced of that.'

He looked at me, a quick, appraising stare. 'Changed your spots, haven't you?'

The question brought me up with a jolt. 'How do you mean?'

'Your background,' he said. 'You missed out on a few details.' His manner had toughened, the friendliness gone. 'Perhaps if I tell you an Inspector Garrard came to see me at my offices in London – to warn me about you . . .'

The tiredness came back, a sense of weariness, of deflation. 'Why the hell didn't you tell me?' I got to my feet, suddenly furious – furious because I knew Garrard had been right to warn him. But to spring it on me like this . . . 'If you want to break that charter agreement, you'll have to buy me out.'

'You'll fight, is that it?'

'Yes. I haven't spent a month of my life slaving to get that trawler ready for sea . . .' But what was the use? Everything I did – all my life . . . that devil Stevens had been right, the past would always dog me. 'I have a police dossier. But how you read it depends whose side you're on.' I couldn't keep the bitterness out of my voice, seeing him, sitting there, a man who had got himself to a position of power by using money the way a militant like Scunton would use a mob – what was the difference?

'Sit down,' he said quietly.

But I didn't move, seeing him as representing everything I

had fought against, and that voice of his, so accustomed to command he didn't have to shout. It was men like Villiers who turned youngsters into anarchists.

'Sit down,' he said again. And as I hesitated, he added, 'Now I've talked with you I have a proposition.'

He waited until I was seated, and then he said, 'Garrard showed me your file, yes. And I agree that most of it is open to different interpretations, according to whether you're a capitalist or a socialist. But it was somewhat alarming from my point of view.' He paused. 'Except for one thing. It doesn't explain what induced you to become a trawlerman, or why a man with your record of industrial action should commit himself so wholeheartedly to the salvage and management of a vessel for gain. That's capitalism by my reckoning.' He raised his hand. 'No, don't interrupt me please. And don't look so stubbornly defensive. I'm not going to enquire your reasons. I wouldn't get a sensible answer anyway. In fact, I doubt if you really know yourself.'

'What's your proposition?' I said.

But he ignored that. 'I have to consider the safety of the men on this rig. And that's not all. There's a lot of money locked up in the rig itself that would be better employed elsewhere if there were any real risk. Also, of course – and this is between ourselves – we are very confident that we are sitting on oil – right here, this minute.' His fingers were drumming a tattoo again as he stared at me speculatively. 'Suppose you were going to sabotage *North Star,* how would you go about it?'

The question, so abruptly flung at me, came as a shock. 'I haven't thought about it,' I told him.

'Well, I have,' he said. 'It's something all rig operators have had to face up to for several years now. Indeed, everything going on to a rig has to be checked for the possibility of explosives. It would have to be explosives, wouldn't it? Pieter van Dam and I were discussing it just before you came in.' Abruptly he got up from his chair and crossed to the corner table. 'Come and have a look.' He unfolded the design sheet again. It was a drawing of the rig's underdeck lay-out. 'There, and there,' he said, stabbing his fingers on the junction points of the cross-struts. 'Two large limpet bombs. Mines perhaps. But if those struts go, then the column towers will fold inwards with the weight of the drill tower and all the mud and fuel and pipe we carry.' He gave me a sidelong glance. 'Our Achilles' heel. That and blasting holes in the pontoons.'

'Why are you telling me this?' My mouth felt dry.

'You don't have to be an engineer to identify the weak points of a rig like this one,' he said quietly. 'Anybody with any imagination can see it at a glance. It would mean divers, of course, and they'd have to be transported out here by sea. You're the guard ship. The orders you'll be given require you to make sure no vessel comes within the circle of the anchor buoys, only the supply ships. The crews on those ships have been thoroughly screened.' He turned, looking me straight in the face. 'That leaves you, doesn't it? That trawler of yours is the only ship that has a right to be here – and that I'm not sure about.'

Put like that I could see his point. 'If you don't trust me,' I said uneasily, 'then you'd better find another ship.'

He shook his head. 'As you say, it's very suitable employment for that trawler of yours. You'd require compensation, and anyway, there isn't another in Shetland, not that's available.' He turned away and began pacing the room. Finally he said, 'No. What I've got to do is make certain of you.' He had stopped and was facing me again. 'That's the answer, isn't it?' He went back to his chair and flopped into it, drumming with his fingers on the table top. 'Vulnerable was the word Garrard used. You're vulnerable – because of an incident in Hull. There's a suspicion you might have set fire to the house yourself.'

'Is that what he told you?'

'He didn't put it as bluntly, but that was the implication.' He stared at me, waiting, and when I didn't say anything, he went on, 'Fuller went into this charter blind, knowing nothing about you. It was a mistake, and now I have to make up my mind – whether to employ you or not. You weren't there by accident, were you?'

'Have you been in touch with the police handling the case?' I asked.

'Yes, I phoned Hull myself.'

'What do they think?'

'Either you threw that petrol bomb, believing the house to be empty, or you were there because you knew something like that was going to happen. They haven't made up their minds, but don't imagine they've closed the case.'

It was almost two months ago, the memory of that night blurred and unreal here on an oil rig, cocooned in power plant heat, the smell of oil and the background hum of the rig's machinery. 'You may not like my record,' I said, 'but I don't go around throwing petrol bombs.'

'But you were there. Why?'

I hesitated. He had no right to question me, but it could be a way of clearing myself with the police so I told him about the meeting I had attended in Hull that evening, how it was packed with militants, most of them brought in from industrial towns farther north and some who had no right to be there at all. 'It was a particularly ugly meeting. A union official, who had come up from London, was howled down and virtually kicked off the platform. They'd got pickets on all the shipyard gates, a busload of them from the Tyne, and some from Liverpool, even the Clyde. Pierson & Watt were non-union. They whipped themselves up into a mood where they were ready to march on the offices and smash them up, and a man kept yelling for them to be set on fire. Then somebody, I don't know who – it was just a voice – shouted that the foreman was the bugger to get. The mood was pretty violent by then, half the room on its feet and everybody worked up. Somebody else shouted, "I'll fix the bastard." That was when I left.'

'To go and watch the foreman's house.'

'To warn him. I knew Entwisle. I'd been mate on a trawler when it was into Pierson & Watt for repairs. But there was no answer when I rang the bell. I thought they were all out.'

'So you hung around.'

'Yes – fortunately as it turned out.'

'And afterwards, why didn't you wait for the police?'

'Why should I? Nobody was hurt.'

'A man's property was set on fire. That's arson.'

'The *Fisher Maid* was sailing at first light. And my hands hurt. They were cut and slightly burned.'

'So you went off on a distant water trawler. And when you got back, instead of returning to Hull, you headed for Shetland and got involved in salvaging the vessel we've now chartered.' He smiled, shaking his head. 'Some people would regard that as pretty strange behaviour.'

'But you don't?'

'Depends what your motives are. I think I can guess, knowing your background – and now that I've talked to you. You want to make something of your life before it's too late. I could help you there.'

I started to tell him I didn't want his help, that his whole outlook was entirely opposed to mine, but he stopped me. 'Of course our outlooks are different. You've been switching from one thing to another, experimenting with drugs and ideological theories. I've kept to one single basic tenet, the profit motive. You probably abhor that. But you're running your own business now. You'll learn. You can't run even a broken-down old trawler unless your cash flow is sufficient to keep the damn thing afloat.'

I stood there, silent, knowing it was true and that I hadn't considered what would happen when the charter ran out. The scrape of his chair as he got to his feet interrupted my thoughts.

'You're an awkward cuss,' he said. 'I was going to make you an offer – a gamble I suppose you'd call it.'

'I don't gamble,' I told him.

'No? Then why did you salvage that trawler?' He was smiling, his tanned, strangely handsome face suddenly alive. 'I'm not talking about cards or betting on horses. I'm talking about pitting one's wits and one's energies against the odds in life. That's what I'm doing drilling out here with this rig. It's what you're doing with that trawler. The rig's old, and so is your ship – both of us taking a chance.' He turned abruptly towards the door. 'Had any breakfast this morning?'

'No.'

'Nor have I.' He pulled it open. 'Let's go and feed. I'll tell you what I have in mind over our bacon and eggs.'

We went down a flight of metal treads to the lower deck of the crew housing. It was hot and airless with the same stale smell of food and oil combined with salt to be found on a ship. The shower was running in the men's room, the glimpse of a fat white body towelling itself, and inside the mess a long aluminium counter with two cooks in white chatting behind it. 'Bacon and eggs twice,' Villiers said. He handed me a plate. 'Try the rolls. They bake their own on the night watch.'

The room, with its three long, bare-scrubbed tables, was almost empty. We got our coffee from a machine set between windows looking out to an empty sea. The wind had freshened, occasional whitecaps breaking across the low line of the westerly swell. The barge engineer was there, sitting over his coffee with a Dutch cigar. We joined him and the talk centred on the drilling crew coming in on the first helicopter flight. A man named Ken Stewart would be relieving him. The toolpusher was American, a hard driver, van Dam said. 'Ed don't waste any time.'

'How long before we start drilling?' Villiers asked.

'Depends on the zeabed. The divers are going down in the bell now. If the zeabed is okay, then maybe tomorrow.'

'Pity, I have to be in Holland tomorrow.'

'Then you give my love to Rotterdam, eh?' And he added, 'Better you go today. Iz full 'ouse ven both drill crews are 'ere.'

The bacon and eggs came and Villiers began discussing gale conditions, up to what wind force the supply boats could keep going and whether the proper tension could be maintained on the anchor cables so that drilling could go on uninterrupted. Except that he was unshaven, it was hard to believe that he had been up all night, his voice quick and concise, his brain sharp. He was brimful of energy and I wondered how many years it would be before he burned himself out. Every now and then I glanced out of the windows, but the sea remained empty, no sign of the trawler, or any other vessel, in that cold northern light.

At last van Dam left, the whiff of his cigar lingering as Villiers reached for another roll. 'How do you ever keep your ship stocked?' he asked. 'Three nights at sea, no exercise, and I'm so damned hungry . . . You know, the time I've spent on this rig, it's given me an idea. City rents have reached a point where it would pay to build an office block on pontoons and moor it off the coast. No rents, no rates, and with the sort of radio equipment we've got on *North Star* there's not much business you can't transact. What do you think of that?'

'Personnel,' I said. 'Drilling, I imagine, is like trawling, it's a way of life.'

He nodded, his mouth full. 'A week on, a week off. Can't do that with office staff. But what about Sparks? His stint is three weeks. It's what you get used to, isn't it?' He was silent a moment, chewing over the idea. 'Sea City . . . The idea's not new, of course. And there are problems, as you say. But this rig is obsolete now. An easy conversion – and if the experiment came off we'd do a lot better than the scrap value.' He glanced at me. 'Where's your wife now? You're not divorced.'

'I've no idea. She was brought up a Catholic.'

'Irish, I believe.'

'Yes.'

'Communist?'

I didn't answer.

'So you hide yourself away at sea. Well, it would make a nice job for a man like you – the first ever sea office block skipper.'

'Is that your proposition?' I asked him.

He threw back his head and laughed, a gold tooth showing. 'No, not really. But it's an idea.' He pulled out his diary and made a note. 'You go and talk to Sparks. If you've got a girl-friend, ring her up – tell him I said you could. I know a lot about planes, nothing about ships or rigs. But I got through to Frankfurt and Sydney yesterday just as quickly as I could from my office in London, and with the FAX machine scrambling teleprint messages can be made safe.' He buttered the other half of his roll. 'That reminds me. I said I'd call Rotterdam . . .' He glanced at the clock over the door and I knew his mind was switching to whatever business deal it was that required his presence in Holland.

'You said something about an offer,' I reminded him.

He looked at me, the eyes shrewd and calculating. It was a mistake, I had been too eager. He smiled. 'Are you prepared to stay on station until we finish drilling?'

'How long will that be?'

'You tell me how many holes we have to drill before we strike oil and I'll tell you how long. We could strike it first go, but if we don't, then we'll go on drilling till we do. There's no other rig available. Not for this year, anyway. And no other trawler, none as suitable anyway. Did you know that when you told Fuller your plans for salvage and took him down to see her?' He smiled, shaking his head: 'No, of course you didn't, otherwise you wouldn't have been such a fool as to sign that charter.' He leaned back, wiping his mouth and screwing up his paper napkin. 'Nor did Fuller. We only discovered that after Garrard had been to see me.'

'You looked for a replacement then?'

'Of course we did. But it would have meant delay, and it would have cost more. On a gamble like this I don't believe in spending a penny more than I have to. But if it comes off . . .' He looked at me, a slight lift to his dark brows. 'If it comes off, I'll see you get a fat bonus, over and above the charter. That good enough for you?' He wouldn't say how much. 'Depends on the strike, but large enough to give you a future.' It also depended on our remaining on station throughout the period of drilling.

I didn't say anything. To him money was the answer to everything. He'd worked it all out, striking a proper balance in that clear, calculating mind of his. But he didn't have to lie out there in the seas that we should have to face if *North Star* continued drilling beyond the end of the summer. 'Well, that's settled then.' He took my consent for granted. He was that sort of man, so sure of himself. 'I must go now or Sparks will be paging me on the Tannoy.' He got to his feet. 'I wouldn't want anybody out there in charge of the guard boat who bears me a grudge.' He was smiling, making a joke of it, but then he added, 'Just don't try anything, Randall. You look after my interests and I'll look after you. Paternalism, I think you people call it. But loyalty to one man can be a lot better than owing allegiance to a faceless bureaucracy. Nobody who has worked for me has ever had cause to regret it. Okay?' He nodded, turning quickly and walking to the door.

I watched him as he went out to his appointment over the ether with some executive in Rotterdam. God! How I envied him that self-assurance! I got myself another cup of coffee, lit my pipe and sat there wondering where it would all end. Would they strike oil? And if they did, would I still be here? I was remembering what he had said about offshore drilling and the country's future, his incredible optimism. By 1980, he had said – *a saving of perhaps £5,000 million in foreign exchange . . . the envy of the world, our industry booming, our currency the strongest in Europe.* Tell that to the men in the shipyards or the docks! But he had believed it, that bloody overbearing self-confidence of his. And I had been swept along by his optimism into making statements just as wild. Did I really believe that the political climate was governed by the state of the country's economy? *You change the economic climate,* I had said, *and the political climate must change, too.* If I were a capitalist, knowing what I did of grass-roots politics, would I back that statement with my own and other people's money?

A sudden scurry of feet in the passageway outside and a voice shouted, 'Coming in now, Rod.' I got up and went out, past a door marked Sick Bay and up two flights into the open where men were already gathering with their suitcases. The sun was shining and there was an air of expectancy. Van Dam appeared at my side looking diminished and somehow ordinary in a dark blue suit and a velour hat. 'Iz come yet?' he asked, and at that moment I heard it. A shadow passed across the pipe deck, the roar of engines growing, then a rush of wind and dust blowing.

Three men in safety helmets dashed out from the shelter of the toolpusher's office. The engines died, the whip of the rotor blades subsiding to a whisper. The passengers began to appear, a motley crowd that would only achieve the coherence of a team when they had changed into the rig gear of overalls, rubber boots, gloves and safety helmets. I watched their faces as they passed me, piling down the stairway to their quarters. Somebody dropped a bundle of newspapers at my feet and I saw the headline – *North Sea Rig Strikebound*. But as I bent down to see what it said, a voice hailed me, a short, tubby man with sandy hair and a bright yellow sweater. 'Remember me? Glasgow, wasn't it?'

I nodded. He was one of the Clydeside men who had been with me when we had clashed with the police outside the Marston yard. 'What are you doing here?' I asked him.

'I'm a motorman now. And you?'

I told him, and he said, 'Aye, I heard ye'd gone into trawlers. Weel, I'll be off now and get settled in.' He gave me a quick grin and I remembered his name as he hurried on down the stairway after his mates. It was Rory – Rory Sullivan. He had been a member of the Boilermakers' Union when I had last seen him. I turned to look again at the packet of newspapers, but it was gone now. The helicopter's engines were roaring and in a moment it lifted clear of the rig, slanting skyward. I watched it disappear behind the derrick, dwindling to a speck as it headed south-east on the 60 miles flight back to Sumburgh Head. Then I went down to the radio room, thinking about Sullivan and unconscious of the bustle around me.

The radio room was on the lower deck of the crew's quarters and had TELECOMMUNICATIONS on the door. Villiers was no longer there, only the radio operator seated at the double-sideband, earphones clamped on his head, his thumb on the key rattling out a message. He wore a white nylon shirt, open-necked and with sleeves rolled up. His arms and face were pale, a cigarette burning in a tobacco tin beside the telex.

There was a chair at a desk in the corner and I sat down, staring at the bank of equipment that filled the far side of the room from floor to ceiling, trying to think out what I was going to say, how I was to get the information I wanted.

It was too good an opportunity to miss. There was so much

traffic going out from *North Star* that it was unlikely anyone would take note of what I was saying, and though Sparks would probably be standing at my elbow listening, it wasn't the same as having my own crew overhear the conversation, rumours flying round the ship and endless speculation.

I was still thinking how I was going to frame my questions when the door opened and two men entered, one of them with a sheet clipped to a board. 'Well, there it is, Ed. Two of them, so you'd better keep your fingers crossed that nobody jams their hand in a winch or gets hit on the head by the kelly.' He was a soft, rather old-maidish little man with a high, piping voice. The other was a big, hard-fisted looking American.

'Split 'em up then, will'ya. Their room mates'll soon tell 'em enough about your ideas of first aid to keep 'em outa that li'l sick bay of yours.' The belly laugh was without humour. 'An' tell 'em this, Lennie – anybody starting a strike on this rig swims for it.' His voice was harsh and grating. 'One Scotch, one Irish, you say. Jeez!' He gave a shrug and walked out.

The sick bay attendant pulled out a bench and flopped on to it, taking a pencil from behind his ear and making a note on his pad. 'Poor bastards,' he muttered to nobody in particular. 'Ed'll pass the word to his drillers and they'll drive those boys so hard . . .' He turned to the operator as he finished sending and spiked his message. 'Any news on *Sunray II*? Ed's feeling sore about it. He knows the toolpusher.'

Sparks nodded, his eyes magnified by his glasses. 'From what I've picked up so far it appears two of the roustabouts came to blows and were ordered off the rig. One of them refused to board the supply ship and his mates stopped work until the order was cancelled.'

'So the strike's over.' The little man got to his feet. 'I'd better tell Ed. He wants to know what happened.'

'Tell him his pal gave in to them. That'll put him in a fine good humour.' And as the sick bay attendant went out, Sparks turned to me, a look of enquiry on his pale face. I asked him if he could get me a London number and I wrote it down for him.

'You from that trawler?'

'Yes.' I gave him my name.

He nodded. 'Mr Villiers mentioned it. A girl friend, he said. Haven't you got R/T on board?'

'It's old equipment,' I said. 'I can talk to you. But Stonehaven and the GPO are outside my range.'

He nodded again and moved over to the big single-sideband set. He had to wait his turn to get through to Stonehaven. Then he asked for the number, listening with the phone to his ear while I stood beside him. 'Ringing now,' he said, and handed it to me.

My mouth felt dry, the ringing tone very clear. Then a voice said, 'Can I help you?' and I asked for Inspector Garrard. There was a long pause. Finally a different voice came on the line. 'I'm afraid Inspector Garrard is not available at the moment. If you care to give your name and tell me what it's about . . .' But it was the voice of officialdom, abrupt and businesslike, and no chance he would understand what I was talking about. 'It doesn't matter,' I said and handed the phone back to the radio operator.

'Not there?' He terminated the call and hung the phone back on its hook. 'Just as well perhaps. I have a message for you.' He rummaged through the papers beside the Morse key and handed me a telex sheet: INFORM MASTER DUCHESS OF NOR-FOLK MRS RANDALL BOOKED ON AIR ANGLIA FLIGHT ARRIVING SUMBURGH 09.15 TOMORROW. The dispatch time was given as 16.35 the previous day, but no indication of who had sent it.

'Do you know where it came from?' I asked.

'Our Aberdeen office.' He hesitated, then said, 'You forgotten to pay the rent or something?' He was looking at me, smiling, and I was suddenly reminded of the radio operator on *Fisher Maid*, his love of gossip. I glanced down at the telex again, wondering who had sent her to the Star-Trion office. And where had she come from? London? Dublin? Belfast maybe. But why? She was city-born. She hated the country, the sea, anywhere that was empty of people. She liked crowds, intrigue, excitement – and argument. I could hear the quick clatter of her tongue voicing the thoughts of her sharp brain, incisive, persuasive, unstoppable as a gorge full of water tumbling over rock. And there had been other times when the Celtic lilt in it was gentle as rain, the hard tinkle of her words softening to seduction. Then she'd had a lovely voice, warm, full-bodied . . . Christ! how was it possible to love and hate a woman at one and the same time?

'Do you want me to contact the office for you? They may know where she's planning to stay.'

'No,' I said. 'No, it doesn't matter.'

Fiona in Shetland. Why? Why now? But I knew. I knew it

in my bones. They weren't sure of me and they were stepping up the pressure. How else would she have known where I was or how to contact me? I turned, walking blindly to the door, and almost collided with the sick bay attendant. He handed me a sheaf of typescript. 'Standing orders for the guard boat,' he said. 'Ken Stewart asked me to give them to you.'

I nodded and went down the passage. I wanted somewhere quiet, time to think. But the quarters were pandemonium, with men changing, moving to their work stations, calling to each other, asking questions, home news mixed with technicalities, like the first day in college. And out in the open there were men already on the pipe deck, climbing the long stairway to the derrick floor, and Villiers in the open doorway of the corrugated iron shelter, a safety helmet on his head. Only the helicopter deck was clear and I went and stood near the edge, looking down at the whitecaps breaking and the *Duchess* small in the distance, rolling sluggishly in the swell.

'What d'ya think you're doing?'

I turned, knowing who it was by the grating voice. 'Enjoying a bit of quiet,' I said, 'before going back to my ship.'

He nodded, the hard face breaking into a smile. 'I know who you are then.' His voice was softer, a Southern drawl, as he held out his hand. 'Ed Wiseberg.'

'Mike Randall,' I said.

'Okay, Mike. You go back to your ship now, you'll get no quiet here. I got another whirly-bird due in shortly.'

'I'll need the divers' boat.'

He shook his head. 'Call up your own guys and have 'em come over for you. Nobody here I can spare. And one other thing.' The mouth had hardened, the tired grey eyes watching me. 'Vic told me something about you. I want you off this barge, and fast. There's been a strike on one of the North Sea rigs. I won't have any trouble like that here. Understand? You stay off this rig. An' if you've got anything to talk about, you talk to me. Nobody else, see. I'll tell the radio op. And I'll have him call your boat for you.' His tone, though firm, was quite amiable and he smiled as he patted my shoulder. 'Good luck then. Glad I don't have to pitch around out there with you.'

I went slowly across to the massive drum of No. 4 winch and started down the long staircase that led into the chill, shadowed world below the platform. As I descended the sound of the sea slopping against the columns became magnified, a hollow, eerie sound, the cross-bracing of tubular girders a visible reminder of Villiers's words as we had examined the design drawing. I reached the bottom and stood waiting just clear of the waves rolling under my feet, the colossal dead-weight structure reared above me, water jetting from cooling and sewer vents, the hum of the rig's machinery muffled now.

It was calm, calm for these waters, the wind westerly about Force 3. I tried to picture it in storm force winds with 60-70 foot waves piling in and breaking. I could just see No. 4 anchor cable running down the side of the corner column leg and stretched taut as an iron bar. What would the tension be with a gale blowing? And the anchor over 500 feet down and more than a thousand yards from the rig.

The boat came, Henrik nosing it into the stairway. I stepped down into the centre of it, and as we came out from under the platform's shadow I was thinking that perhaps I would rather be on the *Duchess*; it might be uncomfortable, but in a trawler there was at least freedom of manœuvre.

CHAPTER TWO

What exactly the divers found on the seabed was not reported on the air, but something caused Ed Wiseberg to have the rig shifted 10 metres to the north-west. They did it on the winch cables, which meant, of course, some 30 feet less cable holding the rig on the side from which winds blow hard at the tail end of a depression. Ken Stewart wanted anchors 1 and 2 re-laid, but with only a single supply ship servicing *North Star*, Ed Wiseberg overruled him. He was spudded in by then and finding the going better than expected. He needed mud and drill casing, and he wasn't going to have *Rattler* wasting time 'frigging around with the bloody anchors'.

We listened in to it all as Ken discussed it with the *Rattler's* skipper, sometimes by walkie-talkie, sometimes on the R/T, bemoaning the fact that Yankee toolpushers didn't know the difference between a semi-submersible off Shetland and a drilling barge moored in the shallows of the Gulf of Mexico. 'It's not right, Jock. It's my responsibility if we drag. But because we're drilling he makes the decisions.' And the other laughing and saying, 'Every barge engineer says the same.

Ye canna win, can ye.'

They had started drilling on the 23rd, and as April ran into May, and the sea stayed calm, the danger of the rig dragging receded from my mind. It was a glorious spell of weather, the wind light and the sun shining day after day, except when there was a sea mist. Often by noon we were stripped to the waist, the ship just lying-to or drifting close along the rig with both engines shut down. We were saving fuel and a lot of wear and tear during those first ten days.

In that time we saw only two other ships, both small drifters out of Lerwick. And with the sun moving steadily north, the nights were shortening, the period of maximum alertness a little less each day. It was a pleasant interlude after all the hard work we had put into the ship, except for the monotony of it and the continuous racket of the rig. The draw-works, the big diesel up on the derrick floor, never stopped, an endless roar that only changed its note when they were using the winches to disconnect and screw on another 90-foot length of pipe to the drilling string that was steadily moving down its casing as the bit thrust deeper and deeper into the seabed sediments. And added to the racket of the draw-works was the steady, continuous hum of the power plant. Even when we had drifted beyond the circle of the anchor buoys, the sound of the rig was almost as loud, the noise of it bouncing off the surface of the sea. And for me there was the sense of waiting, the certainty that this was no more than an interlude. Pacing the bridge in the dark hours, or in my bunk turning restlessly and trying to sleep, there was always at the back of my mind the fear that the work permits would be refused or something else would happen to disturb the new life I was trying to build for myself.

It was the loneliness more than anything else. It preyed on my nerves. I was so goddam lonely stuck out there beside that steel monster, drifting back and forth over the same patch of sea, with nobody to turn to, no living soul I could discuss it with. Once I started writing to Gertrude, but I soon gave it up. The things I wanted to say were not the things I could put in a letter. And she was so businesslike, always concerned about our supply of fresh meat, vegetables and fruit. *Rattler* was based on Aberdeen, but periodically the supply ship put into Scalloway, and then, as well as stores, there was always a note for me. Because Gertrude had sailed so often in the *Duchess,* she understood very well that our chief enemy would be the monotony and emptiness of life out here. She sent us ground tackle so that we could amuse ourselves fishing, and incidentally augment our food supplies for free. She sent out records and the new cribbage board I asked for after Henrik, in a fit of temper, had thrown the old one overboard, intending it for Flett's head. Little things were already beginning to assume larger-than-life proportions, the atmosphere among some members of the crew moving towards flashpoint.

Then the weather broke and we had other things to keep us busy. The wind, which had been mainly north-easterly, backed into the south-west – Force 7, gusting 8, low cloud and rain. A series of deep Lows swept up between us and Iceland and we had three fronts pass over us in quick succession. After that it was unsettled and, with a big sea still running, we had difficulty going alongside *Rattler* when she finally came out to us. With the stores was the usual note from Gertrude. I didn't read it until we had finished standing by the supply ship while she hitched herself stern-on to the rig below the crane, with both spring-loaded mooring hawsers made fast.

A woman came to see me today. She says she is your wife.

I was in my cabin then and I stood with the note in my hand staring out of the window. The wind had veered a little and increased in strength, but I barely noticed it, balancing automatically to the swoop and twist of the ship. It was hard to imagine Fiona in that house by The Taing – Fiona with her pale pointed face, the small determined chin, the high white forehead surmounted by the black fringe of her pageboy cut, and deep-socketed eyes, the small mouth, that bitter tongue. And Gertrude, big and fair and solid as a rock, utterly reliable. Pity I could not fuse the two of them. I laughed at the thought, thinking of the result and wondering, if it was true that the attraction is towards opposites, what these two had got that I hadn't, other than a bosom and the means of satisfying me?

But Fiona had meant more to me than that, much more. She had been a force in my life – for a time at any rate. We had met in Glasgow, at a teach-in on Ché and his place in the self-awareness of emergent peoples. I was remembering how she had looked . . . *She is nice I think, but very nervy. She stayed for tea and we talked, mostly about you, or I think perhaps it is more accurate to say that she do the talking while I listen. Some of it I do not understand. She is I think a most political woman. She talk and talk, that is the nerves I would suppose. Is that why you are separated? She told me. She also told me*

*you are wasting your life in trawlers, that you could be a very
important man. She is a Progressive, she tells me —*

I could not help smiling at that. Fiona had been so many
things, at various times, a Trotskyist, a Maoist. She had been
a member of the WRP, the PD; now apparently she was a
good old-fashioned Progressive. *She want to know how she
can get in touch with you. I tell her if she wish to write she
must send it to Aberdeen to go out by the supply ship. But
she don't agree to that. She want to meet you. It is not easy
to convince her that you are out there for a long time and not
coming ashore. I think maybe you get a letter from her by the
boat after this one. What do you want? She seems very worried
about you, for what reason she do not say.*

The last I had heard of Fiona she was in Dublin. But that
was more than a year ago, and even if she had been working
for the IRA, I doubted whether she would still be with them.
Her allegiances never lasted long. There had to be a Cause,
but always something different. She had never been consistent,
except that she was anti- the present social order. And for her
that had always meant the British social order, presumably
because it was the one she had grown up with and was thus
able to identify as the root of all that was wrong in society.
To claim she was a Progressive could mean almost anything.
But whatever her current Cause, it didn't explain what she
was doing in Shetland visiting Gertrude Petersen and trying
to contact me.

I called up *Rattler* on the R/T and asked them to come
alongside again before they cleared for Aberdeen. Then I
handed over to Johan and shut myself in my cabin to compose
a letter. But to explain Fiona to somebody like Gertrude was
impossible. If I could have talked to her . . . But even then it
would have been difficult. I didn't understand Fiona myself.
We had lived together almost four years, in a miserable little
tenement house looking up the Clyde to the old John Brown
shipyard. There had been times when we were happy together,
fleeting moments in each other's arms, or when she was high.
But mostly I remembered the arguments, the over-intense
voice, the relentless pressure of her restless mind.

I never knew what she took, only that it had the effect of
soothing her nerves. She was very emotional then, often
lovable, with something of the kitten about her. Even now the
ache was still there. But none of this could I explain to
Gertrude. Twice I started that letter and tore it up. Then, as

I tried again, Lars called to me that I was wanted on the R/T. It was the rig's radio operator with orders for me to report to the barge engineer on board.

'He can talk to me on the radio.'

'He wants to see you personally.'

'Why?'

'He didn't tell me why.' The metallic voice sounded remote and uninterested. 'If you can get yourself on to the supply ship he says they'll lift you on board by crane. Okay?'

'Roger,' I said.

Johan took the ship in for me and I made the leap from the high point of our bows, *Rattler*'s crew watching with their fenders out. They put me in the net, clipped it to the big hook on the end of the crane hoist and I was whisked up to be dumped like a sack on the oil-slimed pipe deck beside a pile of stores and new drill bits. It was van Dam's week on duty and I found him waiting for me in the same little office where I had talked to Villiers. 'Ah zo, they get you up all right an' no bones broken, eh?' He had a telex in his hand. 'Virst you read this,' he said and held it out to me. 'Then you tell me vat it eez all about.'

It was from the Star-Trion office in Aberdeen and read: INFORM CAPTAIN RANDALL, STANDBY BOAT DUCHESS OF NORFOLK, WE HAVE RECEIVED NOTIFICATION FROM THE CLERK OF THE CROWN COURT IN HULL THAT HE HAS BEEN CALLED AS WITNESS FOR THE PROSECUTION IN A CASE OF ARSON DUE TO BE HEARD ON JUNE 5. SOLICITORS FOR THE CROWN INSIST THAT THE WITNESS BE IN HULL AT LEAST 24 HOURS BEFORE THE CASE OPENS AND HOLDS HIMSELF AT THE DISPOSAL OF THE PROSECUTION. YOU ARE TO NOTIFY ETA SUMBURGH AND WE WILL BOOK ONWARD FLIGHT. CONFIRM PLEASE.

'Vell?' the barge engineer enquired as I stood gazing down at the flimsy, my mind leaping to the courtroom and the Crown's QC questioning me. Cross-examination would follow. And the court listening, faces in the public seats. *You'll never know a moment's peace* . . . 'It eez an order of the court. I do not know the law in your country, but I think you 'ave to go, eh?'

I nodded. Two weeks. In just over two weeks I would be in that court, a witness, and the shadowy figures I had seen running would be standing in the dock facing me. Scunton would be there, others too, watching me, waiting to hear what I said.

'Vat I tell them?'

And I would be under oath. How Fiona would laugh! She had never believed in God. She was an atheist, and the oath an Establishment trick, an anachronism harking back to an age of superstition when there was a Heaven and a Hell and fire and brimstone.

'I think you 'ave to go, is it?'

I nodded. 'Yes, I'll have to go.' For all the marching and the talk, the strikes and demos, the System was still the same. 'Tell your office to book the onward flight so that I get to Hull on 3rd June. Accommodation, too.'

'Okay. I tell them. Iz not very nice I think appearing for a prosecution.' He was smiling sympathetically. 'That is vy I do not tell you over the radio. Then everybody know.'

'Kind of you,' I murmured. And conscious of the need to say something that would satisfy his curiosity, I added, 'Two youths set fire to a house and I am supposed to identify them.'

'Vandals, ja. Ve haf that in Holland alzo. Too much.'

I went back to my ship, morose and silent, cursing myself for not having gone to Hull directly the *Fisher Maid* docked in Aberdeen. It would have been over and done with then, my statement given to the police instead of in open court, and no threats, nothing they could have done about it. Now, whatever I said, one side or the other would hold it against me.

May ended as it had begun in a blaze of fine weather, the days passing in the slow monotony of patrolling back and forth. The crew were relieved one at a time and the Norwegians stayed. Fuller had succeeded in fixing their work permits. There had been an outcry about it and there was a picture in the local paper of some fishermen demonstrating in front of the Star-Trion office in Scalloway. Gertrude did not bother to send us the national papers, knowing the rig was supplied by helicopter – anyway we got the world news over the radio. But she did send us the *Shetland Times* and in the issue of 16th May there had been a short paragraph stating that Mr Ian Sandford of the Root Stacks Hotel, Burra Firth, had acquired the Hamnavoe fishing vessel, *Island Girl,* built in 1947. He now intended to use her for supplying oil rigs operating off Shetland. Gertrude had marked the news item and in a note to me she said, *I think this is possibly why we have had no more trouble from him.*

On the evening of 2nd June, the day before I was due to leave for Hull, the draw-works suddenly went silent. They had

113

started pulling pipe shortly after noon, and *Rattler*'s skipper, Jock Fraser, told me over the radio the rumour was it was a dry well. This was confirmed when *Bowstring* came on the air to say she had cleared Aberdeen and her ETA would be around 15.00 hours next day.

I went on board the rig shortly after 07.00. The draw-works were running again and Sparks told me they would be lifting anchors and moving to a new location just as soon as they had cleared the seabed. The helicopter that would take me to Sumburgh was not due until 08.30. I left my case under the sick-bay attendant's desk and went in search of Ed Wiseberg.

I found him down on the spider deck with Ken Stewart and several others. They were standing just inside the pump room in front of a big steel cabinet equipped with a TV screen. The picture was vague, a flickering image of some white object that wavered uncertainly. 'Guess we'll have to trim again, Ken. The angle's still wrong.' The barge engineer went over to the pumps and stood considering, the mud tanks rising in bulky curves behind him. He stepped forward, pressing levers, holding them as the pumps hissed. Ed Wiseberg was at the console of the TV cabinet, the picture shifting, the object becoming clearer as he adjusted the position and focus of the camera on the seabed. The atmosphere was tense, electric with frustration and concentration. Through the open door I could see the spider with its girders slotted in to the deck structure and the guidewires leading down into the depths.

It was the retrieving tool that showed up white on the TV screen and they were trying to stab it over the top of the casing which protruded through the main guide base. This was on the seabed and the casing had already been cut about 12 feet below the MGB.

I chose what I thought was a suitable moment to tell Ed Wiseberg I would be gone for a few days, but he ignored me, his face like granite, his eyes on the screen. 'Jeez, we nearly got the bugger then. A little more, Ken.'

'For'ard again?'

'Yeah, for'ard. A little starboard, too.'

I watched as they juggled with the positioning of the rig, the casing suddenly quite clear on the screen, the retrieving tool seeming to float above it. Occasionally a fish swam in front of the camera. It was just after 08.00 that tool and casing merged, the white engulfing the black. The toolpusher was on the phone, ordering the hydraulic rams to be closed, and in a moment the whole rig was shaking as the draw-works laboured to break the casing out. A sudden jolt, the big diesel up on the derrick floor changing into high gear, running fast now and everybody smiling. Ed Wiseberg put the phone down with obvious relief. 'Looks like we'll make the first flight after all.' He was smiling, looking pleased. 'Goddam your bloody regulations,' he said to me. 'At that depth, what in hell's it matter if we leave a bit of pipe?' He put his hand on my shoulder. 'Where you making for when we get ashore?'

'Hull,' I said.

'Oh, yeah. I remember. You're a witness, eh? Well, mebbe we can have a drink together in Aberdeen. Christ! I could sure do with one right now.' He turned in to the workshop, a tired man, moving slowly. 'We bin juggling with that damned retrieving tool since four this morning. It'll be good to get home.'

'You're married then?'

He nodded. 'Twenty-two years. And you?'

I told him and he said, 'Yeah – well, I guess there's not much difference between trawling and drilling. Some women can take it, some can't. Enid and I, we've lived so many goddam places. We got married in Tampico. She had one boy in Curaçao, the other in Edmonton. The two of them are just about grown up now so she gets lonesome at times.'

'Why don't you retire then?' I asked him.

'Retire?' He pushed his hands up over his eyes, pausing and staring round him as we reached the changing room full of oil-stiff overalls and safety helmets, a litter of discarded clothing. 'Yeah. Mebbe I will one of these days. But I bin drilling all my life. I don't know.' He shook his head, smiling quietly to himself. 'There's always the next hole, you see. Right now we drilled a dry one. Next time – next time we strike it, eh?' He grinned and pushed open the door to the quarters. 'I gotta change now. See you on the chopper.'

But I didn't get a chance to talk to him on the helicopter. He slept all the way to Sumburgh, and on the Air Anglia flight to Aberdeen he sat with Ken Stewart. He was two seats ahead and I could hear his harsh, grating voice. They were discussing the new breed of anchorless drill ships that maintain station by computerized control of a dozen engines. Ken Stewart was a much younger man. He had only come into the oil business when the North Sea started up. But Ed Wiseberg, with his experience – it seemed strange that he was content to operate on an old rig like *North Star*.

His wife was waiting for him at Dyce Airport, a thin fair woman in a BMW. I watched them greet each other perfunctorily and drive off. I was the only one booked to Newcastle and from there I caught a train, arriving at Hull in time for a late meal at my hotel. The strike was over. It had been settled almost a month ago, but the shipyards were still working overtime to catch up. Before turning in I went for a walk. There was not much traffic about, the streets almost deserted. It had always been a quiet place after about ten o'clock. I thought a walk would help me work things out, but my mind seemed disorientated by the sudden switch from the endless empty sea to the atmosphere of a big town.

I must have been tired, for I slept heavily that night and I had barely finished breakfasting in my room when the phone rang. It was Edward Hall of Morley & Hall, the solicitors. He wanted me to make a statement to the police. 'As you were not called at the committal proceedings before the magistrates, a copy of your statement as additional evidence will have to be served on the defence before the trial.'

'And if I don't make a statement?' I asked.

'Then you will have to be subpoenaed.'

'I see.'

'On the presumption that you are a willing witness I have arranged with the police –'

'I'd rather see you first,' I said.

He tried to press me, but in the end he arranged to see me in his office at two o'clock. I had only just put the phone down when the desk rang to say a Detective-Sergeant Gorse was asking for me.

I saw him in the lounge, a big man with a slow, not unfriendly manner. 'Now, Mr Randall, you recall the night of 28th February. We wanted to interview you then. But you know that.' There was a mild note of censure in his voice. 'You've had a somewhat isolated job recently, but I presume you know we're holding Bucknall and Claxby on remand. That was the decision of the magistrate's court and the case is being heard in the crown court tomorrow. They are charged with arson.'

I nodded.

'You were there and you saw what happened.'

'I was there,' I said.

'You broke into the house, got the Entwisles' little girl out and handed her over to one of the neighbours, a Mrs Fenton. Then you vanished from the scene.'

'I was a mate of a trawler sailing at dawn.'

'We know that. And we radioed the *Fisher Maid* to say we wanted to interview you. But, when you landed at Aberdeen, you booked out on an Air Anglia flight to Shetland under an assumed name. Why?'

'I don't have to answer that.'

'No. But it's something you'll certainly be asked in court. If we had known where you were – ' He pulled out a notebook, settling himself in his chair. 'No matter. We got a committal and now if I could have your statement.'

'I'm seeing Mr Hall this afternoon.'

He frowned, but his manner was still mild as he said, 'Don't you think you've delayed long enough?' And when I didn't say anything, he added, 'Now, let's start at the moment you arrived in Washbrook Road. What time was that?'

I shook my head. A statement to the police was official and irrevocable. I didn't want that. Not yet. 'If you don't mind, Sergeant, I'll leave any statement I'm going to make until I've seen Mr Hall.'

He hesitated, reluctant to leave it at that. 'It would save a lot of time.'

'I've already spoken to him and explained that I prefer to see him first.'

He sighed and put his notebook away, getting heavily to his feet. 'As you wish.' His tone was distant and there was a hardness in his eyes as he stood looking down at me. 'I think I should tell you we know about you hotheads meeting in the Congregational Hall. You'd be wiser to make a statement now.' He hesitated, and then with a sudden burst of feeling, he said, 'Don't be a fool, Randall; don't try and shield those bastards. Little Amelia could have been anybody's child – yours, mine, anybody's.' He turned abruptly, as though regretting his outburst, and went out through the swing doors walking quickly.

Time passed slowly for me that day. I had nobody to talk to, nobody to turn to, and like a fool I put off going to the trawler owner's office to collect the pay and bonus due to me. I couldn't face it. I didn't want to have to talk to people I knew, and with only myself for company my nerves were on edge when I finally had my interview with Hall. He was a small, deceptively quiet man in a grey check suit, and at first I thought

117

him rather lightweight. He went through the police report of what had happened that night, his voice quick and very quiet, almost a mumble. He had been in court all morning and I got the impression he was reading it as much for his own benefit as mine.

They had all the details, even the time I had arrived in Washbrook Road, where I had stood. And I sat there, feeling dazed, conscious that I was being involved in legal procedures and still uncertain what I was going to do. It was an untidy, musty-smelling office, most of the space taken up by the over-size mahogany desk at which Hall was sitting. Behind him were dusty-looking shelves stacked with books, ledgers and files. I think it was the books and papers that gave the place its musty smell. The windows were shut against the noise of the traffic. Deed boxes, some of them open, lay strewn around on the floor. But though the office was untidy and archaic, the desk in front of me was equipped with the latest tape recorder, phone and intercom.

Hall came to the end of his reading and looked across the desk at me. He had taken off his glasses and was polishing them gently with a very white handkerchief. There was a lull in the traffic, the room suddenly very quiet, his eyes fixed on me, and I found myself swallowing, knowing this was the moment of decision.

I had had all the time between Gorse's visit and this meeting in which to think about it. For much of that time I had remained in the hotel. I had been expecting Scunton, or one of the others, certain they would try and pressure me, or at least appeal to my brotherly feelings. But nobody had come. They had left me strictly alone.

Hall leaned forward. 'Were you listening while I was reading that?'

'Yes, of course.'

'You didn't comment.' His voice was crisper now. 'Then I take it you accept the report as being correct?'

'More or less.'

'What does that mean? That you have reservations?' He didn't wait for me to answer and his words had a bite to them as he went on, 'You realize your absence hasn't made it very easy for the police. In the magistrate's court they had to rely on the depositions of other witnesses. In your absence these could hardly be conclusive, but the magistrates were satisfied that there was a prima facie case, and because a child's life had been endangered, they committed the accused for trial at the crown court.' He paused, looking at me over his glasses. 'Well, now you are here, let's try again. Is that account correct?'

I hesitated. In the main it was, so what else could I say but Yes?

He nodded. 'That's better.' He looked at the report again. 'You notice there is no reference to the reason you were standing there in the dark watching the foreman's house. Also, of course, nobody knows what you may or may not have seen prior to the moment you broke down the door and got the little girl out.' He stared at me, the silence dragging and his long hands stretched out on the desk in front of him. 'Now, I am going to ask you three very simple questions.' His voice was quiet, but very determined, his eyes fixed on mine. 'I want answers to those three questions, and I want the truth.'

I suppose it was the reference to getting the little girl out, but all I could remember as I faced the hard stare behind those glasses was the sergeant's voice that morning, shaken by the violence of his feelings as he said – *She could have been anybody's child – yours, mine, anybody's* . . . 'I'll tell you the truth,' I heard myself murmur.

He nodded briefly. 'Just answer Yes or No please. First question: Were you waiting in the dark because you suspected an attack would be made on Entwisle, or his family, or his property?'

'Yes.'

'You saw the petrol bomb thrown. Can you identify the persons who threw it through the window?'

My voice sounded thin and remote as I answered, 'Yes.'

'And they are the accused you will see in the dock tomorrow – Harry Bucknall and John Leonard Claxby?'

'Yes.'

'Good. And now one final question: You realize, of course, that you will now be the chief witness for the prosecution, that if we succeed we will be putting two dangerous young men behind bars, I hope for a long time. I know something of your background and it could be that you will be under considerable pressure – not only from some of the men you know in this port, but also from within yourself. When you are in the witness box, will you give the same answers to those questions that you have given me here?'

I hesitated. But there was no turning back now. 'Yes,' I said.

'Good. George Sayre will be acting for the crown and he'll be glad to know we've got a statement out of you at last. Particularly as Lawrence Mendip is defending. A willing witness is always better from counsel's point of view.' And after that he took me through the events of that night, writing the statement out in longhand. When he had finished, he read it through to me, made a few alterations, and then called his clerk and arranged for it to be typed. While this was done I waited in the outer office. It took about half an hour, and then I was in his office again, reading it through. Finally I signed it.

He rose then, holding out his hand to me, a flicker of warmth in his eyes. 'I realize this has been very difficult for you, but truth is something absolute, a rock on which the conscience of man can rest secure.' His words, as I set them down, sound pompous, but they did not seem so at the time. And then he went on, 'A copy of your statement will have to be served on the defence as additional evidence and I should perhaps warn you that Lawrence Mendip has something of a reputation.' But then he added quickly, 'Of course, Sayre will have established everything by then and cross-examination can never shake a witness who is telling the truth.' He smiled encouragingly as he showed me to the door. 'I think you will find it all very simple and straightforward. I'll expect you at the Guildhall at ten tomorrow morning.' A brief nod and I was in the outer office, going past the counter, down the stairs into the crowded street.

Walking back to my hotel, my mind was on tomorrow and the court, wanting to get it over now. Tomorrow – one day in my life. And, once that was behind me, it would be finished. The past, everything . . . I could forget about politics, the tortuous, twisted minds that had shattered so many of my ideals. I could concentrate then on simple material things. I was thinking of the *Duchess,* still riding out there beside the rig, and Gertrude, down-to-earth, matter-of-fact, with not a political thought in her head. How much simpler life would be if one were not involved.

That evening I had an early meal and went out to the cinema. A man followed me, but not anyone I had ever seen before. And when he sat a few seats away I knew I hadn't imagined it and that it must be the police keeping an eye on me. The film was an old Charlie Chaplin and to laugh at the eccentricities of human behaviour did me a lot of good.

Back at my hotel, I had a quick drink at the bar, then got

my key and went up to my room. I hadn't been there more than a few minutes when the phone rang and a man's voice said there was a woman in the lobby asking for me. I thought for a moment it must be a reporter, but he said, no, she wasn't anyone from the local press and she wouldn't give her name.

I think I had a premonition then, tension gripping me as I asked him to describe her. I knew who it was before he had even finished. 'All right,' I said, 'tell her to come up.'

'I'm not sure that would be wise, sir. She seems a bit disturbed. Better if you see her down here.'

'It's my wife,' I said.

There was a pause, and then he said, 'Very well, I'll send her up.' There was a click and the phone went dead, leaving me standing there, my nerves taut. So this was why they had laid off me. They were relying on Fiona. It was so typical, getting at me through her. Why didn't they come themselves? Did they think, after all these years, she still meant something to me? There was a knock on the door, a light, almost hesitant tap. I opened it and she was there in the passage, facing me, her eyes enormous. She smiled. It was a tentative flicker of a smile that betrayed her nervousness. 'Come in,' I said and the tone of my voice was not exactly welcoming.

She came in, moving slowly as though uncertain of her reception. Her face looked very white. The pageboy cut was gone, her jet-black hair swept back from her forehead and falling to her shoulders. It made her look more feminine. It also accentuated the pallor of her skin – that and the little black coat she was wearing, the long sensitive fingers poking out of the sleeves, white with blue veins showing.

I closed the door and for a moment we stood looking at each other in silence. Finally I said, 'What do you want?'

She tossed back her hair, a new gesture to go with the new cut. 'That's a fine way to greet me.' The smile was suddenly easier, her nervousness receding. 'Aren't you going to kiss me?' And when I didn't move she laughed. It was a brazen, excited sound. She was enjoying the drama of the moment and I knew she had taken whatever it was she took. I could see it in her eyes, in the sudden changes of mood, the loss of control. 'I used to be able to turn you on, just like that.' She clicked her fingers, her mouth wide open, laughing at me.

'We're both older,' I said.

'You may be,' she said tartly. 'I'm just the same.' She slipped the coat off and threw it carelessly on the bed, her movements as sensual as they had always been, and the little pale blue dress very effective in revealing the slim boyish shape of her body, the small firm breasts.

'What do you want, Fiona?'

She turned, her voice low as she said, 'What do you think?' And she came slowly towards me, her lips parted, the white teeth showing and her hands held out to me. 'We can talk later.' I saw it in her face then. She really did want me and I was shocked. After almost six years. She came close, her body touching mine, her hands moving.

'Stop it,' I said.

'Why should I?' Her face was lifted to mine, her eyes staring up at me, irises and pupils merged to form dark pools, and she whispered, 'My poor Mike. You're starved.'

I took hold of her arms, pulling them away, and pushed her down on to the only chair. 'Now stop it,' I said. 'Just sit there and control yourself and tell me why you're here.'

'You fool!' she said softly. 'You stupid fool!' And suddenly she burst into tears. 'They'll get you. You know they'll get you.'

'Who will?'

'They – they. You don't expect names, do you?'

'How long since you were in Ireland?'

'I've never been involved with the IRA.'

'Who then?'

'CFJ.' And she spelt it out for me – Community for Freedom and Justice.

'What is it – Leninist, Trotskyist, Maoist? Another of those splinter groups operating under the IS umbrella?'

She shook her head, tears in her eyes as she stared up at me. 'I came to warn you.'

'About what? Who sent you?'

'Nobody. You know I went all the way up to those islands, the Shetlands, looking for you.'

'So I gathered.'

'She wrote to you, did she? She said she would.' The tears were drying on her cheeks and I sensed another change of mood coming. She smiled. 'What's she like, that woman?' She stared at me, then burst out laughing. 'Don't tell me you're running her trawler on the basis of pure altruism.'

'It's a business arrangement,' I said. 'Now please explain –'

'A business arrangement!' She giggled. 'And me thinking it's in love with her you are because why else should a man spend weeks at sea if not to build up enough steam to close his eyes and make an image of beauty out of a big, blonde, blowsy lump of a girl, her fat buttocks strapped into patched denims, her big bosom encased in Shetland wool –'

I slapped her then, not hard, but enough to stop the spate of words. She gazed at me, wide-eyed. 'You are in love with her.'

'Would it matter to you, after all this time?'

'It might.'

I shook my head. 'We're finished. You knew that, so why did you go to Shetland? Who sent you?' She didn't answer and I reached down to her bag, which was lying on the bed beside her coat. She tried to take it from me, but I pushed her away, shaking the contents out on to the coverlet.

'What are you doing?' Her voice was high, a little wild.

There were no instructions, nothing in writing. But she had money. Five ten pound notes and some ones. 'Where did you get these?'

'My job.'

'What is your job?'

She turned away. 'None of your business.'

I caught her by the shoulders and swung her round so that we were face to face. 'Somebody paid your fare to Shetland. Paid you to come down here. Who?' She stared at me, wooden-faced. 'Was it a man called Stevens?'

'I don't know any Stevens.'

I described him to her and I saw the flicker of recognition in her eyes. But she wouldn't admit it. 'Let me go. You're hurting.'

'How long were you in Ireland?'

'It's my own country.'

'Were you in Ulster?' I caught hold of both her shoulders, shaking her. 'Is that where you met him?'

But she only shook her head.

'What's his real name?'

'I don't know. I don't know who you mean. I came because you were in trouble and behaving stupidly. What's it matter that a man's house was burned down. The insurance company pays. It had to be burned. A warning. Men like that, men who stand in the way of progress – you can't reason with them. You have to force them to see sense.' She pulled my hands from her shoulders, holding them tightly. 'You must understand, Mike. It's like Ireland. Nobody listens to reason until you make them. Stormont, the "B" Specials, all the everlasting persecution of Catholics . . . Nobody likes bombs, but without bombs nothing would have changed.'

'And a lot of innocent people would still be alive.' All the old arguments that had bust up our marriage. Then it had been wildcat strikes and pickets using force; now it was bombs.

'If the Cause is right—'

'Oh yes, I know—the end justifies the means. Even if the whole fabric of society is destroyed, and the people with it.'

She began to cry again. 'Can't I make you understand? Don't I mean anything to you any more?' Her grip on my hands tightened, her fingers interlaced with mine. 'Please, Mike —don't do it. For your sake. For mine.'

'Do what?'

'Don't shop those boys. They did their duty. That's all. You're a witness for the prosecution tomorrow. All you have to say is that it was too dark to be certain who did it. It doesn't matter what you told that lawyer man this afternoon. Tomorrow, when you're in the witness box—'

'How do you know I saw Hall?'

'They had the offices watched. Hall came back from lunch sharp at two. You were there a little before. You left about three-thirty. They're convinced—'

'Who's they?'

She stared at me. 'The Community, the organization, the militants if you like. What's it matter who they are? They're organized. They know what they want and how to get it. I don't have to tell you that, surely. And they stick by their own people. You shop those boys tomorrow and they'll nail you.'

'Scunton and his crowd?'

She shrugged. 'I'm just warning you, that's all. They thought it was your doing when those boys were arrested, that you'd shopped them. That's why I went to the Shetlands. Oh yes, you're right—my fare was paid, all expenses. I was to talk you into a more sensible view of things. It never occurred to me you wouldn't be coming ashore, that the Petersen girl . . .' She let go my hands, turning quickly away and starting to gather up the contents of her bag. When she had put them all back, she got into her coat. 'Well, that's it, Mike. I've done what I promised. I've warned you.'

'Who did you promise?'

'Myself.' She smiled a little sadly. 'Chiefly myself . . . I know we argued a lot, and fought. But it was good while it lasted.

At least it was for me. Wasn't it for you? She stared up at me, a wistful look. 'Wasn't it, Mike?' And when I didn't say anything, she gave a snort. 'You've changed. A sea change, my God! And I loved you. I loved you, you fool.' And with sudden violence she shouted at me, 'Go on. Shop them. I'll be there in court to see you do it. So will others. Shop them, you bastard, and see what happens.' She turned so abruptly that the skirt of her coat swirled and I watched her storm out. The door banged behind her.

I sat down on the bed, the room suddenly empty and nothing to do but think about tomorrow with the smell of her scent lingering and her words of warning still in my ears.

CHAPTER THREE

The Guildhall was in Alfred Gelder Street and when I arrived there a crowd of about a dozen had gathered around the entrance, mostly students by the look of them. Somebody called out 'That's him' and they surged round me. I don't recall what they said, only their hostility. It was an unpleasant experience and the uniformed constable on duty had to clear a way for me.

The courts were on the ground floor and the witnesses in all the day's cases waited in the corridor. Time passed slowly. Occasionally, as police went in and witnesses were called, the door to the crown court momentarily opened and we caught a fleeting glimpse of the dark-panelled interior.

It was just short of eleven when the usher came out and called 'Michael Randall'. I got up and followed him into the courtroom to take my place in the witness box. Standing there, the testament in my hand and repeating the oath, I had a clear view of everybody – the judge, Sayre, a tall, thin man looking dignified in black gown and wig, the massive bulk of counsel for the defence, the two men in the dock. Bucknall, his pallid, freckled face framed by long hair and wearing a suede jacket over a gaily-coloured shirt, constantly shifted his feet, his eyes downcast; Claxby, much tougher, an older, heavier face with a drooped moustache and long sideburns, stared back at me, sullen and watchful.

The clerk finished administering the oath and there was a

general stir as people settled themselves. I glanced up at the public gallery. Most of the seats were filled, the back of the court, too. I saw Scunton there, several others I recognized – and Fiona. I think she smiled at me, but I couldn't be sure. It might have been a nervous fluttering of the mouth.

'You are Michael Mouat Randall?' Sayre was on his feet facing me across the court, his brief, all his papers, on the desk in front of him. Quietly, crisply, he took me through the events leading up to the moment when I had stood waiting outside No. 5 Washbrook Road. 'And you walked from the Congregational Hall to Washbrook Road?'

'Yes.'

'Was it a dark night?'

'Yes, pretty dark. Raining, in fact – a light drizzle.'

'When you left the hall the meeting was still in progress.'

I nodded.

'How long did you have to wait before the bomb attack took place?'

'Less than half an hour.'

'You were standing in the shadow of some bushes at the entrance to an area of wasteground known as the Stonepit. You remained in that position all the time without moving?'

'Until the light in the porch was broken, yes.'

He reached down for a sheet, holding it and looking at the judge. 'Milord. I have here a plan of this section of Washbrook Road, also copies for the jury. It shows the distance from the gate of No. 5 to the bushes where the witness was standing as forty-seven feet. It also shows the distance to the nearest street lamp. This is on the opposite side of the road twenty-two yards from No. 5 and thirty-five yards from the witness. All measurements taken by a member of the Surveyor's Office, who also prepared the plan.' He handed the sheet to the clerk, who passed it to the judge, and copies were distributed to the jury. Sayre turned back to me. 'Was there any light on in the house?'

'Not in the house. There was a light on in the porch. It was the first thing they broke.'

'But you were able to see who they were. You recognized them?'

'Yes.'

'Are they here in court?'

I nodded.

'The witness must answer so that we can all hear,' the judge interposed.

Sayre looked at me and I said, 'Yes.'

'Would you point them out to us please.'

I indicated the prisoners in the dock and he nodded. 'We have already heard from another witness that they parked their car in neighbouring Ellsworth Terrace. Presumably they were on foot as they approached No. 5.'

'Yes.'

'Was it the street light that enabled you to identify them?'

'No. They were on the opposite side of the road to the light, the same side as No. 5. They had their heads turned towards the houses. I think they were probably checking the numbers.'

'So at that point their faces were in shadow. When did you positively identify them?'

'When they opened the gate to No. 5.'

'An earlier witness, who had picked them out at an identity parade, has admitted under cross-examination that she could have been mistaken. If she could be mistaken, how is it you are so positive?'

'Because the light from the porch was full on them. They had their collars turned up, but from where I was standing –'

'It's a lie.' Claxby was thumping the edge of the dock. 'He's lying. I was never there.'

'Go on, please,' Sayre said, ignoring the outburst. 'From where you were standing . . . ?'

'From there I had a clear view of both their faces as they turned in at the gate.'

'What were they wearing?'

'Cloth caps and raincoats.'

'Both of them?'

'Yes.'

'Can you describe their clothes in greater detail?'

'The raincoats were rather shapeless, and one of them had a muffler. No particular colour. I think it was Bucknall and his cap was in some dull check.'

'Anything else?'

'Not that I recall.'

'Who broke the light in the porch?'

'Claxby.'

'And who threw the petrol bomb?'

'Claxby,' I said again. And he yelled at me from the dock, 'You bloody liar. I was never there, an' you know it. You threw that bomb. You're just trying to cover . . .' A policeman grabbed him from behind. There was a scuffle and then quiet as Lawrence Mendip, moving with remarkable speed for such a heavy man, began whispering to him urgently.

In an icy voice the judge said, 'I must warn the prisoner that if he interrupts again I shall have him taken down to the cells.' He leaned a little forward over the high desk, addressing himself directly to Claxby. 'Outbursts such as you have just made tend to leave a bad impression on the jury. Proceed, Mr Sayre.'

And so it went on, Sayre taking me step by step, and in great detail, through those few vivid, crowded minutes. And all the time, at the back of my mind, was the thought of Claxby's outburst . . .

'And by the time you got the child out the neighbours had already gathered.'

'Yes – three of them, I think. Two women and a man.'

'And you handed the child to Mrs Fenton?'

'I didn't know her name. But one of the women, yes.'

'Did she say you must wait for the police?'

'No, I think the man said that.'

'Why didn't you?'

'I was mate on a trawler. We were due to sail at first light, and my hand was cut by the broken glass. I wanted to get a dressing on it.'

'Thank you. That's all.' And he sat down.

There was a rustle of movement in the courtroom, the sound of feet shifting and people coughing. Lawrence Mendip was on his feet, standing with his head bent, staring down at his papers. His head came up and he was looking at me, his eyes small and very sharp. 'You say it was a dark night. A light drizzle I think you said, yet you saw the faces of these two young men very clearly.'

'In the light from the porch. It was only a few yards from the gate to the porch.'

'And as they went in through the gate, did you move to get a better view of what was happening?'

'Not immediately. Not until I heard the bulb break.'

'But you didn't show yourself?'

'No, not then.'

'And you didn't call out. You didn't try to stop them?'

'I wanted to see what they were going to do. If I had known – '

'And when the bulb was broken, it was suddenly quite dark. Then how did you know it was Claxby who broke the bulb?'

'There was still the light of the street lamp across the road.'

'Oh yes, the street lamp. A single bulb lamp, not a fluorescent standard. And his back towards you. Are you sure it was Claxby?'

'Quite sure.' I felt easier now. It was like all the courts I had been in before, the defence trying to shake the witness on matters of detail. 'I had reached a point where I could look over the hedge as Claxby came out of the porch.'

'Did he try the door?'

'I don't know. All I saw was him coming out of the porch.'

'And going round to the window.'

'Yes.'

'Where was Bucknall?'

'He was already facing the window.'

'His back towards you?'

'Yes.'

'There is virtually no difference in their height. Bucknall is five foot ten and Claxby five foot ten and a half. How tall are you?'

'Five foot eleven.'

'And what were you wearing?'

'A blue raincoat.'

'And a cap?'

'A seaman's cap.'

'So, according to your evidence, there were three of you there, all about the same height, all dressed roughly alike. You say you were in the road peering over the hedge and there were these two figures standing in the little garden facing the window. And you say Claxby threw the petrol bomb. How do you know it was Claxby?'

'I saw him come from the porch. The two of them were standing together for a moment. They seemed to be arguing. Then Bucknall took something from the pocket of his raincoat and handed it to Claxby.'

'Could you see what it was?'

'It looked like a bottle.'

'You've heard the phrase – a Molotov cocktail. Would you say it was that type of a bomb?'

'I imagine it was something like that.'

'A Molotov cocktail is a very simple form of petrol bomb. It has a wick in the top of the bottle. This has to be ignited. Who struck the match?'

'I'm not certain. I think it was probably Bucknall since

Claxby was holding it.'

'But you can't be sure?'

'No. At that point they were crouched down.'

'So Claxby might have set the bottle on the ground and lit the wick himself?'

'Yes.'

'In fact, it only needs one man to ignite and throw the thing. Is that right?'

I thought he was trying to establish Bucknall's partial innocence and I said, 'Yes,' not seeing it as a trap.

'You have identified the accused as the two figures crouched in the front garden of No. 5. Did you know their names at that point – or have you only realized who they are since you decided to give evidence?'

'No, I knew who they were.'

'You had seen them before, in fact.'

'Yes.'

'Could you tell us when you had seen them before?'

I explained that I knew Bucknall's father and had seen them together several times, that I didn't know Claxby, but had seen him at the meeting.

'Was Bucknall at the meeting?'

'Yes.'

'What was he wearing?'

'I didn't notice.'

'But he was there?'

'Yes.'

'And Claxby. He was there, too?'

'Yes.'

'What was he wearing?'

'A leather jacket.'

'You particularly noticed that?'

'I saw what he was wearing.'

He began asking me about the meeting then, about the atmosphere of it and why I was there. 'And you had a hostile reception?'

'I was shouted down. Anybody speaking moderately –'

'In fact, you left the meeting, and went straight to Washbrook Road, thinking somebody was going to attack the Entwisles or their house. Wasn't that a somewhat extraordinary supposition to arrive at?'

'You weren't at the meeting,' I said.

'You mean, if I had been I would have done the same?' He

didn't expect an answer, for he went straight on, 'There is, of course, another interpretation that could be put on your behaviour – that you went to Washbrook Road for the precise purpose you impute to the accused. That you went there with the purpose of proving you were as militant as the others at that meeting.'

I saw what he was driving at then and I said sharply, 'Are you suggesting I had something to do with the attack?'

'I am.' His massive jaw thrust suddenly forward. 'I am suggesting that you are lying, that all your life you have been trying to prove your militancy. That's what your record suggests. Well, doesn't it?' And before I could think of an answer he had picked up a sheet from the desk in front of him and was reading it out. He had been very thoroughly briefed, for he had it all there, all the convictions, everything, and when he had finished, he turned to the judge. 'Milord, I think you must accept that this is not exactly a normal witness. If he were, he would have waited for the police, or at least come forward when he knew they wanted to question him.'

The judge nodded. 'You are, I think, suggesting that the witness had a motive in not coming forward. Is that it?'

'That is exactly it, Milord. I am not only suggesting he had a motive. I'm suggesting his whole testimony is a tissue of lies.' He swung round on me, his heavy jowls quivering and his finger pointing: 'I'm suggesting that you threw the bomb, that you went to Washbrook Road with that intention, with a bottle of petrol in your pocket, that you broke the porch bulb, that you lit the wick and threw the bomb through the downstair window.'

I stood there, gripping the brass rail, shocked into numbness and remembering Fiona's words, remembering, too, the words flung at me on the *Fisher Maid* in Aberdeen. I had been warned, but I still couldn't believe it. Nor could the judge. He leaned quickly forward, his voice quite sharp as he said, 'Am I to understand that you are accusing the witness?'

'Yes, Milord. I'm saying the police made an error when they arrested the prisoners. They should have arrested Randall. Furthermore, I intend to prove it.'

'Are you also saying he did not save the little girl's life?'

'No, Milord. I'm saying that he thought the house was empty when he threw the bomb, but the little girl heard the crash of broken glass, and when he saw her face at the upstairs window he panicked. There is no other explanation of his subsequent behaviour – avoiding being questioned by the police, abandoning his job with the trawler *Fisher Maid* and vanishing, under an assumed name, mark you, to the remotest part of the British Isles, to Shetland.' Most of this had been addressed to the jury, not to the judge. Now he swung round on me again. 'Isn't that the truth? I put it to you that you threw the bomb, saw the child, got her out and then fled.'

'You don't believe that,' I said. It was such an incredible reversal of the truth. 'You can't believe it.' But I knew my voice had failed to carry conviction. I was too appalled by the deadly reasonableness of it, the certainty that the net was closing. Sayre was on his feet. 'You're just trying to confuse the jury. You can't prove that. You've absolutely no –'

'Oh, but I can prove it.' Mendip turned to the judge again. 'Milord, since the accused were before the magistrate's court very vital additional evidence has come to light.'

'A new witness?' the judge asked.

'Yes, Milord. A man who has only recently come forward, rather like the witness here.'

The judge nodded, making a note, and counsel for the defence sat down. The courtroom stirred, and I stood there, remembering Hall's warning about Mendip's reputation. His cross-examination could not have ended more dramatically, and though Sayre re-examined me, trying to nullify its effect by drumming home the identity of the accused, it was obvious that the jury, everyone, were now waiting upon the defence.

My evidence closed the case for the prosecution. By then it was lunchtime, the court adjourned, and as I stepped slowly down from the witness box, I heard Sayre saying to Mendip: 'That's an old trick, and a very dirty one, if I may say so.' And the other laughing and patting his shoulder as they went out together. Hall came across to me.

I was feeling slightly sick by then, the stuffiness of the place and my stomach knotted. 'He can't prove something that isn't true. Last minute evidence like that . . .'

'You did much the same, and the defence not sure how damaging your evidence would be.'

'Not damaging enough apparently.' Anger was taking hold, overlaying the nervous tension. To them it was just a game, these lawyers bustling past with their wigs and their briefcases, full of their own damned importance.

'Wait here, will you. I'll just have a word with counsel in the robing room.' Hall left me and I stood there, feeling suddenly conspicuous as several members of the public came out of the courtroom. And then Fiona's voice at my elbow. 'I warned you, Mike. I told you they'd nail you.'

I looked at her, the high forehead, the thin crimson mouth in the pallid face.

'I tried to warn you,' she said again.

'Yes, you did, didn't you.' My hands were clenched tight. 'If they think they're going to get me shut away in a bloody prison for something I didn't do . . .' And Fiona clinging to my arm and saying, 'Mike, for God's sake listen. Get away, now, while you can – while you're still free.'

'Run for it?'

'What else? You wouldn't listen and now they've got you.' Her fingers tightened on my arm. 'Get out now.' Her voice was urgent. 'Nobody is watching you. There's nobody to stop you. But after this afternoon . . .'

'Is that what you've been told to do – scare me, get me on the run, so that truth becomes a lie?'

'No – no, Mike, you're wrong. That's not the reason. I just don't want to see you in prison. I don't want you convicted for something you didn't do.'

'If you know it, then the court will know it.' I had to believe that.

'Oh, my God!' she cried. 'You bloody intellectuals, you never understand until it's too late, do you? Truth isn't some sort of knightly armour. Truth is what determined people persuade others to believe.' She looked at me a moment and I thought how that had been at the bottom of so many of our arguments. But, to believe that, was to believe that man was a soulless, servile creature without dignity.

I think she misread my silence, for she said, 'How can I make you understand?' Her hand was on my arm, the nails digging into me. 'They don't care about those two boys, they're expendable. It's you they're after.'

But I didn't believe her. 'I'm not that important,' I said. 'I never was. You know that. But if those two are convicted, it's intimidation. That's what –'

'You idiot!' Her grip on my arm tightened. 'Intimidation! Who cares whether it was intimidation. It's that trawler they want. The target is North Sea oil now. We're hitting at the oil companies, hitting at capitalism where it hurts, where it's most vulnerable, and with the sort of headlines –'

She stopped there and I said, 'Villiers?' But her mouth was

a tight-shut line. 'Get out now,' she breathed urgently. 'Go while you can. You'll be safe then.'

I laughed. 'With the police after me?'

'Better the police than a bomb – or a shot in the back.'

I stared at her, shocked by her words. 'So you were in Northern Ireland.' Why else would her mind run on bombs and murder? 'You're crazy,' I said, seeing the wildness of her eyes, and the distortion of the pupils. 'Your imagination always did run away with you when you got yourself – '

'Oh, my imagination, is it?' Her voice was high and strident. 'And you accusing me of being drugged. That's what you're saying, isn't it? You always accused me of that when you couldn't think of anything else to say, when you'd lost your temper as well as the argument.' Her tone had become venomous. God! It took me back. 'One day,' she breathed darkly, 'I'll tell you why I do it. Then, Mother of God, maybe you'll understand.' She was staring up at me, breathing heavily. 'But why should I bother? Why the hell . . .' And then in a quieter voice: 'Just so long as you're out of the way. That's all that matters.' She said it like somebody in a dream, but when I asked her what she meant, she shrugged and turned away. 'Go to hell!' she said in a choking voice. 'And don't say I didn't warn you.' And she left me then, walking listlessly down the corridor. It was almost empty now. I watched her go, thinking about what she had said. *There's nobody to stop you. But after this afternoon . . .* I was still thinking about that, wondering how she knew and who had sent her, when Hall returned. 'He says we'll just have to see what the defence has turned up.'

'But what about the other witnesses?' I demanded.

'I'm afraid they didn't stand up too well under cross-examination. I told you Mendip had something of a reputation. Old Mrs Rogers from No. 7 became a little flustered and confused. She was wearing glasses and Mendip concentrated on that, finally getting her to admit her sight wasn't all that good, especially at night. Sayre didn't press her very hard on re-examination. He was relying on you.'

'And what about the witness who saw them park their car?'

'A young man standing against some railings with his girl friend. It's not conclusive, and Mendip leaned on him heavily, getting him to admit that he was otherwise occupied. He thought they went into Washbrook Road, that was all, and he was vague about the time.'

So it was as Stevens had said – my word against that of his new witness. I asked Hall who he was, but he didn't know. 'Better get yourself some lunch. The court resumes at two.'

I think at that stage I still believed Sayre could dispose of a witness I knew to be lying. But when the court resumed and I saw the man in the dock I wasn't so sure. His name was Edward Bradshaw, a pale, rather gaunt man with thinning hair and a hesitant, slightly earnest manner. He claimed he had watched it all from the front room of No. 8. Prompted by counsel, he gave his evidence in a quiet voice that had hardly any trace of a local accent, and his evidence was totally different from mine. No, he had not seen either of the accused that night. 'There was only one man in the garden across the road.' And he added, 'I remember quite clearly. He stood up suddenly from a crouched position, and I saw his arm swing back, then he threw something and the window shattered. I thought it was some hooligan heaving a brick – then the flames started leaping and spreading. The curtains caught fire and I saw the little girl's face at the upstairs window.'

Counsel stopped him there. 'You're certain only one man was involved?'

'Definitely.'

'And you saw his face?'

'Not in the garden, but when he came up the street.'

'You saw him in the street light?'

'That's right. He was the same side of the road as me then and I saw him plain as – well, very clear. I was a bit nervous laike, so I was watching him and thinking he might – '

'Never mind what you were thinking,' counsel's voice cut in quickly. 'Do you see him in this courtroom?'

'He's raight there, behind you.' He lifted his arm, his finger pointing at me.

'Thank you. That's all.' Lawrence Mendip sat down.

Sayre did his best to discredit the man. Under cross-examination Bradshaw admitted he was not the owner of No. 8, or even a visitor. He had happened to be passing, had seen the gate open and had gone in out of curiosity.

'I think you said you were actually in the house when observing what happened at No. 5 opposite. How did you get into the house?'

'Well, the back door was open, you see.'

'So you entered the house – out of curiosity.'

'That's raight.'

'Where were you when you saw Mr Randall pass under the street light?'

'In the front room.'

'Doing what?'

'Just looking round.'

'Casing the joint would be a more accurate term, wouldn't it?' There was a moment's silence, and then Sayre said, 'This is not the first time, is it? You've been caught breaking and entering before.'

'I didn't steal anything, not a thing. You can't pin that on me. An' I wouldn't be here but for a sense of pooblic duty. When I read that these two young men had been accused for something they never did – '

'You admit you went into that house with the intention of thieving.'

'Just looking for some spare cash, that's all. You'd do the same, I wouldn't wonder, with five kids and no work because of the strike.' He was facing towards the jury then, not Sayre. 'All raight. I would have taken any cash left lying about. I admit that. But if some fool leaves his door open . . .' He turned back to Sayre in answer to a question. 'No, I never used force on it. The door was open, I tell you, and then I was in that room, in the dark, when I heard his footsteps. That man – ' He nodded towards me. 'I didn't know what he was. And then standing in the shadows opposite, naturally I watched to see what he was up to. That's how I saw what happened, an' that's the man sitting there.'

Sayre was able to show that in one particular Bradshaw's evidence was inaccurate – the curtains could not have caught fire because Mrs Entwisle had taken them down for cleaning two days before. He also got an admission out of him that he had served a sentence for theft. But he could not shake him. The man stuck to his story, and the fact that the occupants of the house were away and that he had entered with intent to commit a felony seemed somehow to make it all the more convincing. It explained his reluctance to come forward. It made his presence in the witness stand, at the risk of prosecution, an unselfish act that called for some sympathy, not disbelief.

Re-examining, counsel for the defence was able to drum these points home. No other witness was called. Neither of the accused gave evidence. And in his first words to the jury, Mendip emphasized that, though they might have reservations about accepting the evidence of a man who admitted he had once been convicted for theft, they had to bear in mind that the main witness for the prosecution had also been in prison, though for different reasons. 'So you have two witnesses, two entirely different statements, both given under oath. They are absolutely contradictory. You are not required to decide which is the truth. All that is required of you is that you determine whether, in view of the fact that there is no satisfactory evidence to support either testimony, you can possibly convict these two young men, both protesting their innocence. I say you cannot. You cannot convict when doubt – extreme doubt, you may feel – has been cast on the case for the prosecution.'

The judge in his summing up took a similar line, but less firmly and with some reluctance. 'Of one thing there is no doubt. The witness, Michael Randall, entered the burning house and rescued Amelia Entwisle at some risk to himself. If the other witness is telling the truth, then you may reasonably ask yourselves why he did not attempt to rescue the child himself, or at least to offer assistance to the man who did. After all, once he was out of No. 8 he ceased to be a trespasser and became just a passer-by. There is, therefore, no reason at all why he should not have gone to Randall's assistance. Instead, according to his evidence, he remained concealed, a watcher, taking no part, offering no help. You may feel that only proves him to be a nervous, perhaps frightened man at the time. Or you may feel it indicates that his testimony is false. Are you to believe him, or are you to believe Randall? It is not easy for the jury when the two main witnesses are suspect. One of these men is a liar and it is for you to decide which.'

But then he added, 'However, this is not your prime responsibility. Your prime responsibility is to the prisoners – are they guilty or not guilty? Here doubt alone is sufficient. If such conflicting testimony raises a doubt in your mind – a reasonable doubt – then you must give the prisoners the benefit of that doubt. But if you accept Randall's testimony, then there is no doubt, just as there is no doubt about his rescuing the child. You will now retire and consider your verdict.'

The jury were out barely ten minutes. They found both the prisoners Not Guilty and there was a murmur of approval from some of the public. And as the judge dismissed the case and ordered the prisoners to be released a constable appeared at my side. I was hurried out of the building by a back entrance and into a police car.

I wasn't taken back to my hotel. I was driven instead to Hull Central Police Station and put in a room with a uniformed constable. I didn't argue. I think I was too shocked by what had happened. I have always differentiated in my mind between law and justice. The law is part of the Establishment, the rules by which the System perpetuates itself – but, strangely, I had always respected British justice. The laws might be wrong, but within the limits set by those laws, I believed British men and women did dispense justice. Now a lying witness, suborned to pervert the course of justice, had led judge, jury and lawyers by the nose, convicting me there in that court, though I was not on trial.

And Fiona had known. She had warned me. *You shop those boys and they'll nail you.* She had known that justice, like truth, could be turned upside down, an image in a distorting mirror. And I hadn't believed her. I had let slip the opportunity to escape, convinced that justice could recognize truth, and Sayre hadn't even recalled me to the witness stand. The rules of the game did not allow it. Instead, he had thrown in his hand, and in doing so had branded me a liar.

The door opened and an officer in plain clothes came in and sat down at the table opposite me. He had the usual form. 'Name please . . .' and he began filling it in as I answered his questions. And when that was done, he said, 'Are you prepared to make a statement?'

'My statement is in the court records.'

But that wasn't good enough for him. He wanted a completely new statement, and he cautioned me.

'Are you going to charge me?'

He shrugged. 'That will depend on your statement. In any case, it's not for me to decide.'

And so I went over it all again and he wrote it down laboriously in longhand, then took it away to be typed. When he returned and I had signed it, I said, 'I want to speak to Inspector Garrard.' And I gave him the slip of paper with the number on it. 'I think he's a Special Branch officer.'

He looked at it and then at me. 'It's unusual . . .'

'So is what happened in court today,' I told him angrily.

'I'll see what I can do.' He nodded to the phone on the table. 'We'll put it through here if we get him.' He left me then and I was alone in the room. Maybe I could have walked out, but it never occurred to me. I was too busy thinking what I would say to Garrard if they managed to get through to him.

It was a long wait, and then suddenly the phone rang and I picked it up. 'Inspector Garrard?'

'Yes.'

'Randall,' I said. 'You told me to ring you –'

'Go ahead.'

I began to explain what had happened in court, but he said, 'I know all about that. What is it you want to tell me?'

I told him then about the man calling himself Stevens, how he had come on board the *Fisher Maid* in Aberdeen. And then about the second meeting when we were anchored off Ham in Foula. The name meant nothing to him, but when I had given him a description I thought I detected a sudden interest. 'You say it's Villiers he's after?'

'Not Villiers personally, but his reputation. It's the rig chiefly.'

'What can he do to the rig?'

I tried to explain, but sitting there in an office in a police station, the rig sounded very remote, the loneliness of the sea area west of Shetland impossible to convey. And then I asked him about my father. 'Is he still alive, do you know?'

'Have you any reason to believe he is?'

'Only that you were right when you said he was brought out of Norway in 1942. The *Duchess* picked him up and Stevens implied that you would know.'

There was a moment's silence. 'What exactly did he say?'

'That rehabilitation is a long process and not many survived. I think he was referring to men returned to Russia after the war.'

'What else?'

'Nothing, except he suggested it might make a difference if I were able to talk to him.'

'But you haven't?'

'No, of course not. Otherwise I wouldn't be asking you for confirmation that he's still alive.'

There was a pause. Then he said, 'I can't answer that. I'm not sure.' And then I heard him murmur reflectively. 'He couldn't possibly – he'd be too old.'

'Too old? For what?' I asked him.

But all he said was, 'No, it's out of the question. And this man Stevens – where's he operating from?'

'I don't know.'

'And you don't know his real name.' A faint sound like a

139

sigh came over the line. 'Well, I'll have the local police check on Sandford. At least we know where to find him. But –' Another long pause, and then he said, 'Look, I'll be honest with you. I talked with Detective-Sergeant Gorse. You're suspected of committing perjury. When was your meeting with this man Stevens – weeks ago, wasn't it? Well, wasn't it?' And when I admitted that it was over six weeks ago, he said, 'Then why the devil didn't you contact me before?'

'I tried to,' I said. 'I rang the number you gave me from the rig, but you weren't there.'

'You could have left a message.' His voice had sharpened. 'You're in trouble and you can't blame me if I'm left with the feeling that you're trying to use me to get yourself off the hook. I gave you my number on the chance you might find yourself involved in subversive activities and be prepared to give evidence. What you've been telling me isn't evidence. It's supposition based on two conversations – conversations that may be no more accurate than the evidence you gave in court.'

I started to tell him that my version of what had happened that night was the truth, but he cut me short. 'Then why didn't you make a statement to the police? You knew they wanted to interview you. I reminded you of that when we met.' And he added, 'I also said you were vulnerable. But that hardly applies now.' He rang off then and I was left with the certainty that he hadn't believed a word I had said.

It was some time before anyone came. Once I opened the door and looked out into the corridor, but the desk was at the end of it and no hope of slipping away unobserved. At last the plain-clothes man came back. 'You can go back to your hotel now.'

I got up, wondering what that meant. 'You accept my statement then?'

'It's being considered.'

'But you're not detaining me.'

'You're requested to notify the duty officer here of your destination on leaving your hotel. That's all for the moment.' He opened the door for me and I walked down the corridor and out past the desk into the street. I was free – for the moment, while they made up their minds. Garrard hadn't believed me. Nor had Sayre. So why should they? At the railway station I bought a copy of the Hull evening paper. It was there on the front page – CROWN WITNESS ACCUSED, and inset a picture of myself being mobbed as I entered the

Guildhall that morning.

They were waiting for me when I reached the hotel, a reporter and a photographer, the flashlight snapping and questions being fired at me. I started to brush past them, but then I stopped. It was a moment to fight back, a chance I might not have again. I took them up to my room and made a statement, accusing Bradshaw of lying, of perverting the course of justice, accusing Scunton, and others I didn't name, but militants who had no connection with Hull or the shipyard strike, of intimidation. 'And the object of it all is the offshore rigs. You find a man calling himself Stevens, a man who has probably had a hand in the Irish troubles – he's the man behind it all.' And I described him to them.

But I could see they didn't believe me. The vulnerability of offshore rigs was too remote, the whole thing too fantastic. And the bitterness I felt, it was in my voice, and that was against me, too. The reporter didn't even bother to write it all down. I couldn't blame him. He was a local reporter, interested only in local news, and what I was telling him must have sounded wild and unconvincing in the mundane setting of that hotel bedroom. In the end they left and I flopped on to the bed feeling utterly drained.

I must have fallen asleep, for I woke suddenly with the light from the street lamp shining on my face. A door banged, the sound of voices loud from the bar. I looked at my watch. It was past ten. I got up, stripped and had a bath. Then I packed my case, wrote a note to the hotel manager, instructing him to send the account to the Star-Trion office in Aberdeen, and went out leaving the key in the door. I had less than £20 in my pocket.

The lobby was empty now except for the night porter behind the desk and a man sitting by the entrance with a paper on his knee. I watched him for a while. He wasn't reading the paper, and I didn't think he was a guest. He could have been waiting for somebody, but he looked more like a man on duty. There was a garage at the back of the hotel and after a little searching I found the door leading out to it. It was not far to the Central Station and a couple just leaving the forecourt of the Royal Station Hotel gave me a lift as far as Melton. It took me a further two hours and three separate lifts to reach the A1 near Pontefract, but a little after two in the morning I was in the cab of a long-distance container truck bound for Musselburgh.

CHAPTER FOUR

I think it was the trawler I worried about more than myself as I sat slumped in the heat of the driver's cab, thundering north up the A1. Perhaps I clung to her as the only reality left to me, so that my mood of depression was overlaid by a sense of urgency. What had happened to me in Hull had made me realize I was dealing with people who did not make idle threats.

It was dawn when we arrived in Musselburgh. I got a bus into Edinburgh, had breakfast in the station buffet and caught the first train to Aberdeen. The Star-Trion offices were in one of the solid residences near Mansfield Road, not far from the River Dee Dock. Some attempt had been made to modernize the place, but the effect was makeshift, as though the company were on a temporary lease and might move out at any moment. There was a telex machine in the outer office and a big fair girl at a typewriter. I told her who I was and asked her to book me a cabin on the night boat to Lerwick.

'Don't you have a return ticket by air?' she asked.

'You can't just walk on to a flight,' I said. But it was the closer check at Dyce that worried me, the isolation of the Sumburgh terminal. Nobody stopped me boarding the boat, and in the morning, when I disembarked at Lerwick, I didn't see a single policeman. It was as though, with the release of those two men, they had lost interest in me. I was so anxious to see Gertrude, and get back to the trawler, that I didn't stop to consider there might be another reason. I grabbed a taxi and drove straight to Taing.

The air was luminous with a light drizzle, the hills all green and the lochs limpid, not a breath of wind. The sun broke through as we came down to the voe, no trawler now and the house solitary and alone, the stonework glistening with moisture. I think I knew she wasn't there before we had even reached the house. It had an empty, deserted look. No answer to my knock, and when I tried the door it was locked. Nobody locks their door in Shetland unless they are away. I tried the back, but that, too, was locked. And then I drove to Scalloway.

I hadn't seen Fuller since that night I had taken him down

to view the *Duchess*. He was wearing the same dark business suit and looked like a fish out of water in that little port. He had taken over two rooms in the local hotel, his only equipment a telex, a telephone and a filing cabinet. Lying on the desk in front of him was a copy of the *Hull Daily Mail*, my picture staring up at me and the headline – CROWN WITNESS ACCUSED. 'So you know what happened.'

'I've read the report.'

'You had the local paper sent up specially . . .'

'No. It came in the post yesterday. Since then I've been trying to get a skipper – '

'You mean you didn't order that paper. It came unsolicited?'

He nodded. 'Sit down,' he said. 'I've also been trying to contact Mr Villiers.'

'It doesn't concern Villiers.'

But he didn't agree. 'He'll have to be told. And now that you're here, perhaps you'd like to give me your version. Then I'll know what to advise him when I get through.'

'Advise him! What do you mean? We have a contract – ' But I saw by the look on his face he had made up his mind. 'Where's Gertrude Petersen? I want to see her, and I want to get back on board. Where is she?'

'She left on a trawler yesterday evening. After she had read the report she insisted she must get out to – '

'You showed it to her?'

'I didn't have to. She'd seen it already.'

'Do you mean somebody had sent her a copy, too?'

But all he could tell me was that she had had the paper with her when she came into his office after lunch. 'Now, if you'll fill in on the details for me.' He sat there waiting, his hands folded across his stomach, his stolid, heavy face impassive. I gave him my version of what had happened and some indication of what was behind it. Finally, I said, 'Somebody wants me out of the way. And they want that contract scrapped so that you're in the market for another stand-by boat.' He didn't say anything, his face blank. 'Have you been offered a replacement?'

He leaned forward, staring down at the paper as though weighing the headlines against what I had told him. 'You think the rig is in some sort of danger, is that it?'

'Yes,' I said. But I could see he didn't believe me, any more than that reporter, or Garrard. He leaned back, his eyes staring beyond me. 'It could be said you're the real risk. And reading

143

this report . . .' His thick fingers dabbed at the headlines. 'Is it true your father was a Russian agent?' He was suddenly looking straight at me.

'Who told you that?'

'An Inspector from Special Branch.' The softness of his voice had gone as he added, 'Well, is it true?'

'I wouldn't know,' I said. 'I never knew him.'

'But you,' he murmured. 'Your record . . .' He was frowning, shaking his head. 'I don't know what to say. If I believe you . . .' He paused, still frowning. 'But it doesn't make sense. It would be very difficult to tamper with a huge structure like *North Star*. Certainly not if the guard ship is doing its job.' And he added, 'That's my difficulty, you see. And yours isn't the only trawler available, not now.'

'You have been offered a replacement then.'

He smiled. 'Oil companies are always being offered things – at a price.' The smile vanished, his lips pursed. 'But if there is the remotest possibility of danger to the rig, then the price becomes irrelevant. And another thing I have to bear in mind is that your view of what happened in court – or rather, what was behind it – is not likely to be the police view. They could arrest you at any moment. In fact, I'm surprised they haven't done so already.'

'They can't arrest me out there,' I said. 'They can't board my ship in international waters – '

'You're employed by us,' he said sharply. 'And we would facilitate any action the police might decide to take.' He got abruptly to his feet. 'Leave it with me now, Randall. I'll have a talk with Mr Villiers and we'll see where we go from there. All right?'

I didn't argue. There was no point.

'Come back after lunch,' he said, opening the door for me. 'I'll let you have our decision then.' The door closed and I went down the bare wooden stairs. The drizzle had lifted, the sun glimmering through. I crossed the road and walked to the pier where a couple of purse-seine fishing boats were unloading their catch. Gulls wheeled screaming and the water calm. I lit my pipe, leaning against the rail and letting the peace of it soak into me, that deep instinctive feeling that this was where I belonged. All that had happened was of no importance then, obliterated by the sense of familiarity, the feeling of contentment.

And then I heard the fishermen talking and reality broke in

again. They were talking about their rights in the fishing grounds. 'Chased off like that . . . What right have they got, any more than us? Just because they're a bluidy oil company . . . Aye, we should have told the bastards to go to hell.' And the skipper, leaning on the bulwarks and saying, 'What d'you expect me to do – risk a collision?' He was a broad, big-bellied man in a Shetland jersey with a brown beret on his head. 'She's bigger than us. I'll report it, but I doubt if the Council can do much. It's the Government in London. They want oil.'

'They don't depend on fish for their living.'

A bitter laugh, the slam of a box and a voice saying, 'Aye, that they don't. And now they're drilling off this side of Shetland. Soon we'll be ringed by oil rigs, fenced in like a lot of puir peerie sheep. Time the Council took note of us.'

The skipper nodded. 'There's a meeting tomorrow and I'll be there. So will a lot of others. We're not the only boat . . .'

I turned away, my peace of mind shattered. Politics! Couldn't I ever get away from politics? I went in search of some food, knowing that it could only have been my own trawler they had been cursing.

Shortly after two I was back in Fuller's office. He had spoken to Villiers and had orders to get me back on board the *Duchess*. 'Don't ask me why.' He sounded annoyed. 'I tell you frankly, it was against my advice. But he's got troubles of his own, so maybe he doesn't want to be bothered by a little matter like you and your trawler.' The London papers had arrived and he had the *Daily Telegraph* in front of him, open at the City page. 'All right then.' He was looking down at the paper, not at me, and I had the impression that his mind was on other things. 'The taxi will be here shortly to take you to Sumburgh. There's a helicopter flight leaving about four o'clock.'

'You passed on what I told you?'

'For what it's worth, yes.'

'What did he say?'

He looked at me then. 'What did you expect him to say – with this hanging over him?' And he slapped the paper. 'Shetland is a long way away and what seems important to you will be looking a lot less important viewed from an office in the City with the pack in full cry. But just remember this, any trouble on the location and you're out. I'll get replacement guard boats on my own responsibility. And if the police decide to arrest you, don't try and rely on the fact that you're in

145

international waters. I won't stand for that. I've enough trouble dealing with fishermen's complaints without getting involved with the police. We come under the law. Is that understood?'

'You may accept that you come under the law,' I said. 'But others don't. I'll wait for the taxi downstairs.' And I turned and walked out of his office, the anger and bitterness back. Why the hell couldn't somebody, just for once, let me get on with the job of running a trawler and making her pay? I was seething all the way to Sumburgh, my mind turned inwards so that I no longer saw the peace of the hills, no longer felt I had come home again. And then, in the little airport building at Sumburgh, I bought a copy of the *Daily Telegraph* and saw the mess Villiers was in.

The details are not important, though I had plenty of time to study them as the helicopter rattled noisily north-westward out to the rig. *Tailor-made to our purpose,* Stevens had said, and now I could see it for myself. The man was being accused of asset-stripping for his own personal gain and the full glare of publicity was being focused upon him, all of it adverse. He had acquired Star-Trion through an investment company managed by VFI. Star-Trion had then been broken up and the assets sold off. These sales, with one exception, had been to companies unconnected with himself. The exception was the oil assets, consisting chiefly of the *North Star* rig and the licences to drill in Blocks 206/17 and 18. These had been acquired by a nominee company controlled by VFI and the price had been fixed by Villiers himself. 'Rigged' was the word used by a solicitor acting for one of the investment company's major shareholders.

Villiers had issued a statement to the effect that the price had been based on an independent assessment of the break-up value of *North Star,* that his decision to operate the rig on the Star-Trion licences had been taken 'in the country's best interests', and that it was being financed by his own company and was a total gamble. He was quoted as saying, 'To commit the funds of an investment company managed by VFI to such a gamble would have been most improper. In the circumstances, no value can attach to the licences west of Shetland and I consider the break-up value of such an old rig the only real basis for disposal.'

It was a specious argument, or seemed so to me as the helicopter slanted down to land on the rig, for there it was, not in the breaker's yard, but out in the Atlantic, a hive of activity with the draw-works roaring and the drill biting steadily into the sedimentary rock deep under the sea.

As I ducked under the turning blades, I caught a glimpse of the *Duchess* out to the north-east, standing guard like a sheep-dog between the anchor buoys and three Shetland boats. She was rolling gently in the swell, the bridge windows inter-mittently reflecting the late afternoon sun. Then I was in the shelter of the toolpusher's office and a thick Dutch voice was saying, 'Ach zo, you 'ave com back, eh?' Van Dam's hand gripped my elbow. 'I am glad.' He told me Alfredo was waiting for me with the divers' inflatable and he added, 'That young woman, she is not tough enough. It needs a man like you out there. Those Shetland boats are a dam' nuisance. They 'ave no business fishing zo close.'

'The Shetlanders don't see it that way,' I said. 'They claim they've a right to fish where they like.'

'Not inside the buoys. Too dangerous. You get them out of 'ere. Okay?'

It was on the tip of my tongue to tell him that there would be trouble if we got too tough, but his relief had arrived and he was being called to board the helicopter. I waited until it had taken off and then went down the iron stairway to the waiting boat. With the sea calm, it didn't take long to reach the *Duchess*. Nobody greeted me as I climbed on board. No sign of Gertrude, and Johan staring at me from the bridge windows like a bear in his den. I yelled for the cook, tossed him my bag and told him to get me a mug of tea. I was in a filthy mood as I went through the gangway and pushed open the door to the bridge. 'Where's Gertrude?'

Johan stared at me as though I were a stranger. He didn't reply, and Lars at the helm looking straight ahead, both of them wooden-faced. 'Can't you answer when you're spoken to?'

'She is in there.' He jerked his head towards the rear of the bridge.

'Then fetch her out.' I saw him hesitate, but the habit of shipboard obedience was strong and he turned towards the companionway. 'Don't bother. I'll go myself.' I had control of myself then and, conscious of the mood on board and who must have caused it, I didn't want to face Gertrude there in the bridge in front of the crew.

She had taken over my cabin, her things strewn about, and she herself lying stretched out on my bunk, her eyes closed.

But she wasn't asleep. I was sure of that. There was a tenseness about her, a feeling of hostility in the air. I stood there, looking at her, not saying anything and the anger building.

'Who's there?' she said at last.

'You know damn well.'

She opened her eyes then, but she didn't look at me. She lay there, staring up at the steel plating over the bunk, and I knew she was holding herself in.

'I've seen Fuller,' I said.

'Then why are you here?' She sat up, swinging her long legs off the bunk. She was dressed in sweater and slacks, her hair a mess and her eyes red-rimmed. 'I was expecting somebody else.'

'Who?'

'I don't know. He said he'd find somebody for me.'

'A replacement skipper?'

'Ja. It was either that or scrap the contract.' She stared at me. 'Why did you do it? Risking lives, burning a man's house – why? I thought at one time all you wanted was a trawler, something to work for. But it isn't that, is it? It's politics, disruption, anarchy, nothing else . . . It's all you care about – destroying things.' The words poured out of her in a sobbing breath.

'Who sent you that newspaper?' My voice sounded cold, and I felt cold, cold with anger that she should believe it of me. 'Somebody sent it to you. Who?'

'Does it matter?'

I started to tell her what had happened in court. I wanted her to understand. But she brushed my explanation aside. 'What do I care – about what happen in that court? It's all there in the newspaper report. And that girl, Fiona – I don't believe what she tell me. I don't want to believe. But now . . . Now I know what sort of a man you are.' She gave an angry shrug. 'And she is your wife. You don't tell me you have a wife.'

So that was it. 'My God!' I said. 'Do I have to share my private life with you?'

'She is your wife. You live together for four years. Now, when you want to be rid of her . . .'

I was across the cabin then, grabbing her by the shoulders and shaking her. 'You stupid little fool!' I was beside myself with anger. She'd infected the whole ship, the crew, everybody against me. 'Get your things packed,' I told her. 'I want you

148

off this ship – now, this evening.'

She stared up at me, her body rigid, her eyes wide with disbelief. 'Is my ship.'

'And mine,' I reminded her. I was bending down, staring her in the face, my hands gripped on her shoulders. 'I can't run this ship with you on board. Not unless I have your confidence. Understand?'

Slowly her gaze dropped. 'Well . . .' She hesitated. I don't think she wanted a row. She wasn't an aggressive person. Emotional, yes – but she was also very practical and this had the effect of concealing her emotions. 'If Mr Fuller has confidence in you still . . .'

'It was Villiers, not Fuller. Fuller is like you. He believes what they want him to believe. Now, get packed and I'll have the boat lowered.' I let her go then, taking my hands from her shoulders and turning abruptly for the door.

'Just a minute, please.' Her voice sounded troubled. 'You asked me who sent that newspaper. Mr Fuller also received a copy.'

'The rig probably has one, too.'

'I don't know who sent it. Your wife perhaps?'

'Perhaps.'

She got up slowly and came towards me. She wasn't crying, but there were tears in her eyes. 'You are in trouble.'

I stared at her, not answering, not willing to admit it even to myself now that I was back in command.

'Your evidence in court . . .' She was standing quite close to me, the lips of that too-big mouth of hers parted, her eyes enormous. 'Will you swear to me that it was the truth. If you swear –'

'Oh, go to hell!' I said and slammed out of the cabin. I heard her call after me, but what did she take me for? What difference would it make, swearing that I had told her the truth? If I were the sort of man she believed . . . The engine-room telegraph interrupted my thoughts. I was in the bridge then, Johan's voice calling for port wheel and the deck trembling to the increased revs. A fishing boat's mast, framed in the starboard window, slid astern and Johan rang for slow again, pushing his cap back on his head and turning to me with a grim smile. 'They play silly buggers like that too many times and somebody get hurt.'

I leaned my head out of the window, watching the little black-painted vessel swinging in our wake. It was a Hamnavoe fishing boat, the white lettering clear on its bows. 'Been having trouble, I hear.'

Johan nodded. 'Ja. Last night is very bad. More than a dozen I think, and some shooting inside the buoys, their seine nets close in to the rig.'

The bloody fools, I thought, risking their nets inside the circle of the anchor buoys. 'Did you threaten to use the hose on them?'

He shook his head.

'Why not? I told you . . .'

'If we use the hose there will be trouble.' He reached for the mug standing on the chart table and passed it to me. 'Your tea.'

'There'll be trouble anyway,' I told him. 'So use it.' The tea was half cold. It seemed to typify the general state of the ship. 'Any boats shooting nets inside the anchor buoys get the hose turned on them after a warning through the loudhailer. Is that understood?' He stared dumbly straight ahead. 'I said, is that understood?'

'Ja.'

'How many were seine-net fishing inside the buoys?'

He shrugged. 'I don't know. Ask Gertrude.'

I turned then. He must have seen her reflection in the glass of the window, for she was standing at the head of the companionway right behind me.

'It was very thick last night. Fog.'

'How long before you chased them off?'

She shrugged. 'What does it matter? There is no law against purse-seine fishing, and it is their nets they risk.'

'And suppose one of them had had divers on board?'

'With bombs?' She laughed. 'Does your mind run on nothing else? I tell you they were just fishermen earning their living, the way we once try to earn ours.'

'How long?' I repeated.

It was Johan who answered. 'The fog came down shortly after midnight. It was about two hours after dawn before the last of the fishing boats made off.'

'Five or six hours then.' I was thinking what a well-trained frogman could achieve in five or six hours. But it was no good telling Gertrude what was in my mind. She wouldn't believe it. She wouldn't believe that there were forces at work planning the destruction of that monster lying motionless off our starboard quarter. I found it difficult to believe myself. 'Were you both on watch?' I asked. 'You and Johan, both of you?'

'Yes.'

'All through the night?'

'Yes, of course. They are shooting their purse nets inside the circle of the buoys, drifting them close by the rig, and in that fog it is very risky. I do not want to steam across the nets. I do not want any trouble with these Shetland fishermen.'

It explained the tiredness, the edginess, the general air of a ship that was without proper order and authority. 'Tell Flett to get me some food right away. Hot food, not lukewarm leftovers like this tea.' I handed her the mug. 'And call me at dusk. I'll stay on watch through the night. After that it will be normal routine.'

I left them and went below to find a vacant bunk, hoping Johan would have the sense to make the most of the night's rest I was offering him. Flett came in with a tray just as I was getting into the bunk. There was coffee as well as a shepherd's pie, and both were scalding hot.

The twilight was darkening in the west when I was called, clouds building up like a ragged mountain range, peaks of cu-nim black against the last dying glow of sunset.

'They have all run for home,' Gertrude said. 'I think you have a quiet night.'

'Has Johan turned in?' Apart from Lars at the helm she was alone on the bridge.

'I think so.'

'Well, check that he has. I don't want a tired mate, or a tired crew. Those purse-seiners will be back, and unless we're tough with them, it's going to be hard to keep the area clear.'

She went through into the chart recess, entered up the log and then turned and went to the cabin behind the bridge without another word, her silence lingering as the last flicker of the day's warmth was snuffed out by the growing cloud cover. Soon it had spread right across the sky, the light fading and the movement of the ship increasing as wind and sea rose. I circled the rig just inside the buoys, the 3-ton cans difficult to see and not a ship's light anywhere, only the rig blazing like a factory, the derrick jewelled with rubies. All the long night stretched ahead of me and nothing to do but think about my situation and what it was I had to guard against. For a time I tucked the *Duchess* close in under the rig, seeing myself as a marauding fishing boat bent on sabotage and trying to work out how they would do it, what method they would employ. But the sheer size of the rig made a nonsense of the exercise.

No bomb carried by a diver could possibly do more than superficial damage, and to get at the weakest section of the cross-bracing a frogman would have to climb well above the level of the sea.

At 23.00 hours I got the financial news. The reference to Villiers came near the end. He had held a press conference and had attacked the directors and shareholders of the old Star-Trion company for letting their assets go to waste. As for the *North Star* rig and the Shetland licences, what had the Company ever done to establish whether there was oil there or not? They hadn't dared risk their money, so why attack him for risking his? Perhaps I was biased by the fact that he had ignored Fuller's advice and supported me, but I couldn't help a sneaking admiration for a man who fought back so strongly when forced into a corner. Somehow it gave me strength.

The forecast for inshore areas followed 15 minutes later; the depression deepening with wind westerly Force 6 rising to Gale Force 7. We were already hove-to, our bows pointing just south of west. I switched off, and after that I had nothing but my thoughts for company. At midnight Henrik relieved Lars. For a moment the two of them were there by the wheel whispering and glancing at me. Then Lars went below. He returned a moment later with a steaming mug of cocoa and handed it to me without a word.

It was shortly after that, when we were nosing westward into a rainstorm to check for fishing vessels, that something hammered at the soles of my feet. I thought for a moment the old girl had fallen off the top of a rogue wave. But it wasn't that. We were in a trough with the sea gone dead in one of those lulls that happen sometimes. The empty mug was on the floor, clattering towards the side of the bridge, and the glass of the rev counter had a crack running across it.

I don't know why I went for the buoys. It was purely instinctive. My hand seemed to leap out for the telegraph and without any thought on my part I had rung for full speed and had ordered Henrik to steer nor'nor'west. I had the spotlight on, but with the rain driving across it, we had hell's own difficulty locating No. 4 buoy. I got it in the beam and then couldn't hold it, but it was there all right, and so was No. 3. Henrik, his mind concentrated on the wheel, hadn't felt a thing. If it hadn't been for the mug and that crack in the rev counter glass I might have thought I had imagined it.

We steamed south and checked Nos. 1 and 2 buoys. Nothing

wrong with them and I turned for the rig, calling the operator on duty to ask whether they had felt anything. But of course they hadn't. They were too high above sea level and the draw-works and the power plant going all the time. I steamed close alongside the five south-facing column legs, then back up the north side. Everything was normal, the big tubular cross-bracings solid and undamaged. By then Gertrude was on the bridge, her fair hair tousled and a duffle coat over her pyjamas. She had been roused by the changes of engine note and the wildness of the movement, and she wanted to know what the hell was going on.

'Nothing,' I said. 'Just been checking the western anchor buoys, that's all.' I didn't tell her I thought I had felt some sort of explosion. It seemed too ridiculous with the rig towering over us and blazing with light, everything so obviously normal. 'Ever seen that crack in the glass there?' I asked her, pointing to the rev counter.

She looked puzzled, staring at it and then at me. 'Yes,' she said. 'It's been there ever since I can remember. Now it is a little more noticeable. Why?'

I shrugged. 'I hadn't noticed it before.' And I walked over to the mug and picked it up. All imagination, and Gertrude standing there looking at me very oddly. Was I beginning to suffer from some sort of persecution mania? I could have convinced myself of that, too, I think, but just as I had told her irritably to go back to bed and get some sleep, Henrik drew my attention to two men high up on the helicopter deck. They were peering down over the edge of it and one of them was pointing to the column leg below winches 1 and 2. A wave reared up and I was flung against the side of the bridge. Gertrude was close beside me. 'What is it?' she asked.

We were coming back on the other roll, the ship broadside to the seas as Henrik took her down the west-facing side of the rig towards the corner where the men standing high above us had been joined by several more, all of them leaning over the edge gazing down at the cable stretched from the winch to the underwater block. I rang for slow and turned the boat head-to-wind, watching from the gangway as men began running to the far side of the rig. 'What is it?' Gertrude called out again, and this time there was a note of urgency in her voice.

I didn't say anything. I didn't know. Ed Wiseberg's burly figure appeared and stood there for a moment. Then he, too, was galvanized into action. The rain slammed down, a sudden squall that blurred the scene. When it had passed I saw Ken Stewart there with a walkie-talkie to his mouth, while he struggled to get an oilskin on over his short-sleeved khaki shirt. I ducked inside the bridge, pushing Gertrude out of my way, and switched on the VHF. 'Barge to *Duchess*. Calling *Duchess*.' His voice was loud and clear above the noise of the wind. 'Do you read me?' And when I had switched to Receive and acknowledged, he said, 'Check No. 2 buoy. The cable's slack and we could be dragging. I repeat, check No. 2 buoy.'

'I already have,' I told him, bracing myself against the radar as a wave rolled under us.

'Well, check again. The tension gauge is right down and it doesn't make a damn bit of difference winding in on the winch.'

It was on the tip of my tongue to tell him I suspected an explosion, but I checked myself in time. This was not the moment. 'What about No. 1 cable?' I asked him.

'We're watching it. Stay out by those buoys and keep your radio on.'

'Roger.' I switched to loudspeaker and rang down for half ahead. We were bucking in to it then, the waves breaking against our bows and seething along the deck. It was almost dark, no twilight now, only the beam of the spotlight sweeping back and forth and showing the break of the waves as they swept down at us out of the night. And all the time my mind trying to sort out what had happened – the cable slack, but the buoy still in position. If No. 2 buoy was still on a line with No. 1, then the anchor couldn't have moved. That could only mean one thing – the cable itself had parted. I was thinking of the colossal strain it was under, a slender line of twisted steel, like an umbilical cord, snaking down in a long half-mile curve to act as a leash between the anchor 100 fathoms deep on the seabed and that huge monster of a rig, and the gusts up to 45 knots now, slamming against its superstructure.

I glanced at the bridge clock, which was on Greenwich Mean Time, the hands at 01.04. It must have happened about ten minutes ago and that slam against the hull, it could have been the tensioned cable parting and curling up to crack like a whip against our underwater plating. Convinced of my reasoning, I made the following entry in the log: *00.50-54 Tension on No. 2 winch cable gone – suspect cable parted deep underwater.*

It took us longer this time to locate the buoy, and then it was more by luck than judgement, for the radar was virtually useless, the object so small and the seas breaking. We fell off the top of a wave and there was one of the buoys right along-side. We wriggled clear and held it in the spotlight till we could identify it as No. 1. Having found that one, it was much easier to locate No. 2, for both buoys were correctly positioned in relation to each other. I reported to the barge engineer, 'Both buoys in position and no indication that either of the anchors have dragged.'

But by then they knew what the trouble was. While we had been searching for the buoys, they had been winding in on No. 2 winch. 'We got most of the cable up now, but the end of it is in a hell of a mess and jammed in the tower block. Looks like it parted close by the anchor.'

'Wind's south-west,' I said, 'and gusting up to 8.'

But he knew that, knew the whole weight of the rig was now on a single windward anchor. His voice was high and anxious as he called to me, 'Stay out there by No. 1 buoy. No, patrol between 1 and 2. I must know any change of position. Ed's hauling up on the drilling string now, but if No. 1 parts, then he'll have to operate the pipe rams, hang off the drilling string at the BOP. So watch those buoys and warn me the instant No. 1 starts dragging. Got it?'

'Roger.'

The door to the gangway slammed and Johan was there, his yellow oilskins streaming water. 'There is a ship out there.' He rubbed a big paw over his wet face, peered at the compass and added, 'About west-north-west of us.'

I switched off the spotlight and peered through the clear-view circle of revolving glass. 'I don't see any lights. Are you sure it was a ship?'

'Ja. She is without lights, but I see the break of a wave against her bows.' He lumbered across to the radar, switching to short range, his big frame very still now in concentration as he watched the sweep. 'There! To starboard.' He shifted to give me a clear view. The screen was flecked with breaking waves, blurred with the rain now sweeping across us again. But there, on our starboard beam, a brighter blip appeared below the sweep, gradually fading to brighten again as the sweep completed its circle. It was just over half a mile away and moving slowly in towards the rig.

I ordered starboard wheel and called down to Per to increase the revs. I had the blip right over the bows then and we were running downwind, the *Duchess* twisting and rolling in the quartering sea, closing the gap fast. But either she had picked us up on her own radar or she could see our steaming lights, for halfway in to the rig she suddenly turned north, and at the same moment Ken Stewart's voice came over the loudspeaker: 'Barge to *Duchess*. Tension gone on No. 1 cable. Report position of buoy. Over.'

The time was 01.27. I picked up the phone. '*Duchess* to barge. Have unknown vessel on my radar screen steaming without lights inside the line of buoys. Am closing to identify. Over.'

But when I switched to Receive it was to hear his voice on a note of panic shouting, 'I told you to stay on station by the buoys. Get back at once and report on No. 1. If it's dragging we may have to go to emergency disconnect. I must know—now.'

I started to argue with him, but I might just as well have been talking to myself, for I got no reply. Hardly surprising if the rig had started to drag. The anchors were his responsibility and I could imagine what Ed Wiseberg would be calling him if the rig was being driven out of position with the line of drilling string still in the hole.

I stood there with the phone in my hand and Johan staring at me, waiting for my order to head back to the buoys. Gertrude, too. They were all staring at me, waiting. But instead of giving the order to turn, I switched off the navigation and steaming lights, picked up the engine-room voice pipe and called for maximum revs. Gertrude was instantly beside me, her hand on my arm. 'What are you doing?'

'Going after her, of course.'

'But why?' And Johan's voice, as he stood over the radar, 'There is no need. She has seen us and is heading away from the rig.'

Henrik, too, was waiting for the order to turn, and I knew so little about drilling that I was blind to the problems of a man with 600 feet of 20 inch casing stretching down to the seabed. I moved to the radar screen, estimated the intercept course and ordered him to steer it. I saw him hesitate, his eyes flickering from Gertrude to me and back again. 'Steer 40°,' I repeated.

'No.' Gertrude was beside me again, two angry spots of colour flaring in the pallor of her face. 'We must turn back to the buoys.'

'When we've got the number of that fishing boat.'

'No, now. You heard what the barge engineer said.'

A wave slammed against the port side. She clutched at me and I held her as the ship plunged. 'Watch your helm,' I told Henrik, letting go of her and moving to the wheel to check the compass as he slowly brought her on to course. 'Hold it at that.' The atmosphere in the bridge was tense. I had a feeling that if Gertrude had ordered him to steer back to the buoys, he would have obeyed her, and with Johan there, I would have been quite impotent, unable to enforce my orders against his massive bulk. But she just stood there, pale-faced and tense, her eyes staring at me with a sort of fascination.

It took us just over ten minutes to close the gap. Then suddenly we were right on top of her, the spotlight pinpointing her black hull rolling on the crest of a wave. She was a fishing boat all right, and I closed right in until I could read her number. I veered away then, steering past her stern, and as it lifted to the seas the spotlight picked out her name – ISLAND GIRL, and underneath the one word BURRA.

Island Girl! The boat that had followed us to Foula with Stevens on board. I turned to Gertrude. 'Sandford's boat,' I said. 'Remember? You sent me a cutting. A West Burra boat from Hamnavoe.' She was staring out at the blunt stern now falling away in a trough, her mouth half open. 'What's she doing out here?' I demanded. 'The paper said he'd bought her as a rig supply boat.'

She shook her head, a surprised, incredulous look on her face, and the bridge silent, only the sound of the engines, the noise of the sea. Perhaps she would believe me now. The boat was gone, the night swallowing it as we swung away in a wide turn and headed back, the rig barely visible, a blurred glow through the rain. 'She certainly wasn't fishing.'

'No.'

'Then what was she up to? What was she doing out here when every other fishing vessel has headed in for shelter?' A breaking wave cascaded over our bows, solid water slamming against the windows. I cut the revs, straddling my feet, bracing myself against the forward pitch as we slammed into the trough. 'You think I'm crazy talking about bombs and sabotage, but –'

'Please.' Her voice was wild, her eyes suddenly bright with tears. 'I don't want to think about it.' And she turned abruptly and went blindly back to the cabin. Christ! I thought. Women! Why couldn't she be logical, face up to the facts? The rig was coming closer, the lit bulk of it rising solid, the red warning lights on the drill tower giving a warm glow to the low-scudding clouds.

I switched my mind back to the fishing boat, trying to understand the reason for its presence. It couldn't possibly have been responsible for the cables breaking. We had been between the rig and the buoy when No. 2 cable had parted. No sign of it then. And it had been well clear of No. 1 cable when that had gone, so a mine, or some sort of a depth charge, was out of the question. Anyway, in this weather there was no way of dropping an explosive device directly on to the slender line of a cable under water, So what *was* it doing?

And then Ken Stewart's voice crackling out of the speaker: 'Barge to *Duchess*. Cancel previous order. Proceed to No. 3 and No. 4 buoys and stay with them. We've got a shift of wind, north-west in the gusts now and we're holding. But there's a lot of strain on the marine riser. If either of those buoys move, call me. Over.'

I ordered a small change of course and reached for the phone. '*Duchess* to barge. I'm heading for them now.' And Stewart's voice again, 'I can't see your lights. Where are you?' He didn't wait for an answer, but added, 'Stay on top of those buoys and if you think they're dragging . . .' His words were cut off, but he still had his hand on the transmitting button and faintly I heard him say, 'What's that – No. 3? Christ! Wind in on that bloody winch. Wind in!' We were so close to the rig by then that I could see him running along the edge of the helicopter deck.

'I think they are in trouble,' Johan said. I nodded. It wasn't easy to visualize the turmoil up there on the high platform of the rig, but in my mind's eye I saw the headlines – *An obsolete rig moored in waters too deep and too dangerous, and Villiers trying for a fortune by risking men's lives* . . . They'd roast him if it ever leaked out that *North Star* had cut adrift in a gale. Was that what Sandford's boat was doing, watching for trouble? I was back with politics again, and I cursed under my breath, visualizing another headline with my own name in black type. 'A blip,' Johan called out, and he made way for me so that I could see for myself. There was the rig showing on the screen like a great moon in the Milky Way of breaking waves. I was remembering Gertrude's words as she had fled from the bridge. I didn't want to think about it either. 'There.' Johan pointed a thick finger. 'Two of them now.' The rain had stopped and we were closing the area north-west of the rig, the two little blips becoming clearer. A few minutes later we picked up No. 4 can in the spotlight. At slow ahead we moved on to No. 3. It was out of position. I tried to report it, but no answer.

Through the glasses I could see men standing around the winches on the corner of the platform nearest to us. I kept on sending as we lay hove-to, keeping station on the buoy and watching for any further movement. But it seemed to be holding, and finally Stewart came through, his voice quieter now, a note of relief. 'We've full tension again. How's it looking out there?'

'Okay, I think. Out of position, but not by much. I've been trying to call you. No. 3 can doesn't seem to have moved much since the rain stopped and we got sight of the two of them.'

'Thank Christ!' he murmured. 'We've definitely got a shift of wind. If we hadn't got that, the riser casing would have snapped under the strain. A hell of a mess. But we're holding on 3 and 4 now, tension constant. Stay on top of those two buoys. Beam your spotlight on us if you think either of them is shifting position. I'll have somebody keep watch on you from up here. I daren't rely on the tension dials only. So watch it.'

We stayed patrolling between those two buoys the rest of the night, the wind gradually steadying in the north-west. Around 04.00 it blew very strong from that quarter, but the two anchors held and by dawn the wind was dropping and the sea with it. The night of panic was over, and *North Star* almost back in position above the drill hole.

Now the hustle was on to clear up the mess and get the rig operational again. Divers were down at first light and the radio traffic was incessant as scrambled FAX reports were transmitted and Ken Stewart called for *Rattler* to bring out new cable and re-lay anchors 1 and 2. And then, just after 09.00, he called the *Duchess* and ordered me to report on board at 10.30. 'Ed's holding a meeting to establish just what happened, and what needs to be done, so bring the ship's log with you.'

PART THREE

STORM

CHAPTER ONE

It took three days to get new cables sent out and wound on to the winch drums. Some of the big oil companies had established a supply base at Lyness in Orkney and were beginning to move back-up facilities to Lerwick, but Star-Trion was an independent and had to get supplies where it could. Mostly that meant Aberdeen, which was a long haul. Another day was lost in retrieving the anchors and re-laying them, so that it wasn't until late on 12th June that the drilling string was connected up again and the rig operational.

The meeting in Ed Wiseberg's office had established nothing. Both the cables had parted at their extremities, close to the length of chain shackled to the anchor. This was confirmed later when *Rattler* winched in both buoys and the anchors at the end of their pennant wires. No. 1 had 15 feet of cable still attached to the chain, No. 2, 7 feet. This seemed to support the conclusion reached at the meeting that the cables were old and suffering from fatigue and that replacement of all anchor cables was essential for the safety of the rig.

Since the discussion had centred on the condition of the cables, I was not involved, except to the extent of justifying my departure from Ken Stewart's instructions in order to identify the fishing boat *Island Girl*. My action was accepted as being reasonable in the circumstances, Ed Wiseberg merely insisting that in future I adhere strictly to the barge engineer's orders. I made no reference to that moment when I thought I had felt an explosion under water. In view of what was discovered later it would have been better if I had, but with everybody convinced that cable fatigue was the cause, it would have introduced a new dimension. I did, however, point out that the fishing boat, *Island Girl*, had been steaming without lights, but they merely put that down to the determination of Shetland's fishermen to shoot their nets close in to the rig. They thought it was a political move, since the purse-seiners normally worked closer inshore, and the absence of lights was attributed to a natural desire to avoid being sighted by the guard boat.

Immediately following that conference I had arranged to get Gertrude ashore. I had never had a woman on board a trawler before and the fact that the crew were so accustomed to her presence that, almost unconsciously, they looked to her for decisions, made my own position considerably more difficult than it would otherwise have been. Johan, in particular, had a great fondness for her, as though she were a close relative as well as the owner. In any case, we needed her back at base to organize supplies. There was no room for her on the helicopter, but when the new cables came out I got her away on *Rattler*. After that I was able to re-establish my authority and get a grip on the ship and her crew.

There was a great deal of activity during the days it took to get the rig fully operational again. But once they had resumed drilling, everything settled down to normal, and the dullness of our patrol, the steady routine of watch-and-watch about, made things considerably easier for me. Throughout this period the Shetlanders gave us no trouble. Indeed, for the better part of a week we never saw a single fishing boat. Johan thought they would be fishing either west of Sumburgh or out by Fair Isle, for the weather was fine and clear. It was midsummer now, the days so long there was almost no night, only a weird pinkish twilight before the sun edged up over the horizon again.

Twenty-third June and another clear, silky morning. I was just coming off watch when the rig called us. I was to report on board immediately – Ed Wiseberg's orders. I found him alone in the toolpusher's office, his hard, leathery face even more craggy than usual. 'You've seen this, have you?' It was a copy of the Shetland paper with a headline – *Dragging Rig a Danger to Lives.*

'No, we haven't had any papers sent out yet.'

He grunted. 'Then you won't have seen the stories in your national press. The *Morning Star* is the worst, of course, accusing Villiers of gambling with men's lives. But they're all on to it – *The Times, Express, Telegraph,* the whole goddam lot, all screaming for our blood.' He flung the pile down in front of me, staring at me angrily as though I personally had leaked the story. The intercom phone rang, and while he answered it, I picked up one of the papers, my eye caught by several lines of print underlined in red: *It is not the first time things have gone wrong for this 51-year-old American driller. In the past six years he has had a fire, a blowout and an accident in which two men were killed. Regarded as something of a Jonah by his fellow toolpushers, it is hardly surprising that he now finds himself in charge of the oldest rig in the North Sea operating west of Shetland in the most dangerous sea area of all.*

No wonder he was angry. I turned to the *Telegraph*. Here, too, the story was front page news, but at that point I suddenly became interested in what he was saying over the phone — something about fishing boats and he had mentioned Gertrude Petersen's name. He reached for a pad, made a note and then looked across at me. 'Okay, George. I think that's a pretty smart deal . . . Yeah, I guess that should cool the whole thing down, locally at any rate. When d'you reckon it'll be on station? . . . That's fine. *Rattler* can stand by till it arrives. Yeah, I'll tell him. He's here with me right now.' And he put the phone down. 'That was George Fuller,' he said. For a moment he didn't say anything more, just stood there facing me, his brows drawn down and his face grim. He was looking older than when I had last seen him, the lines of his face deeper, the shoulders sagging. The effect was to make him seem less than life size, as though the weight of responsibility had diminished his stature.

The silence hung heavy. 'What was it about?' I asked him.

'You.' He paused, still frowning. Then he straightened up, squaring his shoulders. 'First, I'd better tell you the results of the laboratory tests on Nos. 1 and 2 cables. We sent the whole lot ashore, including the broken ends from both anchor chains. It wasn't what we thought. No indication of cable fatigue. Know what it was?' He was suddenly leaning on the desk, his head thrust aggressively forward. 'Sabotage.'

I was so shocked by the boldness of his statement that all I could think of was that moment on the bridge when something, some force, had slammed against the soles of my feet. So I'd been right. It had been an underwater explosion.

'That surprise you?' He glowered at me. 'No, I bet it doesn't. I can see it in your face. You know damn well they were ripped apart by a bomb.'

'Are you accusing me?'

'I'm not accusing you of anything. All I know is that your

political record stinks, and yours was the only boat with the opportunity – '

'What about that purse-seiner I reported steaming without lights?' But I knew *Island Girl* hadn't had time to undertake what would have been a very tricky operation. He knew it, too.

'That fishing vessel's got nothing to do with it. Mebbe you haven't either. God knows how it was done. But there it is. There's the laboratory report.' He picked up a telex and tossed it across to me. 'Read it if you want to. The frayed ends of those cables all showed indications of heat metamorphosis. Traces of carbon, other more technical details. It all adds up, the findings conclusive. And something else you should read.' He reached for the local paper and handed it to me, his finger pointing to the second column of the front page story. 'That boat you saw. It wasn't fishing. It was tailing you. Read it.'

'But it couldn't possibly – '

'Read it. Then I'll tell you what we've decided.'

It was a statement by Ian Sandford:

The rig's only stand-by boat is the Duchess of Norfolk, *manned partly by foreigners. This is not the sort of boat that should be permitted to harry our fishing boats, which have an age-old right to fish those waters. Nor should a man with a police record be in command of the one boat with the right to come and go around the rig. This should be a Shetland responsibility. My own boat was, in fact, present in the neighbourhood of the rig at the time it began to drag. The man on watch saw the* Duchess *out by the windward buoys, but then she forced* Island Girl *to leave the area.*

The implication was obvious, and it went on: *Mr Sandford, who was recently elected to the Zetland County Council, drew a hair-raising picture of what could happen if this rig were to break adrift at the moment when the drill bit had penetrated an underwater oil reservoir. 'It could mean,' he told our reporter, 'vast quantities of crude oil gushing out into the waters west of Shetland. Every fisherman knows the effect this would have on his livelihood. But it's not just the fishing that would be hit. With the prevailing winds, all the west of Shetland could be totally polluted, the whole coastline black with crude oil. The beauty of our islands, the bird life, everything that attracts the tourist, would be ruined.'*

His solution: A modern, self-positioning drilling ship in place of the obsolete North Star. *And in the interim, proper sur-*

veillance with two Shetland boats sharing the guard duties, and manned by Shetlanders.

So that was it. The man had turned politician and was using his new position to get us out and his own boats in. I looked across at the big toolpusher and knew by the look on his face I hadn't a hope of changing his mind. 'You're ditching us, is that it?'

'Call it that if you like. I told you, when I first met you, I didn't want you on my rig. Now I don't want you anywhere near it – or your ship. Nor does George. You're a political liability, and to my way of thinking a potential danger to the rig.' He was looking down at the paper again, his voice thick with anger as he said, 'A dynamic stationed drill ship! That shows their goddam ignorance. A dynamic stationed ship in these waters! There's no heave compensator invented could cope with the pitch and movement of a drill ship in the waves we'll be getting out here later in the year.'

But I wasn't interested. To hell with drill ships and technicalities. All I cared about in that moment was the *Duchess* and Gertrude. Myself, too. 'We've a contract,' I said. 'And provided we can keep on station – '

His fist came down, hammering at the desk. 'I don't give a damn about your contract. No doubt you'll get compensation, if that's what you're worrying about. George can sort that one out with the Petersen woman. Now get back to your ship and get it out of here. Okay? *Rattler* takes over from the *Duchess* as of now.'

I was so angry I had to push my hands down into my pockets to stop myself doing something stupid. 'Have you thought about how an explosive device could have been attached to the cables – close to the anchor stocks in 500 feet of water?' I was holding myself in, my voice tight and controlled. 'You think about that. A bomb slid down the pennant wire from buoy to anchor would cut the buoy adrift and mark the anchor when it exploded. I saw those anchors as *Rattler* hauled them up. They were undamaged. And the buoys didn't break adrift. Both pennant wires were intact. And if you think somebody could slide a device down the cable from the rig end of it on a snap block, then you just try it, see whether it gets anywhere near as close to the point of break on those two cables.'

I had his attention then. 'Okay. How do you think it was done then?'

It was a matter I had given some thought to, but I hesitated, suspecting a trap. When a man has virtually accused you of sabotaging his anchor cables, you don't expect him to enquire about the method used without some ulterior motive. But Ed Wiseberg wasn't built that way. He was a rugged, straightforward drill operator and there was no guile in the grey eyes waiting upon my answer. Their expression was one of puzzlement, and it came as a shock to realize that the man was out of his depth and profoundly worried. He really was seeking my advice. 'Christ! You expect me to tell you?'

'Not if you had a hand in it. No.' He shrugged, and then suddenly that craggy face broke into a smile. 'But I'm asking you all the same. You know about the sea. I don't.'

I laughed. I couldn't help myself. 'You asking me!' The bloody nerve of it! 'All right,' I said. 'I'll tell you.' And I cursed myself for a fool. But you couldn't help liking him, and he knew how to handle men. 'It could only have been done by a ship towing a grapnel. I can't think of any other way. If a grapnel were towed just the rig side of one of the anchor buoys it would be bound to grab hold of the cable. The device could then have been slipped down the grapnel line. A good lead weight on top of that, then cut the line adrift and let it sink.'

'And how do you set it off – delayed action?'

'Either that, or fasten a thin connecting wire to the side of the anchor buoy so that you can detonate by radio signal.' Even as I said it, thinking the method out as I went along, the real reason for the presence of that fishing boat flashed into my mind. 'Since they need a gale to make the operation worthwhile, radio signal would be the sensible method of triggering the bomb off.'

'So we inspect the buoys, a daily routine.' He nodded. 'Yeah. That's the answer.' He came round the edge of the desk. 'I guess you think I'm being pretty rough, hm? Well, nothing I can do about that. I got the rig to consider and the bloody Shetlanders on my back.' He held out his hand, the tough, leathery features lit by a smile of surprising charm. 'I hear the fishing's good now, so no hard feelings, eh?'

I shook his hand. What else? It wasn't his fault. And no good telling him that in getting rid of me he was losing the one person who knew enough to give the rig some protection. 'Good luck!' I said, and I meant it, remembering that paragraph in the *Express* underlined in red.

He nodded, reached for his safety helmet and gloves, and

then he was gone, striding out on to the helicopter deck. I watched him through the window as he headed for the derrick floor, back to the world that was his life, the world he knew and understood.

I thought then, and still think, that the division between toolpushers and barge engineers is a dangerous one. How can you expect a man who has spent most of his life drilling on land to adapt himself to the sea in middle life? Ed Wiseberg at 51 couldn't be expected to think in terms of a real Shetland gale. He couldn't even conceive what it was like. Yet so long as *North Star* was drilling, he was in charge.

I went slowly out on the deck, pausing a moment to see his heavy figure climbing the long iron stairway at the base of the derrick that led from pipe deck to derrick floor, climbing with a sort of punchy swagger. He flung open the corrugated iron door and stood there for a moment surveying the scene, a lone figure standing right above the pipe skid, the noise of the draw-works blasting out and the men inside dancing a strange ballet around the kelly, the tongs in their hands and the winches screaming. Then he stepped forward into that hell's kitchen of machinery and closed the door behind him, safe now among the tools that were his trade.

God help him, I thought, as I turned away, wondering how he would measure up if he was caught in a real storm.

The *Duchess* was wallowing in the bright sunlight out by No. 7 buoy. I went down the stairway then to the waiting boat, and as the outboard pushed us clear of the cold cavern of the rig's undersection, I was considering how I would break it to the crew. They had been out here for over two months now, sacrificing shore time for the benefit of their ship. I wasn't angry. I was past that. But the humiliation of it sickened me, knowing that they would have nobody to blame but myself. And later, when we reached Shetland, there would be Gertrude to tell.

I climbed on board and went straight to the bridge. Lars was at the wheel and I told him to turn in towards *Rattler*. She was still moored stern-on to the rig unloading stores. I steamed close past her bows, hailing her skipper and telling him it was all his now. He wished us luck and I was thinking I could certainly do with some as I swung away to point our bows towards Mainland of Shetland. Then I called the crew to the bridge and told them why we were leaving.

I could see the shock and dismay in their faces and I didn't

166

wait for the inevitable questions, but ducked into the chart recess to lose myself for a moment in the practicalities of working out the course for Scalloway. Johan followed me shortly afterwards. 'So we get compensation and Gertrude pays off the mortgage, then we go fishing, ja?' He was smiling and I guessed what he was thinking. That close positive relation between them would be resumed and everything would go on as it had before. He put a great paw on my arm. 'What will you do then?' To my surprise there was real concern in his voice.

'I haven't thought about that,' I said.

He nodded. 'Well, time you think about it.' He hesitated, his head turned away from me, staring out through the doorway as he said, 'You are a good captain, a good seaman, ja – but for you it is not enough to fish.' He spoke slowly, awkwardly, as though afraid of giving offence. 'Fishing is a good life. But not for you. You need something bigger. Politics per'aps, or oil.'

'You may be right,' I said and gave him the course. He didn't say anything after that. For him it had been a long speech. We had moved into the bridge and we were silent, both of us wrapped in our own thoughts, the only sounds the sounds of the sea and the hum of the engines.

The evening was deepening into twilight as we steamed through the Middle Channel into Scalloway, and we had barely dropped our anchor under the castle ruins when a boat put out from the shore and came alongside. The old man at the oars wore a fisherman's cap. He said his name was McIver and that he had a note for me from Gertrude Petersen. All this in a high piping voice like the call of a curlew. I bent over the bulwarks and took the note from his outstretched hand, ripping open the envelope and reading it by the light of the deck light. It was dated 23rd June at 14.15:

I think perhaps you do not come into The Taing but go direct to Scalloway. In case, this is to tell you that a Detective-Sergeant from Hull came to the house this morning. He is asking for you, but will not say why. His name is Gorse and he is waiting for you at the hotel in Scalloway. I think you may like to know so I am leaving this note for Terry McIver of Dun Croft to give you as soon as you arrive. It is more trouble for you, I think, so let me know if there is anything I can do. G. And she had added a PS: *Sandford now has the Star-Trion contract. He is providing two Shetland boats to replace the* Duchess.

I looked across at the lights of the little port, thinking there wasn't much time now to do what I had to do. Any moment a boat would put out from the pier and I had no doubts as to why Gorse was here. 'Do you have a car?' I asked the old man. But he shook his head. 'Know anybody who could run me over to Taing?'

'Aye. My son. He's got a Ford van.'

I told him to wait and went to my cabin, hurriedly stuffing the things I'd need into my grip. I took my anorak, and sea boots as well, shouted to Johan that he was in charge now, and a moment later I was in the boat and being rowed ashore. Money and a vehicle, those were the two essentials, and I just hoped Gertrude had meant it when she had asked if she could do anything.

McIver's son Robbie was just going to bed, a short, broad-shouldered man with his father's high voice. He accepted my request quite cheerfully, pulling on his gumboots and going out to the barn to get the van. Overhead a child began crying and Robbie's wife appeared in a dressing gown with her hair falling to her shoulders and began heating some milk. The atmosphere in the croft kitchen was warm and friendly. The old man poured me a dram. 'I was with old Petersen when he first began fishing out of Hamnavoe. That was quite a while back before my father died and left me the croft.'

'Did you live at Hamnavoe?' I asked.

'Aye. My wife, she's dead now, but she was from Hamnavoe.'

'You'd know the Sandfords then.'

'Albert and Anna?' He nodded, cackling to himself. 'There's a rum pair. And that son of theirs – ' He paused, his glass half-way to his lips and the moist blue eyes fixed on me. 'Randall? There were Randalls at Hamnavoe once.'

The door banged open and Robbie McIver came in. 'Ready when you are.'

I got to my feet, but he waved me back. 'No, finish your drink. And I'll have one too, Father.' It gave me a chance to ask him whether he had ever met Alistair Randall. But he hadn't. 'It was after the war that I came to Hamnavoe. Your father, you say?' And after that he seemed to close up, staring at me curiously as though the revelation had somehow produced a barrier between us.

'You were saying something about the Sandfords' son. Is Ian

Sandford the only son?'

'Aye.'

'What were you going to say about him?'

But he shook his head. 'It's getting late. You'd best be going now.' And he nodded to Robbie, who downed the rest of his drink and opened the back door for me. I was conscious of their curiosity as I stepped out into the northern twilight. There was a light drizzle falling and I realized that here in Shetland it was hardly the normal hour to be visiting a young widow alone in a remote house. Robbie maintained a discreet silence, driving carefully and nursing the old van on the bends.

It was just past eleven when we turned down the track to The Taing. There was a light on in one of the upper windows of the house. 'Looks like she's just going to bed. Do you want me to wait for you?' He said it carefully, his eyes on the track and his tone innocent of any attempt to pry.

'No,' I said. 'Not if the Land-Rover's there. I have some business . . .'

'Oh, aye.' He nodded to show his understanding and I knew he didn't believe a word of it. 'Well, it's there all right.' We were coming down the hill to the house now and the headlights showed the Land-Rover standing at the door, the black waters of the voe beyond.

He drew up beside the Land-Rover and I got out, standing uncertainly, looking up at that lighted window. The night was very still, the fine drizzle soft on my face, and I was suddenly seeing it from her point of view, the contract cancelled and myself coming like a fugitive out of the night. I dumped my things in the Land-Rover and then moved hesitantly towards the door, no longer sure of my reception and conscious of Robbie watching me curiously. My knock sounded loud in the stillness. Light streamed out as the bedroom curtains were whisked back. Then the window opened and Gertrude's voice called down to enquire who it was.

'Mike Randall,' I said. 'Can I talk to you a moment? I want to borrow the Land-Rover.'

There was a pause. Then she said, 'Wait a minute and I'll come down.'

She came to the door in her dressing gown. Her hair was held with a band of ribbon and she had an oil lamp in her hands. 'It's very late.' She was staring past me at the van. 'Is that Robbie?'

'Yes, Mrs Petersen,' he answered.

Her gaze came back to me. 'You put in to Scalloway then.' There was a long pause, her eyes looking directly at me, a puzzled expression, as though she couldn't make up her mind. And then suddenly she was smiling, to herself, as though at some private joke. 'So that's why you've come – for the Land-Rover.'

I nodded.

'How long do you want it for?'

'Three or four days,' I said.

I could see her working that out and then she nodded. 'All right. You'd better come in then.' She pushed the door open wide and called to Robbie that he needn't wait. 'Captain Randall will take the Land-Rover and I will settle with your father.'

'Okay, Mrs Petersen.'

'Thank him, will you please,' she called as the van's engines started up again. I raised my hand, but he was already backing and turning. I watched as the red tail lights climbed the hill and disappeared over the top. Everything was still then and we were alone. 'Are you coming in, or do you want just to take the Land-Rover and go?' She sounded uncertain of herself, her voice sharp and trembling slightly.

'I need some money,' I said. 'For petrol.'

'Then you'd better come in. You need to explain, too.'

'All right.' I went in then and she slammed the door behind me. 'You like some coffee or something stronger?'

'Coffee please. I'll be driving all night.'

She led me through into the flagstoned kitchen, and as she set the lamp on the table, she looked at me angrily. 'You don't think of my reputation, do you – coming here at this time of night. It will be all over Hamnavoe.'

'I'm sorry,' I said. I was thinking of the last time I had been in this house, the difference in my reception. 'I needed transport –'

'So you come to me.' She began filling the kettle. 'First my ship, and now –' She turned the tap off. 'Anybody else, anybody at all, and we would have been all right, the contract running all summer and the mortgage paid off. But no,' she added, busying herself with lighting the butane gas stove, 'it has to be you who come here out of the blue.' She slammed the kettle down on the lit ring, turning suddenly and facing me, her face flushed. 'Why do you want the Land-Rover? Where are you going?' And when I didn't answer, she said,

'You're going to Burra Firth. Well, isn't it? Isn't that where you're going?'

'Look,' I said. 'Just give me some money, whatever you can spare. You'll get compensation and I'll sign anything –'

'I don't care about the compensation.' She said it with a stamp of her foot, and then she turned quickly, fumbling for the cups and saucers. Her head was bowed and I knew that if I turned her face towards me I would find it wet with tears. I hesitated, thinking suddenly of Fiona, remembering how she would turn tears on and off. But this was different. This was a determined, self-reliant woman. The cups rattled on the tray and I took a step forward. Then my hands were on her shoulders, I don't know why. Sympathy? The desire for human contact in my loneliness, knowing she was lonely, too?

I felt her stiffen, heard her whisper, 'Why did it have to be you?' And then her body seemed to relax, leaning back against mine, as though giving up some sort of struggle. My hands slid down to the softness of her breasts and she put her head back, turning her face towards me, and I kissed her, feeling her lips tremble under mine. There was no passion in that first kiss, just a mutual longing for sympathy and understanding, and her face was wet with tears.

We stood like that for a long time, oblivious of everything. And we were relaxed. We were no longer fighting each other. We had surrendered to something stronger than ourselves, and standing there with my arms round her, the softness of her body, the pressure of her lips, I felt a strange surge of confidence, a feeling that I had found myself at last – that I knew where I was going now and had the strength to get there. It was a marvellous, quite ecstatic feeling, and not explainable in any way.

'The kettle,' she murmured, and pushed me away. The kettle was boiling its head off and we were suddenly both of us laughing for no apparent reason, except that we were happy.

She leaned forward and switched off the gas. She was smiling now, holding out her hand to me and leading me out of the kitchen. The bedroom looked straight out across the voe and I remember a pale line of light to the west reflected on the water.

Then we were together, and for a long time, it seemed, the world stood still and there was just the two of us, everything beyond that tiny room, beyond the absolute harmony of ourselves and our bodies, as though it had never been, all stress gone, an obliteration in ecstasy.

I had never had this sort of an experience before, the giving and taking without restraint. Love is not a word normally used by trawlermen, but at least I knew it when it happened. And afterwards, there was a lot to talk about, sitting smoking together over coffee in the kitchen.

She put up a parcel of food for me and by then it was full dawn with the cloud all gone and the greenish pink glow of the sun just beginning to limn the line of the hills on the far side of Clift Sound. We kissed and she clung to me a moment, murmuring something about being careful and not doing anything stupid. But she didn't try and stop me. She knew it was a thing I had to do. 'There are ordnance survey maps behind the seat,' she called to me as I drove off. I waved, and then I was up the track and over the hill, with time to wonder what the hell I thought I was doing when I could have stayed with her. But that, I knew, would have been anti-climax after what we had just experienced. At least I was doing something, not waiting around until Gorse arrived.

Up by Scalloway I turned on to the main road and kept going north along the shores of Asta and Tingwall lochs with the sky a brilliant green shading to duck's egg blue and the steep slopes of the hills standing back above the water as the sun's glow increased in the east. There were flecks of mackerel cloud ahead and soon all the great bowl of the dawn above the peat hills was aflame. By then I had put Gertrude out of my mind; my thoughts were now concentrated on the journey ahead and what I would find up there at Burra Firth.

The sun was bright in the mackerel sky and it was warm as I drove through the dale between the black peat hills of Mid and East Kome. Coffee and sandwiches by Loch of Voe, then more black-peat diggings to Dales Voe and up over Swinister to Sullom Voe, where a ship was offloading material at the jetty and the wartime camp had been adapted for the use of the contractors building the oil terminal for the Brent and Dunlin fields. I was able to fill up with petrol here, and in the hotel, now full of contractors' men, instead of tourists, a surveyor who had just arrived gave me a copy of one of the London papers. I hadn't had a chance to read a newspaper for several weeks, but the world didn't seem to have changed. I glanced at the headlines over my coffee and it was all gloom — strikes, disruption, shortages, and Britain as always on the verge of bankruptcy. It seemed incredible that union bosses and more of the media men didn't come to Shetland and see for themselves the brighter hopes for the future.

An hour later I was at Toft, a north wind driving down Yell Sound, the waters broken and streaked with white. Standing on the pier I couldn't help thinking what a target Shetland could become when half the lifeblood of industrial Britain was passing through these islands. On Mainland of Shetland the people were of fairly mixed race, infiltrated over the years by Scots and others, but when I crossed into Yell, and farther north to the last island of Unst, I would be among purer Viking stock, men closer to the Faroese, the Icelanders and the Norwegians than to Britain. And if Iceland became wholly Communist, or the Russians moved across the Pasvik River into Finnmark in the north of Norway, how would these men react? In this watery land, touched with the old glacial hand of the last Ice Age, England seemed very remote and London a whole world away.

Sitting in the Land-Rover, reading the paper while I waited for the ferry, I came across the headline: VILLIERS HITS BACK AS VFI SHARES TUMBLE. It was an account of the DTI Enquiry in London into the Star-Trion deal and Villiers was challenging his detractors to risk their own money on the West Shetland shelf – *The trouble with our country is that politicians and their bureaucratic masters are only interested in equality in poverty – in how a meagre cake can be shared more fairly – when they should be bending all their energies instead towards increasing the size of that cake by every means in their power. This is what I am doing, and shall go on doing – whatever the cost, whatever the risk. Call me a buccaneer if you like – that is a term of abuse thrown at me by Mr Swingler, my own Conservative member. All right, I am a buccaneer, and when times are hard, as they are now, Britain is the loser that there aren't more of us, but when North Star brings in another field – as I am confident it will – you won't call me a buccaneer then. You'll pay tribute to my sagacity, claim me as the shareholders' friend, while others will call me a capitalist and scream for nationalization of my company.*

The ferry was halfway across now, and I sat watching it crawl like a steel beetle across the foam-flecked waters of the Sound, seeing in my mind the man I had talked to on *North Star* at bay in that courtroom, angry and obstinate, fighting back with all that extraordinary vitality and energy of his. I turned to the City page. There had been a run on VFI shares, now standing at a new low and less than half the price they

173

had been when the market as a whole had bottomed after the Arab oil embargo. I was thinking of *North Star* then, of its loneliness out there in the march of the westerlies, and of its extreme vulnerability under the orders of a man near desperation and periodically under the control of a toolpusher whose luck appeared to have run out.

Tailor-made to our purpose.

The ferry berthed while I was thinking about that purpose, about who would gain. Not the workers. Nor industry. Certainly not Britain. The direction my thoughts were taking scared me and I drove on to the ferry feeling as though, in crossing the Sound, I was moving into another world, a step nearer the destiny to which all my life had been a preparation. It was not a nice feeling.

From Flukes Hole on the other side I took the lesser road that ran up the western coast of Yell. From Gutcher it is only just over a mile across Bluemull Sound to the island of Unst and then six miles on a good straight road to the main port of Baltasound, another two to Haroldswick. There, in a little house behind the harbour, up near the school, an old man who understood the use of words took me into a strange wild world of myth and legend. He had bright bird-like eyes, intensely blue in the dark wind-wrinkled face, large gnarled hands, and a voice so soft, so lyrical in speech, that to hear him talk was like listening to music. His name was Robert Bruce – 'That's no' a verra good name to have in the island of Unst.'

I thought he was referring to the early Scottish king, but no, he was harking back to a Laurence Bruce – 'the Great Foud of Zetland', he called him – a tyrannical land-grabber who, from his castle at Muness, had held all Unst in the thrall of Scottish law during the last days of the first Elizabeth when James was still only king of Scotland. It was a strange, haunting story, a Romeo and Juliet legend of the north, and at first I did not understand why he was telling it to me.

When I had arrived in Haroldswick I had gone to the Post Office, and because I had to explain my need of accommodation, I said I was an ornithologist. Birds were the main attraction for visitors and it would allow me to walk the hills around Burra Firth without exciting comment. The Bruces had just had a cancellation, so I had been sent to them. But Robert Bruce, a retired schoolmaster living with his sister, now occupied his time helping with the preservation and marking of seabirds on the western cliffs and I don't think it took that shrewd, beady-eyed little Scot long to realize I was no ornithologist. So instead of talking about birds, he told me the story of Edwin and Helga, and how, to escape the wrath of her people, whose leader had been murdered by one of Bruce's minions, she had rushed her lover to the family's little boat and sailed for Yell in a northerly gale, past the great cliffs of Vallafield, to be lost for ever in the roaring tide race off the entrance to Bluemull Sound.

It is too long a story to repeat, and I have forgotten much of it – and in any case the beauty of it was in the telling. But what I do remember is Bruce's guile and greed, his despicable ruthlessness, and the fierce, law-abiding determination of the islanders who had sailed an open boat three hundred miles to Scotland to lay their just complaints before the King in Edinburgh. 'And do you ken why the Scots were in Zetland?' Bruce asked me, his bright eyes fixed on me like the Ancient Mariner. 'Because the islands were handed over to them as a pledge for a Danish princess's dowry. The people were subject only to the Scots king, retaining their own laws and customs, but history is strewn with conditions of treaty unfulfilled and Bruce, as gauleiter for the Crown, violated them with a vengeance.' Looking at me very closely, he added, 'In this lonely island of Unst we are very vulnerable to big northern shifts of power.'

And then, as his sister took the blackened kettle from the hob and made the tea, he began telling me an older island story, of the Pictish inhabitants a thousand years ago who, when their brochs were destroyed and all their lands taken by Vikings from the fjords of Norway, had been forced to retreat into the great caverns of the south-west from which they emerged only at night. 'They were the trolls, you know, the little people of superstition – call them dwarfs, gnomes, fairies, it's all the same – you watch for them at night, mind your children don't get stolen and put out offerings to placate them. That's what the early Norse did and only Coul, the old priest man, captured from the Celts of the south, ever saw the caves in which they had found refuge, and he died just after they had let him go.' He told me the story then of Gletna Kirk, the church Coul tried to build and which they destroyed in the night, thinking it was to be another of the invaders' strongholds.

But by then my head was nodding. It had been a long day and I drank my tea and went to bed, to wake once, briefly, in the night and remember how the old man had harped on successive waves of Northern invaders.

In the morning, after breakfast, I went with him up the road to Burra Firth, about a mile and a half to where a track branched northward. 'You'll not be finding many birds up there, not unless you go right to The Noup and that's a good long tramp by Saxa Vord.' The blue eyes watched me curiously from under his peaked cap. 'Better you come with me up Milldale to Tonga. There's all the birds you could ever want there and I can show you Goturm's Hole.'

I thanked him and he nodded. 'Suit yerself.' He half-turned, then paused. 'Take the right fork in half a mile and it'll bring you to Buel Houll. There's a good view there of The Ness on t'other side of the Firth with Fiska Wick beyond and a fishing boat close inshore. You'll see in your map there's a track from just near Buel Houll that winds round Housl Fiel and straight back by the School.' And then he asked me, 'You've no glasses?'

'No.'

He slipped his own from off his shoulder. 'You'll need them I'm thinking to see what you want to see.' He nodded then and left me, walking with a steady, tireless stride, his body bowed a little into the west wind. I examined the glasses he had given me. They were Zeiss, small and very compact, but of extraordinary clarity and brilliant magnification. Birdwatchers' glasses, but he'd known when he handed them to me it wasn't birds I had come to watch. I went up the track, and before I had reached the fork, I could see the black hull of the fishing boat anchored off a sprawl of buildings on the far side.

I took the left fork, and where the track ended I turned north along the edge of the firth. It was very quiet, only the sound of the seabirds and the lap of the water on the rocks. Root Stacks was right below me and I lay in the grass watching the buildings opposite, across the narrow strip of water. White puffs of cloud sailed over the hills and it was warm, the breeze-block sprawl of the Root Stacks Hotel basking in the sunshine. Through the glasses I could see the sign quite clearly, a painted board on the stone-built front of what must have been part of the old original steading, and just below it, on a wooden bench, an old man sat dozing in the sun, his face strangely twisted. He had a stick beside him and there was a dog at his feet, a black and white collie curled up on the sheep-cropped grass.

It was all very peaceful and nothing stirred for a long time. Then, shortly after eleven, the dog uncurled itself and began to bark. A Land-Rover was coming down the track. The old man stirred and lifted his head, the disfiguring line of a great scar showing. The Land-Rover stopped and three men got out. One of them was Sandford. The old man shook hands with the other two and they all went into the house, including the dog, and after that the stillness and the quiet descended again.

I must have fallen asleep, for I woke suddenly to the sound of the dog barking. Five men were loading packages into the Land-Rover, the old man watching them, leaning on his stick. They piled into the Land-Rover, Sandford driving it up the track that disappeared behind The Ness to where my map showed the narrow gut of Fiska Wick. Ten minutes later the quiet was shattered by the sound of an outboard and an inflatable with four of them in it nosed out from under The Ness and headed for the fishing boat.

I watched them as they climbed on board, but it was impossible to tell whether they were Shetlanders or not, and though the sound of their voices reached me across the water, I couldn't hear what was said. The Land-Rover was back at the hotel now, not a soul in sight. The vessel's engine started up, figures on the foredeck and the clank of the chain coming in, and when the anchor was housed, she steamed down the firth, hugging the farther shore and disappearing westward through the gap between Herma Ness and Muckle Flugga. I lay back in the peat moss again, thinking of the rig and that damned fool Fuller exchanging the *Duchess* for one of Sandford's boats.

I lay there, scarcely moving, until late in the afternoon, when the clouds thickened and it began to drizzle, and by then I knew I was wasting my time. I had discovered nothing except that in the right weather Sandford used the firth as a base for his boats, and I got to my feet, climbing towards Housl Fiel and the track that led back to Bruce's cottage.

He came in a little after me, the tweed of his jacket glistening with moisture, his ruddy face flushed with exertion. 'I could have shown you a snowy owl,' he said, his bright eyes laughing at me. A snowy owl meant nothing to me and he knew it. 'You saw the purse-seiner leave, did you? I watched it from the top of Libbers Hill. It was steaming south-west to clear The Clapper and the islands north of Mainland.'

He talked about birds until we had finished our meal, and

then he began telling me the story of Goturm's Hole, how the son of the jarl of Stackhoull had been killed returning from a raid into Norway and the man who had killed him had had his boat wrecked on the rocks north-west of Unst. 'He climbed the cliffs to the hole named after him and there he would have been killed but for the young man's sister, who had some contact with Christianity and couldn't stomach vengeance for vengeance's sake. Goturm was a Dane and became a king of the Danes, and years later, when the Norse people in Unst had been overrun by yet another invasion from Norway, he repaid the debt he owed for his life, sending one of his captains with a great treasure to the girl who had saved him, now a woman and no longer living in the great hall at Stackhoull, but in a little cot on the Milldale burn. I may well have walked on the ruins of it this very day. A wild place, Captain Randall, this island of Unst – and nothing ever certain in an uncertain world.'

'Why are you telling me this?' I asked him.

'Bobbie loves telling the old legend stories,' his sister said.

'Aye.' He nodded, filling his pipe and watching me, his eyes full of curiosity. 'Y'see, I taught history as well as English and geography. A bit of natural history, too, of course. I love this land of ours, so rugged, bleak and beautiful. It fascinates me.'

'But you had a purpose,' I insisted. 'All your stories are of invasion and retribution – '

'Your name,' he said. 'And you salvaging the *Duchess*. We may be lonely island people, but we do get the *Shetland Times*.' I waited while he lit his pipe, staring at me over the flame. 'Now that's a strange coincidence. You and the *Duchess*. It was during the war and that same trawler putting in to the firth here in a westerly gale. The winter of 1942 it would be and I rowed out to her. A young naval lieutenant was in command and she was on her way back to Sullom Voe from the Norwegian coast. There was a Randall on board there, a man with his face all twisted and the scar of a gash that had bit deep into his skull. I heard he was some sort of an agent – a Russian agent, so the story went, but it was later I heard that.' There was a long pause and I thought I knew what was coming. But then he said, 'There's nobody here walks the cliffs of Tonga, Saito, Neap and Toolie, all the way out to Humlataes, as often as I do. Not much happens in the neighbourhood of Herma Ness that I don't know about. And often I catch a glimpse of those big trawlers that hang around our coast with more aerials and scanners than they have fishing gear. About two months ago it would be and I was up on Tonga with the sun shining brightly and a grey greasy-looking bank of fog hugging the sea. Sticking up out of it were the masts and antennae of one of those big trawlers, and coming in from the north the tip of a single mast, cleaving the fog like a submarine's telescope. It was a queer sight I can tell you, the two of them coming together and voices drifting up through the swirl and the shriek of the birds.'

'What's this got to do with the man you saw on the *Duchess* all those years ago?'

'Aye, it'd be thirty-two years now. But a man so disfigured –'

'He's come back, is that what you mean?' The man on that bench in the sunshine, old now and walking with a stick. My God! And the two of us separated only by that narrow strip of water. 'He's at the Root Stacks Hotel. That's it, isn't it?'

He nodded and his eyes gleamed with the certainty that here was another story. 'A week after I had seen that trawler rubbing shoulders with a fishing boat in the fog, I came down off Sothers Brecks to join the track at Fiska Wick and there he was.'

'Are you sure it was the same man?'

'No doubt at all,' Bruce said. 'Though his name is not Randall now. But a name doesn't matter, not with the mark of a terrible wound like that.' And he added, 'He was sitting there this morning. You must have seen him.'

I nodded, feeling it couldn't be true, but remembering the old man's face in the glasses, the twisted, broken features. About the right age, too, and Root Stacks run by Anna Sandford's son.

'Mouat, he calls himself now.'

His middle name, and mine, and I knew it must be true.

Bruce leaned towards me. 'That's a common enough name in Shetland. But Mouat isn't his real name. It's Randall.' His large hand gripped my knee. 'And your name is Randall, and whatever you may say, Captain, you're not here to look at the birds.'

'No.'

'Then what are you here for?'

I shook my head, not sure I had really known until this moment. 'I think that man may be my father,' I said. And after that I told him a little about myself, enough at any rate to satisfy his curiosity. 'Do you know if a man calling himself

Stevens is ever at the hotel?' But he shook his head, and when I gave him a description, he said he had never been to the hotel, had never seen any of them close to. 'Is he Irish?' he asked. 'I know there's an Irish lad works there. And others, they come and go, claiming they're birdwatchers, same as you, and a mixed lot they are by all accounts.'

'I'll be going up there this evening.'

He nodded. 'Ask Mouat where he was in 1942. It'll be the same man I'm sure.'

I left just after nine and he walked with me as far as the neck of land that separated Loch of Cliff from the Burra Firth. There was a lot of cloud and the light was fading. 'If a new invader were to come to our islands,' he said, 'this is as good a place as any. It's happened many times before – but so long ago nobody remembers, only old men like me who know the history of the islands.'

I looked at his weatherbeaten, gnome-like face, the bright blue eyes, a man so deep in the legends of his land, so close to the wildness of it, that for him the prospect of a new horde landing on the rocks was not beyond the bounds of credibility. 'There are more subtle ways –' I checked myself, conscious of the dark hills against the clouds and my thoughts running away with me. A light gleamed down the track beside Burra Firth, a door opening; then it was gone. 'Don't wait up for me,' I said.

I saw him hesitate, but then he nodded. 'The door will be on the latch.'

I left him and went down the track along the water's edge. The Root Stacks buildings were dark in the shadow of Mouslee Hill and, as I approached them, I was thinking back to that night on board the *Fisher Maid* with Shetland's hills black lumps against a cold green strip of sky. It was then that I had decided to come north to the islands, seeking some knowledge of my father that would help me to understand myself. Barely three months, yet it seemed an age, and now, here in the dark of Unst with my mind stuffed full of the ghosts of old legends, in the dark shadow of these buildings . . .

My pace faltered and for a moment I stood listening, unsure of myself and reluctant to face him. The dog was barking, and I walked quickly up to the door and knocked. I could hear voices, but it was some time before anybody came, the dog protesting from its kennel at the back until a shout silenced it. The door opened and a man stood there, short and squat in an island jersey. 'What is it? If it's a drink you're wanting—'

'Mr Mouat,' I said. 'I'd like a word with him.'

'Mouat, eh? Are you sure of the name now?'

'Quite sure.' I thought he was going to close the door in my face and I put my foot against it. 'Better call Sandford,' I said.

He hesitated, looking at me curiously. Finally he turned and called out, 'Ian. There's a man here asking for Mr Mouat.' The lamp-glow in the stone-flagged hallway brightened as a door was flung wide and Sandford appeared, his shirt open at the neck and a drink in his hand.

'The skipper of the *Duchess,* eh?' He was smiling. 'All right, Paddy. He can come in.' He waved his glass in invitation. 'I wondered how long it would be before you called on us.'

'You knew I was here.'

'Oh, sure. Word of a stranger gets around pretty fast in a place like this. Come on in and have a drink. You're out of a job, I hear.' The same harsh, breezy manner, but there was something in the eyes, an uneasiness, and the cheerful smile seemed somehow forced. 'Come on. You don't hold it against me that I've got the *North Star* contract now, do you?'

I stepped into the narrow hallway full of stuffed seabirds in glass cases. 'The old man's gone to bed,' he said, leading me through into the lamplit room where a quiet bearded man sat at a table littered with glasses and the remains of a meal. 'Whisky?' Sandford picked up a bottle and poured me a drink without waiting for an answer. 'We're short of a skipper. Interested?' There was a peat fire burning in the grate, and it was warm, his round smooth face shining with perspiration as he handed me the drink, small eyes watchful, waiting for some reaction.

'You offering me a job?' I asked. The whisky was colourless, a home brew from some local still.

'Could be. It depends.'

'On what?'

'How badly you need it.'

'I didn't come here for a job,' I said. 'And I didn't come to see you. I came to see the man who calls himself Mouat.'

His eyes flickered towards the farther door, the uneasiness there again, and his face changing, a hardening of the mouth. 'I told you, he's gone to bed.'

I moved to the farther door then, something he hadn't expected, and before he could stop me I had thrown it open.

The old man was sitting there, in a wing chair, a lamp beside

181

him and a book open on his lap. The gashed side of his head was in shadow, so that all I saw was the smooth transparent skin of an older version of the face that stared at me every time I shaved. The likeness vanished when he turned his head, but the shock of that moment of recognition was so great that I didn't resist the grip of hands seizing hold of me.

'Let him be, Ian.' His voice was very quiet, his eyes glinting in the lamplight, a searching stare. 'He knows who I am. I can see it written all over his face.' They let me go then and I stood there, feeling numb as he went on, 'It's something of a shock, isn't it – at your age to find your father isn't safely dead and buried?'

Was there a note of bitterness there, of regret? 'Who put that plaque in Grund Sound Church?' I asked, my voice so choked it was almost a whisper.

He contrived a smile that was more of a grimace. 'I did. Or rather I arranged for it to be placed there.' The twist of his mouth gave a curious lisp to his words. 'Leave us alone now, Ian. We have much to talk about – and things must be said that I'd rather you didn't hear.'

But Sandford stood there, frowning angrily and unwilling to leave us. He didn't trust me and the old man laughed. 'The two of you, here together with me for the first time. We should kill the fatted calf.' That ghastly smile and the blue eyes gleaming wickedly up at me in the lamplight. 'You met Anna, I believe – Anna Sandford in Hamnavoe.' His eyes slid away from me, still with that terrible smile twisting his face, and I turned and stared at Ian Sandford, knowing now what it was he had meant with that reference to the prodigal returned. Christ Almighty! Two sides of the same coin, and I was looking at the other half, wondering how much of the same blood each of us had, whether hidden behind the smooth roundness of my half-brother's face was the same devil of self-doubt.

CHAPTER TWO

I was alone with my father in that room for about an hour. It was a difficult, very disturbing interview, for the twisted features, that terrible gash left by the shell splinter that had ploughed the side of his skull, shocked me deeply. It had marked all the left cheek, split the ear and cut deep into the side of his head, and the wired up remains of his jaw gave a lisp to his speech. Yet he wasn't a man you could pity. He was too withdrawn, too self-contained. And old though he was, he still had some of the fire that had driven him to fight for a cause he admitted he knew was lost before ever he had embarked for Spain.

'That plaque?' I asked him.

'What about it?'

'Making out that you were dead when you weren't. What was the point?'

'You have your mother's tidy mind,' he said harshly. 'How is she, by the way?'

'She died two years ago.'

He didn't say he was sorry, just shrugged as though accepting the inevitability of death. 'But there's something of me in you, too, isn't there?' He smiled, grimacing. 'You see, I've checked up on you.'

'Why?'

'Why not? You're my son, aren't you? As soon as Ian told me . . .' He hesitated. 'I've been expecting you, knowing you were bound to come.' He leaned a little forward. 'What brought you to Shetland seeking out my past? It wasn't affection or filial regard. It was something else. Something you'd been told?'

'No.'

'What then?'

I tried to explain, but it wasn't easy with him sitting there smiling crookedly. He was remote, a stranger, and I sensed an underlying hostility as I told him of the doubts that had gradually ended my early admiration for him.

'So I was a hero to you, eh?'

'At first.'

'And you left your mother, turned your back on the capitalist wealth of her new husband and set out on your wanderings.'

'I wanted to live my own life.'

'We all want that – when we're young. Later it becomes more difficult.' I thought he sighed. 'And for you more than most. You were pulled two ways. That's your nature, Michael. You don't mind me calling you Michael?'

'Most people call me Mike.'

'Your friends and those you work with perhaps. Have you any friends?'

I stared at him angrily, thinking he probably had a liking for getting under people's skin, the bitterness of a man forced into loneliness.

'You're a solitary, is that it?' He nodded, and again that crooked smile. 'I think I know you now. A wanderer. A boy who has never grown up to be a man. Isn't that right? Every time you come up against the rawness of the world we have to live in you run away from it, seeking escape in drugs or . . .'

'That was only a phase,' I said quickly, annoyed that I felt the need to justify myself.

'. . . or some eastern religion.' I had never told anybody about that, only Fiona. 'Buddhism, wasn't it? Then playing with Communism, and running away to sea.'

'You went to sea yourself.' I was angry now, and that annoyed me even more, for I knew he was goading me. And the knowledge that Fiona must have been here, before she had gone to see Gertrude presumably . . . 'What are you after?' I demanded. 'Prying into my private life, asking questions of my wife.'

'Just trying to understand you. When you've never met your son before —'

'You've a reason,' I cut in hotly.

'Perhaps. But it's natural, isn't it?'

And so it went on, a verbal duel between us, each trying to learn something about the other. But he was more adept at it, side-stepping direct questions and shrewdly needling me until there wasn't much he didn't know. Only once was I able to probe a little beyond the ruined mask of his features. He had introduced Gertrude into the conversation, not very nicely since he had implied that the only thing I had ever done that showed any promise of success was going into partnership with a woman. 'Maybe that's the only way you can demonstrate your manhood.'

'What do you mean by that?'

'You wouldn't have gone into partnership with Ian, for instance, would you?'

'No.'

'Or any other man.'

'I never had the opportunity.'

'Feel safer with a woman, eh? Think a woman's easier to handle. Or are you in love with her?'

'What would you know about love?'

He was silent then and I remembered the strange letter he had written Anna Sandford. 'Like you, I never had the opportunity – not after this.' It was just a flat statement, no bitterness, his hand touching the scars. But he kept clear of Gertrude after that, switching to the *North Star* contract, and to Villiers. 'You're a loner, that's your trouble. Now Ian's got the contract, and deserves it. He gets around, that boy, lots of friends, and he's a Shetlander. Oil companies, men like Villiers, they don't think about the islanders or their livelihood, just as they never thought about the Arabs until it was too late. You've met Villiers, haven't you?'

'Yes.'

'Admire him?'

'Somebody else asked me that – a man called Stevens.'

'Well, I'm asking you now.' The name didn't seem to have registered. 'When a man changes his mind about the social structure he wants, he often leans so far over in the opposite direction –'

'I haven't changed my mind,' I told him. 'If anything has changed, it's the society in which we live. Militants are less concerned with justice. They want anarchy now.'

'Do they?'

'You know they do.'

'I know nothing of the sort. I think it's you who have changed.'

'I'm not an anarchist,' I said. 'I never have been.'

'So now you're against all progress towards a fairer, more equitable world.'

I laughed. 'You don't believe that any more than I do. The world's never been fair, never will be. Men are not born equal. And if you don't recognize that, then all I can say is that it's you that has never grown up. You're still a Communist, I take it?'

He hesitated. 'Yes.'

'A Russian-style Communist?'

'If you like.'

'You came here from Russia during the war.'

'From Norway.'

'In 1942. On board the *Duchess*.' And I added, hoping to get something positive out of him. 'You were an agent up in the north of Norway. A foreign agent?' I saw his eyes narrow. 'Whose side were you on – Russia's or ours?'

'Britain and Russia were allies.'

'And that salves your conscience. But now? What side are you on now?'

He sighed. 'Does there have to be sides? Nobody is at war. Not here.'

'No, not in the old sense of the word,' I said. 'But a new style of warfare – economic war.'

'Ah, yes, the London School of Economics. Just because your head has been stuffed with economic fallacies, you don't have to turn your coat at the first whiff of the real thing. And even if the world is temporarily short of energy, it doesn't mean that men like Villiers should gamble lives and risk the future of the Shetland fishery to keep themselves and their City friends afloat. Villiers, in particular. He's stripped others' assets so often, it would only be poetic justice if his own assets were stripped for a change. You surely don't support men like that?'

'Of course I don't.'

'Then what are you doing, coming up here, trying to resolve your doubts by digging up your father's past, and then salvaging a trawler and pretending you're a capitalist?'

'Only this,' I said. 'I think it's time we started picking up the pieces, instead of trying to destroy everything – before it's too late.' And I added, 'You ask my reasons, but what the hell are you doing here?'

'You forget, I'm a Shetlander. I belong here.'

But that was not the answer. 'Stevens,' I said. 'A man calling himself Stevens.' Not a muscle of his face moved, no sign of recognition, not even when I described the man to him, the hard mouth, the slight squint. But when I repeated what he had said about rehabilitation and not many surviving, I thought he winced, a muscle on the right of his jaw tightening. 'Were you returned to Russia, after the war?'

He laughed, a conscious effort. 'What are you, a Nationalist now? An Empire Loyalist? Patriotism in place of Communism that you speak of Russia as though it were a hostile power?'

'I was never a Communist,' I said. 'In theory, yes. But not a Party member.'

'And now? What are you now?' He was suddenly leaning forward, his eyes fixed on my face. And when I said that perhaps that was what I had come to Shetland to find out, he smiled. 'Seeking the answer in me, eh? In my life.' He let his body fall back, the wings of the high chair framing his face. 'Well, now you've found me and I have no answer for you.' He sounded tired then, as though talking to me had proved too exhausting. Or was it the memory of the long years that were a locked secret in his mind? 'You mentioned a need for picking up the pieces. I could help you there.'

'How?'

'I have some influence with Ian. Otherwise I wouldn't be living here in his hotel. You and he have this in common, you both want to be owners. You know he's got three of the larger fishing boats working for him now. Two will share the stand-by job on *North Star*, the other, which he has just arranged to charter, will ferry stores out to one of the rigs on the Dunlin field.'

'And that doesn't worry you, that he's working for Villiers and the oil companies?'

A slight movement of the shoulders, almost a shrug. 'He wants to make money. Why not? He's only doing what every-body else is doing.'

It was on the tip of my tongue to ask if he knew *North Star* had had two of its anchor cables cut by an explosive device, but I checked myself. 'Where's he find the capital?'

'Borrows it.'

'From you? Are you providing him with funds?'

'I never had any capital. I don't believe in it.'

'How long have you been here?' His mouth was a tight line and he didn't reply. 'Was it a fishing vessel put you ashore about two months ago?'

'You ask too many questions,' he said, and I knew by the set look on his face that he would never disclose where he had come from or what he had been doing all these years. 'It's your own position you have to consider, not mine. I'm told you're out of a job. And on the run. Is that right?' Suddenly his manner, the atmosphere between us, had subtly changed. 'Ian had a call yesterday to say the police were making enquiries about you in Lerwick.'

'Why should anybody telephone to tell him that?' My throat felt dry, the net closing again and my liberty threatened.

'The boy's in local politics and his friends keep him in-formed.' He paused, and then he offered me the way out: 'He needs a skipper for his new boat. He'd give you the job if I told him to. And on a supply run to the Dunlin field you'd be clear of the police.' He left it hanging in the air and reached for his stick. 'No need to make up your mind immediately. Sleep on it.' He got to his feet. 'I'm going to bed.' He smiled, and now that I could see the other side of his face more clearly the smile sent cold shivers down my spine. 'Be nice for an old man to have both his sons with him for a while.'

'And if I don't take the job?'

He looked at me, the smile gone and the blue eyes hard. 'You will.' He said it emphatically. 'You've no alternative. And nor have I in view of some of the questions you've been asking. You can't keep your mouth shut and if the police got hold of you . . . I can't risk that.' He was frowning, the scars showing in the glow of the peat fire. 'And then there's that girl of yours,' he added. 'I don't know what you've told her about me, but if she were to learn that you had found me, still alive and here at Burra Firth . . .' He moved slowly to the door. 'Think about it, my boy. You're committed now. You're one of us.' He was at the door then and he smiled at me. 'Just remember that.' And he nodded, 'Good night.'

I couldn't help it. I suddenly blurted out, 'So you're the organizer, are you? They sent you here to organize the—'

'Organizer of what?'

'The oil—' My voice faltered before his steady gaze. 'Oh, I don't know,' I said. 'I just thought—'

'You should have learned by now to keep your thoughts to yourself.' And he turned and went out, leaving the door open behind him. I don't know whether he meant it as a warning or whether he was simply giving me the benefit of his own experience. I heard the sound of his voice, then the tap of his stick, the slow tread of his feet on the stairs, and I went out into the other room to find Ian Sandford waiting for me. The others had gone and he was alone. 'Well, now you've talked to him, do you want the job?' He was smiling, a gleam of humour. 'He says you can have it if you like.'

'You do what he tells you, do you?'

He laughed. 'Sometimes.'

'Why didn't you offer me a job that day you took me down to see the *Duchess*?'

'Didn't know anything about you, did I? Besides, I'm just the old man's bastard. Makes a difference, doesn't it?'

'I didn't know,' I said.

'Well, now you do.' He turned and reached for the bottle on the table. 'Like another drink before you go?'

'No thanks.'

But he poured it all the same, handing me the glass and topping up his own. 'Here's to our better acquaintance.' He was grinning.

I raised my glass perfunctorily, the whisky raw in my throat and my mind on the future. 'He said you needed a skipper to run supplies to a rig on the Dunlin.'

He nodded. '*Deepwater IV*. That's right. You'd be skippering the *Mary Jane*. That's the boat I've taken on charter. The usual diesel job, about 65 feet long, registered tonnage 45.' He finished his drink. 'The old man said you'd like to sleep on it.'

'Why offer the job to me?' I asked.

He shrugged. 'Why not? You're my half-brother.' He was grinning again. 'There's always fiddles running supplies for big contractors whose only concern is speed, so keep it in the family, that's what I say. Makes sense, doesn't it?'

'Maybe,' I muttered, and I put my glass down. 'I'll be going now.'

He nodded, seeing me to the door, the lamp in his hand, and the likeness to his mother very pronounced. 'I'll see you in the morning,' he said. The door closed and I was alone in that strange twilit world that was neither day nor night with the glimmer of water lapping the rocks below me. The moon was just rising, ragged patches of cloud drifting across it and a glimpse of stars.

I walked slowly back up the track, going over in my mind that strange meeting and feeling trapped – trapped by the sort of person I was, and by the system which didn't allow me to escape from my own past, the things I had done before I turned to the sea. If only they would leave me alone. But I knew they wouldn't. And now my own father, the man whose past I had come north to seek – for support, for strength – and he was there in that straggle of buildings, a part of the net that had closed around me. What had he been doing all those years?

He hadn't said, of course. He had evaded all my questions. But instinctively I knew, some deep communication between us – that plaque, that quote from Browning, it still applied – a man deeply unhappy, alone and embattled within himself. It wasn't just the face, the terrible twisted features. I had seen it in his eyes. He, too, was unable to escape the things he had thought and done as a young man. I felt weighed down, utterly crushed by this glimpse of an older, distorted reflection of myself. My God! Was this the road he had trod, drifting along the line of least resistance? And myself doing the same, knowing what my answer would be.

I had known it ever since he had offered me the job. I couldn't face another court, the police, prison, and my own world against me – anything was better than that. Even working with that little bastard Sandford. I laughed at that, laughed so loud I frightened a seabird from the verges of Loch of Cliff, the shadow of it taking wing against the clouds. If only I were a bird and could take wing! But I was grounded and the earth hard and hostile, his face grinning in the lamplight.

I reached the cottage at last and went to bed, alone and my mind in a turmoil of self-hate, as it had so often been. I couldn't sleep and the moon came clear, its shadows moving slowly across the tiny room with its sloping ceiling close under the eaves.

Two days later I took over the *Mary Jane* in Balta Sound. She was a typical island fishing boat, her wooden hull painted black, two tallish masts and a neat little white wooden wheelhouse. The crew were all Shetlanders and she stank of fish. We hosed her out and scrubbed her down, but in the three and a half months I operated her for the Sandford Supply Coy we never entirely got rid of the smell and I suspect that everything we carried out to *Deepwater IV*, particularly the meat, became tainted in the course of the passage.

In all that time I had no word from Gertrude. Ian had delivered the Land-Rover back to her, and when she had read my letter, she had just taken the keys and slammed the door in his face. I hadn't expected her to understand. How could she when I didn't understand myself? All the labour of getting that trawler back into service, the problems and difficulties we had faced together, the shared experience of that one night, all thrown away. I had asked her to phone me, but I knew she wouldn't. It was finished – an episode. The reality was here, on this scruffy boat, with a bunch of men who, among themselves, talked a language that was almost foreign, even Jamie, the mate, who came from Yell.

At first we loaded at Toft on the Mainland side of Yell Sound. Later, when Ian learned that the police were satisfied I had shipped out in some trawler, we loaded direct at Lerwick to save the cost of the truck journey north. He was careful with his money, the only new piece of equipment on the boat a ship-to-shore radio. And he had a signwriter paint the name of his company on each side of the wheelhouse. He was inordinately proud of the fact that he was chairman and managing director of The Sandford Supply Coy Ltd.

It was a fairly good summer for weather, and with not even a gale to relieve the monotony I seemed to live in a sort of vacuum, unconscious of the world outside. Once, when we were in Lerwick, I took a taxi out to The Taing, but the house was locked, the voe empty, so presumably it was true what Jamie had heard, that the *Duchess* had gone back to her old trade of fishing, and Gertrude with her.

We listened to the radio a lot, and sometimes I heard the news, but it didn't seem real – little but gloom and violence, and North Sea oil the only ray of hope. They seemed to think the drillers could magic the stuff ashore and in the Utopia that would follow, inflation and unrest would disappear in a cloud of fairy smoke.

At the end of August, I think it was, Ian came on the R/T to tell me *North Star* had drilled another dry hole. And the very next day, on our way into Lerwick, I heard on the radio that half the board of VFI had resigned. A fortnight later the results of the DTI enquiry came right at the beginning of the news bulletin; the Company's licence to operate as a bank under Section 123 revoked and the report such a damning indictment that I wondered where Villiers would find the money to go on drilling, his VFI shares almost worthless now and his financial reputation equally low.

And then *Deepwater IV* reached her planned depth in a dry hole and we stayed with her on stand-by for the three days it took them to clear the seabed and move to the nearby Cormorant field. She was on summer contract only up here in northern waters, for she was one of the new generation of drilling ships that maintain station over the drill site with variable direction screws linked to a computer beamed on the seabed. No cumbersome equipment like *North Star,* no anchors, no cables and winches. It was impressive to see the economy of time as she moved from Dunlin to Cormorant, the divers down in their bell the instant she was locked on to the seabed sonar and no supply ships risking men's lives and costing money to anchor her.

As soon as she was spudded in we were relieved by a large trawler. The Deepwater contractors were operating for a different consortium now and a spanking new supply ship, straight from a Norwegian yard, began ferrying sealed containers of food with the drill pipe and other equipment. We were out of a job and Ian ordered us back to Balta Sound.

During the whole of this period I had only seen him twice. On each occasion he had been in Lerwick for a meeting of the Zetland Council and he had had little time to spare for us, coming on board for a quick look around and then leaving in a hurry as soon as I produced my list of requirements. But at Balta Sound he sat down in the wheelhouse and went through my whole list, agreeing almost everything. 'Have you had a win on the pools or what?' I asked him. 'I've been badgering you for new warps, new anchor chain–'

'Think I didn't look the boat over before I chartered her?' My sarcasm seemed to have caught him on the raw, for his voice was tense as he went on, 'You've never worked an island fishing boat before. Distant water, that's all you've known, and a wealthy company to foot the bills.' He leaned towards me, speaking very loudly the way some people speak to a foreigner. 'I grew up in the post-war years when every penny counted and everything was scarce. If you wanted something, then you looked around until you found it, or made do with something else, even though it was rusty as hell or half-rotted through with damp. That's the world I grew up in, and that's why I don't throw my money around.' And then with something near to a sneer he added, 'But I don't expect you to understand that. Your world was very different. You never had to scrimp and save, not in the home you grew up in.'

'Not then,' I said. 'But I've made up for it since.'

He grinned and that made me like him a little better. 'Well, nobody gets it good all the time, not even men like Villiers. They say he's bust if *North Star* doesn't hit it with the next hole.'

'Then you'll have two boats out of a job.'

'Oh, not me. I got other jobs lined up for them. And there's always the fishing to fall back on.' He got to his feet. 'Let's have a word with Harry Priest now.'

'He says he needs at least a week to do a complete overhaul on that clapped-out old engine of ours.'

'Well, he can have it – a week, but that's all.'

'What about spares? Or is that the owner's responsibility?'

'No, it's mine now,' he said. 'The boat's no longer under charter. I've bought her. 'There was pride in the way he said it, an air of cockiness, and I laughed, seeing him in his own imagination already halfway to rivalling the big Greek ship-owners.

'Who's paying for it?' I asked. 'Your father?'

'The old man?' He shook his head. 'Borrow from the masses, that's what he says. Banks, insurance companies, pension funds. Or from the oil companies. Never risk your own capital. He's a shrewd old devil. But just not interested, not for himself, anyway.'

'Is it that easy to borrow money now?' I was thinking of all the problems we had had with the *Duchess*.

He grinned at me. 'It is so long as the boats earn more than my backer charges in interest.'

I asked him if his backer was a local man, but he shook his head. 'A property dealer from the south who likes playing around with boats.' There was a note of envy in his voice. 'It's just a leisure occupation, like birdwatching is to some of the visitors I used to have. Goes out periodically and tries new ways of fishing whenever he's up in Shetland on business. Owns some land on Sullom Voe, and with all the oil companies negotiating for terminal facilities – well, it helps my being on the Council.'

'Is that how you met him, through your work on the Council?'

'No, it was the old man. He put me in touch with him.' But when I asked his name, he closed up on me and got to his feet. 'None of your business,' he said sharply as though afraid I was about to steal the source of his capital. He poked his head out of the wheelhouse door, calling for Harry Priest.

He was about two hours on board and when I saw him over the side – we were anchored off at the time – he said, 'See Harry keeps at it. A week, that's all you've got. Then you'll relieve *Island Girl.*' I stared at him and he nodded. 'That's right. On stand-by to *North Star.* I've had to send the other boat down to Lerwick for repairs. Damaged herself alongside one of the supply ships and sprang a leak.' He jumped down into the row boat. 'See you in a few days' time.'

That night I lay in my bunk listening to the lap of the water against the wooden sides, conscious of the quiet on board, with all the crew, except Priest, gone to their homes, and wondering who wanted me back with *North Star,* and why. An accident, Ian had said. The *Island Girl*'s relief boat damaged. And he had bought the *Mary Jane.* On the old man's advice? Was Ian Sandford just an unwitting pawn in a game he didn't understand, or was it all in my imagination, the feeling that I was cast in the role of scapegoat?

In the week that followed, as Priest overhauled his engine and new gear came aboard, I thought a lot about that half-brother of mine and the strange father we shared. I could have taken time off and gone to see him at Burra Firth, but I didn't. Somehow I couldn't face him again, that twisted face. The fact is I was scared of him.

We sailed on 3rd October and Ian came down to see us off with two bottles of Scotch and instructions that all R/T communications were to be handled by Jamie.

'Does Fuller know who's skippering this boat?' I asked him.

'No. And if he did he wouldn't care. He's got other things to worry about, with men leaving and difficulty with mud and other supplies. Everything is in short supply and Star-Trion has to compete with companies that carry a lot more weight.' He shrugged when I asked him why men were leaving. 'They say the rig's bad luck and the man driving them a Jonah.'

'Ed Wiseberg, you mean?'

'That's right. And Villiers's name stinks.'

'You realize my name is on the ship's papers,' I said.

He laughed. 'Nobody's going to look at them. Not with the heat on and those that have agreed to stick it out on *North Star* hell-bent to grab the bonuses they've been promised.'

It was getting late in the season, too late, I thought, for an old rig anchored in those waters. *North Star* was farther north and a lot farther west than *Transocean III* when she went down. 'They must pull out soon.'

But he shook his head. 'Not till they've drilled hole No. 3. There's even talk that they'll stay out there all winter if necessary.' He finished his whisky and pushed open the door of the wheelhouse. 'Anyway, not your worry, and not mine.' He held out his hand to me, something he had never done before. 'Have a good trip and stay off the R/T. It gives them confidence if they hear only Shetland voices.'

It was a dull grey morning with a light rain falling as we headed out round The Nev, turning north to take the tide round the top of Unst. The glass was falling, the forecast bad, and by nightfall we were bucking a heavy sea. It was dawn before we sighted *North Star*, the rig slowly coming up over the horizon and the waves breaking in a white smother of foam against the columns of her 'legs'. Long before we had reached the eastward anchor buoys, *Island Girl* met us, the skipper wishing us joy of it over the loudhailer as he steamed past. I left Jamie to talk to him, keeping out of sight until he was well past us, headed for Scalloway with the wind behind him.

We had an uncomfortable week of it, doing the round of the buoys, rolling our guts out and lying hove-to head-to-wind as a series of small fronts passed through. *Rattler* did not come out once during the whole week. The sea was too rough for her to lie stern-on to the rig, and anyway they were fishing for a broken bit. We heard about it over the radio, van Dam trying to explain the hold-up to Fuller. And then, late on the Monday morning, when they had started drilling again, I picked up Villiers's voice, clear and very controlled, wanting to know how long before they reached depth, and van Dam answering, 'Two weeks maybe if ve don't 'ave no more trouble.' Information like that, given over an open line to London, indicated the urgency of Villiers's situation.

Nobody had any time now for lifting and re-laying the windward anchors. I had Jamie check with the barge engineer on duty. It hadn't been done since they had spudded in on the new location, and when I did manage to get a proper fix, I found they were well to the west of the first drill position.

The water was deeper, the risk greater. And the summer gone now. They were into the period of deepening depressions and stronger winds. No time for a small supply ship like *Rattler* to be fooling around with anchors. And it would probably mean hanging off the drilling string in case *North Star* dragged. A man as desperate as Villiers must be to go on drilling into the start of winter would hardly tolerate such an apparently unnecessary delay.

The wind turned northerly at the end of the week, and when *Island Girl* relieved us on the Saturday morning the sky was clear and cold with cross-seas breaking on the westerly swell. She came close alongside and the skipper shouted across to Jamie, 'Ye're to proceed to Rispond in north-west Scotland to pick up some equipment. Ian Sandford's orders. There'll be a lorry on the jetty there at 19.00 hours tomorrow evening. Three cases. And you're to deliver them back to Burra Firth. Okay?'

Jamie nodded and swung the helm, turning away to the south. Fortunately we had Chart 1954 on board and Jamie knew the place – 'A wee gut they used to call the Port o' the

195

North. Ah knew a man once who could remember the time when they sailed open boats oot of Rispond round John o' Groats and all down the east coast to Great Yarmouth for the fishing. Aye, they wore like Vikings, hard boggers, all of them.'

Rispond was a tiny inlet on the north-western point of Loch Eriboll, completely sheltered from the north and east. The distance was about 150 miles. I had the engineer check our fuel. There was plenty to get us there, but not enough to get us back to Burra Firth. 'We'll be able to take on diesel at Kinlochbervie,' Priest said. They all seemed to know the area.

Running south that evening, the crew grumbling about how they could have been coming into Scalloway with the prospect of four days ashore, I wondered why Ian was sending one of his boats all the way to Scotland to pick up a few cases when it would have been so much cheaper to ship them up in the steamer from Aberdeen. And why such a tiny, unfrequented little gut? 'You go in on the top of the tide,' Jamie had said. 'You've got to. An' if ye can't load the cases fast, then ye're stuck there for twelve hours dried out alongside a bit of a stone jetty.'

I didn't like it. Kinlochbervie would have made more sense, unless there was something about those cases and secrecy of prime importance. But at least we were running, with the cold north wind up the old girl's skirts, and we made fast time of it, arriving at the entrance to Loch Eriboll shortly after 15.00. The wind had backed westerly and we lay hove-to under the lee waiting for the tide to make. The sky had already clouded over, and as the daylight began to fade, mists came down thick over the flanks of Creag na Faoilinn to form a black mass at the bottom of the loch.

Shortly before seven o'clock we began closing the entrance to the little bolthole, nosing very slowly into the gut till we could see the small stone jetty and a trade van waiting. At least Ian had got his timing right, the tide now almost at the full, but even at high water it was still only a gut. The rocks closed in on either side as we crept forward watching the echo-sounder. And then we were through the rocks and there was a house, a nice house standing white beyond the jetty, with a gravel drive and a bit of a lawn right beside the water.

A man got out of the van as our bows touched the stone-work. He took our warps and told us to hurry. He sounded nervous. 'There's the cases.' He had the doors open before we had made fast, and when we had got the cases aboard he made me sign for them and then he was into his van and away.

'A mick,' Jamie said and spat.

I looked at the cases. All three of them had HANDLE WITH CARE stencilled in black across the top and MARINE ELECTRONICS on the side. 'Better get them below.' They weren't heavy enough to contain explosives, but all the same I wanted them out of sight. Time enough to consider what was in them when we were out of the gut. I let Jamie handle her and he worked her on a springer round the end of the jetty until our bows were facing outwards, and then we steamed out on a stern bearing, the break of our wash against the rocks unpleasantly loud.

We lay the night under An t' Aigeach and in a cold green cloudless dawn we hugged the coast round Cape Wrath, taking advantage of the constant west-going stream, and carried a fair tide southward to Loch Inchard. Coming into Kinlochbervie, Sutherland looking a wild land with the great humps of Arkle and Ben Stack looming over the end of the loch, I was very conscious that I was in mainland Britain now, not in the remotest islands of the north. It was the first time in over four months and I felt suddenly uneasy as the little port opened up to the north and we turned in to drop our hook astern of two Scottish trawlers. There were others moored along the quay, a line of buildings, and more activity than I had expected.

I sent Jamie ashore to see about re-fuelling and he came back with the information that the two trawlers anchored ahead of us were waiting to re-fuel and more expected that evening. 'Ah told him we'd only be alongside a few minutes, just for water and fuel, and he agreed to squeeze us in if those two boggers don't take all afternoon.'

We had a meal and hung around waiting until shortly after five when the second of the two trawlers pulled away from the quay and we were signalled in. We had barely got the fuel line aboard when a brand new trawler with flared bows steamed in, a sister ship close behind her. They had fish to land and they lay close off the quay, their engines throbbing gently in the evening stillness.

By six we were anchored off again. There was a Mission for Deep Sea Fishermen on the quay and I sent the crew ashore in the boat. They needed a break, and I wanted to be alone.

197

As soon as they had gone, I went down into the hold. It was dark down there, the fish smell lingering, and in the beam of my torch the three cases looked strangely menacing, alone there in the dark hollow of that empty space. I stood staring at them for a long time, wondering what the hell they contained, where they had come from?

There was only one way to find out, and I got a hammer and cold chisel and went to work. They were nail-fastened and no possibility of breaking into them without it showing. But by then I didn't care. I had to see what was inside.

The result was puzzling. The first case contained what appeared to be some sort of radio equipment, a grey metal box with tuning dials, and an electrical lead neatly coiled, the whole thing carefully packed in a moulded plastic container. The second contained a completely sealed torpedo-shaped object. There was a large towing eye at one end. It was swivelled and had an electrical socket in the centre of the eye. The case also contained a heavy reel of plastic-coated wire, one end of it fitted with a watertight plug.

I stood there for a long time staring down at those two pieces of equipment. In the light of my torch, against the rough boards stained black with fish oil, they had a deadly, futuristic gleam. Or was that my imagination again? Explanations leapt to mind. I knew nothing about electronics, but the torpedo was obviously for towing behind a vessel, and the other for sending or receiving some sort of signal. It could be some advanced scientific way of locating a shoal of fish, in which case Marine Electronics was a fair description. I was remembering what Ian had said about his backer trying new ways of fishing, remembering too what had happened out there by *North Star* in June. It was four months ago now, but the memory was still vivid. This sort of equipment could equally be for locating something on the seabed – an anchor, for instance, or a well-head after the rig had left the site, or broken adrift.

In the end I packed them back in their cases and nailed the boxes down again. I did it as neatly as I could, but the marks of the chisel were there for anyone to see, and the wood was split in places. I didn't bother about the third case, and when I went up on deck, glad to be in the fresh air again, I was sweating. Several more trawlers had come in. I lit my pipe and sat on the bulwarks, staring across at the lights on the quay, thinking about *North Star* out there to the west of

Shetland. A trawler was pulling away from the quay, another nosing into the vacant berth, but my mind was so engrossed in considering whether the equipment we carried in our hold was connected in any way with the future of the rig that it was some time before the shape of that trawler registered as familiar. And then suddenly I was on my feet, staring across the water at her as she moored alongside the quay.

She was against the lights, in silhouette, her hull black as the water that separated us. But when you have worked on the hull of a ship, when you know every inch of her, you cannot mistake her lines. No doubt at all – it was the *Duchess* lying there against the quay. And my boat ashore, no means of getting to her.

I forgot about Marine Electronics after that. I was thinking of Gertrude, of what I would say to her when we met. Would she slam the door in my face? And if she didn't, what then? All the explanations, the fight to try and clear myself. Nothing else would do. I knew that. And suddenly I realized she was the crossroads in my life. She was the focal point of all my doubts, the centre around which I could rebuild my life – if I had the guts.

The boat came back about ten o'clock. By then the *Duchess* was anchored off and I had drunk a lot of whisky. I decided to leave it till morning. In the morning I would be sober enough and clearheaded enough to face her. But when I went across to her in the cold grey light of dawn her decks were deserted. The other trawlers had all gone or were getting under way, but the *Duchess* lay there silent and asleep.

Nobody answered my hail, and when I climbed on board and went through the starboard gangway into what had been my cabin, it was empty. Her things were there, her clothes in the locker, but the bunk had not been slept in. I routed Johan out and he stared at me as though I were a ghost.

'Where's Gertrude?' I asked him.

'Ashore,' he growled.

'At the hotel?'

'No. She is gone to Inverness.'

I felt at a loss, utterly deflated. The confrontation for which I had prepared myself was suddenly not there. 'What the hell's she doing in Inverness?'

'A message we have over the R/T when we are fishing.' And there was hostility in his voice as he added, 'It is about you, so we have to haul our gear and come in here.'

'About me?'

'Ja.'

'What was the message?'

'That is for Gertrude to say.'

I hesitated. But it was obvious I wouldn't get anything more out of him. The relationship I had so carefully built up with the big Norwegian was gone now. I left him and went back to my boat. I didn't even bother to leave a note. I had nothing to say and not much hope that he would have delivered it anyway.

We sailed immediately, and as we motored out, I could see the crew of the *Duchess* – my crew, all the old faces – standing on the deck staring at us. We passed less than half a cable from her, her hull showing streaks of rust, her superstructure dirty with lack of paint, and there was a green fringe of weed along her waterline. I would have given anything to be back on board her.

It was a grey dirty morning with cloud low on the Sutherland hills, and it stayed grey all the thirty-nine hours it took us to raise the light on Muckle Flugga. The time would have been about ten-thirty, a pitch black night, and we lay hove-to with a good offing till dawn. By then we had the tide against us so that it was an unpleasant passage until we were out of the stream and into the quiet of Burra Firth. Ian came off as soon as we had anchored to check the cases. I left him to go down into the hold on his own, and Jamie followed him.

A few minutes later he came storming up into the wheelhouse, banging the door to behind him. 'There's two of them been broken into. Jamie says it was you.'

I nodded. He had discovered it when they had lashed the cases down on our way out of Loch Inchard.

'Why did you do it?'

'They might have contained contraband, or explosives.'

'Explosives!' He snorted. 'You have the most fertile imagination.'

'Why send me all the way down to Scotland for them?'

'If you own a ship, you might as well make use of her,' he snapped. 'And it's not for you to query your orders, or break into cargo. You'd no right.'

'It would have been a lot cheaper to have them sent up on the boat from Aberdeen.'

'And a lot slower.'

'Why the hurry?'

'Because Dillon is due up here this weekend. He's my backer. He's had this equipment made specially and he wants to try it out.'

'Where?'

'How should I know? Wherever there's fish, that's where.' He turned to the door and a shaft of watery sunlight showed as he opened it. 'I've told Jamie the men can go ashore as soon as they like. They're due a few days' rest.'

'What about the cases?'

'They'll remain on board. An engineer will be out shortly to install the equipment. And don't go monkeying around with it when the crew have gone and you're on your own.'

He left me then and I sat there smoking my pipe and wondering what sort of a man Dillon would prove to be and how he was going to get a weekend's fishing with the crew gone to their homes and only myself on board.

Later I went out to see the men away in the boat. The sun was glinting on the water and the old man sitting on the bench outside the hotel. The left side of his face was in shadow so that he looked like any harmless old gentleman taking the sun. He was so still I thought he must be asleep, but when I looked at him through the glasses, I could see his eyes watching me below the hooded lids and his lips were moving as though he were mumbling something to himself.

I could have hailed him and asked to be brought ashore. Was that what he wanted? I could almost feel him willing me to come to him. It would have been the natural thing for me to do, but in other circumstances. What would be the point now? To resume our probing of each other? I sat on the deck in the sunshine, my back against the side of the wheelhouse. It was warm and I closed my eyes. But I couldn't sleep. Too many thoughts were chasing through my mind.

The sun went in and I wished I had gone ashore to stretch my legs on the steep slopes behind the hotel. I could have walked across Mouslee Hill to Goturm's Hole, perhaps had a word with Robert Bruce. Bored with myself, I went into the wheelhouse and switched on the R/T. Almost without thinking I turned to the frequency used by *North Star*. But there was no traffic. Probably I was too far away, and I began idly playing with the dial, picking up scraps of talk, but all very faint. And then suddenly a voice said through a blur of static, '. . . ready for me.' I was almost on the frequency for the

Norwick voice channel and something about that voice made me hurriedly adjust the tuning. I went too far and missed something, but then the same voice came in loud and clear; '. . . the hurry? Where are you speaking from?'

I knew who it was then, that slight lisp.

'The ferry. Have Ian meet me in the Land-Rover. And he's to take the boat back to Lerwick, tell him. As a member of the Council, that's where he should be now. Got it?' And then a different voice came on – 'Thank you, Norwick. That's all. Over and out.'

I switched the set off and stood there, thinking about that scrap of conversation. Dillon presumably. And in a hurry to get to the *Mary Jane*. Why? I was still thinking about that when the inflatable came alongside. Ian was at the outboard and another man in the bows. He was young with a wisp of a beard and shoulder-length hair blowing in the breeze under a grey woolly cap. He looked like a student, his eyes magnified by round glasses as he handed a metal toolcase up to me. 'The old man wants to see you,' Ian said to me as the engineer climbed aboard.

I hesitated, torn between a desire to talk to the man who had come to install the equipment and the urge to get ashore. 'All right,' I said and got my anorak from the wheelhouse. But when I joined him in the boat he knew nothing about the telephone conversation. He had only just got back from Haroldswick.

We landed on the little beach at Fiska Wick and walked to the hotel. The old man was waiting for me in the room where we had talked before. There was a peat fire still glowing in the grate and the single window looked out on to the green slopes of the hill behind. He fixed Ian with his eyes, a hard, flat stare, waiting until he had left and the door closed behind him. Then he turned to me and said, 'It's some months now since we had our first talk. Now it's time for you to reach a decision.'

He was silent a moment, trying no doubt to think how best to put it to me, but I didn't give him the opportunity. 'Was that Dillon on the phone a while back?'

He looked surprised, and when I explained that I had picked up the conversation on the boat's radio, he said:

'Then you know?'

'What?'

'That *North Star* has struck oil.'

CHAPTER THREE

The news came as a shock. We had had our first flurry of snow the previous evening and there had been a drift of white on Hermaness Hill as we had come into Burra Firth. Winter here, and *North Star* striking oil, everything suddenly come at once and my father demanding I make a decision. What decision? But I knew. I could see it in his cold blue Nordic eyes. 'Who is this man Dillon?' I asked him. And I think I knew that, too.

'You'll be meeting him in a few hours.'

'A property man, Ian said, with an interest in fishing. But it's not fishing, is it? The equipment in those cases – '

'You broke into them – why?' I don't think he expected an answer, and after a moment he said, 'Sit down.' He waved me to a seat on the far side of the fire, then slumped into the wing chair. 'There's no more time.' His voice was so quiet it was almost a whisper and there was a look of weariness on his face. 'I wish now you hadn't come.' He gave a little shrug. 'I suppose it was inevitable, but . . .' He took out a packet of cigarettes and lit one, twisting his mouth around it. 'I could have wished it had been some other time.'

'It's *North Star*. Is that what you're trying to tell me?'

He didn't answer, sitting there watching me. 'You have to make up your mind now.'

'What are you planning to do?'

But he ignored that. 'I've given you a job, kept you clear of the police – '

'What are you planning to do?' I repeated.

'That's not for me to say. It's not my plan. Once, yes – but I only came into this because of Ian and the hotel here.' That twisted smile again. 'I hardly expected the two of you.' And then he said, 'I'm getting old, you see. And it's been a hard life.' He seemed to brace himself. 'But I'm still alive. Very much alive. And he's right. We can do a lot with this rig. It's a very good situation, if it's handled right. And it will be.' His eyes were closed, his voice very quiet, and I had the feeling he was talking to himself.

'Is Ian in on this?'

His eyes flicked open. 'Good God, no. Of course not.' He made a dismissive movement of the hand. 'Money. That's all he's interested in. It's the be-all and end-all of his existence.' The weariness was back in his voice. 'Anna was like that, under the skin, under the lovely bloom of youth –' He shook his head. 'Perhaps that's why I didn't marry her. So pretty, so sweet, but under the skin – nothing, no love of poetry, no inkling of the ideological turmoil, the reaching out to the stars . . .' His voice faded.

'Yet you wrote to her – from Spain.'

'Oh, yes.' He smiled. 'She showed it to you, did she?'

I nodded.

'And asked you for money?'

'I hadn't any.'

He smiled at me, and the twisted mouth made a mockery of it. 'You're different, aren't you? Different stock. And you had it as a child. Money, I mean. You could afford to turn your back on it. Nobody can buy you.'

'Did you buy Ian?'

'Ye-es. I suppose you could call it that.'

'To what end?' And when he didn't say anything, I told him how we had sighted *Island Girl* that night the rig had had her windward anchor cables cut. 'There was no other vessel there, so Ian must have been responsible –'

But he shook his head. 'Ian wasn't on board.'

'Dillon?'

He nodded.

'It's not fishing he's interested in then – it's sabotage.'

There was a long pause, and he sat there, drawing on his cigarette and staring at me. 'It's a rough world,' he said very quietly, the peculiar lisp coming through strongly. 'Some day man will learn to organize it so that he can live in peace. But not yet. You have to accept that. You have to accept the reality of the world in which you live.' He leaned forward, his voice urgent. 'Life is a battlefield, a political struggle, you see. And we're all a part of that struggle. We take sides, get involved –' His cigarette stabbed at the air. 'You. Me. All of us. You made your decision. You involved yourself – just as I did. And now – you can't escape that involvement now.'

He paused, breathless, and I said, 'What are you trying to tell me? That I should be a party to locating a wellhead and then destroying it?' His eyes widened slightly and I thought I had guessed the purpose of that equipment. 'A man calling himself Stevens followed me into Foula, when I was skipper of the *Duchess* and we had the *North Star* contract. He said what you've just been saying. He said Villiers was vulnerable, capitalism at its worst, and that there was political advantage to be had out of it. And with Ian on the Zetland Council –'

My God! He had manipulated it all so cleverly. 'And you a Shetlander,' I cried. 'You were born on the west coast. Are you prepared to see the whole of that coastline scummed with oil, a massive pollution that will destroy the livelihood –'

'I tell you, it's a rough world,' he said sharply. 'And there are always sacrifices. Think of the loss of life in the war, twenty million in Russia alone, the destruction, the appalling conditions.'

'And this is war.'

He nodded slowly. 'As good a name for it as any.'

'And I'm to be in the front line, with you. Bringing unnecessary pollution –'

'Michael, you can't help yourself.'

'I bloody well can.' I had got to my feet and stood over him, hating him for what he was, for what life had done to him. 'You're so twisted in your mind it's a pity that shell didn't kill you.'

He sat very still, looking up at me, and there was something almost pitiable in his expression. 'You didn't mean that.' And when I remained silent, the two of us staring at each other, his face gradually hardened. 'That's your answer, is it?' He got slowly to his feet, reaching for his stick. 'I had hoped . . .'

'That I'd co-operate?' The anger and disgust in my voice seemed to touch him on the raw.

'That you'd have more sense,' he snapped at me. And then that strange, disfigured face softened again. 'Would you like some lunch? It's almost time.'

'No thanks,' I said. 'I'll go for a walk.'

He nodded. 'Good idea. Give you a chance to think it over.'

'There's nothing to think over.'

'No?' He smiled. 'Well, maybe not. But just remember what I've said. There's no escape, the police against you and your ship the only one they know was there when the cables of that rig were cut. Go for your walk and think it over. Your liberty, your future . . .' He left it at that, still smiling and a devil lurking in his eyes, as though in me he saw a reflection of himself. 'Come back not later than five. Dillon will be here then and we'll be running tests in the firth before dark.' And he added, 'The *North Star* strike is only a rumour based on core samples flown to Aberdeen. There's still some time yet.'

Still time. I went out on to the track and walked slowly back to Fiska Wick. The little beach was empty, the inflatable gone, and the water was like lead under a leaden sky. I went out on to The Ness where I could see the *Mary Jane* lying like a black rock against the pale glint of the water. She was swinging to the tide, the inflatable snugged against her side, and the cases were all on deck, the engineer and another man opening them up and getting the equipment into the wheel-house.

I watched for a while, but it was cold and no way of getting out to her, so I turned to the slopes behind and began climbing Mouslee Hill, regretting now that I had refused the offer of lunch. Still time, he had said, and I could claim that he misled me. But it wouldn't be true. Where a decision is required the fault lies always in ourselves. From my experience of the sea I should have known that mistakes compound to produce disasters. The mistake I made that afternoon was to do nothing.

There were things I could have done. I could have gone into Haroldswick and phoned the police, or made an anonymous call like the bombers do. I could have gone aboard the ferry and radioed to *North Star* direct. Or I could have simply gone to Bruce's cottage and lain low there, watching to see what happened. But instead, I did nothing. I couldn't make up my mind.

I walked west across the backs of the hills to the high bold cliffs of Tonga, not a soul to be seen, not even Bruce, and conscious all the time of the solitude, the remoteness of this wild northern land, and of my own isolation. I stood for a while on the peat moss slopes above Tonga Stack, which is joined to the land, and north and south of me there were other, isolated stacks with the seas breaking against them. Birds everywhere, the air flecked white and shrill with their cries. And below me the water seethed, a chill north-westerly wind churning the flood tide into a welter of overfalls. The wildness and the solitude were overwhelming.

It was not the place to consider the merits of political activities and the role of economic warfare in an industrial society. Here only the elements counted. Nothing else. I walked south across Libbers Hill and Sneuga, as far as the brough on Flubersgerdie, and all the time I was walking I had the feeling that nothing beyond the peat moss hills and the distant glimpses of granite cliffs had any reality under that vast expanse of grey sky. Here was nothing made by man, nothing controlled by man. All was free and uncontaminated, and power lay in the wind, in the drive of the great depressions endlessly marching up to the white fish grounds from their birthplace far out in the Atlantic.

I was tired and hungry, and no nearer a decision, when I came down the slopes above Fiska Wick, the *Mary Jane* looking like a toy ship in the pale slash of the firth. The inflatable was back on the beach, the Land-Rover backed up and two men loading cardboard boxes. They were the same two I had seen when I had first come to Root Stacks and they were waiting for me as I came down the beach.

'Will you be going aboard now?' the Irishman asked. They were standing in the water in their sea boots, ready to push off. 'The old man said to take you out if you wanted.'

'Has Dillon arrived?'

But he only motioned me to get in, the two of them holding the tubed sides to steady the boat. It was only when we were under way that I realized they had their own gear with them. 'You're going out tonight then?' I had to shout to make myself heard above the noise of the outboard.

The quiet bearded man nodded. He was lying sprawled across the stores, spray whipping over him as the laden boat slapped into the wavelets. 'If everything works all right.'

I asked him what his name was, but he just stared at me. He had a soft, gentle face, very full in the cheeks. He didn't look like a seaman, more like an intellectual – a teacher, possibly a writer or a lecturer. And there was a tenseness about him, his brown eyes staring.

The engineer was waiting for us as the outboard died and we came alongside. There was a big fair man with him. They called him the Swede and the way he grabbed the painter and made us fast I knew he was used to boats.

I gave them a hand with the cases, and when it was all on deck, the outboard started up again, the Swede casting off and the inflatable swinging away from the side and heading back for the Wick. I went straight to the wheelhouse, but the door was locked. The engineer stood watching me. 'Where's the key?' I asked him.

'In my pocket.'

'Give it to me,' I said. 'You don't keep me out of my own wheelhouse.'

He backed away at the tone of my voice. 'You don't give orders. You're not the skipper now.' He said it with the truculence of a young man who resented all authority.

I held out my hand. 'Give me that key.' But the Swede moved between us, and his hand closed on my arm, holding me gripped. 'Nobody goes into the wheelhouse now, only Mr Dillon.'

I stepped back and the grip on my arm relaxed. 'When will Dillon be here?' I asked.

The man with the beard glanced at his watch and said in a voice that was as gentle as his manner, 'Any minute now.' The engineer brushed past me. 'I got to get the engine warmed up.' And he disappeared down the after-hatch. The other two began humping the stores below and I went with them to the little galley. The diesel started into life as I was cutting myself a hunk of bread and some ham.

I was still eating when I heard the outboard alongside and the clatter of feet on deck. I poked my head up out of the after-hatch to see the Swede making fast. The outboard stopped abruptly and a dark face with lank black hair appeared above the bulwarks. He might have been a South American Indian, or perhaps he was Arab – it was difficult to tell against the leaden glimmer of the water as he vaulted on board. And then he leaned over to help my father up.

The old man steadied himself against the wheelhouse, looking at me and breathing a little fast. 'I was told you were here.' The grimace of a smile came and went. 'I'm glad.' And for the first time I saw a glimmer of warmth in his eyes. He turned at the sound of a voice and his hand reached out to my arm, a restraining gesture. I could see Paddy's face as he stood holding the boat alongside and another man just swinging his leg over the bulwarks, his back towards me. He was wearing a dark blue anorak with a Shetland wool cap on his head. 'Dillon,' the old man murmured in my ear, and there was a note of warning. The man turned and I was looking at the hard set face, the cold elusive eyes I had last seen at Foula. 'You know each other I think,' my father said.

Dillon nodded, staring at me stonily, and I thought he smiled, but I couldn't be sure, the tight-lipped mouth compressed. 'So you're coming with us?'

My mouth was dry and I didn't answer, wondering if he knew how the sight of him affected me – the feeling of being trapped.

His wandering gaze appeared to fasten on my father. 'He's your responsibility,' he said. 'Not mine.' There was a note of censure in his voice. Then he turned to me, the hard mouth smiling grimly as he said, 'No doubt we'll find a use for you.' He seemed amused, but there was a tenseness about him, and then the engineer was there and the two of them went into the wheelhouse. In less than ten minutes the inflatable was lashed to the stern, the anchor up, and we were moving down the firth, the man with the dark Indian features in the wheelhouse connecting up the electronic gear.

Just beyond The Fidd they streamed the little torpedo like a tin fish from the stern, letting it out on a Terylene line and unreeling the wire connecting it with the transmitter. We motored almost to the entrance, then slowed to take bearings.

The old man came and stood beside me. 'You don't like him, do you?'

The straight line of our wake was bending now as the *Mary Jane* swung away in a wide circle. 'No,' I said.

'You should try to hide your feelings more.'

'Why?'

'He's one of our top men.'

We were standing in the shelter of the wheelhouse facing the stern and I watched as we completed the turn. 'What's his background?'

'A professional, like myself. But the right age. And the right time, too – democracy finished, all the countries of the West, even America, degenerate and vulnerable.'

We were headed north again, the speed picking up and the beat of the engine increasing. 'Where's he come from?' I asked. 'What nationality?'

'Scots-Irish. Started in the Midlothian coalfields. Moved to Liverpool docks. He's politically astute and quite ruthless. Remember that and do what he says.'

I thought I detected a note of respect, of envy even, as though in the pecking order of that shadowy world to which they both belonged my father knew his place.

The wake was straightening out now and I kept my eyes on the pale taut line to the submerged torpedo. Somebody joined us from the wheelhouse, but I didn't shift my gaze. If the marine electronics gear was some sort of an impulse transmitter, then I knew what to expect and I wanted to see it. The light was fading, the clouds very louring, and suddenly our wake erupted in a jet of spray, the sea heaving beneath it. Then the shock wave of the seabed explosion hit the soles of my feet as it had done that night in the *Duchess* out by No. 2 buoy.

I turned my head. It was Dillon standing beside me, a quiet look of satisfaction on his face. Our eyes met and he nodded. 'North Star,' he said, and there was tension in his voice. 'The charges are already laid.' And he added sharply. 'A job you could have done.'

'The anchor cables again?' I was thinking of the rig adrift in a big sea and the driller working in a frenzy to disconnect the marine riser. 'There are safety devices,' I said.

'Pipe rams, blind shears, the whole emergency disconnect drill.' He nodded. 'I haven't wasted my time in Aberdeen. I guess I know almost as much as a driller about how the blow-out preventer works. But it takes time, and there's always the human factor.'

'So you're going for pollution. You're going to try and flood the whole sea with oil.'

He looked at me, that thin-lipped smile, and a sardonic note in his voice as he said, 'Still worrying about moral principles?' He clapped me on the back, the only time I had seen him in high good humour. 'With luck we'll set that rig adrift at the critical moment when they're testing for pressure, and you can watch it.' The smile vanished, tension in his voice again. 'But don't try to interfere. And stay out of the wheelhouse.'

Darkness was falling as we turned west under Muckle Flugga. We were very crowded with only two on watch and the tiered bunks all occupied. I couldn't sleep for thinking how utterly defenceless that rig was, a sitting duck to the heterogeneous group we had on board. The forecast had not been very good, a cold front passing through and a deepening depression moving in from the Atlantic. About 02.00 I went up on deck. The wind was nor'nor'-westerly Force 4, a beam sea and the old girl rolling like a cow.

I found the man with the dark Indian face clinging to the rail capping of the bulwark and shivering uncontrollably. He was moaning, and when I asked him if he was all right, he only groaned and retched with a rasping empty sound into the back of a breaking wave as it rolled under us.

'What's your name?' I asked him.

'Paulo,' he gasped.

'Where's your home?'

'Mexico.' He pronounced the 'x' as an 'h' so that I didn't get it at first. And when I asked him what he was doing over here, he looked up at me, his face green in the starboard navigation light, his teeth showing in the flash of an exhausted smile. 'You are not a freedom fighter or you know. We are international, like a – a club, eh?' The boat swooped sickeningly on the long Atlantic swell, twisting and rolling as her bows ploughed into the sea, white water creaming past. Stars showed through ragged gaps in the clouds and it was cold.

I got him into the wheelhouse and he leaned shivering against the side of it. Paddy was at the wheel, nobody else there. 'This your first trip?' I asked him.

He shook his head, speechless.

'You're the electronics expert, are you?'

He stared at me uncomprehendingly. The bows slammed down, spray slashing at the windows, and above the roar of the water I heard Paddy's voice – 'You're not supposed to be here.'

I looked at him, at the tough, low-browed, unimaginative features. 'He might have gone overboard.'

'Sure and he never has. He's always sick the first few hours.'

'He's done this trip before, has he?'

There was no answer and I turned to the Mexican. 'How many times?'

He was still shivering, his brown features a sick grey. 'Two times,' he murmured.

'Why? What do you do?' He frowned in concentration. 'You're an expert – at what?'

'Ah, si.' The teeth flashed. 'Explosives. I am trained in explosives.'

I glanced at the impulse transmitter at the back of the wheelhouse and the vessel yawed as Paddy left the wheel. 'You better get out now.'

We stared at each other, but he was a compact, powerfully-built man. 'Watch your helm,' I said as the bows fell away in the trough, the top of a swell breaking against our starboard side, solid water crashing against the wheelhouse.

'Okay. You steer then.'

I took the wheel and he lit a cigarette, standing right behind me.

'You've been a trawlerman, have you?' I asked.

'Coasters.' But he wouldn't say what run or where he came from, and after a while I handed the wheel back to him and went below to my bunk. That short spell at the helm, the feel of the boat under my hands, had relaxed me and I slept.

I woke to a change in the motion. It was just after 06.30 and we were hove-to. The light was on and I heard somebody moving in the bunk below me. I stayed there, wrapped in the cocoon of my blankets, my eyes closed and unwilling to stir. Twelve hours. Just about the time we should reach *North Star*. But there was no movement on deck and when I did open my eyes all the bunks were occupied, only my father getting into his clothes. 'Are we there?' I asked him.

'Not yet. We wait here till nightfall.'

'And then?'

'We relieve *Island Girl*.'

So I still had a whole day. I closed my eyes again, sleepless now and wondering what the hell I was going to do. What could I do? And cutting the rig adrift wouldn't necessarily result in massive pollution. I didn't know much about drilling operations, but I had seen the blowout preventer panel in the toolpusher's office. I had seen how quickly they had been able to operate the pipe rams to hold the drill string suspended in the hole that night the windward anchor cables had been cut. There had been a strong wind then. Now there was very little. I knew that by the feel of the boat. She was rolling to the swell, but that was all. I turned over, away from the light, and dozed for a while.

It was eight-thirty when I finally got up, only two of the bunks occupied now and the ship still hove-to with the engine running slow. There was coffee on the galley stove, eggs and bacon beside the pan. I was just sitting down to my breakfast when Paulo came down.

'Feeling better?' I asked him.

He nodded. 'Okay now.'

'What's happening on deck?'

'Nothing. They wait to make a radio telephone to the other sheep.'

'What time?'

'Nine-thirty.' He went past me, through the door we had cut in the bulkhead to the hold. He had a torch and a plastic case that looked as though it contained tools. I finished my breakfast, then went through into the hold to see what he was up to. He was crouched over a butane gas cylinder, screwing a plug into the head of it where the control valve is normally sited. Just behind him was another cylinder with two wires trailing from it. 'What is it – a depth charge?' It had to be something like that.

He looked up at me, puzzled. 'Detonator,' he said, pointing to the head of the cylinder he was working on.

'An underwater bomb?'

His eyes shifted nervously, the whites showing in the torch-light. 'Bomb – yes.'

'What's it for?' I was thinking of the force that would be generated by gelignite, or even a home-made explosive, packed into such strong cylinders, and the inflatable still with us, lashed to the stern. They could float the cylinders down in that, and if they were detonated against the riser when oil was coming up the pipe on full pressure . . . I was suddenly very scared, seeing in my imagination the vast explosive burn-up, the whole rig engulfed in a searing mass of flame. 'Christ Almighty,' I exclaimed. 'You can't. Just think . . .' I had reached down, gripping hold of his shoulder. 'There are more than sixty men – '

But he had leapt from under my grasp, a reflex action like a coiled spring triggered at the touch of my hand. The torch blinded me, but I saw the knife in his hand, heard the tension in his voice as he hissed, 'You go please.' He was poised like a man cornered.

'It's all right,' I said soothingly. 'I didn't mean to alarm you.'

But he just stood there, the steel blade of the knife glinting in the torch beam, and in the silence I could feel the tautness of his nerves. I turned with deliberate slowness, anxious not to upset him further as I moved to the bulkhead door, the skin crawling between my shoulder-blades.

Back in the galley I glanced at my watch. It was almost nine-thirty and I got my anorak and went up on deck to find the sun glimmering through a layer of cirrus. The wheelhouse door was closed, but through the glass side-panel I saw they were all there and Dillon with the mike of the R/T trans-mitter to his mouth. I slid the door open and heard his voice:
'. . . *Island Girl. Mary Jane* to *Island Girl*. Come in, please, *Island Girl*. Over.'

No answer. He tried again, and then loud and clear over

the loudspeaker came a Shetland voice identifying himself as *Island Girl* and asking why the hell they hadn't been relieved that morning.

'We'll be with you some time tonight,' Dillon said. 'I'll call you again at 19.00 hours. What's the weather like out there? Over.' He knew damn well what the weather was like, for we must have been just over the horizon from the other boat, but he waited while *Island Girl*'s skipper talked about a heavy swell with a layer of cirrus overhead and the morning's weather bulletin forecasting a series of depressions moving in from the Atlantic. Then he asked what was happening on the rig. 'There's rumours ashore that they've struck oil. Over.'

'Aye, there's been a great coming and going these last two days. They've been running an electrical log and getting ready for what they call a drill stem test to check the pressure and rate of flow of the oil. Did you not listen to the news this morning? It seems the Company announced the strike officially late last night.' But when Dillon asked him whether they had started testing yet, he answered, 'Not yet. But there was a helicopter flight came in yesterday with service company lads. They're running a gun down the hole and there's a bloody great steel boom rigged out over the side. Ed Wiseberg was on the R/T to us a few minutes ago warning us to keep clear of it from noon onwards, so I reckon you'll see some fireworks when you arrive this evening.' And he added, 'Who's that I'm talking to? It's not Jamie?'

'No, it's his relief,' Dillon said. 'Jamie and his lads were due for a bit of a break.'

'So you've a different crew, eh?' And the voice went on, 'Have you a man called Randall with you? I heard there was, 'cos the trawler *Duchess of Norfolk* arrived last night with Gertrude Petersen on board asking for him. Is he there now? Over.'

The mention of Gertrude, the memory of that explosives expert crouched over the cylinders . . . I flung the door back, Dillon denying my presence and my voice shouting, 'I'm here. Randall. Tell Ed Wiseberg . . .' But Dillon had dropped the mike.

'Grab him.'

I saw Paddy with his head low and out of the corner of my eye the big Swede, and I leapt at Dillon in the grip of fear and a sudden terrible desire to smash him before they got me. I saw his hand reaching into his anorak, his eyes widening, and

214

then he ducked. My fist caught him on the side of his head, slamming him back against the radio. I saw him fall, a shocked, surprised look on his face, and then a hand gripped my shoulder, swung me round and something exploded in my belly. The Swede was a blurred image as I doubled up with the pain and then his fist crashed into my jaw and I lost consciousness.

The next thing I knew I was being dragged to my feet and a voice, Dillon's voice, said something about the chain locker. I saw my father, the twisted side of his face, and his eyes hurt, as though in doing what I had I had done him a personal injury. He looked at me and didn't say a word. No attempt to stop them as I was dragged out of the wheelhouse. Unconsciousness closed in on me again, the pain in my guts overwhelming, and when I came to it was in darkness with the hard feel of the anchor chain under me and the occasional slam of the bows reverberating through my head, a hanging length of chain sliding across my body.

I don't know how long I lay there in a half coma, dimly conscious of the salt sea smell of the stowage locker and of the links damp and hard against my limbs. It was freezing cold and I thanked God for my anorak, conscious of the roll and swoop as the boat lay motionless, head-to-swell, but conscious of little else until I had recovered sufficiently to drag myself to my feet.

And with consciousness I cursed myself for my stupidity, for the blind rage which had sent me for Dillon. I should have gone for the impulse transmitter. I should have found something with which to smash it. And I cursed myself for not having thrown those cases overboard. Guessing what they were, why in God's name hadn't I got rid of them when I could, instead of delivering them to Burra Firth? The excuse of time. Time on my side. Christ! All my life I seemed to have been living on borrowed time, and Wiseberg, Stewart, men I had met – a total of more than sixty – all at risk. And myself to blame, their executioner. No, not their executioner. But a party to it.

I stood there, in the blackness of the sea-stinking hole, the chain coming down through the hawsepipe, coiled like a cold steel snake under my feet. And nothing I could do. Nothing. Nothing. Shut in behind a thick barred wooden door, in a space I couldn't even stand up in properly, my head bowed by the wooden deck beams.

I sank back on to the dank hard bed of the steel links, breathing deeply, easing the pain until it was no more than a numb ache. Time passed slowly, the luminous dial of my wristwatch the only visible companion in the darkness, and nothing there that I could use on the door. Nothing to do but wait. And waiting, my mind focused incessantly on that scene in the hold, the cylinders with wires trailing from the detonators. A freedom fighter – my God! What sort of freedom was that, to roast sixty innocent men alive! Increasingly, as the power to think returned, my mind dwelt on the *Duchess,* the knowledge that she was out here, fishing in these waters – and Gertrude asking for me.

At irregular intervals one or other of the men who had jumped me came into the hold to check the door and make certain I was still there. The first few times I answered them, demanding water, food, anything to get a brief respite from the cramped hole. But they didn't even reply and the next time I stayed silent. It was Paddy, and he called me several times. Then he went away and a few minutes later he came back with the Swede, the door opening and the beam of a torch blinding me. I hesitated, and then, as I moved, the door slammed in my face.

Shortly after midday the door was opened again and a mug of beer with a thick wadge of ham and bread was set down in a coil of the chain, the Swede watching me all the time. I tried asking about the weather, anything to get them talking, but they didn't answer. I knew the weather was worsening. There was considerably more movement, the bows lifting and falling so violently that at times I had to grip hold of the chain, otherwise my body was left suspended for an instant to be slammed down on the hard steel links as we hit the troughs. Sometimes I thought I could hear the wind. I could certainly hear when the seas broke, could feel them, too, as the vessel staggered, flinging me against the wooden side of the chain locker. It was after a particularly bad slam that the ship came alive with the prop turning, the sound of it merging with the increased power from the engine to produce a steady vibration transmitted through the timbers.

All the rest of that afternoon we were under power in order to stay head-to-wind, and slamming into it like that, the swoop and plunge of the bows became unbearably, exhaustingly violent. I no longer cared about anything. All my energies were set on keeping myself from being battered to pieces.

And then, when I thought I could stand it no longer, the vibrations of the engine increased and the vertical movement eased, changing to a slow, deep roll. We were under way, with the seas almost broadside, and through the thickness of the hull I could hear the water hissing and creaming past.

The time was eight thirty-four. It would be dark now and I thought of the rig again, wondering how long it would be before we reached it and what was happening on that huge platform. Half an hour later the beat of the engine changed. It was no longer under power and we lay wallowing with occasional waves breaking aboard. I thought we had arrived, but then I heard the sound of a much more powerful engine. I could hear it very plainly, a solid, throaty roar, magnified by the fact that I was lying below the waterline. That, too, slowed and I thought I heard, very faintly, the sound of a hail and voices shouting. They were still shouting when the churn of a propeller close alongside drowned all sound, merging with the heavy beat of an engine's exhaust so close beside me and so loud that it seemed like a hammer drill attacking the walls of my prison. I thought my eardrums would split, it made such a thundering noise. Then it faded into a churning of water close alongside. We lay wallowing in its wash, and after a while we got under way again.

I thought it was *Island Girl* that had come alongside us and that we had now taken over the stand-by duty from her. But time passed and we held our course, rolling wickedly with the waves breaking against us on the starboard side, so that I knew we were steering south. We stayed on the same course for almost three hours, then the engine slowed and I heard the beat of another boat passing us to port, and after that it was all I could do to save myself from injury, for the seas were big now and we were headed straight into them, the fall and crash of the bows sudden and very violent. I heard the sound of movement on deck, orders being shouted, but only vaguely through the din of the waves. And then we turned and the roll threw me against the side.

I was still lying against the side, clutching the links of the chain under me, desperately trying to hold myself there, when I felt the first explosion through the timbers at my back, not heavy, more like a sharp tap against my shoulders. But I knew what it was, and lying there in the dark I could visualize the scene on deck, the fishing lights probing the darkness for the anchor buoys and that wicked little torpedo trailing astern,

217

sending its impulses through the water to some submerged reciever on the end of a trailing wire that went down five hundred feet to the explosive device grappled to a cable on the seabed.

Clinging to the links, I counted the minutes on my watch – four, five, and at five and a half the second tap of a detonation hit the timbers. Two of the anchors gone, the windward ones presumably. And then we were turning, but not into the seas – away from them, downwind. Footsteps in the hold and the door opening, the beam of light dazzling after the darkness. 'On deck.' A hand grabbed hold of my arm, hauling me to my feet, pulling me out of the locker and I was so cramped and exhausted I could hardly stand.

They dragged me up the narrow companionway that led direct into the wheelhouse and forced me to stand, propped against the closed door. I saw Dillon's face, but only as a blur, the wheelhouse lit by a weird glow. It shone on my father's twisted face, and I blinked my eyes, weeping after the long darkness. 'You heard the anchor cables go,' Dillon said. 'You heard, did you?'

I nodded, wondering what he wanted of me, and desperately trying to recover myself. I was sore all over, a deep ache.

'Your ship has cut numbers One and Four.' *Your* ship! What did he mean by my ship? His face was strangely lit, a livid red, his cheek puffed and a scab of dried blood on the side of his head where I had slammed it against the R/T transmitter. Slowly I turned, my weeping eyes narrowed against the glare. The bows swung wildly, the break of a wave lashing the windows, and suddenly I saw it, heaving and tossing in the glass panel opposite, Dillon's face no longer red, his head in silhouette.

It was the rig. It rose up out of the wildness of the seas no more than three cables away, towering above us and lit the way I had so often seen it, like a factory complex with the tall finger of the derrick climbing into the night, a tier of ruby lights. But now, from the very top of it, a long gas jet streamed in the wind, and at deck level, thrust out from the side of the platform at the end of a steel boom, a huge tongue of burning oil, a great flare of flame like a dragon's breath, pulsed into the night, spray jets of water shooting out in a lurid flare.

'The moment we've been waiting for.' Dillon's voice was tense, his eyes glowing with a deep inner excitement. 'Only two anchors holding her, the wind around thirty knots, gusting forty, and yours the only ship here.'

I looked at my father, sitting wedged in the corner of the wheelhouse, a crumpled, silent figure. *Quite ruthless.* His words came back to me as Dillon's voice, tight with tension, said, 'We're turning now for the final run. And when we cut those two remaining cables she'll go, just like that.' He banged his hand on the flat of the ledge we used as a chart table, and the boat, completing its turn, his face was lit again by the red flaring of the oil, the skin shiny with sweat, his eyes glowing. 'They won't have time to disconnect or operate the kill and choke. And at the end of it all it's you they'll blame.' And he added, 'But once you're in the inflatable you won't care. You won't care about anything, you'll be too frightened.'

My mind was slow and confused, unable to grasp his meaning, still thinking of the rig and the cold ruthless drive of this man who could see the killing of so many men, a group of fellow workers, the destruction of the rig, as justified, as part of the struggle . . .

'You could have done it for us,' he said. 'You could have done it, so easily. And I asked you. I came to you – '

'I'm not a murderer,' I said, my voice strained and hoarse.

'You think it's murder?' His voice had risen. 'How can it be murder when you're fighting a war?' The man at the helm reported 'On course', but he took no notice. 'Korea, Vietnam Angola – a soldier doesn't call it murder when he destroys defenceless villages, or a pilot when he bombs a town, spreads napalm and burns up innocent children. And if anybody dies out there, it'll be their own fault. They've got safety rafts, scrambling nets – '

'They're testing,' I said, cutting short his outburst of self-justification. 'There's oil flowing up from thousands of feet down, under pressure – and this ship's a floating mine.'

'And who will they blame? – not me.' He laughed, but no mirth in it and his eyes cold with contempt. 'I gave you the chance to prove yourself. Think of Villiers, with the oil flowing and his shares booming. He'll make millions out of this. Is that the sort of world you want?'

'Destruction doesn't build a new world,' I said.

'What do you care about a new world? You're not a fighter. You're not one of us. You're nothing. A little shit of a bourgeois radical who can't make up his mind which side he's on. Radicals!' He spat the word out. 'Get him into the boat.'

The old man stirred in his corner. 'He's my son,' he said,

but hands were gripping my arms, the wind roaring in, solid with spray, as the door slid back. I was thrust out into the gale and I saw a buoy in the spotlight, riding the crest of a breaking wave, and right below me the inflatable bouncing alongside. The vessel rolled in the trough, hands thrusting me against the bulwarks, and above the noise of the sea I heard a voice say, 'Let him be.'

A wave rolled under us, the deck heaving and I turned on the Swede as the roll caught him off balance, hitting out at him, and in that moment I saw the old man standing in the gap of the wheelhouse door. 'Let him go.' The grip of their hands relaxed. I was suddenly free, the twisted side of my father's face lit by the oil flare, the deep gash a lurid red, his voice saying, 'He comes with us.' He was facing Dillon, and Dillon saying, 'No. He takes his chance, and whether he survives or not doesn't matter – he gets the blame.' The bows crashed down, a roar of water, the ship staggering under the impact and his voice whipped away in the wind: '. . . out of this. You were only brought into it because you're a Shet-lander and knew . . .' The rest I lost as another gust hit us, the ship leaning away from it and the old man clutching at the door frame, not looking at Dillon now, but at me. I thought his lips framed the words 'my son' again, but there was no determination, no fight – only acceptance.

I shall never forget that helpless, hopeless look on his face, a man acknowledging his own son, yet acquiescing in his destruction. There were tears in his eyes and the wind tore them away. And that's all I remember – that and Dillon's face and the fist in my guts as I tried to wrench myself free of them. And then the hard top of the bulwarks against the small of my back, a voice high in the wind saying, 'Over the side,' and I was falling, the black plastic fabric of the boat coming up at me on a crest. It was half-full of water and for a moment I lay clutching at the smooth rolled air cushions as the wave broke over me, lifting me almost to the level of the deck. The Swede was fumbling at the painter, the nylon cord difficult to handle, a riding turn.

In that moment, with the Swede right above me, holding a torch and working at the cord with his other hand, the mean-ing of Dillon's words dawned on me, the reality of my situation suddenly very clear. A wave broke under me, lifting me in a smother of foam, and I heard the Swede call to Paulo, saw him reach out his hand for the knife, and in that moment I dived for the bows, gripping the cord, shortening up on the painter. That torch was my only hope. The next wave broke hissing behind me, the inflatable lifting me to the bulwarks again, the Swede sawing at the cord, and on the crest of that wave I reached out and grabbed hold of the torch.

The boat fell away in the trough, my whole weight on his arm, and the fool didn't let go, the trawler rolling and his body coming with the roll, sprawling over the side to hit the airtight slippery curve beside me as I fell back. The nylon cord parted, the *Mary Jane*'s hull sliding past, faces looking down, the whole scene vivid and red in the glare.

I lay in the water, gasping, and the Swede's face close beside me disappeared, his hand scrabbling at the drum-tight curve of the fabric. Then suddenly I was alone, the boat's engine, a distant beat in the wind, gradually fading. It was quiet then, the wind almost soundless as I drifted with it, and only the hiss of the wave crests.

I didn't even feel the shock wave as they cut No. 3 cable. Sprawled in the bottom of the boat, my fingers gripping the slats of the floorboards and my head lifted to peer over the side, I saw the *Mary Jane* steaming across the line of the buoys, and twisting round I could see the rig growing in size, the gas jet high in the sky, the oil flare licking the night. Soon I could hear the roar of that flame, the sound of the power plant, the whole factory blaze of the giant structure going on about its business, apparently oblivious that only one of the windward anchors remained. And the wind and the sea sweeping me towards it, to pass I thought just seaward of that blinding, searing tongue of flame now looking like a beautiful frilled monster with the spray-jets gleaming red, a glorious coloured ruff, a mouth wide open, pouring out fire.

Already I was only catching glimpses of the *Mary Jane,* and then, when she, too, was on the top of a wave, I thought she had turned and was heading north, and at the same moment a klaxon blared on the rig. I could hear it even above the wind, the platform so close above me now. The gas flare at the derrick top was snuffed out, the tongue of flame at the end of its boom flickered, withdrawing itself into the darkening circle of spray. Suddenly it was gone, the sea black, and only the lights of the rig to show the white of the waves rolling under me.

I was almost abreast of the rig then, drifting fast downwind to pass a cable, perhaps a cable and a half, to the north. Then for a while the rig seemed stationary again. Spotlights picked out the underside of the platform, the round fat columns with the waves breaking against them and the big tubular bracings smothered in foam. I could see the guidewires leading down to the seabed and the casing of the marine riser, and guide-wires and riser were no longer vertical. They were slanting away from the wind, the angle increasing. And I was moving down past the rig then, the whole huge structure held anchored by a 20 inch casing reaching down almost 600 feet to the BOP stack on the seabed.

And then it snapped and the rig was moving with me, the guidewires trailing, men crawling like monkeys high in the night, releasing scrambling nets, checking the winch drums at each of the four corners of the platform. The rig stayed with me for perhaps ten minutes, the time it took to drift over her downwind anchors, to drag the cables, and then she held and I was being swept past it again.

Lying there, clinging on to the slats, my head twisted side-ways watching the rig, I was too scared of what might happen to think of myself. At any moment I had expected the whole structure to be engulfed by flames. But something had given them the few moments they'd needed to choke the oil flow. Maybe Dillon had been so tense, so disturbed by the loss of the Swede overboard, that he had mistaken No. 1 buoy for No. 2. That would explain the quick turn and the northward run. Whatever it was, the rig was safe – for the moment. No drill hole run amok and blazing oil, nobody roasted alive in a holocaust of fire.

It was only then that I remembered the torch, my urgent reason for grabbing it, and I shone it up at the small figures loosening the nets high above me. Three dots, three dashes, three dots. I kept flicking it on and off until my thumb ached with the pressure and I was losing sight of the rig in the troughs. It was when I stopped sending that hopeless SOS that I realized I was shaking with cold, the water I was lying in warmer than the wind blowing through my sodden clothing.

I never saw her come up on me out of the night. She was just suddenly there, a trawler with her fishing lights on, her spotlight swinging back and forth across the waves. I began using the torch again and for long minutes I thought she'd never see me. Then very slowly she began to turn, her bows swinging till they pointed straight at me and she was growing larger.

She lay-to a short distance to windward, rolling her side decks under and drifting down on me, smoothing the seas out and blocking the wind. A heaving line came rushing through the glare of her lights, missed me by a few feet. Another whistled straight across me and I grabbed it, wrapping it round my body as the rusty steel plates of her side rolled down on top of me. Then the line tightened round my chest, dragging me into the sea and yanking me up to swing in a blinding crash against the ship's side. I remember nothing after that until I found myself sprawled on the deck and Johan's bearded face hovering over me.

CHAPTER FOUR

I remember putting my hand up to my head, blood on my fingers, and Johan saying, 'It is Gertrude you must thank.' And the next thing I knew I was on a bunk with the light in my eyes and they were pulling off my clothes. I felt dazed and I wanted to be sick. A voice, a long way away, said, 'He's coming round.' It was Gertrude's voice and I tried to raise myself, wanting to ask about the fishing boat, but I couldn't form the words. Instead I was sick, leaning over the edge of the bunk and retching up seawater.

I was shivering then and Gertrude said, 'You are all right now.' Blankets were heaped on top of me and I tried to push them away, thinking of the old man and Dillon, the Swede's hands scrabbling, and the little torpedo, echoes to the seabed, the anchor cables exploding – a kaleidoscope of impressions with the blurred vision of Johan's bearded face and Gertrude looking down at me with huge eyes full of pity. And at last I found my voice, heard myself say, 'The radar. Get that boat on the radar.'

'It's all right. The rig is all right and no need for you to worry.'

'It's not all right.' A big hand thrusting me back, myself struggling – 'Stop them – if those bastards blow the last four anchors . . .'

And Gertrude's voice: 'Relax. Nothing you can do.'

But I knew there was. If the rig went adrift . . . If they succeeded . . . 'It's a lee shore,' I gasped. I saw it in my mind, the rig stranded and battered on Foula, or on the Mainland shore of Shetland. And the disaster blamed on me. The boat gone, nobody else but me . . . 'Get me some clothes.' I pushed the blankets back, holding on to my stomach and forcing myself up on my elbow.

'You can't, Michael.'

'Some clothes. Quick, for Christ's sake.' I swung my legs off the bunk, forcing myself up stark naked, thinking only of that deadly, dangerous little man and what he had planned. Not the others. The others didn't matter, not even my father. It was Stevens, Dillon, whatever the cold-hearted bastard liked to call himself. 'Some clothes, damn you,' I said, through gritted teeth.

A jersey, trousers, carpet slippers much too large for me; somehow I got into them and dragged myself through the door to the bridge. Lars was at the helm, Henrik at the Decca. Beyond them the rig wavered, a lit tower block canted at an angle and rising and falling in the glass of the windows as the *Duchess* steamed at slow ahead into the waves. The bows fell away and I lurched down to push Henrik away and watch the sweep lighting the screen in its steady radial circling.

'It is all right,' Gertrude said again. She was close behind me. 'It is holding on the other anchors.'

The screen, blurred by the break of the waves, was difficult to read, my head throbbing, my eyes not focusing properly. 'Where's that boat now?' I asked Henrik. 'Is that it over the bows?'

'No. Is a buoy, I think. The boat is starb'd bow.'

I waited till the sweep swung round through north-east and there it was, out beyond the pinhead blips of the two buoys, beyond the first distance circle. I reached for the telegraph, rang for full ahead. The bell answered just as a voice crackled out of the loudspeaker. It was Ken Stewart calling on us to stay by the rig and patrol the buoys of the four anchors that were still holding. 'Is Randall able to talk now?'

I reached for the phone. 'Randall here.' And I told him briefly what had happened, how his own stand-by boat had cut the four windward cables by trailing a sonic beam transmitter. 'She's out by Nos. 5 and 6 buoys, but we're going after her now. She won't cut any more cables, and we'll keep after her.'

By then we were almost on top of the two buoys and the blip was moving away to the north, fast. He wanted us to stay by the buoys, of course, but I ignored him, blowing into the engine-room voice pipe and calling for maximum revs. I was remembering the Mexican fixing the cylinders in the hold, the powerful engines of that other vessel hammering at the wooden sides of the chain locker, and Gertrude behind me said, 'No. No, there's no need for that.' A hand fell on my shoulder, gripping me tight, and Johan said, 'You hear what Gertrude said.' His voice was thick and obstinate, and still gripping me, he reached out for the telegraph and put it back to slow again.

I think I was crying then. Crying with frustration. Certainly there were tears in my eyes as I faced Gertrude, telling her how I had been set adrift, Dillon intending my body to be the only evidence and my father acquiescing. The scene was still so vivid, my anger, my hatred of that man so intense that when I turned on Johan, hitting out at him, there was a wildness running through me. He was a beer-drinker, too fat in the belly, and that is where I hit him. Gertrude screamed at me, but then the voice pipe whistled and I picked it up and heard Duncan asking what the hell was going on. But I couldn't answer, my legs suddenly weak and buckling under me. I heard Gertrude say something, but her voice was a long way away, and then I was being lifted up and the next thing I knew I was on the bunk again and she was holding a mug of something hot to my lips. 'Drink it. Then you feel better. You shouldn't have hit Johan.' Her voice was reproachful.

'Tell him I'm sorry,' I murmured. I don't know whether it was exhaustion or the sedative she had mixed with the drink, but I was asleep before I had finished it.

When I woke dawn was just breaking and we were running before a big sea. I knew that by the swooping corkscrew motion, the pitch of the engines, the occasional sound of a wave breaking aft. It meant that we had left the rig and were headed east for Shetland. I closed my eyes again. Nothing I could do about it now. Nothing I could do about anything, and I was tired. God! I was tired.

I didn't wake again until Gertrude brought me some food on a tray. It was past nine then and when I asked her where we were she said, 'Approaching Papa Stour. It is blowing very hard, so we go to Aith. It is nearer and soon we will be under the lee.'

'What about the rig?'

'When we leave it is dragging, but not much, and they have

sealed off the drill hole. The choke and kill, that is what Ken Stewart call it, and they do that before the marine riser casing broke. So eat your food. There is nothing to worry about.'

It was eggs and bacon and a mug of coffee. Just the smell of it made me hungry. 'I haven't thanked you,' I said. 'If you hadn't been standing by *North Star* –'

'It is not me you have to thank. It is your wife.'

'Fiona?' The coffee was thick and sweet in my mouth as I gulped at it. 'What the hell's Fiona got to do with it?' I was staring at her, seeing her large-mouthed competent face, thinking how comfortable and practical she was in comparison with Fiona. 'I don't understand.'

'She did a very wonderful thing – for you.' She spoke very softly, a note of sadness, almost of pity in her voice. 'She loves you I think very much.'

'It's finished,' I said. I didn't want to talk about it, not with her. I began eating, feeling confused and wondering what was coming.

'For you maybe,' she said quietly. 'But not for her.' There was a long pause, and then she said, 'She is something to do with those men on the fishing boat I think.'

'Probably.' I was remembering how she had followed me to Hull, what she had said the last time I had seen her, in the corridor outside the court. 'What happened to the boat?' I asked.

'You don't have to worry about the boat. It made off to the north.'

'You didn't follow it.'

'No.'

Would the police accept that? Would they accept that there had been a boat and that it was Dillon, not me, who was responsible for cutting the cables? I was still thinking about that and eating at the same time when she said, 'You do not want to know what Fiona did?'

'Does it matter?'

'Yes, Michael. It does matter.' And she went on, a note of urgency in her voice, 'Listen please. We came into The Taing and there was a letter for me, from Aberdeen. She wanted to see me urgently, about you. A matter of life and death, she say, and God help me I think she is just dramatizing. So I don't do anything until we are fishing off the Hebrides and I get a telegram from her over the R/T. A telegram is something I cannot ignore, so we put into Kinlochbervie and I telephone her. We arrange to meet in Inverness the next day. And it is there she tells me what is going to happen.'

'About the rig?'

'Ja.' And she nodded, her fair hair falling over her face. 'But it is not only about the rig. She is convinced the man in charge of the operation will make it look so that you are responsible. She is afraid for you. She thinks perhaps it is your dead body –'

'Did you report this to the police?'

'No, that was a condition she made. She was concerned for you, not the rig.'

'Surely you warned Ed Wiseberg?'

'Yes. As soon as we reached *North Star* I talked with him by loudhailer. I tell him something is planned to happen to the rig. But he thinks the *Duchess* is there to cause trouble – to frighten the men or something. He tell us to Eff Off.' She smiled. 'He is very tense, you know, already occupied with his testing. So then I ask the stand-by boat if you are on board or perhaps on the relief boat. But they don't know anything about you, so we stay around the rig, watching. And when it is dark and the relief boat arrive, we keep downwind of her with our lights turned off.'

'She told you I was going to be put in a boat?'

'No, she don't say that. But Johan and I, we think it is possible. We just don't know what is going to happen, only that we must stay in the vicinity of *North Star*. Then Ken Stewart say there is a torch blinking an SOS in the water and that's how we come to pick you up.' And she added very quietly, 'So you don't owe your life to us, but to Fiona.' She was gazing at me wide-eyed, waiting for some reaction.

But there was nothing I could say, and I went on eating, feeling helpless, propped up in the bunk and thinking of Fiona risking her liberty, perhaps her life, because of something that was finished, dead, buried in the past. What the hell could I say?

She sat there waiting until I had finished my food, then she took the tray and stood there, holding it in her hand and looking down at me. 'Do you want me to send a message? I know where she is staying.'

'Tell her I'm safe,' I said.

'I already send a telegram to say that. But she will expect something more – a message from you.' She reached down to the locker beside the bunk and handed me a writing pad and ballpoint. 'You think it out. We will be in Aith in about an hour. Then you can send it yourself.'

She left me then, apparently thinking my reluctance due to her presence. I stared at the pad, knowing there was nothing I could say that wouldn't encourage Fiona to think there was still something left of our marriage. *She loves you, I think, very much.* It was Gertrude I wanted to think of, not Fiona – Gertrude who had brought her trawler north, to stand by the rig in the hope of finding me. And she had done that after three months without a word from me, knowing that I was somehow involved.

One hour, she had said. Then we would be in Aith, tied up at the pier. I thought of all the telex messages being sent out by *North Star* – to Fuller, to the Aberdeen office, to Villiers in London. And the news broadcasts. It would have been on the radio this morning. TV would have it by midday, newspaper presses rolling the story out, a rig broken adrift and suspected sabotage. Aith might only be a small place, but it was on Mainland, and once we were in, press, reporters, police, they would all be there.

A wave crashed aft as we were pooped, but I barely noticed it. I hardly heard the strange noises the hull made as the plates worked under the pressure of the seas. I had one hour, just one hour to myself to get a clear statement down on paper. I was still tired, my head throbbing, but I knew it had to be done. And, once I had started, I found myself writing fast and with concentration, so that I barely noticed the decrease of movement, the growing quiet as we came in under the lee.

I hadn't quite completed it when I felt a bump on the starboard side, the sound of feet on deck and voices. We were alongside, and a moment later Gertrude came in followed by a tall, stooped figure in a tweed jacket. 'Inspector Garrard,' she said. 'He wants to see you alone.'

The inspector came forward, ducking his head to avoid the steel angle irons of the roofing. 'Before the reporters get at you,' he said. He waited for Gertrude to leave, then pulled up a chair and sat down, opening his briefcase. 'Since I'm not sure whether you're one of the villains or not I suppose I ought to caution you.'

'You want a statement, is that it?'

He nodded. 'Yes, I'll need a statement.'

'I've just been writing it for you,' I said and handed him the pad.

'Good. That saves a lot of time.' He took it and there was a long silence as he read it through. When he had finished, he said, 'With what Mrs Petersen has told me and the messages we've had from *North Star*, this is about what I had expected.' He hesitated, smiling slightly. 'We kept tabs on you, of course. From the moment I had them release you from the Hull Central Station we've been following your movements, but at a distance. The trouble was we weren't sure exactly who was involved and how it would be done. We hoped you'd lead us to that. But then it all happened too quickly.'

It was a shock to realize that this quiet academic-looking man had been making use of me so deliberately. But my reaction was only one of relief. 'What about Dillon?' I asked.

'His real name is McKeown. Until now he's always worked in the background. We've been trying to – '

'Yes, but what's happened to him? Where is he now?'

He shrugged. 'You're probably right in saying they've destroyed the fishing boat after transferring to another vessel.'

'But you don't know. You don't know what's happened to them.'

He shook his head. 'A navy ship is out there now, searching. But I'm afraid we moved too late.' And he added, 'We've pulled in Sandford, of course. He doesn't seem able to tell us much, but what he has told us tends to corroborate your statement.'

He stayed there for about half an hour, asking questions and checking my answers against information in a file from his briefcase. Finally he rose. 'I have to be getting back to Lerwick now. Like you, I wish we knew what happened after the rig's cables were cut. But it's been a bad night out there. *North Star* has dragged about three miles and one of the remaining anchor cables snapped under the strain. But the forecast is for less wind, so the rig should hold. And Villiers arrived by plane this morning. He's in Scalloway now. He'll want to see you. Also, the media. They'll want the story, too.' He put the file back in his briefcase and snapped it shut. Then he stood looking down at me and I sensed a sudden awkwardness. 'One other thing. Mrs Petersen said she told you your wife was in Aberdeen.'

I nodded, something in his expression warning me so that I think I knew what was coming.

'You saw her in Hull, at your hotel. And she was in court that day. We kept track of her after that, so we knew where to pick her up for questioning.' He hesitated. 'I'm sorry about this, Randall, but I had a call from the Aberdeen police just before I left Lerwick. When they went to her lodgings last night, they found she'd been taken to hospital that morning suffering from an overdose of barbiturate.'

He didn't have to tell me. I knew from the expression on his face. 'Dead?'

'Yes, I'm afraid so. She was dead on arrival at the hospital.'

I didn't see him go. I just lay there staring at the rusting paint of the roofing, thinking of Fiona alone in some wretched boarding house. Was it my fault? Was I to blame? If I'd been there, if I hadn't left her . . . If I'd gone back to her that night when she had come to my hotel room . . . But it wouldn't have been any use. I knew that. It was something in her make-up, the restlessness, the nervous vitality, the constant shifting from one cause to another. And drugs her only solution. Poor Fiona! I should have wept for her, but my eyes were dry and I felt no loss, only a sense of relief that it was over.

The door opened and Gertrude came in. 'He told you, did he?' Her eyes were enormous and I saw they were full of tears. 'I'm sorry, Michael.'

'There's nothing to be sorry about,' I said, and I meant it, remembering the lost years and what her life had been.

'How can you say that?' And she went on, 'You don't see her as I saw her that day in Inverness.' Her voice was trembling with emotion. 'She was so lost, so alone – and frightened I think. But not for herself. For you.'

I got out of the bunk then, going to her, shocked that it was she, not me, that was crying for Fiona, and I wanted to comfort her, to tell her that Fiona was all right now, the long internal struggle over. But she pushed me away, swallowing her tears and saying in a quiet, matter-of-fact voice, 'There are people, journalists, wanting to see you. They are in the bridge. I came to tell you.'

I got dressed and went through into the bridge and saw them there, rain beating at the windows and the hills on either side of the little port lost in cloud. It was still raining when the last of the reporters left, but the clouds had lifted slightly so that the long bank of Burgins was just visible and the island of Papa Little at the end of the voe. I was just going below for lunch when a taxi drew up and Villiers got out, standing bare-headed in the rain talking to the driver, a bright red anorak slung carelessly over his shoulders. Two other taxis followed, nosing between the houses. He glanced at them, his hair already wet, his square jaw jutting angrily. Then he turned, walking quickly on to the pier, climbing over the bulwarks and coming straight to the bridge.

'Randall.' He held out his hand. 'Glad to see you safe. I saw Inspector Garrard on the road. He showed me your statement. You're lucky to be alive.' He glanced round the empty bridge. 'Where's Mrs Petersen?' And when I told him she was below, he said, 'I'd like to see her please – both of you. I've got to get out to the rig and in this weather yours is the only boat can get me there.'

He didn't waste time. As soon as I had called Gertrude and we were both of us with him in my cabin, he said, 'Now, can we come to some arrangement? We've got an ocean-going tug on the way, but it won't be there for another twenty-four hours at least. George Fuller got me a Met. forecast just before I left Scalloway. There's a break coming in the next six to eight hours, but there's another Low moving in and worse to follow. Did Garrard tell you we've had one man killed and two injured? Apparently they had been winding a new cable on to No. 2 winch drum with the intention of trying to hold the rig on a spare anchor when the cable got out of control. Unfortunately, it was Ken Stewart who was swept over the side. The other two men, they're all right – one has a broken arm, the other cracked ribs. But with Stewart gone, there's nobody I trust on board to handle navigation if the rig starts drifting again.' He was looking straight at me. 'How fit are you? I want somebody out there with me who can take charge in an emergency.'

'I'm all right,' I said. 'But how do you think you're going to get on board? Even if there is a break, there'll still be a hell of a sea running.'

He nodded. 'I appreciate that, but it's something I've got to try.' He hesitated. 'We already owe you quite a lot – you and Mrs Petersen. But there's no stand-by boat with the rig now and this is the only trawler in the area big enough to stay by *North Star* till the tug gets there. You can state your own terms, but don't let's waste any time. Okay?'

The terms we agreed covered any damage, gave us a hefty bonus if the *Duchess* stayed by the rig until it was re-anchored, and provided for a long-term charter thereafter at favourable rates. I called to Johan to get the crew up and we cast off with the TV cameras set up on the pier taking pictures and the producer shouting for Villiers to come out on to the deck. Gertrude was already writing out the charter agreement and it was signed before we were in to Swarbacks Minn and meeting the full force of the north-westerly wind. The tide had only just turned against us and I took her through the Sound of Papa, a big sea running as we came out from under the lee of Papa Stour.

It was no more than 25 miles to *North Star*'s new position, but it took us almost six hours. Twice Villiers talked to the rig and on each occasion Ed Wiseberg was not available. The anchors were still holding apparently, but they had done nothing further about the spare anchor and I got the impression they were simply waiting for the tug to arrive. I don't know who he was speaking to, Sparks probably, but on the second occasion I heard him say, 'Well, for Christ's sake tell Ed I want to talk to him. He's got to get that bloody anchor rigged and over the side, then he's got to think of some way of getting us on to the deck.' I didn't hear any more for our bows fell off the top of a breaking wave and a great burst of spray crashed against the bridge. Then he was beside my chair, leaning over me, peering down at the chart folded on my knees. 'How far off now?' His voice was tense, anger only just controlled.

'A little over five miles.'

He glanced at his watch. 'Another hour?'

'More,' I said.

'Then you must increase the revs.' And when I shook my head, he said, 'It's past five already. At this rate –' Our bows slammed again and he was sent flying across the bridge. But he was back at my side almost immediately. 'It's useless to ask Ed how he's going to get us on deck. You got any ideas?'

'We'll see what the sea conditions are like when we get there.'

I put down my pencil and looked at him then. He wasn't scared, only very determined, almost desperate to get on the rig. 'You any good at jumping and clambering up heights?' I asked.

'I've done a bit of rock climbing. Why?'

'They've got scrambling nets. I remember seeing them being unrolled as I was drifting past the rig. With a bit of luck Johan could get the ship in close enough for us to jump. That is if you're prepared to risk it.'

I was looking at him, but all he said was, 'Good God! As

232

simple as that. Why the hell couldn't they think of it?'

'Because they're not seamen,' I told him. And then, sensing that he was a man who needed to have action in mind, I said, 'Half an hour from now, get on the blower to them and have them unroll the nets. And we'll want oil. Tell them to have some containers full of oil ready to pour into the sea on the windward side.'

There wasn't much light left when we finally raised the rig. Visibility was less than a mile in steady rain, so that we saw it as a blur of light, the factory blaze just as I had seen it so many times, except that the tier of red warning lights on the derrick were no longer vertical, but tilted at a slight angle. I had Johan take us in close. The nets were down, hanging like a wide mesh curtain below the catwalk that ran the length of the crew's quarters. Unfortunately, the nets faced north, almost into the wind. I was looking at the seas cascading through the columns, a welter of foam and broken water, trying to estimate the height of the waves against the meshes of the net. 'There's a hell of a rise and fall,' I said.

'What about the oil?' he asked.

'It won't make any difference to the height of the waves, but there could be a little north-going tide left, so it may help. Tell them to start pouring it – but slowly, so that it spreads, and not on to the nets.'

I had already briefed Johan and he was on direct engine control. 'You think you can do it without the ship slamming against the columns?' I asked him.

'Ja. But can you make the jump?' He was laughing.

I looked at Villiers. 'You realize, if you miss, there's not much chance of being picked up?'

He nodded. 'It's the same for you.'

I looked at Gertrude. 'If either of us misses the net and falls into the sea, you'll only search clear of the rig. You're not to take any chances with the ship. Is that understood?'

'Of course.' She was looking at me searchingly. 'Are you fit enough, Michael?'

'I'm fine,' I said.

She nodded, accepting my assurance. 'Good.' And that was all, no argument, no doubts, both of us in harmony, knowing what the risks were. 'You'll make it all right,' she said smiling. 'Both of you.'

'I put you right into the net,' Johan said.

And he was as good as his word. He took the *Duchess* in a

233

wide, slow turn upwind of the rig, and when she was stern-on to the waves and drifting down on to it, Villiers and I went up into the bows. Neither of us had life-jackets. We had both decided the restriction of movement outweighed the safety factor, but crouched on the stem of the boat, clinging to a ring bolt, I wasn't so sure. The wave height averaged 14 feet, but it seemed much more, the movement very violent, a vertical lift and fall that was like riding the National on a giant steeple-chaser.

It seemed an age that we were clinging there, the rig gradually appearing to lean over us as the slant of our drift brought us under the superstructure, the net coming closer. And then suddenly we were falling off the top of a wave and the net was there, right above us, bulging, wide-meshed and streaming water. The bows touched it, dragging it taut, then something caught, tearing a gap in it, and we were rising again. I felt the screw going full astern and I yelled to Villiers to jump, saw him lean out and grab hold. And then we were on the net, both of us clambering like spiders in a web as the bows fell away beneath us. The net sprang tight under my hands and I clung there, not moving, feeling it rip again. Then suddenly it was slack, the trawler backing clear and another wave rolling in, water licking up to my sea boots and my body being swung under the rig, into the welter of foam thrashing through the columns and the cross-bracings.

It was like that all the time we were climbing, our bodies swung back and forth, faces peering down at us, our arms aching, the roar of the sea and the damp smell of metal, the reek of oil. Then at last hands reached down, gripped hold of my arms, and a moment later I was standing exhausted on the catwalk beside Villiers. 'Not as bad as I feared,' he said, his dark, handsome features streaming water from the spray, his dripping anorak globuled with oil. He turned to one of the men who had hauled us on to the catwalk. 'A complete change of clothing for both of us and a pot of coffee,' he said. 'In the barge engineer's office, I think. I want Ed there and Ken's assistant – what's his name?'

'Hans. Hans Smit.' The high voice, the old-maidish manner; it was Lennie, the sick bay attendant.

'Another Dutchman, eh? Well, get those clothes quick, and a couple of towels.' Villiers nodded to me and led the way into the quarters, ignoring Lennie, who seemed scared and wanting to tell him something.

It was quiet in the barge engineer's office, no sound of the sea, only the hum of the power plant. 'You reckon they can get that spare anchor rigged without any more casualties?' he asked me as we stripped off our clothes.

'Let's get a forecast first,' I said. 'And then we'll need to know when the tug will arrive and whether she can start the tow in the sea conditions then expected. There are three anchors still out. If we get another one rigged, that's four to retrieve or cut loose before the tow can start.'

A galley hand came in with coffee, followed almost immediately by a lean, sallow-faced man of about thirty with a crew cut and heavy horn-rimmed glasses. 'Hans Smit,' he said. 'Sorry I am not there, Mr Villiers, when you come up, but I am talking vit the tug. Conditions are no good. It vill be at least twenty-four hours before he is here and he thinks he must go through Pentland Firth, zo it vill even then depend on the tide.'

Villiers nodded. 'What's the latest forecast?'

But Smit didn't know. The last weather chart he had seen was for noon. 'But is improving all the time, I think.'

'What's the helicopter situation then?' Villiers asked. 'Has Ed arranged to fly the drill crews off?'

'No. Nothing has been decided. You see —'

'Where the hell is Ed?' I could tell by the tone of his voice that his patience was running out. 'I want to see him — now.'

Smit's mouth opened, a look of surprise giving place to doubt. 'Didn't Lennie tell you?'

'Tell me what?'

And at that moment the sick bay attendant came in with towels, a bundle of freshly laundered clothes, overalls, gloves and safety helmets. Smit turned to him. 'Didn't you tell Mr Villiers?'

Lennie shook his head, looking nervously round the room. 'I tried, honest I did. But I couldn't seem to —'

'What is it?' Villiers demanded. 'Where is Ed?'

And Smit answered awkwardly, 'Ve don't know. Ve think —' He gave a shrug. 'But that is just a guess. The last I see of Ed is at midday when he is eating alone in the mess. Ve don't know what happened to him.'

'He's disappeared? Is that what you're telling me?' Villiers's voice sounded incredulous. 'You've searched —'

'Ja. Ve search the whole goddam barge. Everywhere.' Smit shook his head.

'When was this? When did you discover he was missing?'

'Ve don't discover he is missing. You see, it is not like that. There are so many places on the rig, so many things he could be checking. Zo, it is not until I don't see him for several hours – ' He shrugged again, an expression of helplessness. 'Then I start enquiring. That was about vife this afternoon. He is in his office for a short time after the midday meal. Then as far as I haf been able to discover, the last person to see him is one of my engineers, who is checking No. 5 winch. Max says he saw him by No. 4. That is close to the stairway leading down under the rig.'

There was a long silence then, and I was thinking of the last time I had seen Ed Wiseberg, sitting at his desk with the papers in front of him and that paragraph underlined in red, his luck run out, and now, on top of all his record of things gone wrong, this rig – possibly the last rig he would ever get – cut adrift and dragging, a barge engineer killed and two men injured. And Villiers, his boss, the man who owned *North Star,* who had given him the job, coming out in a trawler to risk his life jumping for the scrambling nets. I could see him walking down that iron stairway, the same stairway that I had gone down to my waiting boat, walking perhaps with that cocky swagger, but not into a calm sea – into a roaring inferno of breaking waves. It was as good a way to end it as any, and I glanced at Villiers.

His face was set, the shadow of this new disaster showing in the sag of his shoulders, in the shocked look of his eyes. 'Start searching again,' he said in a hard, tight voice. 'Have every man on board who is in charge of anything search his particular area and report back to you when he has done so.'

Smit nodded and went out quickly, obviously glad to escape, glad of the excuse to do something instead of just standing there trying to explain the loss of the top man on the rig. Lennie scuttled out after him and Villiers turned to me. 'Not much hope, I'm afraid.' All the vigour and decisiveness had gone from his voice. 'And they'll blame me, of course. At Scalloway, there were about half a dozen of them, reporters, and their questions . . .' He shook his head. 'I could tell by their questions what they were thinking.' He picked up a towel and began drying himself vigorously. 'Get some clothes on and we'll go to the radio room and see about that forecast.' It cost him an effort to make even that show of decisiveness and I knew that Ed Wiseberg's disappearance had hit him very hard indeed.

The latest Met. information was that the next depression was moving in from the Atlantic faster than expected and would reach us probably by midnight. It was already 976 millibars and still deepening, wind Force 8, gusting 9, possibly more. Two further depressions were building up in the Atlantic, one of 988 and the other 982 millibars. We were still in Telecommunications when Smit reported that all areas of the rig had been thoroughly searched and no sign of Wiseberg.

'Are you sure they've checked everywhere?' Villiers asked. 'All the compartments with doors that could lock or jam?'

Smit nodded. 'I go down in the lift and search the torpedo compartments myself. All storerooms, refrigerator plant, ve even open the store on deck for sea safety equipment – he is nowhere on the barge.'

Villiers didn't say anything. He didn't thank him. He just stood there, staring at the bank of radio equipment. In the end he sat down and drafted a telex message to Ed Wiseberg's wife. He read it through, made several corrections, then handed it to the operator. 'Send that right away please.' And we went to the galley for a meal, which he ate quickly, hardly saying a word.

Afterwards I went up on to the helicopter deck. It had stopped raining and the wind had fallen right away. I could see the trawler's lights quite clearly bobbing up and down about four cables to the south of us. I was there about half an hour, thinking of the big Texan toolpusher, and about his wife and the sons that had been born in different oil areas of the world, a strange, wandering life. It must have required a lot of courage for him to end it in this alien element, going down into the seething surge of the waves beneath his last rig. And Fiona, the two of them so different, each seeking a way out.

I felt sad and depressed as I turned at last to go below in search of Smit. The wind had already backed into the south-west and increased a little. It was raining again and I could no longer see the lights of the *Duchess*. I found the Dutchman in the radio room talking to Sparks and I suggested he get the spare cable and anchor ready just in case. Then I went in search of Villiers.

He was in the barge engineer's office again, standing at the table with Chart 1118B spread out in front of him. 'If the remaining cable broke,' he said, 'how far do you reckon we could drift in 24 hours?'

'Depends on the wind force.'

'Of course. Say an average over the whole period of 30 knots and the general direction westerly.'

I had joined him at the table, staring down at the chart. 'I have a pretty good idea of the drift of a trawler. But this thing.' I shook my head. I just didn't know. 'The windings must be colossal.'

'What would a trawler's drift be?'

'Ignoring tidal current, about 1 to 2 knots – say around 30-40 miles over the full 24-hour period.'

'And Papa Stour only 25 miles to the east of us. We could be on the rocks there in less than twenty-four hours.'

'Not necessarily,' I said. 'Against the windings you have to reckon on the pontoons, the drag of the columns. It could work out about half the drift of a ship, perhaps even less. But if the cables don't break under the strain, then the anchors will hold us – or if they drag, the drift will be slowed until the anchors hold again as we drag into shallower water.'

'So we're all right if the anchor cables don't break?' He nodded thoughtfully. 'Better see if you can organize Smit and his men –'

'I've already advised him to get that spare anchor ready. But I don't think we should drop it unless we're in real trouble, and then only in much shallower water.'

We argued about that for a time. In the end he agreed. But as I was leaving to go on deck, he said, 'So long as nobody gets hurt. I don't want anybody else –'

'Men don't try and get themselves killed,' I said sharply. 'And no good warning them, it only makes them think about it and then they get scared. These things either happen or they don't.'

I left him then and went up to the pipe deck, where the engineers and a whole gang of roustabouts were working in the glare of the spotlights to wind the new cable on to No. 4 winch. It would have been better if they could have rigged it on No. 1 winch, which was facing due west now, but as Smit pointed out to me, it had to be a winch within reach of one of the two cranes, since there was no other way of hoisting a 15-ton anchor out over the side.

It was past midnight before they had it all set up, the anchor shackled on and bowsed down to the deck. By then the wind was strong to gale force from the south-west. We all went down to the mess for coffee, then turned in. Villiers and I had taken over Ed Wiseberg's quarters and he was already occupying the upper berth of one of the two-tier bunks. It was very hot in the cabin, the blowers full on, and he stirred as I switched on the light. 'Everything all right?'

'Blowing hard,' I said. 'And there's a big sea running.' Down here I was more conscious of the movement of the rig, a slow rise and fall, the floor of the cabin sloped and rolling slightly under my feet. 'They've rigged the spare anchor and set a watch on all three cable tension indicators.'

He grunted. 'We'll just have to hope for the best then.'

I switched from the overhead light to my bunk reading lamp, stripped to my borrowed underwear and was asleep as soon as my head touched the pillow.

It was Villiers who woke me, shaking my shoulder and telling me the last anchor cable had just parted. The light was on and he was fully clothed, his rig issue overalls gleaming wet, a safety helmet on his head. 'What's the time?' I asked.

'Just on six-thirty. The tension indicators were showing over three-fifty kips on the dials. I don't know what that is in tons, but it was too much. The first cable parted shortly after four.'

I swung my legs off the bunk, reaching for my clothes. 'You should have woken me.'

'Nothing you could do.'

That was true. 'What's the wind force?'

'Between 50 and 55 knots – a lot more in the gusts. And it's coming out of the north-west now.'

So the depression was passing to the north of us and moving away. 'We'll need to fix our position hourly to check the rate of drift.'

'I think Hans is doing that. And the radio operator on duty is getting on to the Met. Office for the latest forecast.'

'And the tug?' I asked.

'Hove-to off the north-east of Scotland. He says the Pentland Firth is out of the question and he can't make the east side of Orkney because it means a beam sea across the entrance to the Firth.'

He waited while I finished scrambling into my clothes and then we went along to Telecommunications. It was the same operator I had met months ago and Hans Smit was still there.

He handed me the weather sheet. *Depression of 977 millibars almost stationary to the NE of the British Isles expected to clear all areas by noon followed by shallow ridge of high pressure with winds northerly 20-30 knots backing SW as deep depression of 958 moves in from the Atlantic. This depression still deepening and storm or violent storm conditions with hurricane force winds locally expected in sea areas Bailey, Hebrides, Faroes, Fair Isle within next 24 hours.*

'Any chance of getting helicopters out before that lot hits us?' I was thinking of all the men we had cooped up on board with nothing to do. And the *Duchess* out there. She ought to run for shelter, now while she had the chance.

'Depends what sort of clearance we get when that ridge of high pressure comes through,' Villiers said.

But we never got any clearance, and the ridge of high pressure did not materialize. All that day the depression to the north-east of us stayed almost stationary, and the wind did not lessen, drifting us south-eastward. It was impossible to stand on the helicopter deck, and clinging to the guard rail just outboard of the toolpusher's office, I stared through slitted eyes at the waste of water below. I was accustomed to seeing heavy seas, but from the deck of a trawler, or in the shelter of its bridge. Perched up here, 60-70 feet above the water, I was looking down on to an ocean on the move, long lines of great shaggy wave crests marching endlessly, toppling and bursting, dense streaks of foam streaming out along the direction of the wind. Flurries of rain, and in between the rainstorms, I caught glimpses of the *Duchess* pitching madly, rolling her guts out, and I thought of Gertrude, worrying about that patch in the hull, worrying about the engines and how long the ship could go on taking it.

Villiers had refused to let me order her to run for shelter. 'She's under charter to stand by us. She's the only boat we've got, the one chance if we're driven on to Shetland. What do you imagine people ashore will say if we let her abandon us?'

That was what worried him most – what people would say. And it worried me, too. The ocean was on the move, wind and water and waves driving us south-eastward at somewhere between a knot and a knot and a half. And nobody coming to our aid. Nobody out here except the *Duchess*. And so I left it to Gertrude and Johan to make their own decisions. I talked to them, I gave them the latest Met. bulletin, our estimates of drift position; twice I had quite a long chat with Gertrude, but at no time did she suggest running for shelter. It was not even discussed.

At one o'clock we listened to the BBC news, and again at six. It was a strange experience, slightly unreal, to hear the dispassionate voice of the announcer stating that the rig *North Star,* after striking oil, had dragged its anchors and was adrift in heavy seas west of Shetland. And that Vic Villiers, the 'well-known and somewhat controversial head of Villiers Finance & Investment' was himself on board the rig supervising attempts to re-anchor. No mention of sabotage. Nothing about the *Duchess* or how we had got aboard. Not even a hint of the danger threatening us, the extreme conditions we were facing. It was only in *The World at Ten* later that evening that the seriousness of our situation was indicated in an interview with the manager of the Aberdeen office and with a Shell expert on North East Atlantic conditions.

By then the depression had moved away and the wind had dropped. The tug took advantage of the lull to cross the entrance to the Pentland Firth. It was now steaming north up the east coast of Orkney. But still over fifty miles away. And still no helicopter had taken off.

Our position at this time was dangerously close to Foula. We had been monitoring our distance off all day, knowing that it lay in the path of our drift and was a major hazard. In the afternoon, when visibility had temporarily improved, we had seen the island quite clearly through the windows of the tool-pusher's office. It was then about 3 miles to the south of us. Visibility closed in again, and after that we relied on radar. There was still two hours of north-going tide and gradually we were pushed clear of it, so that by the time we had listened to the news the north end of the island was almost 4 miles west of us. No danger now of the tide carrying us south on to the rock shallows of Hævdi Grund, only Foula Shoal still a possible hazard.

For anybody going about his routine business in the body of the rig, or for the drilling crews who had nothing to do now but lie in their bunks, reading, and waiting for the next meal, it was very difficult to appreciate the danger we were in. There was a film being shown that night in the recreation room and Villiers took the opportunity to tell the men what was happening and what was being done on board and ashore to meet the situation. But he did not attempt to explain to them what conditions would be like in the morning. Though he flew his own plane, he still did not have any real idea of what a severe storm in the North Atlantic would be like. He could not even explain to them clearly why the tug was tucked under the lee of Orkney, only 40 miles away. To them, that made it four hours' steaming. They talked about it, of course, as they dispersed and went to their bunks. But I could see they had no conception, everything around them so solid, so orderly, themselves cocooned in the hot warmth of the heating plant from the elemental forces building up in the night outside. They were technicians, and in their pride I think they really thought man had nature licked.

We went to the barge engineer's office then. Villiers had called a meeting of senior staff and it lasted just over half an hour. There were clearly only two ways by which we could reduce the speed of our drift. We could increase the seawater ballast, thereby lowering the height of the rig and so reducing the windage, or we could let go the spare anchor. Smit had already experimented with ballast control during the day, but as the waves had increased in height and strength he had been forced to de-ballast for fear the quarters would be stove in. He wanted to use the anchor. The others agreed. Finally, Villiers asked for my opinion.

I didn't expect them to like it. I wanted the anchor held in reserve as a last resort when we reached shallow water. I advised that all personnel be evacuated from the quarters up to the derrick floor and the rig submerged to maximum depth. All day I had been gradually coming to this view. I hadn't suggested it before because of Foula. Until we had cleared Foula it might have increased the danger of our drifting on to the island.

'If I submerged to maximum,' Smit said, 'and this depression becomes as bad as you say, then everything goes — quarters, mess, communications, offices. The deck will be swept clean of pipe. Everything will go.'

'But not the rig,' I said.

He rounded on me then. 'Vat do you know about it?' During the last few hours he had been carrying a heavy load of responsibility and his face was tense and overstrained. 'You know about trawlers. But this is a drilling barge. You don't know anything about drilling barges.' And he turned back to Villiers. 'It is my responsibility.'

'All right, Hans. It's your responsibility, I agree. But what do we do?'

'Let go the spare anchor, now, while it is more quiet.'

'And if the cable breaks?' I asked him.

'Then the cable break. But ve don't know about that until ve try. And you don't know,' he added, glaring at me resentfully. 'You don't even know the breaking strain of a 4 inch cable or 'ow many tons the anchor shackles are manufactured to stand.'

It was difficult for any of them to realize what a depression of 958 millibars that was deepening could mean in terms of wind force. They were all of them, including Villiers, thinking of damage to equipment and machinery, the problems of replacement, the lost time, and in Villiers's case I am quite certain the financial cost. At this stage their minds refused to face up to the prospect of total loss. They just could not envisage what it would be like stranded on rock in hurricane force winds. How could they, sitting there in the barge engineer's office, no sound of the wind outside, just the hum of the power plant, the movement under their feet no more than the gentle bowing of a colossus to the sea.

And so Villiers agreed to let Hans Smit send the spare anchor overboard, and after that I went into the radio room and asked the operator to call the *Duchess* for me. It was Johan who answered, not Gertrude, and that made it easier. I told him to make up towards Foula and get into the shelter of the island. 'You speak with Gertrude,' he said. 'That is for her to decide.'

'No, it is for you to decide,' I told him. 'There's nothing you can do for the rig. If anybody is swept overboard he's gone. No hope of your saving him.' And I asked him how the patched plates were standing up to the hammering. He admitted that Duncan had had the pumps going all day. 'There's worse to come,' I told him, 'and you know it.' And I added, 'Once it really starts blowing, you won't be able to make up to the island against it.'

There was a long silence while he thought it out. 'Ja, okay. We lie under Foula. But you talk to Gertrude first. Over.'

'I'll talk to her when you're safe in Ham Voe,' I said. 'Not before. Over and out.' And I cut him off before he could argue further.

Villiers's voice, sharp and angry behind me, said, 'You've no right to dismiss that trawler without reference to me. It's under charter to stand by us – '

'Under charter?' I had turned and was staring at his tired,

243

handsome face, seeing the selfishness of the man, his certainty that agreements, money, power, was everything. 'Charters don't buy lives,' I said. 'Have you any idea what it's been like in that trawler today, what it could be like tomorrow? Do you want to stand in the toolpusher's office, with the stability of this huge structure under you, stand in your shirtsleeves in warmth and comfort and watch a little ship founder with half a dozen people on board? Is that what you want?'

'You're thinking of that girl,' he said waspishly.

'Yes, I am. I'm thinking of her, of a Scots engineer named Duncan, of Johan, a big bearded Norwegian, of men who saved my life – and by their seamanship got you on to your bloody useless obsolete rig.'

He was silent then, and I was suddenly sorry for him. 'Do what you like,' he said quietly, the anger gone and his voice lifeless. Then he turned and went quickly out.

The spare anchor was hoisted over just before midnight. The wind speed was then 30 knots, gusting to 37. I took the reading myself. Unbelievably, the rig was not equipped with a proper anemometer, only a hand speed indicator for the use of the radio operator. Smit and his engineers, the crane driver and quite a little crowd of technicians and drilling crews were gathered round the winch. Villiers was standing a little to one side, a lone figure, his back against the guardrails. Nobody said a word as the needle suddenly came alive, swinging with a jerk round the dial, wavering and settling at around the 300 mark.

The anchor was holding and there was a sigh of relief.

Now that the wind had lessened the seas had become higher, the vertical movement of the rig under our feet considerable. As the crowd drifted off to bed I saw the indicator needle begin to move. Soon it was fluctuating wildly, reflecting the snatch on the cable as the rig rose and fell. Smit stood there watching, his face set. At one point the needle seemed to swing right off the end of its range. I think he was wishing then that he had waited until we were in shallower water, and I left him and went to my bunk, anxious to get some sleep while the going was good.

Villiers came in just as I had put my bunk light out. 'It's holding,' he said. 'But the strain on it must be very heavy.'

'It won't last long,' I told him.

But there I was wrong. It held for almost 5 hours, for shortly after 01.00 the wind dropped right away. If the helicopter crews, who were supposed to be standing by at Sumburgh, had been quick off the mark, it is just possible they could have snatched most of the men off, for the wind stayed light for almost three hours. Just before first light, however, it veered rapidly to 200° and within less than half an hour it was blowing a gale from that quarter.

The next depression was upon us and it had already deepened to 947.

To appreciate the problems we faced that day, it is necessary to realize the large number of men we had on board; also their trades, because, in the event, our lives were to depend on some of the skills we could call upon. On board at that time were: junior toolpusher, assistant barge engineer, 5 rig technicians, 2 motormen, 2 crane operators, 8 labourers or roustabouts, 2 welders, 2 electricians, 2 radio operators, sick bay attendant, 8 cooks and quarters staff, 2 divers, and two complete drilling teams of 8 men. A total of 52. In addition, there was Villiers and myself and the service company personnel who had been flown out to operate the pressure tests.

According to the log kept by the barge engineer, the anchor cable had finally parted at 05.42. But I didn't see that until shortly after eight. Nobody called me, and when I finally opened my eyes, it was because Villiers had switched on the light. He was dressed and I could see by his face he had been up half the night. 'Couldn't sleep,' he said after he had broken it to me that we were adrift again.

I dragged on my clothes and dived up the tilted stairway to the toolpusher's office. The wind was already screaming out of the south-west, rain and spray lashing the windows, and intermittent glimpses of the sea showed that the waves were shaggy combers 30 feet or more in height. A hurricane all right. I had brought the hand anemometer up with me and when I held it outside for a moment, clinging to the rail, my eyes half shut against the wind and driven spray, the force of it was already beyond recording. Back in the radio room I got the *Duchess* on the R/T and talked briefly to Gertrude. They had two anchors out, but even close under Foula the cables were bar taut and the surface of the water being lifted off the voe. 'Will you hold all right?' I asked her.

'Maybe. I don't know. We watch and hope, ja. What about you, Michael?'

'I can have a hot bath or eat myself sick, watch a film show, read a book –' I stopped there, for Sparks was just changing the figures against the Low on the weather chart. It now stood at 941.

And then Gertrude's voice was saying. 'But you have Shetland. It is a lee shore.' There was a pause, and then she said, 'Johan says the tide could help you.' I told her I knew that and she said, 'Fine,' and signed off, wishing us luck. It was the last time I was able to speak to her.

There was no Decca Navigator on board. *North Star* was not a ship. It was not equipped to ride the seas unanchored and alone, and once we lost sight of Foula the rate of drift was largely guesswork. I did some rough calculations, knowing there could be only one answer – total disaster. The rate of drift affected the time, the wind direction the place, but nothing could stop us hitting the rock-bound coast of Shetland – except possibly the speed and direction of the tidal flow.

Smit's view was the same as mine now – evacuate to the derrick floor and submerge to maximum depth. It was the only way to slow the rate of drift, to give us more time. Tugs were gathering, but even if any of them could have got out to us, there was no hope of fixing a towline. But when we reported to Villiers, who was lying stretched out in his bunk, it seemed impossible to make him understand the gravity of the situation. I thought at first he was thinking of the damage to the rig, the difficulty of raising finance, all the problems he would have to face when, and if, he ever got ashore. But it was more than that. He had withdrawn inside himself. In the heat of the cabin, in the warm security of his bunk, he had reached the point where he felt that if he ignored it all the storm would go away.

But even down there, in the depths of the quarters, it was impossible to ignore what was happening outside. The howl of the wind overlaid the sound of the power plant, the crash of the seas pounding at the steel columns of the rig shook the whole structure, the noise of it so loud we had to shout.

Finally he said, 'All right, Hans. Do what you like. You're the barge engineer. It's your responsibility.'

Hans shook his head, looking bewildered and scared. 'My responsibility, ja. But vith you on board it is impossible that I tell the men to leave their quarters and go up into the vind. They vill not accept it from me.'

Villiers didn't say anything. He just lay there, his eyes closed.

'You must tell them,' Hans said. 'To go out into the vind is like going over the top into battle. And the ballast control engineer, who vill have to leave after he has flooded the torpedo tanks, vill be lucky if he is not killed. They vill do it for you, but not for me – not vith you 'ere on board.'

Villiers didn't answer.

Time was passing, and we had no time. I ripped the blankets off him and yanked him out of the bunk. 'Come on,' I said. 'For God's sake tell them, now.'

He stood there in his underpants looking vague. 'We're more than twenty miles from the coast,' he muttered.

'Seventeen,' I said. 'Nearer sixteen now.'

'It's not necessary.'

'I'm telling you it is.'

But he shook his head, unwilling to accept it.

I grabbed hold of him then. 'Why the hell did you bring me on board if you don't accept what I'm telling you? I need you to advise me, you said. Somebody to take charge in an emergency. All right. The emergency is now and I am advising you. Get the men up to the derrick floor and submerge to depth.'

He stared at me, his eyes blank. And suddenly I knew what it was. He was a financier, not a leader. He could read a balance sheet at a glance, could figure out assets and financial gain like a computer, he could talk a board of directors into submission by the cold logic of figures – but he was no bloody good with men. Last night, telling them about the storm to come, it had been facts and figures, not the reality of a hurricane blast and huge seas. Now, with the prospect of death a cold, terrible battering, he was opting out.

'Okay,' I said. 'You got me on board and my life's at risk. Get dressed now and come to the messroom. I'll do the talking, but you'll be there, and you'll go with them up to the derrick floor. You understand?'

He nodded, accepting it slowly. 'Yes. Yes, of course.' And he began to dress. It was incredible, under orders the blankness had left his eyes.

I told Hans to get every single man on board into the messroom. As an outsider, with Villiers standing there, I thought I could do it. And I did. It was, in fact, easier than I had expected. They weren't seamen, but most of them had lived with the sea long enough to understand its power, and they weren't fools. They could hear the wind, feel the seas thundering against the base of the structure. They were ready for action.

It took almost an hour to get them all up to the derrick floor, with their life-jackets on and the rig submerged to depth. Hans stayed with the ballast control engineer, insisting that it was his duty. It meant two lives at risk instead of one, but they both made it, though they were caught by a wave on the catwalk above the pipe deck and Hans was swept against a crane and badly bruised.

In that hour, before the rig was down to maximum depth, the galley staff had managed to get food and drink up to the derrick floor, Lennie had collected his first aid kit, and blankets, clothes, bedding, the welders had got their equipment up. Every department had thought for themselves and brought whatever they considered necessary. The divers had even dragged their inflatable up. And in that wind it was remarkable that they achieved so much without loss of life, for the work went on after the ballast tanks had started to flood.

In the end, of course, the quarters were left deserted and Sparks closed the radio room. After that we had no means of communicating with the outside world. But somebody had brought a portable up and we huddled round it, listening to the one o'clock news describing the build-up of tugs and ships and aircraft, all waiting to get out to us as soon as the storm had passed. The wind was westerly now. I don't know what the force was. High up on that platform, I felt it was beyond anything I had ever experienced. The forecast had not been specific – hurricane force winds with speeds over 100 knots. The depression had now deepened to a shattering 938 millibars; worse still, its rate of movement had slowed and it was not expected to clear the north of Shetland before midnight.

The derrick floor, normally a demoniac centre of activity with draw-works roaring, winches screaming, the clatter of tongs and the turntable turning, was now still and packed with men. But not silent. There was more noise on that platform than ever there had been when *North Star* was drilling, the wind roaring through it, howling at the doors, banging and slamming at the corrugated iron shelter sheets, tearing them loose, whirling them away. And below us, the pipe deck, even the helicopter deck, a welter of foam as the combers roared and broke aboard.

The toolpusher's office was the first to go, the sea breaking it into matchwood, the wind picking it up and hurling bits of it past our refuge. Pipe, and great lengths of casing, were swirled back and forth till the guardrails were torn out of the steel deckplates and they went over the side. The catwalk was buckled and curled up like the slide in a giant child's playground. And all the time we worked to keep large pieces of equipment from breaking loose, to shore up and fasten the flapping shield of iron sheet that was all the protection we had. Everything chaos, and the thuds of the waves thundering beneath the rig, crashing against it, could be felt through our bodies, the movement sickening. The half-submerged rig had a dead feeling. It was like a rock awash.

One of the roustabouts, a man called Wally, was the first to sight land. That was shortly after two o'clock and he only caught a fleeting glimpse of it. I didn't doubt him, because it was downwind of us, just where it should be, and he said it was low-lying. The wind was still westerly by the handbearing compass I had brought with me, and on my calculations, we would go ashore on the West Burra coast, possibly just south of it. I thought perhaps it was Havras Island he had seen, and I wished Johan was with us. He would have known, because the Havras marked the entrance to Clift Sound and the *Duchess*'s home voe of Taing. But, in fact, it must have been St Ninian's Isle.

That brief sighting, the knowledge that we were so near to disaster, finally decided me on a desperate course of action – something I had wanted to do, but had not dared for fear it would kill us all. I looked at Hans, leaning over my shoulder staring at the chart and helping me to hold it flat on the oil-scummed floor. 'The tide turns in just over an hour,' I said, and he nodded, knowing what was in my mind. I knew what he was thinking, too – if only we had that spare anchor, if only we could use it now, now that we were in shallower water. It could have held us till the tide turned.

But then, of course, we could never have got it over the side. There was no electric power, and anyway, the crane nearest to No. 4 winch had already been forced off its mountings, the jib leaning at a drunken angle and banging to and fro. I got up and lurched across to Villiers, who was working with a gang of men to shore up the sides of the driller's office. I told him what I wanted, and he nodded, cheerful and seeming almost to be enjoying himself. 'Okay. Go ahead.'

And he turned and continued with his work, seemingly indifferent to the risk and the ultimate cost if we survived.

It seemed an age that the two welders were hanging in their chairs, held by ropes as they worked with their torches to cut through the windward legs of the derrick. They cut them one at a time, and as they worked on the second, the rig was slowly turning. There was a moment when I was sure I had made a terrible error of judgement and that the whole hundred-odd feet of steel would collapse on top of us. Standing there, watching them, I could see in my mind the ghastly result as the weight of the crown wheel crashed down on to the packed group of men around me.

But the rig kept turning, and suddenly there was a rending sound. Somebody screamed a warning. A rope flew and one of the welders swung across our heads, his torch still burning, to be brought up short by the oxygen hose, and looking up, I watched incredulously as the whole Eiffel Tower structure trembled and began to move, the crown wheel and the traveller swinging dizzily across the scudding clouds. The scream of steel on steel, the whip-crack of metal breaking. And then it was gone, just like that. I don't think any of us really saw it go. One minute it was there, the next there was nothing over our heads.

The tide must have turned about the time the derrick went over the side. And I think the absence of it may have made all the difference, for in that force of wind, the air almost solid with the power of it, the derrick must have been acting as a great sail. At any rate, just over an hour later, we began to hear a deep thunderous noise like an artillery barrage. This gradually got louder until it was an appalling, shattering sound. Visibility was poor, rain and spray screaming past us, so that we seemed almost into the backwash surf of the wave breaks before we saw the land. The roar of sound was so great then that we were just standing there aghast, holding on to whatever we were clinging to, frozen into stillness. And then, downwind of us, through the torn and battered iron sheets, there was a darkening of the waterlogged air, a great mass looming up out of the maelstrom of broken water.

Ever since the barrage of sound had started, Hans and I had guessed what it was – the Atlantic hurricane waves pounding at the near-1,000 foot cliffs of Fitful Head. We both of us knew what that could mean, but now that we could all of us see the towering mass itself, I do not think there was a man among us who did not believe his last hour had come. But though it seemed so near, we were still out beyond the 10 fathom line, and the cliffs were moving, sliding past, the rig being carried south-east by the tide at almost 3 knots. Soon we could see the headland of Siggar Ness, and when the tide swept us past it, there was open sea, wind and tide with us, both carrying us south-east towards Horse Island and the Sumburgh Roost.

It was almost dark then, and as night fell, nothing to see in the pitch black fury, all our senses were in our ears and in the feel of the rig under our feet. I don't know when we hit the Roost. The rig was like a half-submerged wreck and there was such a pandemonium of breaking waves and crashing gear that it was impossible to tell whether the chaos was the effect of the race or shallows. But I didn't care. We were in the clear, and so long as the pontoons did not strike a reef, I was sure a structure as massive as a rig would survive it. And then, suddenly, Sumburgh light came clear of the land, its revolving beam haloed in the wind-driven spray.

The light bore roughly 20°, and within a very short time it was due north of us. I knew then that we were in the grip of the great tidal race that streams round the southern tip of Shetland. I remembered reading all about it in the Pilot, and on the *Mary Jane* I had found an old Admiralty tide book: *Ships in it frequently become unmanageable, and sometimes founder.* Those words had undoubtedly been written with the fishing boats in mind, but the statement: *It should be given a wide berth* was as applicable now as then.

When we entered the race the tidal flow was with the wind, so that we were moving eastward at a considerable speed. But the Pilot, which I had brought with me from the barge engineer's office, warned that in the Roost the tide only ran eastward for about three hours. There was then a 'still' of about half an hour, after which the tidal flow was westward for 9 hours. Thus, we had only a short period of the eastward thrust left. The 'still' came and there was less sea, the light on Sumburgh head blurred and almost stationary, bearing roughly 350°.

That night I was convinced the rig would break up. Shortly after midnight there was a terrible rending of metal, the whole structure shaking to a series of power-hammer thuds. The mud tanks had broken adrift. They went on rumbling and crashing hour after hour as we lay huddled together for warmth, our bodies soaked and shivering with cold. It was a terrible night, and the pounding went on and on.

They finally smashed a way through and went over the side shortly after four. It suddenly seemed almost quiet. The seas were lessening, too, and Sumburgh Light bore north-east. We were out of the Roost.

An hour later we were back in it again. The tide had turned and was carrying us eastward. No rain now, and with visibility much improved, we could check our progress by the bearing of the light. In the space of just over an hour it moved from north-east through north to almost north-west. That was when we were finally spewed out of the Roost by the eastward flow and came under the lee of the land. The wind died away, and the sea with it.

Dawn found us roughly 4 miles east of Sumburgh Head, a battered wreck being carried slowly northward on the tide. An RAF Nimrod came over, flying low, and an hour later the first tug was coming up over the horizon. We raised a cheer as it steamed close alongside. But though we cheered the tug's arrival, we were too cold, too dazed to do anything about it. The iron staircase to the derrick floor was gone, the pipe skid our only way down. Nobody had the energy to be lowered on a rope, to struggle through the tangled wreckage and get a towline fixed. We had been inactive so long that we clung to inactivity, immobilized by the long, dreadful night, by the memory of our fear, of death so narrowly averted.

It wasn't for another two hours, when there were three tugs and a navy ship milling around us, that men boarded us and one by one we were got down from our refuge, lowered into boats and taken on board the destroyer. Villiers was with me in the naval pinnace and I remembered my surprise at the extraordinary resilience of the man, the sudden return of confidence. His square-jawed face was dark with stubble, his eyes red-rimmed and bloodshot from the shattering force of the wind, and his right hand, lacerated by a piece of flying metal, was still wrapped in the bandage Lennie had fixed. And yet he could talk about the future, about the huge possibilities of the oilfield *North Star* had found.

Maybe it was nervous reaction, words pouring out of him as he thought aloud, but I couldn't help admiring him. If he had had phones beside him, he would have been rapping out orders, raising finance. 'The rig doesn't matter. If we lost half a dozen rigs, the cost of them would still be nothing. I'd still have merchant bankers falling over themselves to lend me money.'

'If you lose rigs,' I said, 'you lose lives.'

But he brushed that aside. 'We didn't lose any. Not during the storm, not one. And the rig is covered by Lloyds. How long do you reckon it will take to get it repaired?'

'I've no idea,' I answered tersely. I didn't care about the rig. I was worrying about the *Duchess*, anxious to check that she hadn't dragged her anchors and been forced to put to sea in that maelstrom of a night.

He pushed his hand up over his face, rubbing at the caked salt. 'I have to think of the future,' he said. 'What this oil strike means to the company. A lot of reorganization, new management.' He looked at me then. 'Room for somebody like you.' And he added, 'I owe you a lot, Randall. And you've got brains, education, financial training, even shipyard experience. The knack of handling men, too.' The boat was slowing now, manoeuvring to come alongside the destroyer, and he leaned forward. 'Would you like to come down to London for a few weeks, get the feel of things?'

'Whatever for?' I asked dully, thinking of Gertrude.

'I don't know yet. The rig for a start. Somebody will have to be cracking the whip. Then there's the Shetland office. That will have to expand fast. It will be first priority, and I'll need somebody with a Shetland background.' He was thinking aloud. And then he said, 'Anyway, you come down to London with me. I'll be needing men like you.'

I looked at him then, realizing he was serious. 'I'll think about it,' I said. But I knew I wouldn't. Not if I had Gertrude. I might be able to handle it, but I couldn't see Gertrude fitting into the sort of life he was offering me. And Gertrude was all I wanted. That's what the night had taught me. She was the rock I was now clinging to. Without Gertrude I would be adrift again. But together, creating something of our own – a service, up here in this wild, beautiful world we both understood. I was thinking of The Taing, that house, the ship lying off and the voe as I had once seen it, in moonlight from the bedroom window. That was what I wanted, my life worthwhile and with purpose. Not something handed to me ready-made and only to be managed, something not my own.

I clambered up the destroyer's side and asked the lieutenant who greeted us if I could use the ship's R/T.

'You're Captain Randall of the *Duchess*, are you? Your ship will be up with us in about an hour. And I have a message for you. Will you check with Mr Villiers that she is to resume stand-by duty under the terms of the charter.'

I looked at Villiers, and suddenly we were both laughing.

AUTHOR'S NOTE

NORTH STAR is a natural progression from earlier travels in search of background. I was in Canada in 1950 when the discovery well at Leduc was flaring and the first rigs were moving into the Redwater field. The result was *Campbell's Kingdom*. Six years later I was ashore in the Oman with the first oil expedition on the Arabian coast of the Indian Ocean and wrote *The Doomed Oasis*. It was inevitable, therefore, that I should become fascinated by the search for oil off the coasts of my native land.

I started writing NORTH STAR in the autumn of 1972 with the intention of finishing it late in 1974, but world events caught up with me – the Arab-Israeli war, the oil embargoes, the shortages, the price rises. And in Britain a miners' strike and the 3-day working week, the unions bringing government down, a general election. Suddenly North Sea oil was on everybody's lips, the one bright spot in the prevailing gloom. In these circumstances, I felt it essential to bring the book forward, and if any errors have crept in, then this is the reason.

However, I have had a great deal of technical help. Primarily I am indebted to Shell, and to Sir David Barran, who made me free of their *Staflo* rig on a long tow down from the Brent to the Auk. Later Tammo Appelman, their seabed expert, cleared up many questions of technical detail. Tricentrol's chief exploration manager, A. F. Fox, was most helpful in pinpointing the location for *North Star's* drilling west of Shetland, and I am also indebted to him for a final check on drilling technicalities. And in the north-west of Scotland Sir Reginald Rootes introduced me to the little Port of the North opposite his house.

North Star was the name of my rig, and also my title, right from the first page of writing, and here I ran into difficulty. At a late stage I discovered that there was, in fact, a real rig called *North Star*. It was of the jack-up type drilling in the Persian Gulf and owned by The Offshore Company of Houston, Texas. However, their President, W. H. Moore, raised no objection when I wrote to him of my problem, and

I would like to express my appreciation of his understanding and emphasize that there is no connection between the semi-submersible *North Star* rig of my story and his jack-up.

Finally, I would like to thank Charles Forret for his help over details of speech in Shetland, Mike Burton of Newington Trawlers and the Lowestoft Fishing Vessel Owners Association and Captain Meen for clarification of equipment and layout of the *Duchess,* Jim Mitchell of the *Hull Daily Mail* for court background, and many others who have been of assistance to me during the very concentrated period of writing this book, including all those on *Staflo* who gave me of their time and knowledge.